DOUGLAS J. HIGHMAN

IN THE DARK OF NIGHT

BLOOD OF THE INNOCENT
A MURDER INVESTIGATION BASED ON A TRUE STORY

TACTICAL PUBLICATIONS

ERIE, PENNSYLVANIA

IN THE DARK OF NIGHT by Douglas J. Hagmann

A TACTICAL PUBLICATIONS BOOK

TACTICAL PUBLICATIONS

ERIE, PENNSYLVANIA

Copyright © 2021 by Douglas J. Hagmann
All Rights Reserved

Cover design by Eric Swackhamer
Cover photograph by Marty Desilets – www.marty.fm

No part of this book may be reproduced, stored in a retrieval system, or transmitted by any means without the written permission of the author and publisher.

Visit the author's website at www.DouglasJHagmann.com

ISBN: 978-0-9796479-3-2
ISBN (eBook): 978-0-9796479-4-9

Published in the United States of America

The dead cannot cry out for justice. It's our duty, the duty of the living, to do so for them.

To the people who have lived through many of the events described in this book but cannot be named for reasons that should be clear to the reader.

ACKNOWLEDGMENTS

The author wishes to acknowledge the following people who have helped me through an unusually long and difficult process of getting this book into print: My wife, best friend, and greatest love Renae, who has the patience and endurance of a saint to put up with me. The last three-and-a-half decades have been the best of my life. The invaluable assistance and patience of Eric Swackhamer, otherwise known as "Eric the Tech," whose technical knowledge surpasses that of any single human I know. I also want to thank Russ Dizdar and his wife, Shelly, who are fearless and formidable warriors against the forces of evil, and his entire team who work in the field every single day. Craig Sawyer, the founder of Veterans For Child Rescue (V4CR) for taking the fight to the enemy, despite enduring relentless enemy fire on and off the battlefield. To my good friend Steve Quayle, who has been an inspiration to me in so many ways, and Pastor David Lankford, who has kept me grounded in my faith. To Daniel Holdings, a great author and friend who has given much of himself in the battle between good and evil. To "Coach" Dave Daubenmire, Paul McGuire, Kevin Fahey, Matt Szyszkiewicz, and so many others who have blessed me with their friendship and inspiration. The friendship, generosity and professional insight of Joni Swackhamer, who selflessly invested her time into turning this work into a reality. From the bottom of my heart, I thank all of you!

Prologue

Tick Tock Mister Big Shot PI
You were warned to stop but you did not
Six are chewed clean, just bones from the slop
No more wagging tongues
Tick Tock your time is short
Go out and kill He commands
Programmed to kill, we operate on a different frequency
In the police and FBI and the papers and TV we are everywhere
We are the Super Soldiers with the silver ring
Our leader is more powerful than yours
Ours serves Moloch who we will give 1-2-3
Before the Owl, Our power is by their fright
That in their blood, dark to light
We drink in the dark of night
Take their innocence then no more
We will drink their blood from our silver cup.
At the moment of 12 hours of light and 12 of DARKNESS
Tick Tock time will be up
There will be No One to Talk For three.
Follow the Yellow Brick Road, Dorothy's paradise awaits to enlighten
For MOLOCH

IN THE DARK OF NIGHT

Friday, September 4, 1987

It was almost midnight when I got to my office after a six-hour drive and a week spent in a cheap motel, working 18-hour days and living on a steady diet of fast food, cold pizza, gas station coffee, and cigarettes. The president of a large trucking company located about 300 miles away called me one morning to ask if I would personally handle a problem he was having. It was a big problem. Someone, or more likely a group of people, stole over a million dollars' worth of computer and electronic equipment from the company's loading docks in just two months, during July and August. The police chief in the town where the company is based led the investigation, and he called in the FBI due to the value of the thefts and the interstate shipment of the goods. Despite these resources, there were no breaks in the case when I received the assignment.

The police chief and lead FBI agent didn't much appreciate my involvement and said as much to my client and me when we first met in the president's office. I've experienced that type of reception before and even expected it. It was with that expectation that I arrived with a box of donuts for our initial meet-and-greet, which I admit was a not-so-subtle passive-aggressive move on my part that was not lost on the company president.

Their perception of my role changed when I opened a suitcase that contained state-of-the-art surveillance equipment I intended to use specifically for this case. That and my commitment to live and breathe this case until it was resolved to my client's satisfaction.

Before I left today, I was confident that the names of the four employees working on the loading dock, one company driver, and two outside accomplices that I turned over to my client and the police would result in arrests. Background data, surveillance video, and recorded witness statements made up most of the damning evidence.

The local police chief personally accepted and logged the evidence I provided. He thanked me and gave me his card, telling me to personally call him if I was ever in the area or had any problems within his jurisdiction. The FBI agent was equally appreciative and gave me an official FBI cap for a job well done as if it was some type of trophy from the director himself. The president of the trucking company, standing next to the police chief, thanked me and wished me a safe drive home. One for the good guys, I thought.

I carried my gear from my car into the office, grabbed the stack of mail Annie left on my desk, and tossed it into my briefcase. The last thing I wanted to do tonight was to sit around at the office and sort through the mail. It was the start of the Labor Day weekend, and I figured that I could take care of this mundane task later. After all, Annie would have told me if there was anything significant in the mail, as she always opened it at my request.

Just then, I saw a note written by Annie reminding me that my final report for the wrongful death case Gina and I have been working on for the last few months was due next Friday. That gave me just a week from today. I've been working the case on behalf of Fidelity Mutual Insurance, my largest client. Absent of finding any mitigating factors to deflect liability from the insured, and depending on the generosity of the jury, my client stands to lose at least five million dollars.

"Marvelous," I uttered myself. I picked up the reminder, opened my briefcase again, and tossed it on top of the mail and whatever other files were already inside. Although I like to be organized, I was mentally exhausted and felt covered in road grime. I would organize everything later.

I was at my apartment ten minutes after locking the doors to the office. I dropped my briefcase by the door and headed to the shower. Exactly one half-hour after getting back in town, I was clean, in my own bed, and about to, hopefully drift off into the most restful sleep I've had in a week. The notes from the case I had just successfully completed could wait. The report I had to finish could wait. The mail could wait. It could all wait, at least for a day or two. It just felt good to be home and on familiar and friendly ground.

****

The man with the dark, soulless eyes turned his cargo van from the main Bayfront road onto a dirt and gravel service road that few people even knew existed. It was exactly 3:33 a.m. according to the digital display of his cassette radio he recently installed in his dash. He liked that number, and the time was no accident.

Darkness seemed to envelop everything around him, even consuming the light from his headlights. The air felt thick and oppressive, the type of oppression that muffled sounds and made even the simple task of breathing feel laborious. The only audible sound was the noise that was made as the tires of the van slowly turned over loose gravel, and the occasional squeak from its underside as it traveled over the rough terrain of the unserviced path. Instead of the pockmarked dirt and gravel service road, he saw a road constructed of yellow bricks. An iridescent yellow brick road that glowed and guided him.

The lifeless four-foot-nine, 98-pound cargo made no sound during this trip, unlike the indescribable wails and cries of pain the young boy made during the murder ritual several hours before.

About 20 yards ahead of the driver stood an old, dilapidated grain silo and elevator. A set of unused railroad tracks sat adjacent to the grain elevator. To the right of the silo was an old shack that once had a purpose, but now, along with the silo, stood in disrepair as a symbol of the urban decay of the port city of Lakewood. The shack's two glass windows were long gone, and the door ceased being a barrier for anything. The two structures stood in stark contrast against Lakewood's newer commercial construction, and as a reminder of a much different era.

The shack was not readily visible from the main road. It sits lower than the silo and is blocked by thick brush and trees that mercifully extended and covered the length of the blight.

"Perfect," he muttered to himself as he eased the van so that the side cargo doors faced the front door of the shack. He moved the stick shift on the steering column from drive to park, turned off the lights, and immediately began to count silently. His cadence matched perfectly with the silent ticks of a stopwatch. The numbers in his head stopped at 333—three hundred and thirty-three seconds, or about five-and-a-half minutes. He didn't know why he counted. He just did. That was the time it took him to move and stage the body of the young boy from the corrugated floor of his van into the shack.

He had no problems lifting and carrying his cargo, although the young boy's lifeless arm brushed the side of his head as he carried him from the van. That excited him, although he did not know why. "Don't forget his hand," he whispered to himself as he walked back to the van to retrieve the amputated appendage. He cradled it like a normal person would hold a puppy. He was sorry to leave it.

He then reset his mental stopwatch and began counting upward again when he moved the stick shift into drive. Thirty-three. It took him 33 seconds to get back on the main road. He was pleased with that number. He completed his assigned task in less than three minutes and under the complete cover of darkness. Despite the stickiness in the night air, he never broke a sweat.

It was well over a mile before he saw any sign of anyone alive or awake, despite being well inside the city. It was safe now, and that part of his job was done.

A lone car passed him traveling the opposite direction, paying him no attention. For a second, he thought about crossing the center line and running headlong into the oncoming vehicle. "It's not time yet," he heard the voice in his head tell him.

As he continued driving away from the Bayfront, he awkwardly stretched his neck and head over his right shoulder to look at the floor behind him. Even in the dark of night, he could see blood and bits and pieces of flesh and hair that sloughed off the young boy's body as he pulled him over the rough floor of the van. He felt a rush of excitement wash over him again, as he savored the moment and delighted in storing the image in his mind. Fighting the exhilaration, he could not afford to leave evidence. No matter, he would take care of that later, maybe back at the barn from where his trip began. For now, his job was done, completed precisely as instructed by his handlers.

As the man with the soulless eyes maneuvered his van into the barn, the headlights cast eerie shadows upon a long, wooden table-turned-altar that was built long ago. It was there as long as he could remember, but it always was kept secured, out of sight and inaccessible to all but a very select few. Anyone unfortunate enough to accidentally stumble upon its existence would never alert anyone. The acres of wooded private property and a nearby pig farm guaranteed such secrets.

He closed the double doors of the barn and locked them with three heavy-duty padlocks, aligned vertically at the center of the closing. He counted, "1-2-3" as he locked each of them. He walked to his cabin, situated about a half football field away from the barn, closer to the road. He entered through the back door as he always did. The noise from the specially handcrafted wind chimes attached to the top interior part of the door made a dull, clanking noise as he entered.

No other wind chimes like these existed anywhere. Like a fingerprint, they were absolutely one of a kind. Even the sound made from the chimes was different, like dried sticks. The dull sound they made as he opened the door seemed to alter the state of his consciousness, his awareness. To him, it was a symphony, an orchestra of instruments only found in the depths of hell, and each note was instructive.

Before retiring, he removed two containers of meat from the refrigerator and placed them on the kitchen counter. He took out a vacuum sealer and carefully cut two gallon-sized bags from the roll, sealing one end of each bag. After transferring the meat into the bags, he sealed each and used a permanent marker to note the date packaged. Below the date he wrote "tenderloin" in neat, block lettering and placed both bags into the freezer above the frozen vegetables.

Chapter 1

<u>Sunday, September 6, 1987</u>

To say that I was not mentally prepared for the sight in front of me would be a considerable understatement. How I found myself to be looking down at such a horrific image on this summer evening in the middle of the long Labor Day weekend began with a series of unplanned events that most people would call coincidences. Of this, I am not so sure.

I stood numb at the sight of the body of a boy who appeared to be barely in his early teens, although the condition of the body made a more exact identification extremely difficult. A cold chill ran through me despite the heat and humidity still clinging onto the remnants of the day. It was almost seven o'clock in the evening, and the sun was already casting long shadows across the tall grass and long-abandoned structures that would soon become part of a particularly gruesome crime scene.

The boy's body was bloated, discolored, and in a state of advanced decomposition, undoubtedly hastened by the hot and humid weather conditions over the last few days. He was completely nude, and his body appeared to be "posed" in a kneeling position with his back against the interior wall of the abandoned shack near the grain elevator at the Bayfront. Both of his arms were tied behind his back at his elbows. The bones in his shoulders jutted out in an unnatural fashion, suggesting that they were broken. Both of his hands appeared to be missing, looking to have been rather crudely cut off. He also had a deep laceration that extended from the top of his chest to his lower abdomen, eviscerating him and exposing his internal organs. Even more notably, his genitals were missing, apparently cut off, although in a more surgical manner than his hands.

Russ casually handed me a small bottle of Vicks VapoRub as we had done for each other many times in the past. I ran my fingers across the ointment and rubbed a liberal amount on my upper lip, directly under my nose, and gave the container back to him. It helped mitigate the unmistakable smell of death but would do nothing to relieve the horrific sight that would be forever burned into my brain.

Despite this involuntary yet indelible imagery, I followed the instructions of that little voice in my head, prompting me to examine this murder closely. That little voice served me well in the past and became the first of what has become known to other investigators working with me as "Stiles' Rules." Rule number one is to "always listen to your gut," or stated differently, "always follow your instincts."

I inspected the body and the surrounding area as carefully as possible without disturbing the crime scene. I suspected that the victim died from exsanguination, and the lack of pooled blood under the body indicated that the boy was murdered elsewhere. It was evident from the color of his skin and state of decomposition of the body that he's been dead for some time before being staged at this location. The oppressive stench of death was overpowering.

My inspection of the body and surrounding area was interrupted by a commanding voice. "C'mon Marc, get back to the rig and wait for Lakewood PD. You know the drill," Russ said, making sure that we wouldn't contaminate the crime scene.

We used to be partners for a few years as first responders and had countless calls under our belts, but that was in my "previous life." I've since traded being an adrenaline junkie for all the glitz and glamor of being a real-life private detective. Now, nearly a decade later, I found myself standing with each foot in two different worlds as I carefully retraced my steps backward, making sure that I did not disrupt the crime scene.

I wouldn't have even been here if Russ and his partner Stan had not stopped at my apartment at my invitation. I've been working a wrongful death investigation on behalf of a large insurance company, and the case would soon be going to trial. The insurance company stood to lose upwards of five million dollars if the claimant prevailed. The investigation dominated my schedule for several weeks during the summer, and it didn't look good for my client. I was running out of time and ideas, and I don't like to lose.

As I was reading through the file yet again to see if I missed anything, I realized that the adjuster never requested or subpoenaed the medical transport form, or "trip slip" as it's called, and on-scene treatment records for that case. Although I was unsure whether the information would be helpful, I called Russ earlier that day to ask for a copy of the trip slip and the entire EMS report. Since none of the bosses or office personnel were working at the ambulance service on this Sunday of a long weekend, I figured my chances were good that he could access the record without any questions being asked. I was right.

Russ eventually called me back and told me that he found the file and made a copy of its contents. Instead of picking it up at the service, I offered to cook him and his partner steaks at my apartment for his trouble. After getting an enthusiastic nod from Stan, Russ accepted my invitation and brought me the report. It would seem like old times, I thought, as we used to grill steaks outside of the ambulance service garage bays every Sunday when we worked the 24-hour weekend shift together. Plus, it didn't hurt to reward someone for saving me from a lot of unnecessary bureaucratic hurdles. Such requests often demand a lot of red tape and request forms, and I hate both.

Russ and Stan just arrived in their unit, designated as A1, which was the very same rig I manned several years previous. Seeing it brought back a lot of memories as I watched Russ back the ambulance into an empty parking space in front of my apartment. Whether ambulances or police cars, my neighbors have grown accustomed to their presence as most of them knew what I did for a living and that I have friends in both emergency sectors who occasionally visit.

The guys just sat down at my kitchen table as I pulled the steaks from the refrigerator. It was at that exact moment when the notably generic call for an ambulance to respond to the building next to the grain elevator at the Bayfront crackled through the hand-held Motorola radio on the table in front of him. Russ quickly picked up the portable radio to acknowledge the call and asked dispatch whether they had any specific information about the nature of the emergency.

"That's negative, A1, an unidentified male caller requested an ambulance to respond to the shed below the wooded area south of the Bayfront and hung up. No further information is available."

About three square blocks in size and butting up against railroad tracks and the southern shore of Lake Erie, that part of Lakewood has its share of problems. Its inner-city location, proximity to the lake, and challenging vehicle access from public streets and sidewalks provide a convenient location for area residents and drifters alike to engage in various illicit activities. Abandoned and all but forgotten and situated at the base of an incline that makes it difficult to see from street level, it hosts a copse of trees surrounded by overgrown bushes and tall grass. High school kids overdosing on street drugs such as LSD and heroin are not uncommon. It is also not unusual for the homeless to seek shelter in that area, with more than a few succumbing to the elements during the colder times of the year. It's not the first call there, and most assuredly won't be the last.

"Ten-One dispatch, unit A1 is code two to the Bayfront call," Russ spoke into the radio.

After acknowledging the call, Russ asked me if I wanted to relive old times and ride along. "What do you think, one for old times' sake?" he asked as he stood up from the table.

"We could probably use an extra set of hands. You know the terrain and how far we'll probably have to carry him," said Stan with more thought than Russ expected. "Are you still certified?" Stan asked.

"As far as you know, I am," I said with a smirk.

Admittedly, I missed the rush and excitement of responding to calls, so I leaped at the chance. I climbed onto the jump-seat in the rear of the ambulance, just behind the driver's seat. It was Russ' day to drive and Stan to ride shotgun. I held tight as Russ skillfully maneuvered the rig through the heavy holiday traffic near the lake, wasting no time getting to the location. I soaked in the sound of the siren that made cars yield and saw the blurred reflection of the rig's emergency lights in the windows of the buildings we passed at three or four times the posted city speed limit. Until this moment, I thought about how much I missed the rush. Now, not so much.

I could hear Russ communicating with the dispatcher from the radio inside the rig. "A-1 to dispatch, code eleven, code twenty-two. Get LPD down here now and tell them to step on it!"

"Dispatch to A-1, roger, code eleven and twenty-two at 1907 hours," indicating that it was seven minutes after seven in the evening in military time.

Code eleven is the radio code for a dead body, and code twenty-two summons the on-duty county coroner to the scene. It's a subtle and sanitary way to get a message across airwaves that are being monitored by everyone who owns emergency frequency scanners that have become so prevalent these days. Just as quickly as he made the radio call for an expedited police response, the three of us could hear the distant sirens of police cars rushing to our location.

Stan was standing at the front passenger side of the rig and began to vomit. After a minute or so of retching, Russ handed him an unopened can of ginger ale he brought from the ambulance garage. Now warm, he used it like mouth wash, spitting the contents several feet away from the scene and rig. He then wiped his face with a towel I removed from the linen cabinet from the back of the ambulance. The three of us just looked at each other. None of us were able to speak due to the horror we just saw.

When the first police unit arrived, Russ pointed toward the location and warned the officer that it was gruesome. "Yeah, you think? I can smell it from here," the cop gruffly said. Without any prompting, Russ handed the officer the Vicks. "Thanks," he said as he rubbed it across his upper lip and gave it back to Russ.

It was evident when the cop reached the scene. "Holy mother of God. What in the hell?" The officer quickly walked back to his car and radioed police dispatch for detectives and the crime scene unit. "Get them out here, now, and get the Chief of D's out here forthwith." The Chief of D's is police slang for the Chief of Detectives.

The officer was walking back to his unit when he spotted me standing next to the ambulance with Russ and Stan. "And just who in the hell are you?" It was a fair question since I was obviously out of place in my khakis and tan polo shirt rather than EMS attire.

"He's with us. He's an approved civilian ride-along," Russ answered with as much authority as he could muster before I could even open my mouth.

"I'll bet you're glad you picked today," the cop said as he proceeded to the trunk of his police car. He took a large roll of crime scene tape and tied it to a small tree about fifty feet from the shack and began taping off the area.

"You better move your rig unless you want to be here all night," the officer said to Russ. Now mostly recovered, Stan was already in the ambulance and moved it to the far side of a secondary access road that ran parallel to the Bayfront.

Unattended deaths involve a lot of paperwork, and murders require a lot more. It promised to be a long night for everyone.

We waited for the coroner to arrive to declare the obvious. As he arrived in the black van with the word CORONER painted in white lettering across the back, I was surprised to see it was Denny McGovern, who I had partnered with for about six months when I was working for the ambulance service. Small world, I thought. I walked toward him, and we greeted each other warmly.

"Good to see you again, Marc. What are you doing here?"

"It's nice seeing you too. I guess I picked the wrong day to be a ride-along," I replied. Denny nodded and kept walking toward the macabre scene that awaited him.

Over the next thirty minutes, additional police cars, detectives, and members of the crime scene unit arrived, followed by members of the local media. By this time, a crowd gathered on the side of the Bayfront road above the scene, and a contingent of local press formed nearby. Both were kept far back from the sight and smell of the scene by police tape and officers assisting in crowd control.

Russ and Stan were finally cleared to leave by the coroner and police about thirty minutes later. Before we left, I asked Denny for his "best guess" as to the cause of death and whether he found any identification under or near the body. "No identification that I could see. As to the cause of death, or COD, I'll know more after the autopsy. Otherwise, take your pick. There are more than enough possible CODs right now," referring to how the young man was killed. "Dear God, just when I thought I'd seen it all." Denny shook his head and walked back to his van.

As Russ and Stan drove me back to my apartment, we barely spoke. "We'll take a raincheck on the steaks, okay?" It was more of a statement than a question. "We've got to get back to base and change," Russ said.

"No problem at all. I've got to bag up these clothes and shower myself. Thanks, Russ, I owe you one for that report. Would you do me one more favor?" I asked.

"What do you need?"

"Would you let me know the inside scoop as soon as you hear anything?"

"Sure. I drew the short straw, so I'm working right through seven on Tuesday morning. You remember how it is on holiday weekends. I'll call you as soon as I hear anything. After dragging you out to see that, I at least owe you that much."

****

As soon as I walked into my apartment, I removed all of my clothes and double bagged them in an outdoor trash bag, including my socks and underwear. The unmistakable odor of death still clung to the fabric. I placed the bag into a plastic trash bin outside my apartment, making sure that the lid was tightly secured. I then took a long, hot shower, wearing down a bar of Irish Spring until I ran out of hot water.

It was almost eleven o'clock by the time I finished and changed into fresh clothes. I grabbed a beer from the refrigerator and turned on the television for the local news, catching the last few minutes of a repeat broadcast of *Married With Children*. The audience's laughter from the ending scenes of the episode did nothing to elevate my mood or help my state of mind.

The discovery of the young boy's body was the top story of the 11:00 p.m. newscast. It gave me a surreal feeling to watch the live footage being shown from the crime scene I had just left. The young female reporter was interviewing the Chief of Detectives who arrived after we had gone. He refused to provide her with any specific information, but his facial expressions conveyed much. He said that the body of a young, unidentified male was found and that the cause of death was "presumed to be a homicide." If she only knew, I thought to myself. If the citizens of Lakewood only knew. If most people only knew.

The image of the young boy's mutilated body was seared into my mind every time I closed my eyes. A young boy possibly in his early teens, not yet a man. How could anyone have such savagery within them? It seemed he had been dead for some time and tortured, perhaps, for a much longer time. That meant he had to have been missing even longer. Somebody somewhere had to be missing him, I thought. He was someone's son, once in the not too distant past, someone's little boy.

My mind suddenly thought about the police officers tasked with making the death notification to the family. I've had to do that, thankfully, only a few times while working in the emergency medical services' field. As horrible and painful it is to receive the news, delivering such news also takes its toll on the messenger. Some mother and father, perhaps sisters and brothers, maybe even grandparents, were about to have their lives changed forever with just one unexpected knock on their door.

The closing footage aired by the news showed the coroner's vehicle leaving the scene, terminating with its taillights disappearing in the dark of night. Left at the scene was the crime scene tape flapping in the light breeze, and the ground still moist from whatever blood and body fluids remained from the victim.

Chapter 2

My name is Marc Stiles. I'm a 28-year-old licensed private investigator working in Lakewood, a city of about a hundred thousand people situated along the southern shore of Lake Erie. I've had my private investigator's badge since early January of this year, although I worked under another investigation company's license for the last half-decade. I've lived in Lakewood my entire life and have already been married and recently divorced. I have two young children, a boy and a girl who live with their mother, although I see them as much as I can.

Currently, I live alone in an expansive single-story, two-bedroom apartment, and have been trying to put my life back together. Although I'm not in a formal relationship, I'm love-struck with a beautiful young woman named Deana Griffiths, who is also recently divorced. She works at a local insurance company and has a young son who is the same age as my daughter, my youngest child. We have a deep fondness for each other; some might call it being soulmates, although issues within our own lives complicate our relationship.

The senior partner of my detective agency is Paul Owen, a man in his mid-fifties with a hardened attitude and general disregard for working within the straight lines of his profession. His dismissive approach toward authority and his no-nonsense demeanor is perhaps the reason we work well together. Our relationship is more of a peaceful coexistence than an actual partnership. Although Paul holds the agency license under which I work, he gives me and another investigator, Gina Russell, the space we need to get things done.

How I got to my present station in life is full of twists and turns. I'm an only child who was raised by loving and hard-working parents. They made sure I received a quality education at a private school during my most formative years, after which I attended a seminary for both the education and perhaps priesthood. After coming to grips with the fact that my interest in women outweighed my interest in becoming a priest, I graduated but did not pursue that vocation. Instead, I enrolled in the necessary schooling to become an emergency medical technician, paramedic, and firefighter.

Although I applied to become a police officer locally, I failed the physical exam due to poor uncorrected eyesight. I also applied with the New York City Police and the Tampa, Florida Police Departments, scoring in the top one percent of all applicants in both written exams. Like the Lakewood Police Department, I was rejected by both due to the same stringent requirements regarding uncorrected vision at that time.

After several years of working as a first responder as both an emergency medical technician, EMT instructor, and firefighter, I found that my interest remained in investigative work. While working in the emergency medical field, I enrolled in the criminal justice program at a local college. There, I received the certification necessary to become a municipal police officer as a way to sharpen my skills. I also became certified in several forensic disciplines in my post-graduate work. The university offered such certifications to graduates of the municipal police officer training course and active law enforcement officers.

My position enabled me to spend a lot of time with cops from various jurisdictions and see numerous homicides and questionable death scenes. Through the professional contacts I made and the personal relationships that I nurtured, police detectives would often allow me to review the files of unsolved homicide cases. I was frequently permitted to scrutinize crime scene photographs and reports, often over beer and pizza. It was over the last few years that I began seeking a position with a local private investigative firm since I could not physically qualify within the public sector.

The most significant motivating factor that propelled me into private investigative work was the brutal stabbing death of my uncle, Gerald Stiles, in 1982. Despite plenty of forensic evidence left at the scene, his murder in Lakewood went unsolved for five long years.

That was the first murder investigation I worked as a licensed private investigator. After being a cold case for five years, the police arrested a man as a result of the investigation conducted by my firm with me heading the investigation. That was only several months ago. That investigation also opened an unpredictable "Pandora's Box" of unfathomable events involving some of the most hideous crimes committed by some of the wealthiest and influential people in Lakewood and beyond.

IN THE DARK OF NIGHT

Chapter 3

<u>Monday, September 7, 1987 - Labor Day</u>

Jim and Angie Carr live on the outskirts of Lakewood, far west of the city limits in a well-established, quiet and upscale cul-de-sac of larger-than-average homes, each well-maintained with excellent curb appeal showing pride of ownership. Both Jim and Angie were born and raised in Lakewood, went to the same high school, married young, and raised three beautiful children together. They celebrated their thirtieth wedding anniversary last December, about six months before their youngest child, Daria, moved out of their home and married. Jim and Angie were both just 53 years old and even shared the same birthday in May. The last several months were a whirlwind of activity.

It was now just the two of them living in their expansive home as empty-nesters, along with their six-year-old, floppy-eared Golden Retriever named Oscar. By all accounts, they were an idyllic couple. Jim spent the last twelve years as an Assistant District Attorney in Lakewood County. At the same time, Angie worked her way up from claims examiner to head the claims department at Fidelity Mutual Insurance, also based in Lakewood.

Angie could not remember precisely when she began to notice a change in Jim's demeanor, although recalled thinking that the marriage of his daughter, his "special princess," might have been a precipitating factor. It was not long after her June wedding that Jim seemed to be overly consumed by his work. He had gone from spending most evenings and weekends with Angie to working until all hours of the night. He seemed distant and distracted, even when he was not working. She initially chalked his moodiness, as she called it, to missing his youngest daughter as they were always close.

Angie tried everything she could think of to lift Jim's spirits, and even talked about taking a Caribbean cruise sometime in the upcoming winter. It was something Jim had long talked about doing once all of their children were out of the house, so she became very concerned when he abruptly refused the idea one night during dinner. He told Angie that he was working on a very complex and important case that he could not pass on to anyone else. He said that it could be the most significant case of his career and the most prominent case in the history of Lakewood. That puzzled her, as she could not think of any matter being handled by the Lakewood County district attorney's office in the news that matched such a description. It also bothered her as he refused to talk about it, even without specific details, unlike other cases he worked.

Jim and Angie just finished an afternoon barbecue at their house with their neighborhood friends Tom and Peggy Bauer, whose only son also recently married and moved out of town. The couples are close in age and share similar life patterns. However, unlike the Carrs, the Bauer family moved to Lakewood from Columbus a few years ago as a result of Tom's expansion of his commercial transport business. Peggy Bauer, now a secretary at McDonald, Cervas & Raines, a large law firm that specializes in criminal defense work, picked out the neighborhood and house in which they have lived since they relocated.

Angie and Peggy are somewhat close and confide in each other as friends do. It was Peggy, more than Angie, who seemed to cultivate a more intimate relationship after both of their children married. While the women worked in the kitchen, washing and putting away the dishes and leftovers, Jim and Tom stayed outside on the patio drinking beer and talking.

"Jim seemed to be in a good mood today," Peggy remarked to Angie.

"Well, I hope he stays in a half-way decent mood. He told me last night that he had finally had enough evidence to give him a big break in the case he's been working since spring. He won't talk about it, but he spent the entire weekend working in his office here at the house. I think he spent all day Saturday talking on the phone and most of the day yesterday meeting with a witness, or at least that's what he said. On a Sunday during a holiday weekend, no less. I wish I knew more about what he's been doing that requires all of this secrecy, even from me. Like I've said, I've never seen him like this before. After this weekend, maybe it's about over."

"Here's hoping," Peggy said as she raised her glass, half-full of wine in the air toward Angie. "Who knows? Maybe my firm will see a surge in business from his big case," she laughed awkwardly and downed the remaining wine in a single swallow.

"Sorry to eat and run, but Tom has an early morning meeting or something, and I've got a doctor's appointment first thing," Peggy said.

"Oh, that's right. I forgot that this is your week in the stirrups and boob press," Angie remarked, trying to move the conversation away from Jim's work. Angie coincidentally received a clean bill of health the week before.

"Good luck. Call me after, and maybe we can meet for lunch."

"Will do. It's not as if my doctor will do the honors after he has his way with me."

After Tom and Peggy walked the short distance back to their house, Angie asked Jim if he wanted to take Oscar for their usual evening walk. "There are not that many more nice days left, you know, and we could both use the exercise after all the food we just ate."

"Sounds good."

Before they left, Jim took an unusual step of locking the door to his home office and placed the only key in his pocket. He patted his pocket as he walked away to make sure it was secure, grabbed a light coat from the hall closet, and handed Angie her jacket.

At the first sound of his leash coming off the hook near the door to the attached garage, Oscar came running, his tail wagging so hard it made a loud tapping noise on the wall. Before turning his attention to a very excited Oscar, Jim checked the locks on the front and back doors of their house. Although this bothered Angie a bit since they lived in a very safe neighborhood, she didn't question Jim lest she ruin his good mood.

Jim clipped the leash to Oscar's collar, and after making sure the front and garage doors were securely locked, they left through the entrance to the patio and began their walk as the sun started to set.

About ten minutes into their stroll and after Oscar marked his usual spots along their standard route, Angie asked Jim if he'd ever tell her about the case that seemed to have consumed so much of his life lately.

"It's just best that you don't know, not right now, anyway." He was abrupt, and she knew when not to push Jim, so she changed the subject. They spent the remaining fifteen minutes of their forty-five-minute walk talking about their week, the kids, and the usual stuff that make up the lives of married couples.

As they neared the back door of their home, Oscar began sniffing the grass, then the brick patio, and then moved back to the lawn. "He's probably looking for food you guys must have dropped," Angie quipped. Jim was not so sure, as Oscar was clearly his dog and spent most of his time at his side. Angie became a bit more alarmed when Oscar stopped sniffing and began barking and snarling in the direction of the window of Jim's office. Jim glanced over in an attempt to see what Oscar was barking at but couldn't see anything as dusk had quickly turned to darkness.

"You hold Oscar and stay here," Jim instructed as he forced the end of the leash into Angie's palm. He then reached into his pants and removed a semi-automatic pistol from a concealed holster hidden in his waistband.

"Where did you get that?" Angie was taken aback by the sight of Jim holding a gun that she had no idea he had.

"Please, be quiet and stay outside while I go in and check things out. If you hear me run into trouble, get over to Peggy's house and call the police," he said forcefully. "It's probably nothing, but I want to check. Please, do what I said." Angie was too stunned to protest and did what she could to keep Oscar calm.

Shortly after Jim unlocked the back door and entered the house, Angie heard Jim yell a string of expletives. She could tell that his reaction was more anger than fear. A minute later, Jim appeared at the door and held it open to let Angie and Oscar inside. As soon as Angie unhooked the leash from Oscar, he scurried directly toward Jim's office, sniffing with extra intensity around his desk and a nearby file cabinet.

"What's going on? Where did you get that gun? When did you get it and how long have you had it?" Angie peppered Jim with questions and demanded answers. "I need to know what's happening. No, damn it, I have a right to know," she protested. Her questions stopped as she looked at Jim's office. Upon entering the house, he unlocked and pushed open the door to find the room in complete disarray. Angie could see a perfect circle cut through the double-hung window that provided a pleasant view of their finely manicured back yard. The window was now fully open, and a chilly breeze rustled the papers that remained across the top of Jim's desk.

Seemingly oblivious to her demands for information, Jim quickly checked the bottom drawer of a locking file cabinet he specially ordered from a safe company a few months back. The drawer was partially open, and whatever contents it once held were gone. Jim slumped into his chair, looking more depressed than his wife had ever seen him. Oscar rushed to Jim's side and put his paw on his leg as if to provide him comfort.

"We've got to call the police," Angie said as she picked up the telephone and dialed. Feeling defeated, Jim listened in silence

IN THE DARK OF NIGHT

Chapter 4

Working in the district attorney's office has its perks. Within minutes, two police cruisers pulled up in front of Carr's house, and two uniformed officers quickly made their way inside. A minute later, one of the officers called for a crime scene unit to respond, something not usually done for "regular" people on simple burglaries. What happened here was no simple burglary.

Upon seeing the flurry of activity and police cars at their friends' house, neighbors Tom and Peggy returned to the Carr's. They sat with Angie at the kitchen table as the crime scene unit dusted for prints and took photographs. One police detective who responded to the scene was taking notes as he talked with the assistant district attorney outside on the patio.

Inside, Tom asked Angie if she knew what was missing and if anyone saw anything. "Do you know if the police have anything to go on? Did anyone else see anything at all?" Tom pressed rather forcefully. They seemed like reasonable questions to ask, but there was something about the way he asked them that troubled her. She didn't answer, partly because she didn't know, and something just seemed to be "off" about the way he asked. She couldn't quite put her finger on it, but for the first time during their friendship, Angie felt uneasy. Perhaps the totality of events was catching up with her. She simply shrugged.

A detective briefly questioned Tom and Peggy. "How about you two? Did either of you two see anything?" Tom said that when he got home, he did some work inside of his garage and neither saw nor heard anything. Peggy also denied seeing anything, adding that she became interested in a television program. Tom returned to the house from the garage about a half-hour later and joined Peggy on the sofa, where they both sat until they saw the flashing lights of the police cars.

It was after eleven o'clock when the last detective left, and Jim and Angie were finally alone. They were both seated at the mahogany table in their formal dining room, finishing what was left of the second pot of coffee that evening. Angie broke the uneasy silence that existed between them. "Now, are you going to tell me what in the hell is going on?" Her question sounded more like an order to Jim.

"I don't like keeping things from you, but it's for your protection."

"Yeah, that's some protection. Somebody came into our house, trashed your office, and took who-knows-what that according to you involves one of the biggest cases this county has yet to see. Then I see you walking around with a gun I didn't even know you had, and the next thing I know, a bunch of cops fill our house, and a crime scene unit comes in and takes photos and prints. They checked every room, opened all the closets and drawers. What a mess." Oscar just then let out a deep sigh from under Jim's feet, almost as if he was following the conversation.

After a pause, Angie snidely remarked, "By the way, I'm not cleaning that up," pointing to Jim's office door, residual fingerprint powder, strewn papers, and broken glass made by a perfect circle cut from the window and falling to the hardwood floor. Jim's grimace turned to a slight smile as he detected a bit of levity in his wife's voice for the first time that night, yet he remained silent.

"Are you ever going to talk to me about this?" Jim's brief period of relief quickly vanished as he was brought back to earth by the realization that all that he had worked for and everything he'd put his wife through over the last several months seemed to be taken from him that night.

"I don't think you'd believe me, even if I told you."

"Try me."

"You might want to switch back to wine or something stronger."

"I'm fine with what I have, and I'm ready to listen. We've been together for so long, and we've been through so much, I think I can handle whatever it is you have to tell me." In a moment of compassion that three decades of life and love have mustered, Angie gently placed her hand on Jim's arm.

Jim began talking. It was as if a valve suddenly opened to release the pressure that built up long past its safety level. It felt good to talk to someone he could trust with his life and would not think he was crazy, considering the information he discovered and the evidence that he and others worked so hard to obtain.

Chapter 5

"Do you remember that five-year-old cold case murder investigation that a private investigator resurrected earlier this year? It involved the murder of his uncle, and the Lakewood Police Department made an arrest."

"I think so. Wasn't it somebody named Stone or Stein?"

"Close. It was Stiles. Marc Stiles is the private investigator, along with his partner and another PI from their firm. His uncle was Jerry Stiles, the victim. He was a school teacher murdered in 1982. It was a brutal murder."

"I thought that they closed the case. You said that the police arrested somebody," Angie insisted.

"They did. I have no doubt that the trial will end with a slam-dunk conviction."

"So, what's the problem?"

"It wasn't too long after the arrest of the perp, a real psychotic dirtbag named Webber, that Marc Stiles asked to see me. I was referred to him by a mutual friend within the police department who we both trust. Marc Stiles asked me to look at the evidence he received or, in his words, "stumbled on" while investigating his uncle's murder. I figured that I'd humor him and give him five minutes at most. As it turned out, I've given him almost five months after everything that he showed me."

"Must've been some evidence," Angie said with raised eyebrows.

"If I did not work to validate and authenticate it myself, I would never have believed it in a million freakin' years. Marc has information about crimes taking place in Lakewood, and I mean hideous crimes involving kidnapping, human trafficking, child sex abuse, and worse." Jim paused and inhaled deeply.

"What could be worse than the sexual abuse of children?" Angie asked.

"Ritualistic abuse and satanic abuse. The things nightmares are made of."

"I've never heard anything about this here or for that matter, anywhere else. Maybe in some East Asian or third-world hellhole, but not here."

"It's not just here. It's happening everywhere. Well, I mean, it's happening across the country and the world. It involves people in high places, with both money and power. It gets worse. It goes all the way into government too, right to the center of power. Their hands aren't clean in the legal sense, either. There are secret government programs that go back to World War II and the Korean War. Mind control, torture, stuff that's found in bad spy novels but never in history books. Rogue people inside three-letter agencies are involved, even today." Jim sat very still, his hands clasped together on the table as if he was talking to a client or another prosecutor.

"You need to know that we've been working on compiling a report to the state attorney, that is the Office of the Attorney General, putting together evidence that Marc, a few others, and myself have collected over the summer on the crimes I've mentioned. They opened a new task force to specifically address these crimes as local agencies have been either loathe to investigate, or worse, maybe even complicit."

"How much longer before you can get it finished?"

"I don't know, but the sooner we get this into their hands, the better I'll feel. Angie, these are evil people. They're sick and perverted. You have no idea. Few people do. Somebody has to do something."

Angie swallowed hard. Her silent response was nothing less than a mix of rapidly changing facial expressions that pained Jim to watch. They ran the gamut from surprise to anger to thoughtfulness to fear and back to anger as she attempted to process the information that she desperately wanted over the last few months.

"I've lived in Lakewood my whole life, and so have you. I've never heard about anything like this. I don't believe it!" Angie became red-faced. Tears began to well up in her eyes. She stood up and began to walk toward the kitchen slowly. She stopped short of the kitchen and stood near his side, slowly turning to look at him. Her arms were folded defiantly across her chest. Jim could almost feel her stare. He continued to look straight ahead as he could not bear to see her like this.

Before Jim could finish his next sentence, he felt the sting of her hand across his cheek. He did not react or even flinch. All he could muster were the words, "I'm sorry."

The sudden tabletop commotion caused Oscar to come out from beneath the table. As if to act as a peacekeeper, Oscar sat down directly between the two, leaning against Jim's leg and looking at his wife. He could feel Oscar shaking, witnessing something that has never happened before in "his" house. Again, Jim softly uttered the words, "I'm sorry."

"Sorry for what? Sorry for not telling me? For putting our lives in danger? What have you gotten us into? I suppose the next thing you're going to tell me is that you're some government spy yourself. After all, that's the way these kinds of stories end, right?" Angie walked into the kitchen. Jim just sat there, stunned at everything that happened.

Jim was still sitting at the table when he heard a knock at the front door. Peering through the side window, he saw Tom and Peggy standing on the porch. Tom was holding a piece of wood and a toolbox. Jim opened the door. Tom was the first to speak.

"I know it's late, but I saw that your lights were still on and figured you could use some help before you called it a night. I've had this piece of plywood in my garage for a while, and I thought it might come in handy to secure the broken window. I didn't think you'd want to go to bed without at least a temporary fix. I brought my tools, and I'd be glad to take care of this for you."

Tom was well-equipped to provide a temporary fix for Jim's window. With his imposing six-foot-four-inch frame and weighing about 275 pounds, he wielded the plywood and tool-filled box with ease. His dark hair was closely cropped to his head and gave him the appearance of a marine just out of boot camp. He towered over Jim by at least six inches.

"Gee, thanks, come in," Jim uttered barely over a whisper. He opened the door to let Tom and Peggy inside. Peggy said something to Tom about wanting to support Angie and walked directly into the kitchen, brushing past the two men, who then walked to Jim's office.

"Wow, what a mess! What really happened here if you don't mind me asking?"

Jim was not much in the mood to talk. He was still distraught over losing something more valuable than the few hundred dollars left untouched in a nearby drawer and his small but valuable collection of watches in a man's jewelry box on top of the credenza. "Someone broke in while we were out walking Oscar." His reply was weak and unconvincing.

"No kidding? Did they get whatever they were looking for?"

Jim did not immediately answer and instead reflected on the rather odd way Tom asked about the apparent burglary. As quickly as he wondered how Tom knew that they were looking for something, he dismissed it to his growing paranoia of nearly everyone and everything.

"Don't take this the wrong way, Tom, but I don't want to talk about it."

"Hey, no problem, I was just wondering. Just curious, you know."

The piece of plywood Tom brought from his house fit perfectly inside of the window frame. It took Tom less than ten minutes from start to finish to install a couple of "L" shaped metal brackets to hold the wood in place while Jim cleaned the broken glass and picked up the strewn paper and other items from the floor. They walked into the kitchen where their wives were seated at the table, discussing the events of the day.

"All fixed, at least for now," Tom said somewhat triumphantly. Ready to call it a night?

With that, Peggy got up and gave Angie an obligatory peck on the cheek while Tom gave Oscar a scratch on his head as they walked out the door. Oscar emitted a low growl at Tom's touch.

It was a few minutes after eleven, and Jim and Angie were both mentally and physically exhausted. Jim checked all of the doors and windows on the first floor to make sure they were closed and locked, closed the blinds and curtains on the exposed windows, and met Angie back in the kitchen. He assured her that the house was secure, and they were safe.

"I was just thinking about tonight," Angie said with more than a note of hesitation in her voice. "I know Tom and Peggy wanted to be helpful, but did they seem…" her voice trailed off into a whisper.

"Did they seem what?"

"I don't know. Did anything feel 'off' about them?"

Jim paused as the question hung in the air while he seemed to be recounting the events of the evening. Despite his observations, he could not bring himself to even broach the subject with his wife. She was already upset enough. "I think they were just trying to be helpful."

"Well, I'm going to bed. Are you coming?" Angie asked.

"I'll be up in a little while. I'm going to clean up a bit, so we don't wake up to this mess in the morning."

"Do you want me to help?" Although the words came out of her mouth, it seemed painfully obvious to Jim that Angie had no desire to help.

"No, please get some sleep. I'll be up soon. If you want, we can talk more tomorrow." Jim walked into his den and shut the door.

IN THE DARK OF NIGHT

Chapter 6

I was jarred awake by the phone ringing on top of the nightstand next to my bed. The big red numbers on the digital clock next to the phone displayed 11:50 p.m. Unexpected calls at that time of the night rarely deliver good news. However, I was anticipating hearing from Russ with more information about the murder near the Bayfront.

"Marc Stiles," I answered, attempting to sound alert and coherent.

"Marc, it's Jim. Are you awake?"

I'm not sure what I hate more; someone who wakes me up from a sound sleep and asking if I'm awake, or the inevitable bad news that follows. On this occasion, I became more concerned about the news as Jim Carr never before called me this late at night.

"Yeah, I am now. What's up?"

"The package you gave me, you know, the evidence from Sadie Cooper, it's gone. Someone broke into my house tonight while Angie and I were out walking Oscar. They managed to get into the safe and took everything." I detected a slight tremble in Jim's voice as he explained the events of the evening.

"Dammit, Jim, how could this have happened? I didn't think anyone knew you had the evidence, especially not at your house." I sat up on the side of the bed, feeling angry and betrayed. "Do you want me to come over? Do you want to meet?"

"No, not now, not tonight. Angie's pretty upset. She's upstairs pretending to sleep, and I can tell you that she's not very happy with me."

"How much does she know?" I asked, holding my breath.

"I told her as little as possible, but as much as I felt I could. I'm not sure she believes it, or me. I didn't give her any specifics except that it involves the investigation into your uncle's murder and that you brought me into the fold of the bigger crimes. I gave her just some of the high points, but again, nothing too specific."

"Marvelous. Does Angie know that we've been meeting over the summer?"

"No, she has no idea, and I'd like to keep it that way for now."

"Of course. How about the DA? I mean he's your boss, so did you tell him? Does he know anything yet?" I asked.

"Hell no! How could he? You know he has no idea about what we've been working on since May. Marc, I even lied to the police tonight. I told them that I thought someone broke in to look for valuables. I said that I had a small coin collection and some cash in the safe, not damn evidence! And I'm an officer of the court!" Jim's voice began to raise a few octaves.

"Did they buy it?"

"What do you think? They passed over my watch collection that was in plain view just ten feet away from my cabinet and didn't bother to take about a hundred bucks I had stashed in my dresser drawer. I'm sure the lead detective thinks that I'm either hiding something or whoever broke in is the stupidest burglar walking the planet. That was a difficult sell considering that this was a professional job. He didn't exactly look convinced when we talked."

"Did the crime scene guys find anything?"

"No, not a damn thing. Not one print and no trace evidence."

"I wouldn't think so, considering the type of people we're dealing with," I replied. Now more alert, I started to run all through possible scenarios, each worse than the last.

"Who else besides you and I know about our investigation and where you kept the evidence I gave you?"

"Nobody at all, and as I told you, my wife didn't even know. Just you, me, and whoever you might have told."

"What do you want to do now? Is there anything I can do?"

"I'll call you at your office in the morning. We'll talk more after I see how this is going to play out after I get to work. In the meantime, make sure you've got eyes in the back of your head." I could tell Jim was in the process of hanging up when I yelled into the mouthpiece. "Wait, Jim, don't hang up!"

"What?"

"Did you hear about the young boy they found murdered yesterday?" I asked.

"Yeah, everybody's heard about it. It's all over the news. Why?"

"The media doesn't know the half of it. I was there. I was at the scene."

"You were what? How in the world did you manage that?"

"I rode along with Russ for old times' sake. The murder was similar to the others," I said.

"Geez, hanging around you is dangerous. I'm sure I'll be briefed on it tomorrow. I'll call you. Go back to sleep." The phone clicked off.

By now, I was very much awake and thinking about the break-in at Jim's house and the timing of the murdered boy. Jim Carr is a hardened prosecutor who's not easily riled. He's prosecuted quite a few cases against some evil people, including mafia members and a few of their hitmen. Even in the relatively small city and county of Lakewood, once a booming industrial town in the era of World War II that has since become part of the nation's rust belt, we seem to have more than our share of criminals.

Jim also received some threats in the past that hit pretty close to home, which, as he told me during the hours and days we spent together over the last few months, comes with the territory. What happened tonight, though, was more than a threat. Moreover, it merely did not hit close to home. It hit home. It hit *his* home.

Going back to sleep now was out of the question. I decided to look over the documents I collected during the investigation of my uncle's murder and the unexpected discoveries made during my investigative work and research. After a brief bathroom visit, I walked into my office that I set up right after the murder investigation was complete.

As the senior partner of the investigative firm, Paul made it clear that he did not want any of "that work" being done inside the agency office as it did not pay the bills. To avoid unnecessary tension, I set up a small command center at my apartment whose existence was known to only a select few people. Paul was not one of the elite few.

My home office has just the right feel to it to be used for this purpose. It was the larger of the two bedrooms, with dark paneling extending from the floor to the ceiling. A large wooden desk faces the center of the room from the east wall, and two brown leather chairs sit strategically in front of the desk.

A matching dark brown leather sofa sits against the far wall, and a credenza to the right of the desk that is home to a recently purchased Smith Corona typewriter. I bought the desk credenza and the typewriter from the same local thrift store in Lakewood.

The sofa and chairs were given to me in July by an attorney instead of a typical cash payment for a case I worked for him last spring. When I initially objected as our agreement was that I was to be paid at an hourly rate, he also tossed in a high-back leather desk chair to sweeten the deal. Although I was in rather desperate need of cash, I knew it was the furniture or nothing. God has an exciting way of guiding and nudging people in specific directions and providing the necessary tools and provisions to do the job of His calling, I thought.

My home office became known as the "war room" to those who knew of its existence. In addition to it being neatly furnished and large enough to fit several people comfortably, I hung a few corkboards and whiteboards on the two of the four walls. I used the corkboards to pin-up newspaper articles, index cards that created visual graphics of leads, and the names of people and suspects. The whiteboards are for timelines and other important reference notes. There were two additional whiteboards on easels, giving the room sort of a command center and war room feel. Moreover, I quickly realized that we were fighting a war that existed not just in the physical world, but as much, if not more, in the spiritual realm.

After grabbing a bottle of Coors from the refrigerator and turning on my radio for some background noise, I unlocked the combination safe from the closet in my office. Removing a handful of file folders, I placed them on my desk. I started to look through the files, unsure of what I was looking for. At least I felt like I was doing something.

Chapter 7

<u>Tuesday, September 8, 1987</u>

Just before seven o'clock, I was awakened by the searing rays of the rising late summer sun coming through the East window of my home office. My mouth was dry, and my neck was stiff as I fell asleep at my desk sometime during the night. I was awake for only a few seconds when the memories of the previous two days came rushing into my head. I surveyed the papers and photographs strewn across my desk, the mostly full beer bottle, and an ashtray filled with spent Marlboros. I felt a sense of foreboding that rivaled the promise of a sunny day.

Living alone, without family or roommates, sometimes has its benefits. By seven-thirty, I had showered, shaved, straightened the unused blanket on my bed, and cleaned up my office without fear of waking anyone or waiting to use the bathroom. I put on a suit that I picked up from the dry cleaners last week and was just about ready to leave. I walked back into my office and looked down at the papers I neatly stacked on the center of my desk. It was at that moment that I felt that living alone, without family, also has its drawbacks.

I sat back down in my chair and looked at the top photograph on the pile of papers I had taken out the night before. Maybe it was because I was tired from the events of last night, maybe it was because of the darkness associated with murder, or maybe it was a combination of everything to this point in my life that I felt an intense wave of emptiness and indescribable sadness.

I stared at the top photograph, which was a picture of my childhood home. It was once my haven. I could almost hear the laughter and feel the good times as I reminisced years past, from being a toddler and growing into adolescence, and being nurtured into adulthood in this modest house, I once considered a sanctuary. Instead of it being inside of a family photo album, it was now just one of many exhibits in the murder case of my uncle. He was stabbed in my old bedroom while my father was working.

IN THE DARK OF NIGHT

I sat quietly at my desk in an attempt to gather my thoughts when I realized that I had not yet turned the radio off from last night. The 1970s song *Forever Autumn* was playing at that moment. The song not only reminded me that the darker days of winter are drawing near but of another intensely painful event that forever changed my life. It pulled my thoughts back to nine years ago, October 21, 1978. I was just 19 years old then and was already working with the Lakewood Ambulance Service as an Emergency Medical Technician instructor and a firefighter on the township fire and rescue squad. It was a Saturday morning at about the same time as this morning when I decided to visit my mother before she began her day. I was on a personal mission that morning to make amends with her for some very harsh things I said in the heat of an argument two days prior. Things that I wanted so badly to retract.

I drove from my apartment that I shared with a co-worker to my childhood home, where she lived with my father, who worked the night shift at a local manufacturing plant. He had taken on a second job at that time that took him directly from his night shift without stopping home. Considering that my father would be working and that I'm an only child, I knew that she'd be alone, and we could talk without distraction.

As it happened, *Forever Autumn* was playing on my car stereo for nearly the duration of my trip. When I reached my parent's home, I knocked on the back door and waited an appropriate amount of time before I used my key to enter the house through the back door. I called out for my mom as soon as I entered the house, not wanting to startle her. Nothing but an eerie and almost oppressive silence greeted me in return. Thinking that she might still be asleep, I walked to my parent's bedroom and saw that the door was open. Pausing briefly at the entrance to the bedroom, I could see her lying motionless and unresponsive atop the bed despite my calls. Even from this distance, I instinctively knew. My heart felt as if a giant fist punched it into the pit of my stomach.

As I slowly approached the side of her bed, it was readily apparent that my mother was dead. By this time in my life and career and despite my relatively young age, I had seen more than my share of lifeless bodies in their many forms of death. It was entirely different this time, though, as I was looking down at the body of my mother. She was just 56 years-old and reportedly died of a heart attack in her sleep, according to a determination made later by the coroner.

Just as quickly as my thoughts wandered back to that day, I mentally jerked myself back to the present. The memories and guilt, however, remained. I briefly wondered whether God was punishing me for the things I said to her the last time we spoke. Things I could never take back, and apologies I could never deliver.

I continued to sit motionlessly, still staring at the photograph. It was in that very same house where my father found the mutilated body of my uncle, Gerald "Jerry" Stiles when he returned directly home from his third-shift job on the morning of April 28, 1982 and called both the police and me. I was off that day and just happened to arrive before the ambulance and police. For the second time in less than five years, I was looking at a dead body in the house where I grew up. Someone brutally murdered my uncle and remained at large for five years. His "cold case" was solved with my assistance, at least in part, just a few months ago.

Lakewood Police arrested Alan Macy Webber and charged him with first-degree murder. He stabbed my uncle about three dozen times in a frenzied attack that left the entire room, from floor to ceiling, looking like a Jackson Pollock painting where blood was the medium of choice.

I could not break my gaze away from the picture of my childhood home and the safety I found there as a child. There were so many happy memories, now shattered by one untimely death and another murder.

It was from my findings related to my uncle's murder that I met Assistant District Attorney Jim Carr. Now Jim Carr might have found himself in a "jackpot" of his own. Not of his choosing, but because he was one of the only people in authority who cared enough to investigate additional evidence of a much more massive and unsavory criminal conspiracy currently taking place in Lakewood and beyond.

Just as I stumbled into a dark underbelly of human and child sex trafficking, satanic crimes involving torture and sacrifice that spun from my investigation of my uncle's murder, Jim received a crash course in these hideous topics throughout the summer. In fact, both of us did, from our own investigations and experiences.

To the public and the press, of course, there is no conspiracy as the facts about such activities are rarely if ever disclosed. If something does not make it in the paper or television news, it simply does not exist, at least as far as the majority of the public is concerned. People can go on living their lives much easier that way, free from worry and insulated from the darkness that exists just under the surface of a false sense of normalcy. I could not help but wonder whether the very unusual murder of the young man found on Sunday was part of this dark underbelly of satanic ritualistic conspiracy. Actually, I am sure of it, just as I am confident that the timing of the break-in at Carr's house was not coincidental to this case.

Chapter 8

As I walked over to turn the radio off, my knee bumped my briefcase that I probably moved a half-dozen times since bringing it into my apartment on Friday, knocking it sideways to the floor where it hit with a thud. In all of the excitement that occurred over the long weekend, I didn't take the time to organize my case notes from last week or look through the mail I had taken from my desk Friday night.

I picked up my briefcase by the handle and slung it to the top of my desk, opened it, and removed the handful of papers from the mail Annie left for me. It was then I noticed the plain, business-sized envelope with no return address. It was addressed to me and marked "personal and confidential," which explains the reason Annie didn't open it like every other piece in the stack. Everything was typewritten on the outside of the envelope, making it appear to be a standard business letter. The postmark indicated that it was mailed locally, from somewhere within Lakewood, at the beginning of last week.

Curious, I hastily opened the envelope and removed a single sheet of white paper. It was creased sharply and folded three times instead of the customary two, with writing on one side. I immediately knew this was no business correspondence. It was tauntingly personal, starting with "Tick Tock Mister Big Shot PI."

Instead of being typed, it was carefully printed in an unusual color of ink that looked like a mixture of brown and maroon, taking on the appearance of dark rust. Although the paper was unlined, each sentence seemed to be perfectly level and centered from right to left and top to bottom, with each letter of each word and every line perfectly spaced. Whoever wrote this did so with great care, I realized, and it must have taken a lot of time.

Despite reading it several times, I was uncertain of the precise message or messages beyond the obvious. It read like a hybrid admission and warning that seemed to contain information that I was supposed to figure out. An inverted pentagram was hand-drawn in a perfect circle under the last line,

"For MOLOCH," which is an obvious reference to the demonic or satanic. It was clear to me that this had everything to do with the satanic crimes we've been investigating and perhaps the murder of the young boy found over the weekend. The immediate impact the letter had on me was somewhat destabilizing.

I put the letter back inside the envelope and put it back in my briefcase to take to the office with me. I looked through the remaining mail, finding nothing else of significance, and left for the office.

I finally got to my office a little after 8 a.m., unlocked the front door, turned on the lights, and made coffee in the well-used coffee maker located in the reception area of our suite. I called our answering service for any messages that came in after hours, taking three messages for Paul from his security clients. Paul had expanded his security services after I became his business partner, leaving me the task of overseeing the investigative side of the agency.

The service then informed me of receiving two calls from a woman who refused to identify herself. The first call came in at about six o'clock yesterday evening. This mystery woman first asked for me by name and wanted to know if I was in the office. When the representative explained that she had reached our answering service, she stressed that she needed to speak with me right away and asked for my home number, which they declined to provide. Less than ten minutes later, she called a second time and asked for Gina, making the same request and getting the same response. Although she sounded almost hysterical and stressed that it was "a matter of life or death" that she speaks with either Gina or me right away, she refused to provide her contact information so we could call her back. She hung up before the service could collect any additional information from the woman.

The answering service established a set of protocols dictating how to handle such incoming telephone calls after our involvement in my uncle's homicide began making headlines. It was not uncommon for us to receive all kinds of calls, from the mundane to the cranks, kooks, and occasional threats, depending on our active caseload. High profile cases, such as murder cases, always generated calls from kooks and cranks. Messages of this type that were handled by our answering service were kept in a separate log and were verbally provided to us whenever we checked in. If the call seemed too far out of the ordinary, a supervisor would page either Paul or me. In this instance, the on-duty supervisor at the answering service felt that the calls from the same woman fell into the "kook category." Moreover, the woman caller left no name or return number, so the service employee who answered the call thought it could wait until we opened the office this morning. I wrote down the information from the service and took back control of our phones to our office.

After pouring myself a cup of coffee and unlocking the door to my private office, which is adjacent to the waiting area, I placed my coffee, the messages, and the briefcase I was carrying on top of my desk. I removed my .38 caliber revolver from the briefcase and put it inside my right desk drawer next to my pager as I do most mornings. This time, however, I carefully inspected it as I experienced an indistinct apprehension by the events of the last few days and now, the letter.

I began thinking about the two telephone calls from the unidentified woman. Something about them made me feel that they were important and relevant to recent events, from the murdered boy, to the break-in at Assistant District Attorney Jim Carr's home, to the letter I received. Something seemed to be brewing, which gave me an uneasy feeling. Not knowing is the worst part.

Despite my uneasiness, I needed to take care of company business, or "precious billable hours" as Paul always called them. I was happy that I was able to short-circuit the system by getting the EMS record from Russ for the insurance case. I placed the field report and trip record into the file and began to write up notes of my work on the case. I began to review the handwritten notes of post-surveillance interviews conducted by Gina and was impressed by her abilities. She is the first female investigator Paul hired in his twenty years of operating a private investigative agency. She was brought aboard five years ago when she was just 25 years old.

Gina earned a degree in criminal justice, joined the police academy, and worked for three years as a police officer for a small department about 30 miles west of Lakewood. She was furloughed when the state disbanded the department she worked for due to budget reasons.

When I first saw her, I thought that she looked a lot like an actress or a model, but with a tough, street-wise side to her. She accomplished much as a cop, from patrol duties to working vice. After being furloughed, she decided not to find employment with another police force, wanting instead to hone her investigative skills without having to spend time patrolling the streets.

She became pregnant in her senior year of high school by a young man she hasn't seen since and is presently a single mother to her 13-year-old daughter. The fact that she is a mother played a role in her decision not to continue her police work, as most of the available police jobs are located in the larger cities with rampant crime and street violence. She recruited herself into Paul's employment, and the rest, as they say, is history. Gina and I became close as we often worked cases together, including and especially the investigation into my uncle's murder.

It was eight-thirty when Gina walked into the office with Annie Knoll, the office secretary Paul hired in January, right before we became partners. At just 25 years old, the same age Gina was when Paul hired her, Annie was proving to be the glue that seemed to hold the office together. She knew more about Paul, most of the cases, and me than she would ever tell, and she kept things running smoothly between all of us and our case load. Attractive, mature, unmarried, and romantically uninvolved at the moment, Annie is focused on her job. She is self-motivated with a penchant for solving complex puzzles. Annie also has excellent observational skills, is superb at recalling details, and is destined to become a fantastic investigator.

"Good morning, ladies," I yelled through my open office door. Annie replied with a cheerful hello, but Gina merely nodded and walked right into my office without saying anything, shutting the door behind her. She walked over to the conference table, sat down, and set her large handbag next to her chair. A look of concern was apparent on her face. Gina's instincts were as good as her sources, which made me value her input.

"Did you hear about the murder of a young man down at the Bayfront Sunday?"

"I did. Do you know anything?" I asked in a hushed tone that matched hers. I moved from my desk to the chair across from her, opting to see what she knew before I said anything more.

"I made some calls and got some information from one of my sources down at the station. There's quite a buzz going around the department that this was a ritual killing. I should have the autopsy report today, compliments of my friendly stalker Petey from the medical examiner's office. I called him yesterday to ask if I could have a copy of the report based on what I heard from my source at the station. He agreed to give me a copy of the autopsy report on the condition that he could finally take me to dinner."

"That sounds fair," I said with a smile.

"That sounds like extortion! I finally negotiated him down from dinner to lunch," Gina said as she rolled her eyes, thinking about having to spend time with a nerdy guy in his early thirties who spends his time working with dead bodies. And if the rumors are correct, he likes to talk to them too. I knew that he'd been asking her out for months.

"I like it! Thanks for taking one for the team. Now, how about grabbing a cup of coffee and coming back to my office? We have quite a few things to talk about," I replied.

Her mood seemed to lighten a bit as she walked toward the door. "So, you do know something, don't you?" Gina said as she cracked a smile. "Hold it right there, and I'll be right back."

I moved to the conference table, where I brought my notepad along with a few files, including the insurance case. Gina joined me, turning on the radio before she sat down. The radio and classical music, as much as I enjoy it, is also a counter-surveillance measure. It's a habit we both developed after working on my uncle's murder case.

"I know you might find this hard to believe, but I was on the ambulance with the first responders who responded to the call. I was at the murder scene before the police," I said to her casually.

"How did you manage that? Don't tell me that you're moonlighting now. Wait, you aren't, are you? Do you know something I don't?"

"No, it's nothing like that. I called Russ for the EMS report for our insurance case, and he dropped it off at my apartment when the call came in. I went with them as a civilian ride-along. It was purely coincidental and very unofficial, of course."

"Sure, it was coincidental and unofficial, of course. It's always unofficial with you," Gina said with a hint of sarcasm in her delivery.

I've lived by the fact that obscurity permits a certain amount of professional traction at critical times, and this was indeed one of those times. It is one of my operational rules, referred to around the office with a touch of humor as "Stiles' Rules."

"Remember Stiles' Rule #14," I said.

"Remind me again, please," Gina insisted, playfully emphasizing the word, please.

"Stiles' Rule #14: Deliberately orchestrated obscurity permits personal and professional traction."

"I guess I'm going to have to start writing these down."

"Don't just write them down, commit them to memory and practice them," I chided.

"How many rules are there?"

"Officially, fifteen."

"Tell me about it. Was it as bad as my source said it was?"

"In a word, yes." I filled her in on all of the gory details while she took notes in a special notebook we both carried for such cases. We documented as much information as possible for use by the state Office of the Attorney General, who recently formed a special task force to investigate human trafficking and sex crimes against children.

"As if that's not enough, there are even more things going on than that right now," I said.

"Like what?"

I told her about the break-in at Jim Carr's house last evening while he and his wife were out for a walk with their dog, and that some of the photographs, documents, and other items that Sadie Cooper gave us were taken from his safe. Nothing else, just the evidence we all worked so hard to protect.

"How did that happen? No one outside of the "Carr Club" knows that stuff even exists!"

The "Carr Club" is the official name Gina created for the small group of "white-hat" investigators dedicated to exposing the people behind the human and sex trafficking, child prostitution rings, ritual crimes, and other hideous offenses taking place in Lakewood and beyond.

Established after we investigated my uncle's murder, the Carr Club has only a few primary investigators. In addition to Jim Carr, who holds the most senior professional position among us and after whom the club was named, it consists of Gina, Annie, and me. The club's name also serves as a linguistic diversion in the event anyone heard the name of our group. Should someone outside of our group hear the name, they would likely think of a few car aficionados rather than discovering the true nature or purpose of our group. As necessary, which became at least once a week lately, we'd all meet at the war room to discuss our continuing investigation into the perverted crimes everyone else refused to believe are happening.

"Well, obviously someone found out. The question is, how? Ours is a tiny and tight-knit group. Whoever hit Jim's house knew what they were looking for." I said.

"Do you know everything that's missing?"

"I'm not sure. Jim said he'd call me today, so I'll know more after we talk. I think we've done a pretty good job of spreading the evidence out and keeping copies of all of our work, so I'm not sure how far this will set us back. I'm fairly certain they got the gold pendant and chain given to us by Sadie Cooper."

"Dammit! I thought you had that in a safety deposit box at the bank," Gina said.

"I did until about two weeks ago when I gave it to Jim at his request. I gave it to him because he said that he was in the middle of preparing a comprehensive report for the state Attorney General and wanted it for evidence. I signed off on the chain of custody form, so I thought that meant we were one step closer to exposing these pedophiles, Satanists, and rich and powerful perverts who've escaped justice for so long."

The gold pendant belonged to Sadie Cooper's husband, Benjamin

Cooper. Her late husband wore it all of the time, and he was wearing it when he was found with a bullet in his brain. She gave it to me in a Ziplock bag when she visited our office at the same time that they arrested my uncle's killer. It was surprisingly heavy and very dense for its size. Upon closer inspection, we learned that the ornate pendant and chain were crafted using solid gold. The pendant was that of a head of a goat inside of the circle, or that of a Baphomet symbol. On the obverse, there were small etchings that included a .999 gold designation, along with the "SS" lightning symbol used by the Nazis.

Mrs. Cooper said that its provenance was authenticated and traced to gold taken from Jews at the Nazi death camps. She was insistent that we knew that the gold that's in this trinket was not from the jewelry of the Jews but extracted from their teeth. The chain and pendant still had the bloodstains of Benjamin Cooper on it as a result of his alleged suicide by gun.

"Let me know when you get the details from Jim. In the meantime, as I said, Petey is going to give me the medical examiner's report when we have lunch," Gina said.

"There are a few more things that I think you should know. First, I'm not sure how or even if this fits into everything that's going on right now, but I've just got a bad feeling about it. Look at these messages I took from the service when I came in this morning." I slid the legal pad across the desk to Gina. She took her time reading each entry and noting the times.

"I don't like this at all," she said. "These came in last night?"

"Yes, the first call came in at six, and the second call came in about ten minutes later. It was the same woman, according to the supervisor."

"This has got to be related to our Carr Club investigation, don't you think?" Gina asked. "Do you have any ideas about who it could be? Considering the events of the last two days, this is no coincidence, and certainly wouldn't involve any of the cases we're working here."

"Well, we don't have a lot to go on. I just wanted to keep you in the loop."

"Thanks, I think."

"One more thing," I said as I reached into the pile of papers next to me. "Look at this," I instructed Gina, sliding the letter I opened this morning across the table to her. I had put it back in the envelope and watched her carefully remove it after spending several seconds studying the outside of the envelope. I sat in silence while Gina looked intently at the letter.

"According to the postmark, this came into the office last week. Why did you wait so long to show this to me?"

"I was out of town all last week on that theft case from the trucking company, remember? When I got back Friday night, I just stuffed all of the mail that Annie put on my desk into my briefcase. She didn't open it as it was marked personal and confidential, and I didn't see it until this morning."

"It reminds me a little bit like the "Son of Sam" letters. 'Tick Tock, your time is short?' That sounds rather ominous," Gina said.

Just then, the office phone rang, and Annie picked it up on the second ring. Gina and I were looking at each other as we strained to listen to Annie's side of the conversation. We didn't need to listen very long as we heard Annie place the call on hold and get up from her desk. She knocked on the office door, opened it a crack, and pointed at me, saying that Detective Jenkins of the Lakewood Police Department was calling for to me. "He said it was urgent."

"Marvelous, I wonder what this is about," I said to Gina as I walked to my desk to take the call while motioning to her to stay seated.

Ron Jenkins is a longtime friend and a dedicated cop who was promoted from patrol supervisor to the position of detective a few months back. He is a genuine white hat and knew about the existence of our side investigations, although not the details. He was not privy to all that we knew, which was deliberate to avoid putting him in a potential jackpot as a police detective.

"Marc, I need to talk to you and Gina as soon as possible. We need to meet, but I don't want it to be anywhere we can be seen by our guys," a reference to other police officers or detectives from Lakewood.

"How about the war room?" I suggested.

"I like the privacy part of that, but it's too close and too noticeable."

"Okay, you pick the location. Just tell me when and where and Gina and I will be there," I responded, although curious about the need for secrecy from the police department.

"Let's make it for eleven-thirty today at The Blue Roof Truck Stop by the interstate. Look for me in a booth in the back." He immediately hung up after confirming the time and location, not giving me a chance to respond.

I looked at Gina. "How do you feel about a change in lunch plans today? Since you're already committed to taking one for the team, do your think Petey would mind an early dinner date instead of lunch? Jenkins wants to meet us at eleven-thirty, and it sounds pretty important."

"Oh, man, the things I do for you. I'm sure he'll be delighted with me for changing the plan back to the original dinner date. I'll call him in a minute and make his day," Gina said before asking Annie to come into my office.

Gina showed Annie the envelope, asking if she recalled seeing it and whether there was anything unusual about its delivery.

"No, it came in the mail on Tuesday, I think. I saw that it was personal for Marc, so I didn't open it and put it on the pile of mail I put aside for him while he was gone. Is something wrong?"

"Since you're part of the Carr Club and have a stake in everything that we're doing, read it and tell us what you think." Gina handed the letter and envelope to Annie, who sat down at the conference table.

"Wow!" Annie said. "Marc, I had no idea what was inside. I would have opened it, but it was marked 'personal and confidential.' I probably should have told you about it when I spoke with you during the week."

"Don't worry about it, Annie. Since you're good at solving puzzles, why don't you make a copy of it and let your analytical mind go to work on it," I said. "Oh, Gina and I have to meet with Detective Jenkins this morning. We're going to meet at the truck stop by the interstate."

"I'll be ready to leave at eleven," Gina said to me as she and Annie walked out of my office together. Pausing at the door, Gina turned and asked if we should show Jenkins the letter.

"Not yet," I answered. "I don't see anything specifically actionable in it, do you?

"No, I guess not."

A minute later, Annie returned. "I made four copies, along with the front of the envelope. I've got one, I gave Gina a copy, and you have two copies along with the original. I'll let you know what I come up with, if anything."

IN THE DARK OF NIGHT

Chapter 9

Gina and I arrived at the truck stop ten minutes early, finding that Jenkins was already sitting at a booth in the back of the busy truck stop restaurant. Judging by the opened sugar packets strewn on the table, he looked to be on his second or third cup of coffee. As we neared the booth where he was sitting, I could see a closed manila folder on the table in front of him. Gina and I slid across the bench opposite him, sitting next to each other. Instead of our usual pleasantries, Jenkins blurted his first question before we were even comfortably seated.

"Exactly how well do you two know a woman named Sadie Cooper?" He asked the question just above a whisper but with a force that matched his authority as a police detective.

"Good morning to you too," I said.

"Not now, Marc, this is serious," Jenkins said.

I could feel Gina tense up, but she chose to remain silent and let me do the talking. I stared at him, not quite knowing how to answer or even if I should answer. I thought for a moment and decided to play it cool as I had a horrible feeling about where this was going, despite our longtime friendship and professional relationship.

Gina and I both know and vividly remember Sadie Cooper, but the backstory is complicated. We met her earlier this year during the investigation into the murder of my uncle. Sadie Cooper was a slender, tan, and bleached-blond fifty-year-old woman who always did her best to appear half her age and made sure people knew she was a member of Lakewood's upper class. Wherever she went, she was always wearing designer clothes and expensive jewelry.

Her husband, Benjamin Cooper, was a person of interest in the early stages of our investigation into the murder of my uncle. We ultimately ruled him out as a homicide suspect, but he eventually evolved into an active suspect of something much different and much more significant. That is, of course, until his untimely death by his purported suicide not long after we began making inquiries and significant inroads with him. Sadie called the police one day last May when she allegedly found him sitting at his desk in the den of their palatial Lakewood estate with a single bullet wound to his head. Blood, bone fragments, and brain matter covered the walls to his left and behind him.

The murder weapon was a .45 caliber Glock that was reported as stolen from a now-retired Lakewood police officer in 1980. Police at the time confirmed that neither Cooper nor his wife owned any handguns before or at the time of his death. How the stolen gun made it into Cooper's possession has never been answered. After his death, the newly widowed Sadie Cooper provided us with a lot of information about the dark secrets of Lakewood. Secrets that included her husband.

Benjamin Cooper was a wealthy industrialist with interests in the steel industry. As that industry began to die off in the late 1970s, turning Lakewood into part of the country's rust belt, Cooper supposedly sold his company to a Chinese firm and mysteriously made a fortune.

She admitted that she married Benjamin for his money and the security it provided and claimed that she was in a loveless marriage. At age sixty-four, her husband was about fifteen years her senior. He considered her his trophy wife or arm candy at elite Lakewood functions, at least in the early years of their marriage.

In reality, however, Benjamin Cooper was not his real name. Our investigation determined that he was born Rudolph Fleischer in pre-war Germany. Growing up, he became a member of the Hitler Youth Party and then a full-fledged Nazi who served a brief stint at a Nazi death camp. He then came to the United States when he was only twenty-two years old. From materials given to us from Mrs. Cooper, we learned that her husband was one of the first and youngest members of the Nazi party to be brought into the United States, courtesy of our government, under a covert blanket program titled Operation Paper Clip. Fleischer graduated early from a German university, where he was well known for his scientific prowess and achievements. He played a role in that capacity at the death camp, although the exact nature of his activities was not publicly known.

After arriving in the U.S., Cooper, or Fleischer, worked at a lab for the government. During our initial questioning of Sadie Cooper, she knew about his academic background but claimed to have little knowledge of her husband's business. She stressed that he was very secretive about it. When questioned about how he got his initial start in business to become among the rich and powerful. she was a bit more forthcoming.

She claimed that her husband got his start with government seed money but denied knowing the specifics of his business arrangements. She added that her husband would leave Lakewood once a year to spend a few weeks in the Washington, DC area, including Virginia and Maryland. Despite his routine annual absences, he refused to speak to her about his activities away from home.

Gina and I knew that patrol-supervisor-turned-detective Jenkins knew Sadie Cooper, was familiar with her single-car accident that reportedly claimed her life, and her husband's alleged suicide. Even though he is not part of our core investigative team, we consider him a white hat investigator and a person we can trust. Because he was not part of the Carr Club as it would be a conflict with his detective position, he did not know the entire backstory about Cooper. I continued to walk that very fine line between these two worlds even as I finally answered him.

"Sure, she was the conveniently widowed woman who was killed in a freakish one-car accident the day my uncle's killer was arrested. She was burned up pretty bad if I recall."

Jenkins glared at me with his steely blue eyes for what seemed to be an eternity. I could tell that he was carefully gauging my reaction as he anticipated my response.

"Marc, don't screw with me. Do not screw with me, not today. Wanna try again? How about you, Gina?" The forcefulness with which he responded startled both of us.

"What do you want us to tell you?" I asked.

"The truth, dammit. All of it. I'm on your side, remember? But I can't risk my career to cover for you if you're withholding information, and neither of you can afford to be charged with obstruction of justice. And dammit, Marc,

I'll charge both of you if I have to. Don't test me."

For the first time in our personal and professional relationship, I had the feeling that we could be in serious legal jeopardy if I did not tell Ron the whole truth. I felt that he was about to read us our rights, something every private investigator and any other sensible person on the planet would typically want to avoid. On the other hand, if we told Detective Jenkins everything we knew about Sadie Cooper, we could put this "dead woman's" life in jeopardy. The information would be made into a report that could then be accessed by anyone within the department. Gina and I did know the truth, or at least some of it, and were holding out on Ron. Moreover, Ron Jenkins, the detective, knew it.

The truth is that Sadie Cooper did not die in that freakish car accident last May. It was not her body that was found in her car that crashed into a ravine and exploded, and both Gina and I knew it. She somehow skillfully faked her death and skipped town to parts unknown. All of this was the result of information she gleaned from her husband about black-ops government experimentation involving mind control, the business of human and child trafficking, and other sordid activities that few people believe exist, except in the movies.

Also, it was Sadie Cooper who played an integral role in shedding light on the murder of my uncle. She was purposely in our office on the day that my uncle's killer, Alan Macy Webber, was arrested. She also provided me with a package of information that exposed the dark underbelly of this perverted world. Until yesterday, Jim Carr had a large part of the information in his home safe.

"Before we tell you what we know, Ron, would you please tell me why you're suddenly so interested in the victim of a four-month-old, single-car, fatal accident?"

"This isn't a negotiation, Marc. I'm the one asking the questions, and I damn well expect you to give me the answers."

I paused again to mentally work through what was happening while Gina sat in uncomfortable silence, squeezing my leg with her hand. I couldn't tell if she was trying to silence me or signal me to be more cooperative. If we were really in trouble for what we knew and kept from Ron, I reasoned, this questioning would be taking place at the police station and not at a truck stop. Given our friendship, which was no secret to anyone within the department, I also doubted that Jenkins would be the detective asking the questions. Having regained some of my inherent cockiness, I decided I'd stay quiet for a few more seconds while meeting his stare head-on. It seemed to work, at least this time.

"Okay. Interpol initially contacted the station this morning. Sadie Cooper or the real Sadie Cooper is dead. She was murdered in London, England, yesterday."

I nearly spat out my coffee upon hearing this news, and Gina covered her mouth with her hand to stifle whatever sound was about to come out. Our surprised reactions were not lost on Jenkins.

"Wait, I'm not done yet. It gets even better," Ron leaned over the table and was now just inches from my face, the odor of coffee coming from his hot breath. "Guess what? They found your business card along with Gina's at the murder scene. She was carrying your business cards before and at the time of her murder, like she was going to contact you guys. Do either one of you care to explain that?"

Gina and I looked at each other as our minds raced back to earlier this morning and the messages that came into our answering service last evening. Whatever doubts either of us had about the identity of the mystery woman caller just vanished. We were now both positive that it was Sadie Cooper who called. It had indeed proven to be a matter of life and death. Her death, in this instance, or her "second" death.

For the next hour, Gina and I told Detective Ron Jenkins everything. We explained how she assisted us in solving the homicide of my uncle. We told him about her intimate knowledge of secret government programs, mind control experiments, human trafficking, sexual slavery, Satanic Ritual Abuse, and all of the perversities that exist below the surface of our nine-to-five world. We explained who her husband really was and how Gina and I uncovered so much about these activities, even in Lakewood.

By the end of our conversation, he had taken so many pages of notes that his hand began to cramp. When we finally finished our dissertation of depravity, he rested his back against the booth and sighed heavily. He seemed to change from detective to friend and from a potential antagonist to promising ally. Nonetheless, he was forced to engage in a delicate balancing act between his position with the police department and our friendship.

After he appeared satisfied that we answered all of his questions and gave him even more than he expected, I asked him if he could tell me what he knew about the circumstances of Sadie Cooper's murder. Suddenly, it was Jenkins who seemed to be on the defensive and appeared to exhibit a growing concern about this latest turn of events.

"First of all, based on what you told me and what I know at this point, I think a crap-storm of enormous proportions is headed your way." He tossed down his pen on the table and rubbed his temples. "I don't exactly know from where or who, but I'm certain that whatever is coming isn't going to be pretty. Unfortunately for you and Gina, you two seem to be right in the middle of it."

"I figured as much Ron, but we're not the ones who declared Sadie Cooper dead or conducted the police investigation into her accident. It seems to me that would fall on your department. We weren't involved with that in any way," I insisted. "You guys closed that investigation."

"It's not about that, or I should say it's not only about that. I read the traffic report and the police file about the accident, and if anything, the guys who did the traffic report might be facing some kind of internal investigation. It's the fact that it was indeed Sadie who tried to call you yesterday just before she was murdered. And it's not just that she was murdered, but how she was killed that is quite disturbing."

"I'm listening," unsure if I really wanted to hear the details but suspected that they might sound eerily familiar.

"I'll know more when a complete copy of the preliminary investigation file arrives from London. What we've already received by Telex suggests that this was no ordinary murder, if there is even such a thing. But here's what I do know. In the last hours of her life, Sadie Cooper was on the run. Two or more people were chasing her. She was ultimately caught and taken to an old warehouse in London that dates back to World War II. The perpetrators, who have not been identified, bound her wrists and ankles and secured her to makeshift moorings on the wooden floor of the warehouse." Ron stopped to take a drink of water that sat untouched on the table since we arrived, which also allowed him to maintain his composure.

"Based on the initial reports, she was badly tortured."

"Is there a good way to torture someone?" I asked rhetorically in an attempt to break the intensity of what I was hearing.

"I guess not," Ron said as he attempted to force a smile while Gina jabbed me in the ribs.

"She suffered a lot before her death. Whoever did this to her not only wanted her dead for real, but seemed to want information from her and send someone a message."

"Ron, this might seem like a pretty far-out question, but are you sure that the victim is really Sadie? From the description of her body, how was she identified?" I asked.

Ron was silent for a few seconds while continuing his stare into my eyes. For a second, I thought I could see the imaginary mechanical cogs working within his brain. He broke his stare by opening and looking at the folder that contained the notes from the London police. He shuffled through a few papers. Finally, he settled upon a page that showed a copy of her passport that was reportedly found near her body.

"Based on the preliminary report, it looks like she was identified through her passport. I don't see anything in here that would cast doubt on her identity. Why would you suspect otherwise? Do you know another Sadie Cooper in London who would be carrying around your business cards?"

"I'm sorry, Ron, of course not. Do you mind if we take a look at the picture you have anyway?"

"Here's what I have. Does this look like the Sadie Cooper you know?"

Ron placed it down on the table between us, right-side-up for Gina and I to view. It was the Sadie Cooper we met in our office, or at least a remarkable likeness. Gina began to weep silently, dabbing her eyes with the paper napkins from the table. I nodded and slowly pushed the picture back to his side of the table. A silence existed between us for what seemed like an eternity. None of us felt like talking anymore. No rational or sane person would.

I finally broke the silence by asking about how the Lakewood Police Department was going to handle the investigation, considering that our names and business contact information was found at the scene and in her possession.

"I don't know yet, Marc, but I'm sure that the London police in the UK certainly will have some questions for you. I'm sure our department and maybe even the DA will as well, in a more official manner," he added. "As I said, I'm expecting more information from the Detective Superintendent from the London police later today or tomorrow, considering the time difference. I don't know what in the literal hell is going on here, and I'm not sure that what you told me cleared anything up. If anything, it just raises a whole lot more questions."

Jenkins looked down at his coffee. "There is one more thing I should tell you. There are two agents from the FBI snooping around, a male and a female agent. They were at the district attorney's office today, and I saw one of the agents talking with the chief. I'm not sure what they're doing here, but it looks like they might be around for a while. I'll let you know more when someone decides that I should know, I guess."

An awkward pause seemed to overtake the table.

"I'll write up an initial informational report, which, as you both know, is less formal than an interview report or statement. Both of you better keep your head on a swivel until we figure this thing out." Jenkins slowly stood up, stretched his legs as he gathered his papers from the table, and gave us a parting glance as he walked from the booth.

Almost two hours after we first began talking, we all left the truck stop together. Ron instructed us to keep the information he shared with us to ourselves until we heard back from him.

Chapter 10

Gina and I got back to the office a little before two o'clock after an unusually quiet car ride. We were both shaken and wondered what would happen next. As we walked in the door, Annie handed me a few pink message slips after greeting us with her natural perky smile.

"Wow, who died?" Annie innocently asked, noticing our apparent dark demeanor.

"Sadie Cooper. You might not remember her. She was in our office back in May. She was reportedly murdered yesterday in London," Gina said matter-of-factly.

"You mean the bleached blond, overdressed woman who popped in our office unannounced on the day Lakewood PD arrested the murderer of your uncle? She was wearing a black cocktail dress, red fingernail polish, and trying way too hard to look half her age? She came into the office and stayed for about 45 minutes, left you guys a package, drank two cups of tea, left our office, and supposedly died in a car accident a short time later. Do you mean that Sadie Cooper?" Annie looked at both of us, waiting for our response.

"Yes, Annie, that Sadie Cooper," I said with a grin.

"How did she die this time?"

"According to Jenkins, she was tortured and murdered in London. Our business cards were found near her body. She apparently tried to call us Sunday night, and the London Police want to know why."

"Are you sure it's her?" Annie asked.

"It looks that way," I answered.

Gina followed me into my office, and we looked through the messages together. One was for Gina from Petey, confirming their 5:30 p.m. dinner date tonight. Two others were for Paul, and one was from Jim Carr. The message from Carr was that he would be tied up in sentencing court until three o'clock, and he would call back when he was free.

"I really don't feel like going out to dinner tonight," Gina said.

"I'm sure you don't, but the stakes have just gotten higher for all of us.

Dinner and the full report from the medical examiner all in one fell swoop. Besides, Petey isn't a bad guy. He's just lonely. After all, he doesn't have too many people who actually talk back to him during the day," I said, again trying to lighten the mood.

"We should schedule a meeting tonight at the war room with just you, Jim, and me if he can make it," Gina suggested. "Even with dinner plans, I'm sure I can make it there by eight if that works for you and Jim."

"I'll check with him when he calls. I think it would be a good idea. We can all catch up on everything that's going on."

For the remainder of the day, Gina and I completed our investigation and surveillance notes on the primary insurance case we were working together so we could submit a preliminary report. We discussed the case and a possible new strategy, although we admitted to each other that we felt like we were just going through the motions.

Jim Carr called just after three and agreed to meet with us at eight o'clock tonight. He was just leaving his office to meet a contractor at his house who was going to replace the glass in his window. He planned to stay at home with his wife until our meeting, which he figured would make up for his later absence. Gina left just after five for dinner, assuring me that she would "report for duty" at the war room promptly at eight. I followed her out the door and drove to the Towne Restaurant, an upscale restaurant and bar conveniently located less than a mile away from my apartment and is a favorite spot for many within the Lakewood professional community. One is likely to see lawyers, city and county politicians, and even judges meeting and mingling here, especially during happy hour.

****

Brenda, the 28-year-old perky, unmarried, and naturally blond manager has been a fixture here for the last five years and was on duty when I arrived. We met on her first day of work when I stopped to privately celebrate the successful closing of a lengthy and complex fraud case involving one of Lakewood's largest employers. I was retained by the CEO of that company before partnering with Paul Owen, and soon found myself sharing information with the Lakewood County District Attorney, who assigned a county detective to work with me for that investigation. After several months of extensive investigation, the District Attorney filed embezzlement charges against the Chief Operating Officer and two of his assistants. Charges were also filed against the Lakewood County Treasurer, who was walked from her office in handcuffs in front of a multitude of television cameras and reporters.

It was that scene, followed by the subsequent press conference to which I was invited and received an "honorable mention," that was playing on the television when I arrived. As she watched me take a seat at the bar, her gaze switched between me and the unfolding drama on the television screen. The timing could not have been better as far as introductions are concerned.

"Hey, that's you on the news!" she exclaimed. "I've been following this case. It's big news in Lakewood. I have to admit that I am a local crime buff, and I just get caught up in these things. It's like a hobby to me, I guess."

"That's quite a hobby," I responded while turning a few shades of red in the process. From that very first meeting, we developed a deep friendship.

Although she's not in a relationship, she knows about my romantic endeavors with Deana. Even so, our friendship allowed us to spend some time together outside of our workplaces. During those times, we shared our hearts with each other about our lives, hopes, and dreams. I've found her to be a very gifted reader of people, and she possesses amazing instincts along with a very high IQ. She's not your typical bartender.

It was during our first meeting that I learned that Brenda holds a degree in criminal justice and planned on entering law enforcement until life, filled with all of its twists and turns, got in the way. Before we met, her father died unexpectedly of a heart attack and her mother became ill. She's an only child like me, and her few aunts and uncles are spread across the country, so she was forced to make certain career choices that permitted her the flexibility to provide care for her mother.

Because we have so much in common, our deep friendship has grown stronger over the last few months. Maybe it's because we're both only children that our relationship developed as it has. Although she is considered by most to be drop-dead gorgeous, I sometimes feel like a big brother to her. A protector of sorts. At other times, I feel something totally different. During one of our deeper personal conversations, she admitted feeling the same way.

As I arrived in the parking lot of the restaurant, I recalled the events of one night earlier this summer. I stopped here after a long surveillance for a quick drink before heading back to my apartment. It was near closing time, and several men were still in the bar area, all who appeared to have had too much sun and more than their share of liquor. When Brenda cut them off before last call, they expressed their disagreement with her decision and began harassing her. The restaurant manager became involved and asked them to leave, although they were slow to move. Once the manager was out of range, a younger man from the group, well known in the community who came from a life of privilege, whispered to Brenda that he would show her how big of a man he really is once her shift was over. The threat was filled with graphic and expletive-laden language that unnerved her. Although Brenda was quite capable of taking care of herself, the threat came at a time when Brenda felt extremely vulnerable. She received news earlier that day that her mother's health was rapidly failing, and full-time hospice care should be considered.

I walked into the bar area that night and greeted Brenda as usual, but I could clearly see that she was upset despite her best attempt to hide her emotions. I sat down at the bar but didn't order right away. Instead, I turned my attention to the small group of boisterous young men dressed in khakis and polo shirts. They were seated at two adjoining tables within the bar area, and each was louder and more obnoxious than the other. I focused on one in particular. He was sitting with his back against the window and facing the bar. I watched as his eyes followed Brenda's every move. He appeared to be in his mid-twenties, had well-coiffed light brown hair and a solid build. He was wearing expensive jewelry and a watch that probably cost more than my car. Second generation trust fund kid, I thought.

I turned back to Brenda, who was now standing close to me, pretending to review the receipts for the night. I gently grabbed her forearm and pulled her closer to me. "Is it them, or is it something else?" I asked.

A tear fell down her cheek as she looked up at me.

"Oh, Marc, it's a lot of things. But right now, it's them. Or at least him in particular," she said, discretely pointing to the man I had in my sights. "He hasn't left me alone all night, and I'm really afraid he's going to do something more than just talk." Reluctantly and after much prodding, she told me what he said to her. Upon hearing what he said, I became angry, incensed, actually.

Before she could say anything more, I left my seat at the bar and walked over to the man who the others called Tommy, deliberately invading his personal space. I bent over and put my face within an inch of his. It was close enough that I could smell alcohol seeping from the pores of his skin.

"Tommy, my name is Marc Stiles, and I just learned that you said some very ugly things to my good friend over there," pointing over my shoulder toward Brenda. "You upset her terribly, and I don't like to see her upset. Now, I'm not going to ask you to apologize, but I am going to demand that you leave now and never talk like that to her again, do you understand me?"

"Screw you," Tommy said loud enough to capture the attention of the others at the table who became quiet as they watched the scene unfold.

I looked away from Tommy while maintaining my posture over him and turned my attention to the others. "Are any of you guys going to take this young man home and teach him some manners, or do I need to do it?" No one said a word, appearing to be transfixed in the moment.

In retrospect, probably should have known better to look away. Tommy took this opportunity to land a punch between my left eye and ear, his college ring ripping a small piece of flesh from the side of my face. Before he could fully stand up and land another, I knocked him back onto his chair with enough force to send him and the chair across the floor and to the far wall of the bar area. Before the others could react, I picked Tommy up by his shirt and slammed his head into the table nearest the wall, face first. I heard a crack as his face hit the table, certainly the sound of a broken nose. When he raised his head, blood was streaming from his nose, and Tommy was crying in pain. "You broke my nose!" His shouts were muffled by blood and mucous that filled his nasal cavities.

In the ruckus, my sports jacket was pulled off my left shoulder enough to reveal the .38 tucked securely in my shoulder holster. The older and much more sober man in the group looked at me, then back at Tommy, then to the others.

"C'mon guys, let's go. Tommy's had too much to drink, and he threw the first punch. We don't need any trouble with the law." I didn't bother to correct his erroneous assumption as they all got up and started toward the door. Instead, I followed the group from a comfortable distance to the parking lot to make sure they all left. I watched as the older man of the group assisted Tommy into the passenger seat of a late model BMW and handing him a towel to stop the blood flowing from his nose. The man then got into the driver's seat as the others filled a second car. I returned to my seat at the bar after I saw their taillights in the distance.

In my brief absence, the restaurant manager had sent two busboys to clean up the mess. By the time I sat back at the bar, all evidence of a scuffle was gone.

"You didn't have to do that, Marc. I'm a big girl and can handle myself, you know. It's just, it's just been a bad day."

"Follow me home. Stay the night, so I'm sure that you're all right and tomorrow I'll take you to breakfast. No strings. Just a safe place for you to be," I said.

"I'm fine, really. A nurse is spending the night with my mother to further evaluate her, so I won't be alone."

"That's even more reason for you to stay under my watchful eye." An agonizing silence persisted between us as I placed my left hand on her arm and brushed a tear from her cheek with my right.

Forty-five minutes later, I ushered Brenda into my apartment.

****

The sound of Brenda's voice pulled me back to the present. "Your usual, hon?" she asked before I even made it to the bar, referring to my preference for straight bourbon. I switched from bourbon and water to just bourbon near the end of the murder investigation, rationalizing that I was "cutting out the middleman."

"Sure, but just one," I said with some hesitance, eyeing her closely. "I've still got a long night of work ahead and need to stay sharp," I responded.

"Wow, it must be some case. I take it that you're going to be needing my exceedingly accurate womanly instincts and sharp detective skills to help," Brenda said with a level of authority she earned during my investigation of my uncle's murder.

She poured my bourbon, neat, placed it in front of me, leaned across the bar, and gave me a kiss on the cheek. "I was just thinking about you. Ya know, I haven't seen you in a while, and I was getting concerned. How long has it been, two weeks? You gotta catch me up on things. Are you still seeing Deana, or are you finally free to sweep me off my feet and take me away from this place?" Brenda said with a forced smile.

"So much for small talk!"

"Well, a girl needs to know these things. At least this girl, anyway." She placed her hand over mine, leaving it there and bent forward to look into my eyes, cocking her head slightly. "I know you're madly in love with Deana, but seriously Marc, I still worry about you, you know, and I don't want anything to happen to you. You've got a bad habit of making enemies with some very nasty people."

"It sure seems that way, doesn't it? Don't worry, my love. I'll be fine," apparently unconvincingly.

"Marc, I've seen the local news. I don't know everything, but my instincts tell me that you're up to your eyeballs in whatever is going on. It feels like there's a bad storm coming, and you're about to be in the middle of it. In fact, I think you're probably chasing it."

I didn't answer, but instead took her hand in mine and squeezed. "You're intelligent and gorgeous, you know that?"

She excused herself and went into the employee area behind the display wall of liquors. I thought I noticed tears starting to well up in her eyes as she turned away. It was unusual, and at this point, a disconcerting emotion to see coming from this strong young woman. I became somewhat unnerved by it.

I had finished my drink by the time she returned. "I've got to go," I said, managing a smile to reassure her.

"Come over here. I want a hug before you leave. Who knows when I'll get to see you again," Brenda said with a shaky voice. I obliged, and we embraced for several seconds, stirring feelings deep inside me that I hadn't felt since that night at my apartment earlier in the summer. She rubbed her hand on my back and whispered, "be careful" in my ear. I gently kissed her on her forehead and left the bar without saying anything else, feeling her stare as I exited the bar. I began to wonder whether she knew something I didn't.

Chapter 11

By 8:00 p.m., I already finished my second pack of Marlboros and a half-pot of coffee. Inside the war room, I dedicated a large whiteboard for this meeting, sectioning it into three columns by black electrical tape. The far-left column contained information about the body of the young man found at the Bayfront. The middle section was dedicated to the break-in at the home of Jim Carr and was mostly blank. The third column was simply titled "Sadie Cooper."

Gina and Annie were the first to arrive. Gina casually let herself in with a spare key I had given her for convenience and in case of an emergency. She was carrying a manila folder with papers sticking out of both ends. Annie had her notebook along with a copy of the letter sent to me.

"How was dinner?" I asked, looking at Gina.

"It was nice. Peter is a good guy at heart, and he's had an interesting life. I think I heard all of it tonight. Better still, he came through for us." Gina held up the file folder she received in exchange for her dinner date.

"So, it's Peter now," I chided.

"He deserves at least that much respect from us. He knows far more than people give him credit for. He's quite intelligent and has a great sense of humor, despite the daytime company he keeps. And he's a man of his word." Gina placed the file and my desk, tapping it with her hand. She was about to say something when a knock on the door interrupted our conversation.

"I'll get that," Gina said as she spun out of the room toward the front door. She let Jim Carr inside and offered him coffee.

"I brought my own, thank you," holding up a large cup from the nearby McDonald's. "Have you tasted Marc's coffee lately?"

"Hey, I heard that. Someday I'll create my personalized brand of gourmet coffee, and it will be a hit! I'll be a coffee tycoon and retire on some tropical island," I said.

With the four of us now gathered inside the war room, Gina kicked off her shoes and sat on the sofa, tucking her legs under her body. She had picked up the folder from my desk and rested it on her lap. Jim sat next to her and leaned forward, studying the sectioned board a few feet away. I sat on one of the leather chairs, turning it away from my desk and toward the others. Annie sat in a leather chair close to me.

"Before we begin, I want to make sure we all agree on something," I said. "Everything we've uncovered during our murder investigation and over the last few months confirms that my uncle was not involved in any of the abuse of young boys. To the contrary, he was trying to uncover the abuse and was murdered as a result of it, or because he saw something he shouldn't have seen. I just want to keep our scorecard of good guys and bad guys straight."

"I'm in total agreement," Gina said.

"No problem here," Jim added. "I also think that what we see now is directly related to us closing in on some very sick bastards who traffic children. Don't forget that everything started when you opened the investigation into your uncle's murder after it went cold and sat around for five years. You and Gina shook a lot of trees during your investigation and stepped on a lot of toes."

"That would be just like us," I replied with a wry smile. "I suspect this piece of fan mail that came in last week supports your assessment. Annie and Gina have already seen it," I added, handing a copy of the letter to Jim.

As Jim studied the copy of the letter, I explained that I forgot about it and left it unopened in my briefcase amid all of the excitement during the holiday weekend. The color of the ink of the original letter, I told him as he looked at the black and white copy, was written with an odd brown and reddish or rust color ink. I added that the postmark was Lakewood.

"Whoever wrote this seemed to go out of their way not to make any actionable threats that would elicit police involvement. From my experience in the district attorney's office, I don't see where any laws have been broken by the person writing and sending this. It looks like it contains some type of cryptic message that I suppose could be viewed as a warning, but not necessarily a threat. It's all kinds of creepy, but not illegal by itself," Jim assessed.

"We determined as much. What's the primary message? Anyone?"

Annie spoke up. "I have a couple of ideas."

Everyone looked up from the copies they were holding in anticipation. "First, it was addressed to Marc personally, so I believe this has everything to do with the investigation into the murder of his uncle, or the continuation of the investigation. Look at the first line of text after the greeting to 'Mister Big Shot PI,' who is obviously Marc," Annie said with a slight smile.

"The first line is a reference to Sadie Cooper's warning that we had a choice to continue our investigation into human trafficking and ritualistic sexual abuse of children or leave it alone."

"And we purposely chose to continue our investigation," I added.

"Six are chewed clean, just bones? Does that mean what I think?" Gina asked. "Six victims somewhere?"

"It sounds that way but is hardly specific."

"If my memory serves, the Son of Sam used the phrase 'programmed to kill' in his spree in New York City a decade ago," Gina said.

"Super Soldiers? Operating on a different frequency?" I asked.

"I don't know."

"What about the reference to the owl?"

"Egyptians associated the owl with death. It could also be a reference to the night," Annie interjected. "It is also considered to be an omen of death, according to the Romans. It also represents a loss of innocence or virginity. In most occult cases, it's not a good thing."

Everyone paused and looked at Annie after hearing her explanation.

"What?" Annie said as she looked around. "I took my classes in ancient history seriously. Don't you guys know about owls presaging and then screeching to signal the death of Caesar?"

"No," Gina replied.

"On the other hand, the ancient Greeks believed the owl represented wisdom," she added.

"Okay, you've made your point!" Jim said.

We continued to peruse the letter and concluded that there would be three additional killings, although we debated whether the Labor Day weekend murder was one of the three.

"If you all don't mind, I'll send this over to Ed Gajewski, who is a friend of mine at the Profiling Section at Quantico. He might be able to find things we don't even see," Jim said. "I'd like to send the original, so they can determine the type of ink used as it appears so unique."

"I think that's a good idea," Gina said. "What bothers me more than anything else is the apparent warning that there will be more victims. How do we stop that?"

"We find the perp who wrote this and take him down, along with every one of his accomplices," I said as I pinned a copy of the letter to one of the boards on the wall.

"Can you send it by express mail? I think that time is of the essence," I said.

"I'll send it by fax first, and then I'll FedEx the original for the ink analysis. He'll have the copy in the morning, and the original the day after."

"Fax?"

"Yeah, I'll send it by facsimile first."

"What's that?" I asked.

"You don't know what a fax is? Are you serious? It's data sent over telephone lines. It's instant transmission anywhere. We have a facsimile machine at the office."

"I'm impressed," I said to Jim.

"Marc, you've got to get up to speed with the times," Gina said. "After all, this is 1987. Maybe we should get a fax machine. And you should trade your typewriter in for a computer and a printer. I see that Radio Shack has a model that would be good for the office."

"There's nothing wrong with my typewriter," I insisted.

Continuing, I asked Jim to give us a rundown of the break-in as well as whatever the scuttlebutt there was at the district attorney's office.

"The break-in at my house has taken a back seat to the body found at the Bayfront. That's a good thing, at least for me. The Lakewood PD is treating what happened at my house as a routine burglary. They've left me alone, at least for now. The body of the boy, though, now that's a different story. The district attorney played host to two FBI agents all morning and for most of the afternoon, and it looks like they are going to be in town for a few days," Carr said. "I met both of them today. They are agents Ted Roberts and Marcy Liu, and they make quite a team."

"That's what Detective Jenkins told us. What are they specifically doing in Lakewood?" I asked.

"They're both from the Behavioral Science Unit, according to their titles. They're profilers, from the same department as Gajewski. "

"Let's get back to the letter for a minute. I'm just curious, why not give the original copy of the letter to them since they're already here?"

"It would just end up in Ed's hands anyway," Jim replied. "I already asked Ed about agents Roberts and Liu before I knew about the letter. Although he doesn't know them personally, he knows them by their reputations. They're the ultimate public relations gurus who usually arrive to 'shape a narrative.' They're better in front of the camera than working crime scenes. Besides, Ed will be very discreet. I'm sure he'll personally walk the letter over to the lab for analysis of the ink and keep it all under the radar."

"Okay, got it."

"As far as Roberts and Liu are concerned, they were assigned here due to the similarities to a few other murders they've been investigating," Jim said. "And, it sounds like they will convince the public that this latest murder is the work of a potential multi-state serial killer who is on the loose. They've already classified him as a sexual-sadist serial killer. They are in full damage control mode and were quick to deny that the Bayfront murder was part of anything satanic. They would rather tell the public that the killing is the work of a highly organized sexual sadist rather than a satanic cult."

"And a sexual-sadist serial killer running around is supposed to be more palatable to the public?" I asked. "That's some PR tactic."

"It's either that or admitting that satanic rituals exist in and around Lakewood," Jim said. "They haven't said anything about the cause and circumstances of death, so I don't know how they'll spin this particular murder. I'm sure I'll know more about what they will have to work with when the medical examiner releases the official autopsy report, which should be early tomorrow morning."

"I can give you a jump on that, Jim. Here you go." Gina lifted the folder from her lap and handed it to him.

"How did you get this?"

"You're not the only one with contacts, you know," Gina said with a teasing smile. Contacts, whether on the street or in essential places, are valuable to cops, private investigators, and members of the district attorney's office alike.

Jim opened the folder and quietly reviewed its contents. Except for a few guttural sounds and whispered expletives, he didn't say anything.

"Since we can't read your mind, how about doing us a favor?" I asked Jim. "Give us the highlights, you know, out loud. I'll put some notes on the board as you read."

"Okay, let's get through some important points for now." Jim scanned the papers and searched out the high points. "Currently an unidentified body of a boy appearing to be twelve to fourteen years of age. His death was most likely due to exsanguination, or loss of blood sufficient to cause death. It took a while, though. His hands were crudely chopped off at the wrists with an ax or an ax-like instrument pre-mortem, while his genitals were removed with more surgical precision, post-mortem." Jim paused as he shuffled through a few of the papers.

"Considering the higher-than-normal temperatures in this area before and at the time that his body was found, the medical examiner estimates that he was dead for about 24 hours before he was moved and staged at the Bayfront."

"It sounds like the medical examiner is hedging on the time of death, doesn't it?" I asked.

"Yes, although he raised some possibilities that the body could have been subjected to 'different environmental temperatures' post-mortem, according to the narrative section of the report."

"Different environmental temperatures?" I asked. "What does that even mean?"

"If I had to guess, it seems like we have a well-traveled corpse. I think it suggests that his body might have been left in the elements after he was murdered, then stored in a cooler environment somewhere, then his body was staged where he was found. It could also explain the length of time between his time of death until his body was discovered."

"That seems like a lot of unnecessary work, but it could account for the more advanced state of decomposition of his body. It also makes me wonder if just one person could do all of that. How did the perp manage to store and move his body, carefully stage him, and get away without anyone noticing?" I asked. No one had an answer.

"Now, this is interesting. It looks like the coroner found his right hand under his legs, although they did not find his left hand or any of his other 'obviously missing' body parts. The medical examiner found all of his internal organs except for his…" Jim's voice trailed off.

"His what?" I asked.

"His heart. His heart was missing as well. The feds are calling it a trophy. You know, serial killers often take something from their victims."

"Were his genitals taken as trophies too?" I asked.

"His genitals were not found with the body, so maybe they were taken as trophies, or perhaps 'something else' might have been done with them. I shudder the think what that could be. He's also missing two ribs and a few pounds of surrounding 'meat.'"

"So, the feds are insisting this is a serial killing and not a ritual killing, even in private?"

"That's why they're here. The FBI will never admit to a ritual killing. Never. As far as they are concerned, ritual killings don't exist. Satanic or demonic ritual killings are the stuff of fantasy and conspiracy, with emphasis on the word conspiracy, according to the feds. They're calling any reference to such actions as 'Satanic Panic' and have done their best to dismiss any such notions that this activity is real. After all, this is the 1980s, not the 1780s."

Gina and I looked at each other but remained silent as Jim continued his narration.

"Gina, did you read through this autopsy report with Pete?" Jim asked.

"No, I thought about it but decided I'd leave that job to you or Marc. My job was just to get it. I thought we could go over the details together, rather than over an Italian dinner," she said.

"Yeah, that was probably a good idea," said Jim. "It's no wonder why the feds were around all day. Like my friend Ed, they are from the FBI's Behavioral Science Unit, or what's now known as the Behavioral Science Investigative Support Unit or just the Investigative Support Unit. They're involved in the use of applied criminal psychology to get a sense of the type of killer or killers we're dealing with, or what some are calling criminal profiling. Most local cops and detectives tend to refer to them as members of the BS Unit, which is probably the reason they changed the name of their department a few years back," Jim said.

As Jim continued to peruse the papers in the folder, I began writing some bullet points on the whiteboard.

"Now this is disturbing," Jim said as he flipped between pages and resumed citing from the report.

"Examination of the body revealed several significant old wounds, including circular type scarred skin on his inner thigh, the area around his rectum and across his buttocks. Additional relatively recent pre-mortem trauma was noted to his anus and surrounding tissue extending into his rectum, likely caused by the likely forcible insertion of unknown objects. Layered scarring was also apparent upon closer internal examination."

"Here we go again," Gina said just above a whisper. "The same or at least similar injuries we documented on abuse survivor Martin Tingsley. Where are his files and the photographs?" Gina asked.

"One set is in the safe," I replied. "The originals and the negatives are in the safety deposit box at the bank."

"I have a duplicate set in my safe. Or I should say that I had a set until this past weekend," Jim said. An uncomfortable silence hung in the air as all of us considered the timing of that break-in.

"I know what you're both thinking, and I agree that the timing of these two events, this murder, and the break-in is somehow related," he added.

"It's more than two events. It's three, or four, if you count the letter, at least that we know about. I take it that you haven't heard about the late Sadie Cooper and our meeting today with Detective Jenkins. Is there anything floating around the DA's office about that, Jim?" Gina asked.

"I spent much of my day out of my office and in court, so I haven't heard anything. What about Sadie Cooper?" Jim pressed.

"She was reportedly murdered over the weekend in London, England," I said, looking for a reaction from Jim. "Supposedly murdered, as in 'for-sure dead' this time," I said.

"What? How did Jenkins find out? How did you find out? What in the bloody hell is going on?"

"It seems that our business cards were found near her body, as if she was either trying to call us or was about to call us," I said. Upon hearing this news, Jim became visibly upset.

Gina and I provided Jim with all of the details of our meeting with Detective Jenkins. He listened with rapt attention and scribbled a few notes in his version of the special notebook each of us carried for this investigation.

"This whole thing has moved up a whole bunch of notches from 'merely strange' to the 'truly bizarre,' and I don't like it," Jim said. "It's as if things are starting to close in or accelerate. Something sure has changed, but I'm not sure what, or why," he added.

Annie spoke up. "The letter and the phrase, 'Tick Tock, time will be up' referring to the 12 hours of daylight and 12 hours of darkness could be a reference to the upcoming Autumnal Equinox. Before anyone asks, I checked with an astronomy professor I know. He said that it most likely refers to the Autumnal Equinox, which occurs on September 23rd this year. That's two weeks from tomorrow."

"Things are accelerating, and just as we're preparing to submit all of our findings to the newly created special investigative unit within the state attorney general's office," Gina noted. "I don't think this is a coincidence."

"I have a sense that we're headed directly into a crap storm, and I don't like it," added Jim.

Interesting, I thought. That's the third time in one day I heard our current set of circumstances described as a storm, and I didn't like it either.

I put more notes on the board and continued going over the recent events in detail. By ten o'clock, though, we had enough. The three of us were in sync as far as current information is concerned. Jim, Gina, and Annie left at the same time, and I was in bed before this week's episode of *Moonlighting* was over.

Chapter 12

<u>**Wednesday, September 9, 1987**</u>

It was 7:15 a.m. when I was in the kitchen, putting the coffee cups and glasses from the previous evening into the dishwasher when the phone on the kitchen wall rang. I picked it up on the second ring and was delighted to hear Deana's voice wishing me a good morning.

"Good morning, beautiful, how'd you sleep?" I asked her.

"Fine," she said. "Do you want to take a lonely girl to lunch today?"

"I'd love to. I've missed you, you know. Our schedules seem to be out of sync lately," I said.

"I know. I thought you might call me over the long weekend, and we could've snuck some time away together, but I guess you had better things to do, huh, my darling," emphasizing the term of endearment just a bit too much.

"Hey, I don't deserve that," protesting a bit. "Okay, well, maybe I do. Should I pick you up at 11:30 in front of your office?"

"Make it eleven. They owe me some time, and it won't seem so rushed," Deana responded.

"I'll see you then."

****

I arrived at the office at 7:45 a.m., going through my usual routine of making coffee and getting settled.

Before I could finish my first cup of coffee, the phone rang. It was Detective Jenkins. "Marc, I've got to talk to you as soon as possible. There have been some developments that you need to know about, the sooner, the better," he said.

Here we go again, I thought. "Just tell me when and where."

"The same place as yesterday. You need to bring Gina with you too,"

Jenkins said. "Make it at nine this time, about an hour from now," he said with a sense of urgency to which I've become accustomed.

"We'll be there." I heard Jenkins hang up the telephone receiver long before mine left my ear.

I began wondering if we were going to want to hear the developments he mentioned.

Gina arrived at the office at 8:30, looking like she slept in her car. She barely mumbled a hello when I told her about our truck stop meeting with Jenkins. "Ah, man, I can't catch a break," she said with a bit more clarity as we walked from our office. Gina made it just inside the doorway. I turned her around and escorted her by her arm to my car.

"Do you want to talk about it?" I asked, obviously surveying her from head to toe. She was wearing tight, stonewashed jeans, ankle boots, and a blouse that seemed a bit out of place from the rest of her clothes. She had dark circles under her eyes that defied her attempts to hide with make-up.

"Man trouble?" I asked.

"I wish. I thought I heard something outside my house last night. Whatever the noise was, it happened just after one o'clock this morning and sounded like someone pounding twice on the siding of my house. I saw a tree limb that I thought could have been the culprit, but there was no wind, and the thumps were too loud anyway, and the tree was not on the side of the house where I heard the noise. I went out to check and didn't see anyone, so I went back to bed. I had just fallen back asleep sometime before four, and it happened again. It was louder this time. I grabbed my gun and was ready to do battle with whoever was keeping me from my sleep, but I didn't find anything. I've been up ever since."

"Are you sure you weren't just dreaming?" I asked.

Her look told me all I needed to know.

"I checked around the outside of my house when it got light this morning. I saw that one part of my flower bed nearest the side of my house and under my bedroom window had been trampled but good," Gina said. "That's where the noise came from," she added.

"Not an animal, then?"

"No, not an animal, unless that animal wears a size 12 boot, has two legs and walks upright. I made a cast from the impression left in the dirt, just in case. I lifted a good tread impression."

"Impressive," I said. "Did you dust for prints too?" I asked with a wry grin.

"Almost, but I left my lifting kit at the office and didn't feel like driving to work twice this morning. Now I think that maybe I should have."

"Jilted lover? Old boyfriend? Angry wife?" I jabbed.

"Marc, don't! Just stop it!"

"Gina, I'm sorry. I truly am. I was just trying to lighten the mood. Did you call the police?"

"No, not after I checked and found no one there. Besides, I did more than the police would have."

"Look, I'm really sorry that I upset you. Let me make it up to you. How about I escort you home later and take a look around?"

She brushed some invisible lint from her blouse in more than a hint of nervousness. "I don't think it's…" Gina paused, allowing me to insist.

"Okay, it's a date, sort of," I responded as soft and kindly as I could, taking advantage of her mid-sentence pause. As we got to my car, I opened the door for her, an act to which she would generally object. As I walked around the back of my car to get in the driver's side, I saw her through the back window dab her eyes with a tissue. I could not think of a time when she seemed this upset.

****

We arrived at the truck stop ahead of Jenkins and took up the same booth in the smoking section as the previous day.

"Back again, I see," said the waitress holding two pots of coffee, regular and decaf. "Do you want some coffee while you wait for your friend?"

"How do you know we're expecting someone else?" I asked, apparently exhibiting obvious suspicion toward the waitress.

"I'm sorry, I guess I just assumed," she said meekly, "you know, from yesterday. I was the one who kept you guys caffeinated."

"Oh, sure," I said, trying to regain a normal countenance. "Well, you assumed correctly, and yes, please fill us up with the good stuff while we wait," I said, forcing a smile in the waitress's general direction.

She hadn't finished pouring the second cup when Jenkins danced around the waitress to take the empty seat made when I moved next to Gina. He was holding a thick binder of papers and slumped into the booth with a thud.

"Regular, please," he said to the waitress.

"Would you like to hear our breakfast specials?"

"No, we're fine, just coffee, thanks," Jenkins spoke for all three of us.

An uncomfortably long pause ensued between Jenkins and us after the waitress left the table. I decided to break the silence. "What's this all about, Ron?"

"To be very explicit, our meeting, this meeting never happened. Are we all clear on that?" His voice was steeped in seriousness, as was his message.

"Sure, Ron," both Gina and I replied in a near chorus-like fashion.

"It's the feds, and they are crawling up our collective asses about the latest homicide at the Bayfront. They want it cleared as soon as possible. No muss, no fuss, and certainly nothing publicly revealed about the manner of death and the condition of the boy's body," Jenkins stated.

"And exactly how do they think that's going to work?" I asked. "There will be a trial, assuming they arrest and charge someone. The facts will eventually come out anyway."

"I don't know, Marc. They're extremely intent on keeping this one quiet. One of the agents even leaned pretty heavily on the coroner and medical examiner. I heard from the coroner this morning, and he wasn't pleased, either."

"Has the victim been identified yet?" Gina queried.

"The identification is somewhat convoluted, so it is not to leave this table until it's official. The coroner and CID identified the victim as Jacob Mitchell, age 13. Do either of you know him?"

Gina and I both shook our heads no in unison. "Should we?" Gina asked.

"Okay, let's try this one. How about Jacob Tingsley?" Jenkins asked, adding an extra-long stare at both of us to gauge our responses.

Gina and I looked at each other. "Did you say Tingsley? As in Martin Tingsley?"

"You got it. The same family, only there's a bit of a twist."

"What sort of twist?"

"Jacob Tingsley legally had his name changed to become Jacob Mitchell before his mother adopted him out to his current family. The family court judge ordered the records sealed, so not too many people outside of his mother, very immediate family, and the courts would know that Jacob Mitchell is actually Jacob Tingsley. As you said, he's the younger brother of Martin," said Jenkins. "So, do either of you want to tell me how you know Martin Tingsley, his older brother?"

"We know Martin Tingsley very well, or we thought we did. Martin was the victim of severe physical and sexual abuse as a child. We took his statement and photographs during our investigation of my uncle's murder. He identified some of his abusers as some well-known public and private figures in Lakewood. We did not know there even was a younger brother in the picture."

"Like who?" Jenkins asked.

"Wealthy residents, doctors, even a judge," Gina said.

"We gave all of this information to your department, but that was before you got your gold shield," I added. "You should have seen the report in your files if you found that the victim's last name was previously Tingsley. That is if you looked."

"I looked, and believe me, there is no Tingsley file anywhere, in either active or closed drawers," Jenkins replied. "I even spent a few hours checking in the records room. I'll admit that I found it a bit strange because I remember you two working on the case, and that name rang a bell. I started to ask around, but I started to get a funny feeling like I better stop sticking my nose in my own department's business."

"If you don't mind me asking, what address do you have for the victim?" I asked, hoping that Jenkins was softening. He thumbed through some papers until he found the victim's address and the names of the other residents of the household.

"It looks like some kind of foster or group home in Pennsylvania. Amish Country, to be more specific. I can't tell by the reverse trace of the address whether it's formally recognized as an actual group home, but the contact at that location is listed to Joseph and Mary Smith."

"Smith, huh, how original," I said to no one in particular. "So, how did you determine that Jacob is Martin's younger brother if the court records are sealed and notifications have not even been made yet?" I asked.

"You can thank the FBI agents who we've been playing host to for the last few days. They made the identification, maybe through prints on his remaining hand. Then at the request of the agents, the U.S. attorney was quick to have the legal records of the name change made available to us for this investigation, and here we are," Jenkins said.

"Just so I'm clear on this, Jacob Tingsley became Jacob Mitchell through a legal, pre-adoption name change. At some point, he was adopted by the Smith family, who reportedly live out of state, but no official adoption papers seem to exist. The Smith's are a foster family, yet no records of Jacob exist anywhere within the family court system. Why not?"

"That's a good question. There's nothing in the file or anywhere, for that matter, that indicates a reason. I'll agree that it is a bit unusual, but I'm sure it's not the first time."

"So how did Jacob go from being under the care of a foster family from another state to winding up dead in Lakewood? Was he abducted? Was there a missing person report filed? How long was he missing?"

"All good questions," Jenkins replied. "There was a missing and endangered person report filed several days ago by his foster parents. We're still looking into the timeline and waiting on investigative reports and specifically the notes from the local police officers who took the initial complaint."

"Have family notifications been made yet?" I asked. "Both to the Smith family, if that's their real name, as well as Martin and Mary Tingsley?"

"Our uniforms are in the process of informing Martin and Mary, while the Pennsylvania notification will be sent to the appropriate jurisdiction for personal service. They might have already done it by now, but I'm not sure."

"Just so you have the full story," Gina said, "We met with Martin Tingsley and his wife Mary in our office during our investigation of the murder of Marc's uncle. He told us that his mother died in a single-car traffic accident by driving her car off the bluffs by the lake. She reportedly talked to a Lakewood detective and was dead shortly after that. I'm not sure whom she contacted or what information she provided, but Martin insists that her death was no accident. He said that the accident happened at night, but she never drove at night."

"Again, I don't believe Martin ever mentioned that he had a brother," I added emphatically.

"He didn't, and neither did Mary. That's certainly something I would have remembered," Gina said. "Is it somehow possible that he doesn't know?"

"I would find that very difficult to believe. So now the question becomes, why would Martin and his wife keep this fact from us."

"So, let me get this straight," Jenkins said as he rubbed his temples. "We've got the mutilated corpse of a 13-year-old at the morgue who shows signs of ante-mortem and post-mortem sexual abuse similar to that of his older brother who claims he suffered the abuse by prominent people in Lakewood. His mother died under mysterious circumstances in Lakewood. Jacob, the freshly dead young man from this weekend, lives a few hours from here in foster care or a group home, yet is found at the Bayfront. Now, we've got feds descending upon us, wanting to keep everything hushed up. Oh, and let's not forget about the pesky little unresolved international issue you two have with the murder of Sadie Cooper in London," Jenkins said as he exhaled sharply. "Does that about sum everything up? I want to know what in the literal hell is going on around here."

"That would be nice," I said. "Things seemed to have taken quite a dark turn over the last few days. I wonder why now," I said aloud, not expecting any response.

Perhaps sensing the seriousness of our conversation, the waitress gave us a wide berth, stopping only to refill our cups.

"Speaking of Sadie Cooper, did you hear anything more from the London police or Interpol?" I asked.

"Not me, although I think the chief might have, along with the feds. When the two agents were in his office, the chief asked me about what I knew about your involvement with Cooper," Jenkins said. "I told him I was in the dark but offered to find out, which seemed to satisfy him. That issue almost seemed to take a back seat to what's happening here."

"Until they find out that the murders are connected. They have to be," I said. "I don't think the timing is coincidental, especially considering that both Sadie Cooper and Martin Tingsley, Jacob's older brother, were at the epicenter of my uncle's murder investigation."

"I don't know what you guys have gotten yourselves into, but I don't like any of this one bit. I told you both yesterday, and I'll tell you again, you both better keep your head on a swivel. I can see a storm coming from a mile away, and this looks like a big one," Jenkins said.

"Ron, there is one more thing I think you should know, something odd that happened to Gina," I said and turned to her. She had her hand under the table and squeezed my leg hard as if to keep me from mentioning anything about her interrupted sleep.

"Gina, what is it?" Jenkins looked at her with his steely eyes, expecting an answer.

"I don't know, I don't think it's anything or anything related to any of this," Gina said, dropping her head submissively. "I don't even want to bring it up."

"Bring it up," Jenkins insisted. "I'll be the judge about whether it's relevant."

"Last night, during the night, somebody was beneath my bedroom window. I heard a noise. Twice. Like a bump against the side of the house. At first, I thought it was the wind, but there was no wind last night. When I checked this morning, I found the impression of a size 12 boot print in the flower bed where the noise came from."

"Did you call the police?" Jenkins asked.

"No, what would they have done anyway? I took a cast from the boot print, but that's it."

"How about you call the police next time," Jenkins commanded.

Gina gave me an annoying look. "While we're at it, are you going to tell him about the letter, Mr. Big Shot PI, or should I tell him?"

"Oh geez, now what? What letter?" Jenkins asked as he exhaled sharply.

"This letter." Gina pulled her copy from her notepad and gave it to Jenkins. He studied it intently, his facial expressions contorting as he read each line of the unsolicited correspondence. Looking closer, he was incredulous when he realized that the letter was printed by hand.

"It was, and whoever did it spent a lot of time doing it. Local postmark but nothing actionable in terms of threats, it seems."

"I should take this to the chief, and I'm sure he'll give it to the profilers."

"Ron, would you mind giving us a little time before you turn it over to anyone else? It's being analyzed by the feds right now, so it's not like we're holding anything back. We are just routing it differently, considering the implications of local involvement of high-profile people. The letter does state that there are police involved. Think about the fact that you were not able to find what we previously gave to the department. Please," I pleaded.

Jenkins sat quietly for a minute, appearing to consider his next move carefully.

"I'll make a deal with you. Let me take this copy for my reference. I'll keep it confidential. I won't turn it in or tell anyone that it exists unless or until we all agree on it. When you get the report back from your fed sources, let me know. Deal?"

Gina and I looked at each other as we considered his offer.

"Deal," I said. "Thanks, Ron. I know you're sticking your neck out for us."

IN THE DARK OF NIGHT

Chapter 13

Because of the time and the lunch date I scheduled earlier in the morning, I dropped Gina off back at the office and picked Deana up right on schedule. Instead of going to a restaurant, we went back to my place after stopping off at a local delicatessen to pick up a light lunch we planned to share in the quiet of my apartment. The trip to the deli and back to my apartment carved out a mere 15 minutes from our unhurried 90 minutes we could have together.

"It's been a while since I've been here, ya know," Deana said as she walked over the threshold and as I jiggled my keys from the deadbolt.

"And how is that my fault?" I said, turning back to give her a warm smile. She smiled too, although I detected a note of regret flash across her face. Was it simply regret, I wondered, or was it the loneliness caused by our different life paths? She's raising a young boy alone, which isn't easy, and I've been immersed in my work, nearly all of it, I reasoned, to which she should not be subjected.

We entered my apartment, and I put the deli bag on the counter that separates the kitchen from the living area. "I'm going to wash up," Deana said as she headed to the washroom between my bedroom and office. I watched her walk down the short hallway in her red and white dotted dress and red heels, closing my eyes after she was out of sight. I stood like a statue, taking in the pleasant scent of her light perfume that seemed to linger in the air in her wake.

Somehow, we lost all track of time, forgetting to eat, or simply choosing not to. It was nearly an hour-and-a-half later that I found myself locking the door to my apartment and walking Deana to my car. Neither one of us ate, but we were both satisfied.

Deana held my right arm and put her head on my shoulder as I drove her back to work. For a minute, I thought she might have fallen asleep as I consciously drove slower than usual to avoid disturbing her. A few minutes passed when she raised her head and looked at me.

"When can I see your war room or whatever you call it? This was the third time I've been at your apartment, and the door is always locked."

"Anytime you want, I suppose. There's not much to see, just some office furniture and a bunch of work files. Just let me know ahead of time, so I can make sure it's clean," I said, thinking instead about the gruesome crime scene photographs and newspaper clippings that seem to be fixtures on the walls of late. No one, I thought, should ever have to see that, especially her.

"Call me tonight?" Deana asked.

"I will. Oh, and if this how you do lunch, I can hardly wait until we have dinner," I said with a smile, pulling away once she disappeared safely inside of the office building.

Chapter 14

As soon as I walked into the reception area of our office, Annie walked around the reception desk and pulled me by the arm halfway out the door. "I wanted to catch you before you walked into your office," she whispered. "Gina is in there with Martin and Mary Tingsley. They're all seated at your conference table. I just took them some coffee and a few Cokes from the machine downstairs. They both seem upset, and I didn't want to see you get blindsided."

"Thanks, Annie. I figured it would only be a matter of time."

Because of Annie's warning, I walked into my office with at least a little bit of mental preparation. By her account, Martin and his wife had only been inside for a few minutes, so I was reasonably sure that not too much had been discussed about his brother's murder. A brother that we never knew he had despite the extensive investigation and talks we had months ago. I don't like it when clients keep information from me, and I was not in the best frame of mind when I walked into the room.

Despite this critical information being kept from us, Martin's story was a sad one. As a child and into young adulthood, he was physically and sexually abused in unspeakable ways. He was also a student and friend of my murdered uncle. During our first interview, Mary said that she met Martin when he was just 16 years old, not quite a year before my uncle's murder. According to her, he was "a mess" when she met him, claiming that he was sexually abused by numerous men on countless occasions, at different times and places, starting a few years before. Prominent men of means and even some well-known and highly respected in the community. Mary ultimately "saved him" from this abuse by telling Martin's mother, who then alerted Lakewood Police and even the FBI to the abuse. Shortly after that, Martin's mother died in a one-vehicle crash.

Despite several investigations and the scars that memorialized the abuse on Martin's body, no one has been held accountable for his abuse and pain. Now in his mid-twenties, only the deep mental scars and painful memories of the unanswered injustices remain.

His story is not merely sad. It is one of many similar accounts we've uncovered since opening the homicide investigation of my uncle and even after the arrest of his murderer. While attending junior high, Martin got caught with marijuana. Instead of receiving punishment or help, certain school officials ultimately recruited him for sex parties in exchange for that and other drugs, including LSD. The men were not only school officials, but the supposed pillars of the community—people of power and influence who themselves were fathers in many cases.

As he got deeper into these underground activities, becoming one of the regulars at these parties, the more drugs they would give him, and the worse they treated him. He described being raped by men and older boys. There were other boys from his school there, as well as some young girls. Except for one other young boy, he knew only their first names.

His story was not just hard to believe, but hard to listen to and more difficult to comprehend. The older men would take turns performing various sex acts on Martin, and make Martin reciprocate. He said there were times when he was tied up to other boys and blindfolded while he was being raped by men and various objects. He said that the longer scar was from a curling iron that was heated and used to rape him. It got too hot, he said, and he screamed. An older man removed the curling iron from inside of him, replacing it with his own manhood. The burn was caused as the older man purposely turned the iron higher and placed it against his buttocks while raping and sodomizing Martin.

Martin was frequently burned at different times, at various parties, by men with cigarettes and cigars. The men would bet money on how long it would take for each boy to scream out in pain, pleading for the hot cherry tip to be removed, or pass out. He described how the men would take their turns, switching between the boys and the girls. Some of the others he saw at future parties. Others, he never saw again. It was difficult to imagine and even more difficult to accept that such things could happen.

Had I not seen and taken pictures of his injuries myself, I might not have believed him. Most of the physical scars remain, some more prominent than others. His previous injuries are so old and the stories of how he got them so difficult to believe that they've had little impact on seeking justice against the perpetrators. Because of the unwillingness of people to believe him, it seems that Martin stopped trying to be convincing. He's lost faith in people and trusts only in his wife.

Now, for the second time this year, he's in my office to talk about murder.

I walked in and approached the conference table where Martin, Mary, and Gina were seated. Martin appeared to be heavily medicated and nearly catatonic. Mary seemed to be on the verge of a nervous breakdown. I looked at Gina, and she looked back at me with a desperation that only such horrific situations can generate. Despite my anger, I greeted them warmly and offered my condolences on the loss of Martin's younger brother, but the words felt hollow, even as I said them. I felt like I failed them in some way since our first meeting. I sat down next to Gina, directly across from Martin and his wife, giving them both time to compose themselves. Showing her compassion, Gina placed both of her hands on top of theirs.

I broke the silence that hung in the air like an ominous cloud. Looking directly at Mary, I opened with the most basic of questions.

"Why did neither of you tell us Martin had a younger brother? Does he have any other family we don't know about?"

"No, Jacob was Martin's only other living family member," Mary said weakly. "You must understand that Martin and I… we… we were not trying to hide anything from you. It was all about protecting Jacob, who we thought was living a normal life with a loving family. Or so we thought."

"What have the police told you?"

"They haven't said too much. The cops asked more questions instead of answering those we have. I don't know if they were just trying to be kind or purposely evasive, but all we know is that Jacob was found murdered, apparently stabbed to death at the Bayfront. They said that he was probably killed someplace else and dumped there like trash. All we got to see of Jacob was his face on a TV monitor at the morgue so we could identify him." As Mary broke down in sobs, Gina provided her a box of tissues. Through an otherwise eerie and stoic silence, tears streamed down Martin's face, which

Gina gently wiped away. "We almost didn't recognize him at first," Mary said between sobs.

I turned my attention to Martin after he appeared to regain his composure. "Martin, I need to know if your brother was victimized by any of the same activities you experienced, the rituals, and the abuse. I'm asking whether he was a victim, or if you, Mary, or anyone else knew or suspected that he was a victim."

"No, we made sure of that. My mother made sure of that. He was well protected."

"How?"

"There's something you both need to know. My mother took extra steps to hide any family connection just in case someone wanted to get to him through us. Before giving up Jacob to his current, er, former family, my mother changed his last name. She did it legally, and she managed to keep the records of the change under seal at the courthouse. I'm not sure how she managed to do that. She also changed his last name to an old family name on my mother's side, which was Mitchell. He was living as Jacob Mitchell, not as Jacob Tingsley. Mitchell is a common name, especially in this area of the country. While she gave him anonymity, she also allowed him to have a connection to his ancestry."

"Martin, did you have any contact with Jacob since his name change and he went into the system?"

"No, and it broke my heart knowing he was out there, that I had a little brother."

"How about you, Mary?"

"No, of course not."

"How about your mother before she died?"

"Not that I'm aware of. It would be stupid and self-defeating, wouldn't it?"

"How was the adoption accomplished?"

"It was all done in private. It was kept out of the court system."

"What about your father?"

"He was out of the picture. Gone."

"Do you know how your mother found the family that adopted Jacob?"

"I think her attorney got that information, but I don't know how."

"Who was her attorney?"

"There might be some papers in storage with his name, but I think it's Marvin Cervas. He's big in family law in Lakewood. We certainly can check and confirm it for you."

"I know the name. I think one of the biggest unanswered questions is why? Why did your mother give up Jacob? There must be a reason, and a damn good one," I said with as much authority as my compassion would permit.

"We don't have any answers for you, Marc," Mary said.

"Are you saying that you don't know, or don't want to provide the answers," I pressed Mary. As I did, Gina shot a disproving glance in my direction, causing me to dial the pressure down.

I turned toward Gina, straining to understand what was going on. "This cannot be one big coincidence that Jacob endured the same abuse that Martin was subjected to. Meanwhile, Martin lives, and Jacob dies. None of this makes much sense," I complained aloud.

Gina was equally confused and baffled. "We're missing something here, and until we find out what we're missing, you two are going to need to be kept safe. They got to Jacob, your mother a while ago, and also Sadie Cooper, who has been living in obscurity in London."

"Sadie Cooper?" Martin said through his drugged state. He appeared surprised upon hearing her name. "That name sounds familiar, but I'm not sure why."

"Maybe you heard it from the local news back in May. They reported that she was killed in a car accident." Gina said.

Mary looked at Gina, then to me. "Martin has been regaining some of his memory, but they really did a number on him. They fractured his mind."

"Who are they? With only a couple of exceptions, we've been talking in generalities, and I think it's time for specifics. Do we know everyone who was or is involved in these networks of trafficking and abuse? We've identified some of the participants, as you know, but I think we need to be casting a much wider net. With the latest flurry of activity, it seems like they are busy tying up loose ends. Now we need names. People we can positively identify."

"They wore masks," Martin stressed. "Hideous, devilish masks."

"You had to recognize *someone*. Is there anyone you haven't told us about?" I pressed.

"I'm sorry," Martin said as he began to weep quietly.

"About Jacob, the question, or I should say one of many questions I have is why now after all of this time? And who's next?"

"That's enough!" Mary objected, insisting that Martin had endured enough for one day. It was evident that the news of his brother's murder was taking an immense emotional toll on Martin. Mary also seemed to be experiencing emotional turmoil of her own, although her emotions seemed to be more challenging to read.

"Is there someplace other than your home where you and your two young children can stay until we figure out what's going on? A place that no one else knows about?" Gina asked.

"There is someplace! Mary said enthusiastically and without hesitation. My uncle owns a cabin outside of Lakewood that he uses as a retreat for his business partners. He's owned it for a long time. It's always well stocked with provisions for that reason. I've been there a few times, but the last time was quite a while ago. It's nice, and woods surround it, and some farmland. It's very private and out of the way, except for a livestock farm and slaughterhouse far behind it, but those face the other direction on State Line road. When I was young, my family would occasionally get our meat, milk, and eggs there. Anyway, I know where it is and exactly how to get to it. It's located on the state line, about ten miles out of town but comfortable. I'm sure we'll be able to use it."

"Great, can you get in touch with your uncle now? You can telephone him from here." I said.

Mary stood up and walked to the phone in the reception area, leaving her purse next to her chair. Returning a minute later, she said that her uncle was more than happy to let them stay there for as long as they needed. He informed her that an emergency key to enter the cabin was hidden under a fake rock in a garden area.

"Would you please give us the address and directions to this cabin, so we know where to find you? We won't tell anyone where you've gone, and I mean anyone. I ask that you do the same. It will just be you two, your uncle Paul, Gina and me."

"Look, we trust you both. The place has no mail delivery or postal address, so I'll just give you the directions." Mary took a Sharpie pen and piece of paper from her purse and carefully wrote the directions to the cabin and drew a detailed map. "There's no phone there either, so if you need to contact us, you'll have to drive there."

"That's even better," I said. "Oh, by the way, what's your uncle's full name? What kind of business does he own?"

"Why do you need to know that?"

"I just like to be thorough. Besides, if we misplace the directions or can't find the cabin for some reason, or in the event of an emergency, we can always contact him."

"His last name is Kruger. It's Paul Kruger, and he owns Kruger Logistics, which is a trucking company and specialized delivery and transport service."

"I know about the company. At least, I've seen their trucks on the roads and know where their terminal is. If I recall, they've been in business for a long time."

"Yes, that's right. I think they just celebrated fifty years in business. My uncle and his father started it right after World War II."

I asked Mary to write his name, telephone number, and home address on the paper with the directions. Although she initially protested as she did not want us disturbing him, she provided the information I requested. Before sliding the paper across the table to me, she asked me to promise that I would not "bother" him. I explained that I would only use the information in case there was some sort of emergency. Mary appeared satisfied with my response.

Mary and Martin left our office a few minutes later, heading to their house to pack a few things for this unplanned vacation and pick up their kids from Mary's mother. They planned to be settled at their new, temporary safe house by supper time.

I walked the couple through the reception area and instructed them to get to the cabin before dark. I assured them that we would check on them within the next few days, but Mary said that there is no rush, insisting that they would prefer to have an extended period of "alone time." She suggested that it might even be best to wait until after the weekend before visiting, which would give them all a chance to rest after the emotional toll they experienced. Despite the family ties, they would not be attending the memorial service, if one was even scheduled.

"Please understand that Martin needs this time without the external stress of your investigation. He's in a very fragile emotional state." Mary seemed quite emphatic with her request for solitude, adding that since the police were "done" with them, perhaps we should be as well.

"Okay, but you came to see us, remember?"

"That's right, only because we knew it would only be a matter of time before you came to our house, upsetting Martin all over again."

Sensing a bit of tension, Gina chimed in. "We'll stop by to check on you sometime next week, then, unless something important rises." As they neared the door, Martin glanced at me with a look of apprehension that I attributed to his loss. Whatever the reason, it was unsettling and nearly caused me to stop him. Instead, I watched him follow Mary out of the office with his head down, staring at the floor as he walked. I heard him mumble something about following the "yellow brick road" as he walked down the hallway behind Mary.

"Did you hear that? Another reference to the yellow brick road," I whispered to Gina. "Thoughts?"

"I don't know, but I'm sure we're going to find out."

Chapter 15

Gina and I returned to my office after they left the building. I closed the door behind me after asking Annie to hold any calls that might come in. We both sat at the conference table in my office in relative silence for the next few minutes, individually contemplating the gravity of the events that occurred over the last few days.

Gina was the first to break the silence. "Marc, I can't shake the bad feeling I've got about everything. It seems like someone is cleaning up loose ends. Someone is eliminating witnesses, stealing, and likely destroying evidence ahead of us turning over our findings to the state attorney. Consider the letter and everything that's happened. It's clear to me that someone is trying to warn us off. I have the feeling we've yet to see the worst part of what's coming. The problem is not knowing who is behind all of this or what will happen next. I'm not embarrassed to admit that I'm getting scared," Gina said, her voice starting to tremble and doing her best to hold back her tears.

I walked over and sat down next to Gina, placing my hand gently on her arm. "I'm sorry that I got you wrapped up in all of this, whatever this is," I said with a whisper of defeat.

"You didn't put a gun to my head. It's not your fault that such horrible people are walking among us, doing terrible things that people don't want to believe are happening. If I wasn't involved in the investigation myself, I might not even believe it."

"But it started with the investigation of my uncle's murder. It spun off from there, taking a life of its own. So I am responsible, at least for bringing you into this."

"Forget it. I'm in for the long haul."

Gina and I gathered our notes from our meeting with Mary and Martin, both of us making sure we had the directions to their temporary safe house and Paul Kruger's home and business telephone numbers.

"Now what do we do?"

Gina said that she was going to go back home to check on things after the incident during the night.

"Let me drive you, or at least go with you. There's safety in numbers."

"Okay, you drive," Gina replied, surprising me by not objecting to my help.

"How is your daughter taking all of this?"

"Melissa? Oh, she's fine. Better than fine. She's been staying with my mother, so she doesn't know all that's been going on. I spoke to her this morning. I talked to my mother a little bit as well. I told my mother that I was working on a big case and asked if Melissa could stay with her for a few days. She's busy with her schoolwork, cheerleading, and you know, just girl stuff in general. My mom loves the company, and you know how much Melissa adores my mom, so it's a win-win situation for them."

It took about 15 minutes to get to Gina's house. She unlocked her front door and entered as I held open the door for her. Everything appeared in order and untouched since she left this morning, a welcome relief from what we've come to expect. We both walked around her house and located the area where she found the boot print earlier this morning. We inspected the area thoroughly. In addition to the footprint and some trampled flowers beneath her window, I found several cigarette butts on a small patch of trampled ground just behind a hedge that acts as a natural barrier between her house and the adjoining property, about 20 feet in a direct line from the window.

"Gina, take a look at this," I said as I motioned her over to where I was standing. "Somebody spent some time here, maybe as long as 30-45 minutes based on the number of cigarette butts on the ground. From this position, a person could see into your bedroom window without being seen." Without thinking, I pulled a plastic evidence bag from my pocket and carefully placed the remnants of L & M filters into the container.

"Marc, I think I'm going to get a room at a hotel tonight."

"Nonsense, you can stay at my place. I insist."

"I don't want to put you out. What about Deana? Won't she be upset that I'm staying with you for the night? What if she calls or comes over? The fact that I'm sleeping in your apartment wouldn't bother her?"

"Given the circumstances, I hardly think she would mind. I believe she would be upset if you didn't stay. She trusts me, and let's just say that our relationship has never been better."

"I'll grab my turnout bag and some clothes. If you don't have any plans tonight, maybe we can work in the war room for a little while."

"Sounds like a plan."

Gina called Annie from her home phone to let her know that we would not be coming back to the office and told her that she could reach us both at my apartment should an emergency arise. We arrived at my apartment 30 minutes later.

I held the door open for Gina, who entered my apartment first. "Well, now, what do we have here?" she playfully asked, smiling and pointing to an unopened deli bag that was left sitting on top of the kitchen counter, untouched from my lunch with Deana. "I don't think I need to be a detective to figure out that you decided on another type of fare for lunch today."

"Oh yeah, I forgot about that."

"You mean the deli."

"Yes, that's exactly what I mean."

"Well, if you want to order out tonight, it's my treat," Gina announced. "We could always eat and watch Magnum PI to see how the other investigators live."

"Or there's Jake and the Fatman if you want yet another alternative in 'must-see TV,'" I chided.

We ordered in and spent the evening in the war room looking over all of the files going back to my uncle's murder. I created several new index cards containing names, dates, and events and secured each to the whiteboards, creating a visual timeline and cast of characters, of sorts.

"You've been staring at the boards for nearly an hour and haven't said anything," Gina said, piercing the silence. "What are you thinking?"

I've been using my whiteboard and corkboard layout for a long time to create a timeline of people, places, and events. It helps me mentally sort out the bullet points and visualize the case I'm working. My criminal psychology professor saw me doing it in a notebook during class one day and called it "case mapping." Since then, I've used the process countless times and have since moved up to using it on a much larger scale.

"I'm thinking that before this is all over, we're going to need more cards. We've got to determine the identity of the people behind the killings. We know some of them and their motives, but have an ever-increasing pool of victims."

"More cards? Heck, we're going to need a bigger board. What do you think about the serial killer angle that the feds are talking about?" Gina asked.

"I think that's a convenient way of hiding a much deeper and more sinister aspect of everything that's been going on. I can almost see how the idea of a serial killer would be more palatable than a group of locals involved in occult rituals, demonic worship, and human sacrifice. You've taken courses in criminal psychology, right?"

"Yes, in college and the special courses offered through the department. I was lucky enough to take one at the FBI academy that was taught by the founder of the Behavioral Analysis Unit when they first began to teach profiling."

"Does any of this fit into the profiles you've seen?"

"A few elements fit, but looking at the larger picture here, not really."

"Remember how this all started, at least for us? We were investigating the murder of my uncle. That led us deep into the homosexual underground. From there, it expanded into something much bigger and much greater. The sexual abuse of young children, especially young boys. The trafficking of children, from the very young to those in their teens. The so-called parties Martin talked about and, in particular, the sexual perversion."

"That part fits the profile of sexual sadists, but I'll agree it's far more than that."

"If we are to believe Martin, and we have no reason not to believe him, we're dealing with some of the most perverted and depraved people on the planet. Predators who prey on young children for sexual gratification and worse. I was just reading the notes from one of our first interviews with Martin back in May. Do you remember him talking about men dressed in robes and an altar of some type? He also suggested child sacrifice, the drinking of their blood, and maybe even cannibalism."

"I remember it all too well. I also remember the three Poloroid photographs Roger Braun gave us while he was on his deathbed. Here they are," Gina said as she reached into a folder and handed them to me.

The first picture showed a young boy, no more than ten years old, fully naked, performing oral sex on an older man wearing nothing more than a devil's mask seen during Halloween. Four other older males stood in a semi-circle around the pair, each holding a lit candle. Hot wax from the candles held by each of the men dripped onto the boy's bare back. The boy had his eyes fixed at the camera. He had a look of pain and fear, while the men sported smiles and grins behind their hideously evil-looking masks.

The second picture showed the same young boy, bent forward over a chair, being violated by another man while the others stood in observance. The image on the boy's face was a horrific combination of pain and fear. The boy's blood was clearly evident running down his leg, a result of the intimate violation. This time, a pentagram was partially visible on the boy's back, appearing to have been crudely carved by a sharp instrument. A towel soaked in blood laid at the boy's feet.

The third picture was, by far, the most horrifying. The boy shown in the previous images now appeared to be laying, face-up, on a raised cot like structure. Six men in total, each one naked and wearing either full or partial masks covering their faces, surrounded the lifeless body of the young boy. Although not completely visible, it was evident that the boy's genitals had been severed, and he was at least partially opened up near the bottom of his breastbone. All six men were holding leaded crystal glasses containing what appeared like blood, presumably from the boy. Like some morbid lipstick, blood stained the lips of the men and the rims of the glasses.

Gina broke the heavy silence. "These are not pictures of some twisted Halloween prank. This is some sick stuff, and it's real. Real people and real victims."

"And then there's Sadie Cooper and her husband. How does anyone even begin to explain that? The gold Baphomet pendant, the stories about mind control by rogue elements of our government, the activities that congressional hearings verified in the late 1970s. If I recall correctly, it was you who first talked about all of this during our murder investigation," I added.

"It was, and I vividly remember our conversations. Even with all the documentation, the evidence, and the photographs, I still have a hard time believing that we could have all of this going on undetected right here in Lakewood." Gina said.

"Why not? Maybe not to the degree it's going on elsewhere, but why not? I mean, everyone has to live somewhere. Why not here? And who said it's undetected? Maybe there's an element of facilitation to keep things quiet."

"This goes beyond serial killings. This is evil to the core, satanic worship. It's demonic, and yet the FBI will not even entertain such an idea."

"So, the feds are here to keep a lid on things or to run interference and damage control. Minimize the 'Satanic Panic' as they are describing it."

"Exactly."

"Imagine that," Gina said.

"Imagine what?"

"That people would more readily accept the existence of a sadistic serial killer roaming among them over what's really going on. That's got to tell us something."

****

It was 10:45 p.m. when Gina and I decided to wrap things up for the night, weary from looking at wholesale perversity and death. As if we were trying to convince ourselves that we had things under control, we assured each other that Martin, Mary, and their children were safe at the remote hideaway, compliments of Mary's uncle.

"Mary was quite insistent about being left alone for a while," I said.

"Wouldn't you be? Let's give them some time. They're together and safely tucked away for the time being. We've got other avenues to explore."

"Okay, but did you notice that she called her uncle without having to look up his telephone number. She also drew a map to a place she claims she hasn't been to in a long time."

"I noticed that. I'm not sure what to think about that. Some people just have great memories, I suppose."

"Do you think we should bring Paul up to speed on what's going on?" Gina inquired.

"Well, we've spent a lot of time on this 'side case' as he'd call it. He's going to see the dip in the billable hours, and I'm sure he starting to wonder whether we took off on vacation together. I'm sure Annie has covered for us pretty well, but he is going to need to know everything for our sake as well as his. I wouldn't want him to find out from someone else."

"How much do you want to tell him?" Gina pressed.

"I guess that depends on what we know at this point. Not what we think we know, but what we know."

Gina looked down at her notebook, flipping the pages back and forth. She must have felt me staring at her engage in this sudden burst of compulsive behavior and stopped, holding a few pages upright in her hand.

"I can tell you what I've managed to compile, and you can tell me if it sounds right," said Gina.

"Go ahead."

"I'll start from the beginning with the highlights so that I can keep this straight in my head too. We know that the investigation into your uncle's murder overlapped into something much larger. His behavior ultimately led to his murder as he was introduced to people who were involved in sex with underage children, mostly boys, at least in his circle of acquaintances. He was not involved in any of that but learned the identities of some who were. Some of those people were in the military, either from World War II or Korea. That touches on our government's 'black ops' programs, either related to Operation Paperclip from the 1940s or later mind control experimentation known as MK-Ultra. Of course, that is connected to the late Benjamin Cooper and his newly departed wife Sadie, as well as the guys we met during our trip to Florida. All of this is in addition to the 'normal' perversions of pedophilia, as if there is such a thing. How am I doing so far?"

"That's a pretty distilled version, but I'm following. Continue, please."

"From there, there's a 'ritualistic' aspect that includes some, but not all of the criminals, sickos, and perverts. I'm referring to what is officially known as

Satanic Ritual Abuse. Now, this is some really sick stuff. This is where the guys in the robes, altars made from bones, drinking blood, and even child sacrifice comes in. Even reports of cannibalism. I can't believe I'm even saying this." Gina looked up from her notes. "Please feel free to stop me anytime."

"Believe me, I'd like to tell you to stop, but continue."

"Mixed in with all of this, we've found evidence of people with multiple personalities, or multiple personality disorders. These are people that have suffered severe trauma, usually at an early age and usually sexual in nature, that possess different personalities within themselves. Does that sound right?"

"I'd say that's about the most basic explanation possible. It's hard to believe that the government is involved in any of this, though."

"I'm not saying that our government is involved, but certain elements inside the CIA, formerly the OSS, and I'd suspect elements of foreign intelligence agencies are involved. Do you remember the congressional hearings about ten years ago? There was an investigation by the Church Committee that uncovered the experimental use of mind-altering drugs like LSD on unwitting people. Do you remember?" Gina asked.

"Vaguely," I said.

"I copied some newspaper reports from the library that go into some detail about the findings. I also have copies of transcripts from the national archives that I asked a friend to send me. They're here somewhere in one of the folders. It's pretty interesting reading."

"Then there's the human and child sex trafficking aspect. Children go missing and are never found— adults too—in some cases. There are also breeding programs, where babies are born for the specific purpose of programming and rituals. This is so hard to accept that it's no wonder few people believe it."

"So, we go from taking on the five-year-old unsolved homicide of my uncle and 'stumble' into this deep underworld of black ops and an even darker world of satanic sacrifice? Yeah, that sounds about right," I deadpanned.

We were both exhausted from the events of the day. I told Gina to sleep in my bed and that I would use the couch in my office. She didn't object to the proposed arrangements.

As Gina walked out of the office, she turned back to me before she reached the door, grinning. "I just thought of something," she said. "You've had two different women in your apartment on the same day. I wonder what your neighbors are thinking if they've been watching."

"It's not the first time," I said with a wry smile.

IN THE DARK OF NIGHT

Chapter 16

<u>**Thursday, September 10, 1987**</u>

I was seated at my desk in the war room by 5:45 a.m., already having showered and dressed. I got prepared for the day quietly and in virtual darkness as I didn't want to disturb Gina. I selected a dark blue suit and pressed white shirt that I had picked up from the dry cleaners, complementing it with a solid red tie. I forgot to remove my clothes from my room the night before, so I was proud of my skills to silently retrieve my clothes without the need to turn on the bedroom light.

After making coffee, I used this quiet time to pay some bills I had put off and organize other investigative files that needed our agency's attention. I was just finishing the mundane paperwork when I caught a glimpse of Gina as she walked into the war room. She was wearing a white cotton nightshirt and carrying a mug of coffee from the second pot I made this morning. She sat down in the leather wingback chair across from me, waiting for me to finish before saying anything. I could feel her gaze upon me and wondered what she was thinking.

"I see you found the coffee. How did you sleep?" I asked her.

"Like a baby. Thanks for letting me stay last night."

"What are partners for?"

"I thought Paul's your partner. Is there something you haven't told me?" Gina asked.

"No, nothing like that. Paul and I have reached a mutual understanding. He's handling the security side of the agency, and I'm handling the investigative side. You're a great investigator and certainly don't belong on guard duty. So, I've claimed you," I said with a smile.

"If you don't mind, I'm going to use your bathroom to take a shower and get dressed. I promise I'll be quick."

About a half-hour later, Gina returned to the war room, this time dressed in a denim skirt and a light-colored blouse that draped over her skirt. Her shirt covered the gun she was wearing inside her waistband on her hip. Her appearance was close to that of the actress Stepfanie Kramer, the character of Dee Dee McCall from the television show *Hunter*. When I told her that, she laughed and said that despite the compliment, I'm no Fred Dryer.

****

"What do we know about Martin and Mary Tingsley? I mean, what do we really know about them?"

"What do you mean? Jim took their sworn statements. He packaged them for submission to the state attorney general. We also have their statements on audio. The documentation they've provided, including Martin's scars and the photographic evidence, is all pretty solid. The physical evidence alone is strong. You can't fake that. Why, what are you thinking?"

"I don't know, but something's bothering me, and I can't put my finger on it. The Tingsleys first appeared on our radar during the investigation into my uncle's murder. We interviewed them a few times, took some photographs of Martin's old wounds from the sexual abuse he suffered, and documented his relationship with my uncle when he was a student. We know he saw my uncle on the day he was murdered. We know about the suspicious car accident that killed his mother just as she was pushing to get answers about the abuse of her son. I do not doubt that Martin is a victim," I said, recounting our interactions.

"But…?"

"Why didn't either one ever mention anything about his father? Where's he been through all of this? What about his younger brother, Jacob? Why didn't either of them let us know about him? Martin entrusted us with the most intimate details of his life but decided not to disclose he had a younger brother his mother adopted out? And now, out of nowhere, the boy turns up dead?"

"You heard him tell us that he never said anything about his younger brother because he was worried about his safety."

"You see how well that worked out. And again, what about Martin's father?"

"I don't know."

"Maybe we should be asking ourselves why we broke protocol and never did a thorough background investigation on them like every other case we handle."

"I think the reason was seeing his injuries and how fragile he was. The way he gave us detailed accounts of his experiences that matched the physical evidence we obtained. I wouldn't say that we've got a protocol for a victim or a case like this."

"Perhaps not, but I refer you again to Stiles' Rule number four."

"And that is?"

"Never trust what someone tells you. Always verify the information yourself. So now, let's do an extensive background investigation like we should've done and see what turns up. We need to know as much about the Tingsley family as they know about themselves."

"And you think we'll find… what, exactly?" Gina asked.

"I don't know if we'll find anything, but we have to look. They're safely tucked away at her uncle's cabin, so we've got a bit of a window. Let's make this a priority anyway."

"I'll get right on it," Gina said, collecting her handbag and notebook. "My car is still at the office, so you'll have to give me a lift."

"No problem. While you're at it, let's do a thorough background check on Mary's uncle, Paul Kruger. Let's find out everything we can about anyone remotely involved in this nightmare."

After taking care of a few things at the office, Gina spent the day at the county courthouse, public library, and in the field conducting interviews of several people who could fill in the blanks about the Tingsley family.

Meanwhile, I began an initial investigation on a fraud case that, until now, was languishing in a file on my desk. By Thursday night, I completed interviews with eight people and typed a report of my findings from my home office. Perhaps out of habit, or perhaps a sign of things to come, I fell asleep on my couch while watching the latest installment of *Night Court*.

IN THE DARK OF NIGHT

Chapter 17

<u>**Friday, September 11, 1987**</u>

    I arrived at the office at 7:30 a.m., watching as Annie parked her car in the space next to mine. We walked into the office together, dodging large raindrops falling from thick, dark clouds that seemed to appear from nowhere. Once inside, we laughed at each other's soaked appearance.

"It's good to see you laugh," Annie said as she blotted herself dry.

"It feels good to laugh," I said as she handed me a fistful of paper towels.

Annie made coffee and called the answering service to check messages and take control of the phones back while I got settled in my office. Considering the morning weather, I opted to get some paperwork done in the office and catch up on some client telephone calls. At the same time, Annie worked on a personnel roster and billing invoices for Paul's security business.

Around noon, I spoke to Gina by telephone. She told me that she was able to spend some time with her daughter and mother the previous evening, after putting in several hours of an extensive investigation of the Tingsley clan. She also explained how she used older editions of the city and county directories at the library to elicit information from the various departments at the courthouse. The tasks were tedious and time-consuming. She told me that she was continuing her research and could possibly have things wrapped up late today.

It's interesting how much information can be cultivated from those publications collecting dust in the reference section at the county library if one knows where to look. One of two directories provides the occupations of the members of the household with surprising specificity and accuracy going back to World War II.

Gina said that she found some "disturbing" information and would attempt to organize the data once she verified it through secondary sources. She suggested that we meet this weekend to supplement the information we planned to submit to the attorney general's office through Jim Carr, adding that she would call me late tomorrow morning so we could schedule a weekend meeting.

Her main focus today was on the Tingsley family, tracing their time and connections in Lakewood using marriage and property ownership records, and conducting field interviews. From that information, she was able to develop a network of possible relatives and associates, including those of Paul Kruger, the owner of the cabin where they are presently staying. One lead seemed to lead to another, and soon, Gina had developed a web of potential names and locations from which to work. Before long, the information became unwieldy. And troublesome.

****

At 12:50 p.m., Annie stuck her head into my office. "Brenda from The Towne Restaurant is on the phone for you. She said it was important."

"Thanks, Annie," I said, waiting until she closed the door before I picked up the call.

"Brenda, is everything okay?"

"I'm not sure, Marc. Two guys just left here. They said that they are old friends of yours visiting from Florida. They wanted to know if you'd be stopping in today and what time you usually come by. There was something not right about them, Marc. They gave me the creeps," Brenda said, her voice shaking slightly. "Are you expecting any visitors from Florida?"

"Not that I'm aware of."

"I didn't think so."

"They didn't happen to leave their names, did they?"

"No, neither one did. One guy was older, probably in his late fifties trim with salt and pepper hair, and the other was much younger, who was all muscle. The younger guy had a head of styled blond hair and didn't say a word. The older guy is the only one who spoke, which I thought was odd. They aren't cops or feds. I can tell you that. Neither one seemed like your friends or the kind of company you'd keep."

"I'm pretty sure I know who these guys are. Did you happen to see what they were driving?"

"Yes, a newer black Cadillac, maybe a 1987 or even an '88. The young guy was driving, and the old guy rode in the back like he was being chauffeured around. The older man was wearing a hand-tailored Italian suit and a couple of flashy diamond rings, while the young guy was wearing a light blue button-down shirt and khakis. He was also wearing a thick, braided gold chain and pendant around his neck, but the pendant was tucked inside his shirt, so I didn't see what it was."

Brenda is not only observant, but she can spot a fake ID or a fake Rolex a mile away. She has impressive skills that can put many FBI profilers to shame, and I've seen her do it ever since we first met. She can tell when something is amiss long before anyone else, a quality that has served her well.

"You said the younger guy was wearing a gold chain and pendant?"

"Yes."

"It's interesting that it caught your eye. I've seen that before, and I think I know what it is. Did they want anything else?"

"They wanted directions to your office, but I told them I've never been there and don't even know where it is. I don't think they believed me. I told them that they could find the office address in the phone book if they looked and pointed to the pay telephone by the restrooms. They also asked for your home address, and I told them I had no idea. I tried to play dumb and downplay how well we know each other, but I doubt that the older guy believed me when I said that I barely knew you and that you were just an occasional customer."

"Anything else?" I asked.

"The older man wanted me to give you a message."

"Go ahead, lay it on me."

"He said, 'Tell him that I will be seeing him.' Then he repeated it, except this time he added something that sounded more ominous than friendly."

"Go ahead."

"Make sure you tell him that I will be seeing him long before he sees me, especially if he stays on the yellow brick road. He said that you would know what that meant, that it was a private joke. Then he laughed and walked out with 'Mr. Muscle' to their car."

"Marvelous," I muttered.

"The yellow brick road he mentioned, is that some kind of code?" Brenda asked.

"Sort of," I said to Brenda. "It's where this guy lives his pathetic and miserable life. You didn't happen to get their license plate number, did you?"

"What kind of junior investigator would I be if I didn't? You know I did." I could detect the hint of a smile in her voice as she asked me if I had something to write with, adding, "but you might not need it."

"Why not?"

"It's an Ohio vanity plate: MONARCH. Rather strange, don't you think? Is the old man that much into butterflies, or is there another meaning to this?" Brenda asked.

As soon as she read the plate to me, my stomach turned. I didn't explain the possible connection to the U.S. government mind control program known by that name. Project Monarch was part of a covert CIA operation known as MKUltra that reportedly began in 1953. The project operators sought victims, especially young children, and allegedly subjected them to torture and extreme psychological and physical trauma to "split" their personalities. Unable to handle the experiences, their minds would fracture or split, causing a type of multiple-personality disorder. From there, their handles could program the dissociated parts of their brains into different, controllable personalities.

"There is one more thing I noticed, Marc. Both were packing. The print from their weapons was evident through their clothes."

"Thanks for the heads up, Brenda. I appreciate you looking after me like this."

"Can you tell me what this is about? Please?" Brenda stretched out the word 'please' a bit longer than necessary.

"Maybe for right now, it's better to keep you out of the loop," I said, genuinely trying to protect her. "I promise, though, I'll fill you in sometime soon. In the meantime, please let me know if they come back or if anyone else asks any questions about Gina or me. Even if you think someone seems out of place, please call me."

"I will, sweetheart. Just promise me that you'll be careful. I need you around, more than you know." I hung up, momentarily wondering more about what she meant by needing me around than thinking about the implications of the visitors from Florida.

****

If there's one thing that's important to a private investigator, it's sources and contacts. Specifically, having people you can call upon who can quickly provide information that's not readily available to the general public, and do so without the need to fill out pesky forms or wade through a lot of bureaucratic red tape. TC is a police officer at the state capital who was introduced to me by my partner. He has a lucrative side business providing private investigators with information from the department of motor vehicles. He offers this service to only licensed investigators he knows will not reveal the origin of the information provided. He does everything by telephone, except for sending out generic invoices to his clients.

"Hey TC, can you run an in-state plate for me? I need the complete owner profile, and I'll take the VIN information if it's handy."

"Sure, I can do it shortly, I'll have to call you back, though. Give me 30 minutes."

True to his word, TC called with information about the owner of the plate and vehicle.

"According to the state DMV records, the tag is supposed to be on a 1987 black Cadillac sedan. It's registered to Porter O. Landers under a business in your area. The name of the business is Oz Enterprises, LLC, PO Box 366, in Lakewood. His operator's license and the vehicle registration is current through January of '88. There are no liens on the vehicle, either. Must be nice, the guy owns it outright."

"Thanks, TC. Send me the bill."

It was just as I suspected. Based on his physical description and what was said to Brenda, it was indeed Landers who was asking for me at the Towne Restaurant. I was unaware, however, that Landers maintains an address in

Lakewood under a fictitious business name. Gina and I conducted an extensive records check in Miami-Dade County, Florida of Landers while we were down there. We learned that he resided there for more than fifteen years and didn't think to look further, particularly in Lakewood. We found nothing to suggest that he had any operational business or mailing addresses here. It was my fault for failing to check Lakewood County and state records at a local level, which would prove to be a critical oversight.

****

Our history of dealing with Porter Landers and Luke was, if nothing else, entertaining. While pursuing leads in the murder of my uncle earlier this year, Gina and I visited him at his estate in Florida. He lives in a large and ostentatious estate that exudes wealth and influence, all supposedly earned from his ownership of a dive of a nightclub aptly called The Yellow Brick Road, located just off of Tamiami Trail in Miami. Landers kept a young, muscular man, who he identified only as Luke, at his residence to service his needs. All of them. Appearing to be in his early twenties, Luke seemed to be playing a dual role as Landers' servant and enforcer. Along with the Rolls Royce parked at the estate, Luke was eye-candy for Landers' perverse friends and associates.

Looking back at our initial Florida meeting with Landers, it was surreal. Our subsequent encounter was even more surreal. We initially met Porter Landers when we made an unannounced visit to his mansion. His boy Luke greeted us at the door and instructed us to wait in the large foyer that extended two-stories and was appointed with the biggest crystal chandelier I've ever seen. Large pots of tropical plants and flowers were set upon a marble floor that spanned across either side of an ornate staircase that led from the second floor to where we stood. The floor of the foyer was constructed from white and black marble, alternated to create the appearance of a checkerboard. It seemed to be a common theme in the homes and businesses of those we encountered. This would prove to be important, we learned.

Our interview took place by his large, inground pool with Luke serving up our refreshments. During our two-hour conversation, Landers exhibited different traits at different times, his mannerisms ranging from nauseatingly effeminate to surprisingly gruff. I recall that it was like interviewing multiple people in one body.

The interview produced seven pages of handwritten notes that we transcribed upon our return. Despite his perverse proclivities and flamboyant lifestyle, Landers had a fascinating tendency to tell the truth. He exposed the good, bad and ugly, of which there was little good but plenty of bad and ugly. He provided us with some much-needed information that shed light on not only what was taking place in Miami but in Lakewood.

While in Miami, Gina and I also checked out his club, which was not open due to the time of day that we were there. It was located in a rather bleak area of Miami, surrounded by industrial-style buildings and warehouses that created a seedy atmosphere, even under the bright Florida sun. An engraved white sign that readily identified his business was affixed to the right of the entrance with the words 'The Yellow Brick Road' spelled out in script. Under that and in the same type of writing but smaller lettering were the words 'Dorothy's Paradise.'

While our initial meeting with Landers resulted in obtaining a lot of actionable intelligence, he was not as pleasant the next time we met later that day. Whether he was having second thoughts about the information he had initially given us or slipped into another persona remains unclear. Just as we dropped in on him unannounced, Landers, his boy Luke, and a few other unidentified 'enforcers' surprised us at our Miami motel.

It happened when Gina was inside the motel room we were sharing, and I was sitting at the motel bar, deciding to take a few minutes to unwind. While seated at the otherwise empty bar, I was flanked by the duo at the same time Gina was forcibly subdued in our room by their associates. I was escorted from the bar to join Gina after having a .45 shoved against my ribs. My guard was down at the time that left us vulnerable to this type of blitz. It was careless on my part.

Whatever goodwill was shown to us earlier that day by Landers had disappeared entirely. Now, it was his turn to give us our marching orders through his delivery of a bizarre monologue he delivered to Gina and me in our motel room. Considering that this took place at the business end of a gun, it's easy to recall this event with absolute clarity.

Inside the room with his captive audience of two, Landers began his soliloquy with the statement, "There are a lot worse things than death. You're not going to die today, well, at least I'm not going to kill you, or have you killed. You're going to leave town now, and not come back. For the sake of your son and daughter Marc, and your daughter, Gina, you're going to go back to Lakewood and stop sticking your noses into places they don't belong. As you can tell, I've got a lot of friends here, and you're making them uncomfortable." How did he know about my children and Gina's daughter, I wondered.

For another five long and uneasy minutes, Landers continued his monologue. During that time, I had thoughts of rushing to overpower him, although I reconsidered that idea as I had no clue where his associates were. Furthermore, we already determined that he had some members of the local police and sheriffs' department in his pocket, and any favorable extrication from that mess would be unlikely. So, I just kept my mouth shut for once and listened.

As it turned out, listening and giving the outward appearance of complete cooperation had its benefits. Through his unholy sermon, Landers had added to the information he provided earlier that day. I recall that he seemed to be in some type of trance created by the sound of his own voice, which oddly morphed into a German accent at times. Thinking about that today, it didn't take a detective to see a common theme developing. He twice referred to the "yellow brick road" that we were "traveling" to pursue the killer of my uncle during his speech. As we would soon learn, we were indeed on a yellow brick road, but not one paved of gold, yet one that could ultimately take us to the wizard.

His mission that day was to make sure that Gina and I understood that we were to leave the motel and the county without delay and to cease our investigation or face the consequences. Although it was abundantly clear that Gina and I had no friends in that Florida county, we only half obliged him.

We did leave the county following those unpleasantries, but never stopped our investigation. Now it appears that he has a problem with me for not heeding his advice.

****

I called Annie into my office and asked her to take a seat at the conference table. As a single and attractive woman, I consider her to be a target who could be more vulnerable than most, especially working at a private investigative agency. I sat down across from her and explained the events of the last several days in detail, including and especially the information relayed by Brenda. I told her that I thought it would be a good idea if we coordinated our schedules, so she never opens or closes the office alone, and when she's at the office, she should keep the outer door locked. I apologized for placing her in the position of having to watch over her shoulder constantly. Before I finished my apology, Annie patted my hand and told me that I had nothing to apologize for, she enjoyed the work. She then stood up and turned her body so that her right side was visible to me. She lifted her beige cashmere sweater to show me that she was carrying a Glock in an inside-the-waistband holster.

Surprised, I asked her how long she has been carrying a handgun. She explained that she had taken a gun class over the summer and also graduated from a more advanced tactical handgun training class.

"You didn't think I'm all beauty and brains now, did you? I'm also quite lethal. I don't want to brag, but I can hit center mass dead-on at 20 yards with a remarkably tight grouping. I feel that I'm better armed than you, Marc. I'd personally feel a lot better if you upgraded from 'your grandpa's' .38," she said with a smile. "And I can field strip and reassemble my weapon with my eyes closed in 90 seconds or better if you'd like to test me."

As my mouth hung open, Annie walked back into the reception area of the office and sat bar down at her desk. I followed Annie to the reception area and told her about the call from Brenda. I asked Annie to be careful when she traveled to and from the office and to be aware of potential surveillance by bad actors. She seemed to be more aware of recent events than I had previously thought.

"Do you want me to let Gina know that Landers and his sidekick are in town?" Annie asked.

"Yes, please give her a 'heads-up' when she calls in case I don't get a chance to talk with her."

The telephone was ringing when I got back to my desk. It was Detective Jenkins, who skipped all pleasantries to tell me that the police have officially cleared Gina and me in London in the case of the murder of Sadie Cooper. They had a suspect in custody and put him in jail, pending their version of an arraignment. When the guards checked on him, they found him hanging from his bunk with a sheet tied around his neck before he could talk to a solicitor, or an attorney to present a defense. According to their medical examiner, the suspect committed suicide in his cell and left a pretty straightforward confession. He admitted to killing Ms. Cooper and two other women. Their investigation found that he was a suspect in two other unsolved murders that had similar pathologically sadistic qualities. Anyway, it's all nicely wrapped up, with the bow on top being his death.

"How did they explain our business cards?"

"They didn't. Or at least, they didn't have to. Again, the case is closed, and the suspect killed himself, saving the 'Crown' the spectacle of a public trial. The victim's body is still on ice pending any family coming forward. They'll keep her there for several more days according to their policy, but the suspect was buried in a public cemetery, or their type of a potter's field," Ron said matter of factly. "If no family comes forward, she'll be buried in the same cemetery."

"How did you find all of this out?"

"From our FBI guests. I learned that the London police had been in communication with the FBI and everyone was satisfied that it was a simple case of being in the wrong place at the wrong time. They believe that Sadie Cooper was stalked for a short time by her killer, and she saw something that alerted her. She ran and became hysterical. Frantic and not being in her right mind, she tried to contact you and Gina while her killer was pursuing her."

"Do you believe that story?"

"It doesn't matter what I believe. The case is across the ocean and not my problem. It's closed."

Detective Jenkins gave me the name of the alleged suspect, as I requested. He added that the suspect was known to the police in London and had a long rap sheet, including violent attacks on women. "His last name was Forsythe, his first name Andrew. He just turned forty-years-old at the beginning of this month. 1 September 1947 was his date of birth, according to this report from Scotland Yard."

"Thanks, Ron, I appreciate you keeping me up-to-date on that."

There was a silence that seemed to prohibit his reply that seemed to last for a few seconds longer than what might be considered polite or comfortable. "Ron? Are you still there?" I asked.

"Marc, there is one more thing I think you should know, but you did not hear this from me. It's about Jacob Tingsley's foster parents and another child." There was yet another uncomfortable pause.

"Another child?" I asked, breaking the silence.

"There appears to be another child, an 11-month-old infant, who seems to have completely disappeared from their care."

"When?"

"The investigators there have been hard-pressed to pin down an exact date, but it happened within the last week or so. The weird thing is that the entire Smith family, and not just the parents of Jacob Tingsley, are denying it. They completely deny having any infant in their care, and we're having a hard time proving that such an infant exists."

"Are you kidding me?"

"I wish I was joking. This is about as bizarre as it gets."

"How is that even possible? Can't the child be traced through medical records or Child Protective Services?" I asked.

"We checked. CPS has no record of any infant placement or any placement at all. There are no county or state birth records that we were able to find. There are no calls or complaints either. We're going on the statements of several reliable witnesses, and observations made by the officer who conducted the death notification about the murder of Jacob Tingsley. Something is going on with that family, it's not good, but I'll be damned if I know what it is." Jenkins said.

"Are you telling me this for any specific purpose, Ron?"

"I know what you guys are doing. I know about your investigation into missing children and SRA victims. After what I've seen with the feds and all the weird things going on, I want to help you as much as possible even though it might not seem that way. I don't know how this all fits in, but I believe it does. Hell, at the moment, I don't know much of anything, but I do know that I trust my gut more than any federal agent or just about anyone else, present company excluded. My gut tells me there is something very wrong here. The feds, the local police, no one wants to investigate this, and since the foster parents deny that there ever was an infant in their care, there's not too much we can officially do."

"Why are you so sure there was an infant there?"

"Among other things, the officer who made the death notification concerning Jacob not only saw the infant, but a crib and some toys in their house. Now, everything's gone. There's no trace of an infant. Since the murder of Jacob, the baby just disappeared. More than disappeared. It's like the baby never existed. No birth record, no medical records, no pictures, and now, no crib or infant toys at the residence."

"Could they have just been babysitting? That would be the most obvious answer."

"Of course, we considered that, and for a while, thought that was the case."

"What changed your mind?"

"The totality of the evidence, from the way the Smith family, including the children, provided answers to our questions. Then, the information we received from a neighbor. She said that one of their foster children, a 15-year-old-girl, was pregnant and delivered a boy not quite a year ago. Then another neighbor of the Smith family provided a similar statement. That neighbor said that she helped decorate a nursery for the child, but now that nursery is a guest bedroom. Yet when they were confronted with this information, the

Smiths stated that both neighbors were either lying or mistaken. They became very irritated by our questions."

"How did the neighbors become involved with a death notification?"

"The media ran a big story on the murder locally. As it was an unsolved homicide, one neighbor called the local department and offered information they thought might help. That led to the contact with a second neighbor and ultimately, an interview with the Smith family."

"What about the infant's mother?"

"Her name is Maggie, now 16 years old. She's still there but denies being pregnant or delivering a child."

"Where are you at with the investigation now?"

"As I said, what investigation? No missing person report, no body, denials by the family, and the foster kids, including the alleged mother. What's there to investigate? Hence, there is no investigation. But Marc, I believe there's something to this. We can't investigate, but…" a silence hung in the air for several seconds.

"But we can. Got it," I said. "And thanks."

"Marc, please do me one favor. Let me know on this one, okay?"

"I will. There's one more thing I need to tell you, Ron. Do you remember Porter Landers from our investigation in Florida?"

"Yeah, queer as a three-dollar bill. He owns some nightclub in Miami if I recall correctly."

"That's him. I just found out that he's in town with his muscle and has been asking about me. He's driving a new Caddy with in-state plates. It's a vanity plate that spells out MONARCH. Would you let me know if you run into him?"

"I've got your back, Marc."

IN THE DARK OF NIGHT

Chapter 18

<u>**Saturday, September 12, 1987**</u>

Jim Carr called me just after 9:00 a.m. from a phone booth near his office. The excitement in his voice was noticeable. "Listen to this," he began. "I stopped by my office this morning, and the two FBI agents, Liu and Roberts, were talking with the district attorney inside his office. I overheard them talking about getting a late breakfast, and they left a few minutes later. Well, guess what? He forgot to lock his door, and even better, the two big shots from Quantico left their attaches in his office. Since no one else was around, I went into his office and found all of their documents, investigative notes, and reports. Everything was there, including the files the feds have been carrying around with them since they got here."

"So, you had access to the documents. Did you read them?" I asked.

"Better than that, Marc. I copied every page I could find while they were gone. I also copied the DA's file that contained an updated investigative report on the Tingsley homicide," Carr said in a hushed but hurried manner. "I was sweating bullets, thinking they were going to come back before I finished, but I made it. I was able to put everything back the way it was and managed to get out of there before they came back. It was close, though. They were walking onto the floor just as I was leaving."

"Well, what's in the files?"

"I didn't look at everything in detail for obvious reasons and thought we could go through it all together. I do know one thing, though. Even though the FBI believes that they are dealing with a multi-state serial killer, the sexually sadistic type, they do acknowledge the ritual aspect of some of the killings. It seems that they have documented a few other similar cases throughout the state as well as in New York and Pennsylvania. There's a lot of information in here, Marc. I've got copies of everything in my briefcase."

"Can you meet me at the war room in an hour?" I asked.

"Let's do it. Angie had to go into work this morning. She's got a big case that's heading to trial, and her boss insisted that she and her team work today. She's going to be working until at least two o'clock, maybe later."

"Damn, I forgot about that," I said out loud.

"Is that the same case Fidelity Mutual assigned to your company?"

"Yes, it is, and I was supposed to deliver the final report to them yesterday."

"If it helps, I don't think that will be a problem for you guys. Angie said that they would not be able to form their defense until next Tuesday when the 'brass' arrives from Columbus. She said that today would be more of a housecleaning to get their files in order before Tuesday. Besides, I told Angie that I was going to the gym and maybe the driving range if the weather stays decent, so if I'm not home when she gets back, she won't think anything of it."

"Okay, I'll put the coffee on and see you in thirty," I said.

"Wait, as I said, there's a lot here. You might want to see if Gina and Annie can help us with this if they're free. We're going to need all hands on deck."

"Right. I'll give them a call."

"Before I get there, I'll stop at Kinko's and make copies, so we each have a set."

As soon as I hung up with Jim, I called Gina at her home and told her what we had.

"Let's meet in the war room as soon as you can make it in."

"I'm on my way, and I'll bring my papers from the research I did this past week with me too. I'll call Annie and ask her to join us, especially now, with the work ahead of us."

"Sounds good."

"By the way, Annie told me about Landers being in town and the ominous-sounding message he left. I'm not sure what to make of that, but we can talk about it when I get there."

"See you in a little bit."

****

Jim arrived first, carrying his newly acquired documents. Minutes later, Gina came with Annie. Within the hour, the four of us were already fifteen minutes into our review of the recently obtained documents inside the war room.

"Remind me again of the penalty for the unauthorized possession of government documents," Gina mused.

"Only some of these are law enforcement sensitive," Jim said as both Gina and Annie huddled closely on the couch.

The total number of pages Jim Carr had managed to copy and bring in for review number just north of one hundred. Of those, there were about two dozen 302s or FBI interview summaries in conjunction with numerous pages of handwritten notes primarily from FBI Agent Marcy Liu.

"She's got nice handwriting, Marc. It's quite legible. You could learn a thing or two from her so other people would be able to read your writing," Annie deadpanned.

Three hours later, we had many of the same insights as the FBI and the district attorney into murder and more in Lakewood and beyond. Gina and I methodically sorted through the notes and made index cards of the names they contained. Several names were familiar, including Porter Landers from Florida, the late Benjamin and Sadie Cooper, and Roland Speirs.

"Why does the name Roland Speirs sound familiar?" Gina asked. "I know the name but can't place him."

We scoured the notes. Speirs' name appeared next to an entry written as The Ruby Slipper Lounge. We located a corresponding 302 that was completed and signed by Agent Roberts just two days prior. The summary indicated that Roland Speirs stated that he was part of the MKUltra program, and his handler was identified as Benjamin Cooper. The 302 seemed to lack a lot of specific information about Speirs' role in the program, although the notes contained many more details that the 302 did not list.

"Damn, Gina, I let Roland fall through the cracks right around the time we took our trip to Florida. He called the office and said he had some information for us. I remember calling him back to set up an appointment. The phone number was for the Ruby Slipper Lounge, and the guy who answered said he wasn't in. I never followed up. Now I think that I missed a huge piece of the puzzle."

"Well, since I don't have a life outside of work anymore, do you want to follow up on this later today or tonight?" Gina asked, looking at me.

"I'm in."

Upon hearing us make plans for a visit, Jim piped in. "Look at the handwritten entry on the notes, about five lines down from Roland's name. It says that he has some kind of journal that the agents are trying to find. They asked him where he kept it, and he told them it was in his safety deposit box at a local bank. He promised to give it to them next week. The word 'journal' is underlined and circled in the handwritten notes, yet no reference is made about it on the 302. Nothing, no mention of it at all. That's curious."

"Yeah, that is interesting, and its omission on the 302 is deliberate too. What do you think the chances are that Roland has the journal in his possession right now? He's had time to get it from the bank. Or maybe it was never at the bank. Maybe he always had it in his possession. Anyway, the agents talked to him on Thursday morning, so I would imagine that he's had ample time to get it by now, wherever he kept it," Gina wondered out loud.

"Let's find out. I'll call the lounge later and see if Roland will still talk to us. Maybe we can beat the feds to his journal."

Gina, Jim, Annie, and I spent another few hours pouring over the investigative work products of FBI agents Ted Roberts and Marcy Liu, along with reports submitted to the district attorney by the Lakewood Police. During this time, I relayed the information Detective Jenkins gave me about the Cooper homicide being closed in London, and the new twist to the Smith family.

"So now we might have yet another potential victim?" Jim asked.

"I don't know what we have, but Ron was very certain that an infant was living with the Smiths at the time of the death notification, but then the infant completely disappeared."

"Gina and I will investigate that angle. It might relate to the letter I got," I said.

By two o'clock, Jim was gathering his set of documents and placing them back into his briefcase.

"I've got to be getting back home. I'd like to beat Angie home for once."

"Have you heard anything more about the break-in at your house last weekend?" I asked.

"A detective called me yesterday and told me they were moving the case to inactive status based on the lack of any evidence or additional information. It's for the best, I guess."

"Do you have any ideas of who might have wanted to steal your investigative report and evidence you've been compiling for the state Attorney General?"

"No, but I've been thinking about it. Whoever broke in had to be watching the house, and had to know when Angie, Oscar, and I left. They could have done things a lot differently. I mean, they could have entered the house and my office, stole the items and documents that they did, and exit without leaving a trace. Whoever did this were professionals. I'm sure that this was not their first rodeo, they seemed to know what they were looking for and where to find it. They could have gotten what they wanted without me knowing they were ever there. I might not have realized that there was a burglary for a few more days if it weren't for the obvious signs of a break-in. Think about it. I have a feeling that whoever did this wanted me to know. I think that in addition to taking what they did, they were sending me a message."

"What kind of message?"

"I don't know. A warning, I suppose."

"Speaking of warnings, did you tell Jim about the message you received through Brenda yesterday?" Annie interjected.

Jim turned his head and began staring at me, expectantly.

"Brenda from The Towne Restaurant called me on Friday. Two guys matching the description of Florida's own Porter Landers and his sidekick stopped at the restaurant asking questions about me. They wanted to know where our office is, which is public information, and where I live, which is not. Brenda said that they both were carrying. They were driving a new Cadillac with Ohio vanity plates, 'MONARCH.' Brenda was a bit rattled by it."

"I am too," Gina said. "Did you forget what he did to us in Florida? How he warned us off, stuck a gun in your ribs, and knocked me around? That guy is as evil and dangerous as they come, and now he's here in our backyard!"

"He's not just a visitor, either," I explained. "I'm not sure how we missed this, but Landers has a Lakewood post office box listed to his company called Oz Enterprises, LLC. I did some checking, and the Cadillac is registered to him under that business name."

"How did we not know this? Or is that tidbit stuffed somewhere in this maze of information, and we just overlooked it?"

"In our defense, it's not that difficult to overlook. As far as I can tell, Landers has no actual physical business address or other property in this county. It's just the post office box. The post office up here forwards his Lakewood mail to his Florida address. I didn't see anything in the FBI papers, either, that mentions his Lakewood post office box, although I might have missed it."

"If it is in there, then we all missed it. I wonder what reason Landers has to have a Lakewood mailing address without any known business presence. It's certainly not for any tax benefits," Jim added.

Gina stood up and gave me a look of concern. I watched as she adjusted her .45 caliber semi-auto into her waistband by her right hip. "This has all gotten a lot more personal, and I'm not taking any chances," she said. Just then, I became aware of my own .38 Smith & Wesson secured in my shoulder holster under my left arm and a speed loader with extra hollow point ammunition in the pocket of my sport coat.

"I've gotta go," Jim said. "I want to get home before Angie does. I don't want to push things right now. See you guys later. Call me later, or tomorrow if you end up talking to Roland tonight," Jim said as he walked from the office.

****

After Jim left, Gina, Annie, and I ordered a large pizza delivered from Mama Rosa's and finished all of it. At four o'clock, I called The Ruby Slipper

Lounge and asked to speak to Roland. The man who answered the phone told me to hold on and put the receiver down. I heard him walk from the telephone, and noise from the bar filled the earpiece in his absence. I heard him walking back and pick up the receiver.

"He's not in his room. One of the guys here said that he was visiting someone and wouldn't be back until later tonight."

"Any idea how late?" I asked.

"Look, pal, I'm not his secretary. Check back later." He hung up, placing the receiver on the phone that made it clear that the conversation was over.

The volume coming through the phone made it easy for Gina and Annie to hear both sides of the conversation.

"Do you want me to stay here?" Annie asked. "Is there anything I can do?"

"No, but thanks for the offer, and welcome to the club," I said. With that, Annie left the war room and my apartment, saying that she would see us both Monday. "Call me anytime you need me," she added.

"If you don't mind, I'll stay here until we meet with Roland. I've got the time," Gina said.

"Please, be my guest. I can use the company."

"So, we wait. Do you mind if I grab a quick shower while I'm here? I'll wear the change of clothes I brought in my turnout bag that's in my car."

"No, go ahead," I said as I turned on the local television news.

"You're not expecting anyone today? What if Deana drops in and finds me in the shower? She won't be upset?"

"I think she'd be more upset if I were in there with you."

"Don't you wish!"

"Clean towels are in the linen closet next to the bathroom."

"That's one thing I'll say about you, Marc. You keep an organized house."

IN THE DARK OF NIGHT

Chapter 19

<u>Roland Speirs</u>

It was back in early May when I received a telephone call from a man who identified himself only as Roland. The number traced back to the Ruby Slipper Lounge, a bar located in a rough area of Lakewood that is plagued by crime commonly found in blighted urban areas. Crimes such as prostitution, drug dealing, assaults, and burglaries. The bar caters to a mainly male homosexual clientele and is owned by Max Klein, who spent most of his life in Columbus before moving to Lakewood in the late 1970s. Klein bought the bar and the attached rooming house in 1978. The rooming house seemed like an attached afterthought of the older bar construction. Klein rents the rooms by the week or month, thus providing a low-cost option to those who would otherwise be living on the street.

We learned that Roland Speirs had been a near-permanent fixture of room number three since Klein first purchased the bar. While he was acquainted with Speirs, he claimed that he didn't know much about him.

A cursory background investigation of Roland Speirs found that he is 62 years-old with a lengthy criminal history dating back into the 1940s, mostly for non-violent crimes across the state. He served a short stint in the U.S. Army during World War II in 1944 when he turned 18 and was discharged in 1946. Roland seemed to drop off the radar between 1953 and 1956, at least on paper; however, he resurfaced with a Maryland address the following year. Then, according to a credit history report, his name was associated with a long list of addresses across our state. He finally settled in Lakewood at about the same time as Klein. He is not married, has no family to speak of, does not work anywhere, at least not on the books, and appears to rely on the income from a small disability payment from the government.

"What kind of a name is Roland? I mean, what were his parents thinking?"

"Maybe it was a 1920s thing," Gina mused, referring to the decade of his birth as she held his file. "Does he actually use that name?"

"You have his file. Are there any aliases or nicknames listed?"

"It doesn't look like it," Gina said as she viewed his rap sheets. "So, how do you want to handle this?"

"Let's just drop in on him later tonight. With the way things have been going lately, I don't want to announce our moves. "

Omega

Just before 11 p.m., Gina and I walked into the Ruby Slipper Lounge. Max Klein, the owner, was standing behind the bar at the end closest to the door, talking with a small cluster of customers. I showed my badge as we approached him, saying that we were here to speak with Roland Speirs, a tenant who is renting a room in the back of the bar.

"Room 3," he said, barely breaking from his conversational stride with his buddies. He pointed to a door at the back of the bar, beyond a pool table and jukebox. The door provided access to four separate rooms that served as the living quarters for those down on their luck.

While speaking with a Lakewood Police Department patrol officer earlier in the day, I mentioned that I was going to be interviewing a tenant at the rooming house behind the Ruby Slipper Lounge.

"I know that place well. Are you current on your TB shots?" A smirk flashed across his face as he asked the question.

"That bad, huh?"

"Yeah, it's that bad. Mostly drug addicts, guys just out of prison and transients rent the rooms for about fifteen dollars a week."

The patrol officer gave me the lay of the land from his many calls to that address. According to him, there are two ways to get into the rooms located behind the bar. The easiest way is to go through the bar when it's open. Otherwise, there's an external door that doubles as an emergency exit for the rooms and the bar.

"If you go when the place is open, I'd go through the bar. The access to the rooms is much easier, and it saves you the trouble of walking across the alley behind the bar, which is a busy place for guys who want to get their 'freak-on' after they hook up inside. I've had to uncouple a lot of guys back there," the patrol officer said.

He said that each room was about the same size, which is about the size of an average bedroom, he estimated. Each room comes sparsely furnished with a metal-framed bed and a small refrigerator sitting on top of an old, wooden upright dresser. Occupants share a common bathroom that is located in the middle of the hallway and consists of a single toilet, sink, and shower stall. "Depressing, to say the least," he said.

He was not wrong. As Gina and I opened the door to the hallway, the smell of burnt food from hotplates, mixed with a sick and musty combination of body odor and something that smelled like bug spray permeated the air. The cement floor was covered by black and white linoleum square tiles laid out in a checkerboard fashion. The walls that were once white are now various shades of yellow and brown. Whatever the temperature outside, the hallway was at least ten degrees warmer and stifling.

The rooms were numbered one through four, spanning from the left side of the hallway to the right. Roland's room was almost directly in front of us as we walked through the door leading into the hall. A black metal number 3 hung loosely from a single finishing nail in the middle of the wooden door.

As I was about to knock, I noticed that the door was slightly ajar. Instead, I pushed the door open just enough to see the bed positioned against the far wall of the room, to our left. A single 100-watt lightbulb hung from the ceiling in the center of the room, casting an offensive glare and creating sharp shadows in an otherwise dank and dingy room.

I took the slightly opened door as an invitation to enter Roland's room. Gina followed close behind me, both of us walking to our right once inside. We ended up facing Roland, who was sitting on the edge of the bed and nearly in the middle of the mattress. The bed was pushed sideways against the far wall. A threadbare sheet, once white and now mostly yellow at best, covered the mattress.

Roland looked as if he had lived a hard 62-years. He seemed to have very rough skin covering his large frame, a prominent bulbous nose, and a large crop of gray hair. A few days' worth of stubble covered his face. He was wearing a long-sleeve flannel shirt, well-worn, stained and dirty jeans, and brown work boots. Tattoos were visible at his neck and on both wrists, apparently extending from his arms to his hands.

He was bent forward at his waist, leaning on what appeared to be his cane with his chin resting on the top, except it did not have the traditional curved handle. He sat motionless as Gina and I stood a few feet away, almost directly in front of him now.

"Roland? It's me, Marc, and this is Gina. You called me earlier this year during my investigation into my uncle's murder. You said you had information to give me, but I never followed up. I'm sorry. Now I hear that the FBI had talked to you last week, and I thought we should talk right away. That's why Gina and I are here. We want to find out what you know about things that have been going on in Lakewood. I'm sorry it's so late, but Max said you were out when I called earlier. So, I thought we'd just stop down and talk."

He grunted and made a motion for Gina to shut the door. She took a step, reached back, and slowly closed the door as he requested. It was then that I saw what Roland was leaning on, and it wasn't a cane at all, but a .12-gauge shotgun. Gina must have seen it at the same time as I heard her stifle a noise of surprise.

"What the hell, Roland? What are you planning to do with the gun?" I asked with an inflection of surprise and annoyance in my voice.

Roland looked up at both of us without moving his head from the business end of the shotgun. His lack of motion caused his face to contort as he looked up. His face and eyes looked a lot like Jack Nicholson's in the movie *The Shining*. His appearance was deeply unsettling.

"You're not going to get anything from me. I've finished my job here." This time his voice sounded deep and guttural, almost unnatural. If Gina noticed the strange sound of his voice, she didn't let on.

"First things first," Gina said, "put the gun away now, Roland." Her voice was authoritative.

Gina and I were each quietly assessing this unexpected and surreal turn of events that were playing out directly in front of us in the brief silence that followed. Neither of us moved for fear of causing Roland to point the shotgun in our direction. Because of the size of the room, we didn't have many options to take cover or retreat. Although we were both armed, our weapons were concealed. I could draw down on him, I thought to myself, but that could cause the situation to go sideways very quickly in several different ways.

"Beta... Delta... and now, Omega," Roland said without moving the position of the shotgun.

"Do what Gina said. Stop screwing with us and put the gun away," I said.

"Why don't you shut up and listen, Mr. Big Shot PI. The problem with you is your mouth. It's too big for your body," Roland said without moving his head.

"Then stop talking crap and tell us about what you know about murders in Lakewood. You can start with what you know about my uncle since that's when you first contacted us. And don't forget, it was you who reached out to us," I said.

"That wasn't me," Roland uttered with the same disturbing inflection in his voice that sounded like it was someone other than Roland talking.

"If it wasn't you, then just who in the hell was it?"

"It was him."

"I don't see anyone else with us, Roland," I said with even more annoyance. "Him, who?"

"Beta... Delta... and now, Omega," he repeated with a higher inflection on the word "Omega."

"I'll take the Greek alphabet for one hundred, Alex," trying to lighten the mood a bit. My lame attempt at humor elicited a look of scorn from Gina, who decided to take a softer approach.

"Tell us what you mean by that, Roland. We want to hear what you have to say, and believe it or not, we can help you," Gina said.

"You can't help me, not now. My assignments are over."

"What assignments?" I asked, having become even more agitated by his theatrics.

"My journal. Everything, almost everything you need to know is in my journal. Only if you're enlightened enough to understand it, though," Roland said as he pointed down by his right foot to a hardcover book that was just barely visible beneath his bed. His voice had returned to normal or more normal sounding.

"We want to hear it from you, not read about it," Gina responded in an attempt to have him put his gun away. "You can help us understand. Right here. Right now. We'll listen."

"I'm not telling you a damn thing." Although the words came from Roland's mouth, the sound was again distinctly different, reverting to the grave and guttural sound.

"Then why did you agree to meet us?" I asked, looking at Gina while trying to detect whether she noticed the difference in voices.

"I did not agree to meet you. I'm just one of many. There are more of us here than you realize. We're in your schools, hospitals, courts, and your police departments. We're everywhere. You cannot stop us." In addition to the change in tone, I detected a slight German accent as he spoke, reminiscent of my experience with Porter Landers in Florida.

"If you know what's good for you, you'll get out of here now and stay away from us. Don't come back," he said, this time with his normal voice.

"Roland, who's the 'us' you are talking about?" Gina prodded as if she knew more of what was taking place at that moment than I did.

"Soldiers."

"How many?" Gina asked.

"There are millions of us. We are legion. It's all there," Speirs said, referring to his journal. Roland moved his right hand and placed his fingers on the trigger guard of the shotgun, moving them closer to the trigger.

"Wait, Roland, don't do anything right now except talk to us. We can help, and we need you to help us," Gina said.

"This discussion is over," was Roland's reply again with the slight German accent, his voice louder than before. "Omega!" We both helplessly watched as Roland rapidly moved his right thumb to the trigger.

"No!"

I don't remember grabbing Gina in an attempt to shield her from the blast, but the blood spatter on my body and clothes suggested that's what I did. The explosion from the barrel was loud and amplified by the small, enclosed room. The room was strangely silent now, with any ambient noise muffled and barely audible behind a constant, high-pitched hum in our ears. The odor of gunpowder mixed with the stench of blood and raw human flesh from a sudden and violent death hung like a dark cloud inside the room. It's an unmistakable and sickening odor that is impossible to forget.

I looked at Gina's face, her horror apparent. The top left part of her head had blood and a small piece of Roland's skull falling from it. Fragments of skull, brain matter, and a few bits of Roland's hair also struck my left arm and the left side of my face.

I looked at Roland's body, which was now almost headless. He was thrown back against the wall by the impact of the blast. His body was now resting almost flat on top of the bed. His feet were still flat on the floor, and the shotgun was propelled forward, landing between his body and where we were standing. A transfer stain of blood, bone, and soft tissue on the wall showed where Roland was forced backward, his lifeless body sliding down the wall before coming to rest on the bed. I saw one cadaveric spasm and heard a sickening "glug-glug" sound as Roland's still-beating heart emptied the remaining blood from his body through the massive hole where his head once was.

With the blast still echoing in my ears, I could see Gina's lips moving but could barely hear her. It was as if she was talking through a thick blanket. I could hardly make out what she was asking. "Are you all right? Are you hit anywhere?"

"I'm okay. I think, anyway. Are you okay?" I shouted.

Gina seemed to be experiencing the same problems with her hearing as she merely nodded while having a confused look at my question. We each patted ourselves, searching for any holes made by the metal or human shrapnel.

I was surprised when Gina suddenly broke away from me and quickly grabbed the journal Roland pointed to during our brief conversation. It seemed to be about the only thing in the room mostly untouched by the carnage sprayed so violently across nearly everything else in the room. She quickly placed it in her shoulder bag right before the door to Roland's room burst open.

"What in the hell?" The voice of the bar owner was barely audible. When he saw the condition of his late tenant, he turned and vomited his supper in the hallway, adding to the overall grotesqueness of the scene.

An ambulance and the police were on the scene within minutes. Since there was nothing that the paramedics could do for the late Roland Speirs, they turned their attention to us. This time, I did not know either member of the crew, but they were gracious enough to wipe us down and check us over for any wounds from errant shrapnel or other objects coming at us at high velocity. They also checked our ear canals for damage and assured us that our hearing would be returning to normal shortly.

When they finished with us, we gave our statements to the patrol officers. The officers told us that we could leave after we spoke with the detective who would be taking over the formal investigation of this incident. Just then, a familiar voice rang out in the distance, recognizable even with our temporary hearing problem. It was the voice of none other than Detective Jenkins.

"Ah geez, I should have known I'd find you involved somehow as soon as I caught this case," Jenkins said as he exited his car and walked toward Gina and me.

"Unless he's yelling at us, I think I'm starting to get my hearing back," I said to Gina.

"I don't think he's yelling, at least not yet. But give him time."

"You two stay right here while I check the scene. Then, we're going to have ourselves a nice, long talk," Jenkins emphatically pointed at both of us, and then put on a pair of rubber gloves and booties he brought with him from his unmarked car. He walked briskly into the rooming house through the bar with a patrol officer guiding the way.

After we gave our statements to the responding officer and Ron Jenkins, Gina and I were officially free to go. Ron was satisfied that this was a suicide, and we were simply the unfortunate witnesses to the final earthly moments of the late Roland Speirs. He told us that although he would likely close the case, he might have some additional questions for us after checking into Speirs' background, his current status, and the "curious" timing of our corresponding visit.

"I'm willing to fill in any blanks you might have, Ron, but I'd like to get out of these clothes and shower," I said.

"That goes for me too," Gina said.

"Oh, I'm sure we'll be talking again. You two seem to be quite the 'death magnets' lately."

We borrowed two white linen stretcher blankets from the ambulance, placing both on the seats and seat backs of my car to protect the interior from whatever pieces of Roland that still might be stuck to our clothes or exposed skin. Although we were somewhat cleaned up courtesy of the paramedics, we still looked like cast extras from a horror film. I started my car and turned in the general direction of our office.

"Hey, do you want to hit a drive-thru or stop for anything at the store?" I asked Gina, again trying to lighten the mood. Despite the horror that we just witnessed, I could see Gina trying to stifle a chuckle. Recovering, she admonished me for my gallows humor.

"What in the hell just happened back there?" I asked Gina after a period of extended silence. "Why did he call us down there? So that we could watch him turn his head into hamburger?"

"I think I might have an idea about that."

"Good, because I'm running a bit low on ideas at the moment."

"Do you remember us talking about the mind control experiments done by our government and other governments going back to World War II? We spoke about a secret government program called MKUltra. Mind control experiments."

"Of course, I remember. Sadie Cooper mentioned it as well. Her late husband was involved at some level. Now that you mentioned it, this MKUltra program seems to be a common theme in everything we've been dealing with since we took on the murder of my uncle."

"Right. You watched Roland tonight. Did you catch him seemingly arguing with himself, or appearing to be two different people inside of one body? Did you notice the change in his voice and the German accent of one of the voices?"

"I was going to ask you the same thing," I said to Gina.

"Well, I think we just witnessed the program in action. The Greek terms Speirs used are known assignment codes for people or, more specifically, personalities created by the mind control programs. Each code, or designation, has a specific purpose."

"Omega, if I remember correctly, is Greek for the end, and that's just what we saw of Roland. But what about Beta and Delta?" I asked.

"I'm not sure, but this might hold some answers." Gina reached into her bag and removed Roland's journal. I noticed its ornate leather cover that was once adorned with raised, gold-leafed symbols around the outer edge, was tattered and now quite worn. The book itself appeared thick, heavy and old, and looked like something from a library or even a museum. It was "perfect bound" and about the size of a college textbook. As Gina opened it, I glanced over to see the first few lined pages filled with entries in small, fine print in the blackest ink I've ever seen. I glimpsed a few symbols carefully drawn on the pages, along with what appeared to be dated lines of text written in some other language.

"I wonder if anyone else, besides the feds, knows that he kept a diary," I said aloud.

"I don't think it's a question of whether they know it exists, I think the better question is how far they will go to find it," Gina said with an ominous tone.

"Do we know who they are? It seems to me that we're getting a lot of bodies piling up all of a sudden, so I think we need to get a good handle on identifying who 'they' are in this mess."

As we proceeded back to the office where Gina left her car, we talked about the best way to keep the journal safely in our hands. We decided that I should store it in the safe in the war room until we could make copies of its pages, and then we would put the original in the safety deposit box at the bank. I assured Gina that I'd make copies first thing in the morning and have the journal in the bank vault the first thing Monday morning.

"Remember, right now, it's just the two of us who know that we have the journal," Gina said.

"For now, anyway. I wonder if our FBI friends will come looking for it."

"We did, so I'm sure they will."

"What happens when they find out Roland doesn't have it? They'll know we were there from the police report, and the journal was not among his inventory possessions."

"I don't even want to think about it, at least not right now. I'm cooked. Burnt. I need to get home, take a shower, burn these clothes, and sleep."

Gina exited my car and took the blanket with her, placing it on her seat. It was heavily stained in a few places. "Great," she muttered as she tucked the top under her headrest. "I hope I don't get stopped on my way home. Can you imagine me trying to explain this to a cop?" She pointed to the multiple blood transfer stains on the blanket. "I'll burn this in the morning too. Let's meet back at your place first thing tomorrow and go over everything we have on Roland, including his journal," Gina said as she entered her car.

"Gina, wait," I said in a manner that came out as almost an embarrassing afterthought. "Look, considering what you just went through, I mean, what we went through, why don't you stay at my place tonight? If you don't have your turnout bag with you, I've got things you can use at my place. I'll even let you shower first. You don't have to be alone tonight, and I imagine that your daughter is still staying with your mom, right?"

Gina gripped the steering wheel of her car with both hands and seemed to be contemplating her next move. I could see that thousand-yard stare in her eyes as she sat motionless, in silence. "I could use the company too. Please. It's not that often that you see," Gina stopped me in mid-sentence. "Okay, I'll follow you," she said, just above a whisper, sitting motionless. The light created by a nearby streetlamp accentuated a single tear rolling down her cheek. She quickly wiped it away. "Okay, let's go."

IN THE DARK OF NIGHT

Chapter 20

<u>**Sunday, September 13, 1987**</u>

After hot showers and a fitful night for both of us, I awakened first at 5:30 a.m., a bit stiff from sleeping on the couch in my office. Over her objections, I insisted that Gina sleep in my bed, hoping that she would be able to get a good night's rest. While she slept, I quietly snuck another shower, shaved, threw on jeans, a dress shirt, sports jacket, and went into the kitchen to make a pot of coffee. For the second time in as many weeks, I thought, my trash bin held another load of discarded clothes.

Just after 8 a.m., Gina walked into the kitchen wearing one of my dress shirts she grabbed from my closet. Her well-tanned and firm legs, and her brown hair that flowed neatly across her shoulders offset the white color of the shirt. For the first time in a while and despite the events of the previous night, she looked good and well-rested. Pointing to my shirt she was wearing, she cracked a smile and said, "I hope you don't mind."

"Of course not. After all, what are partners for?" I smiled and squeezed her shoulder as I filled her coffee.

We sat together in silence for several minutes, pondering the events of the previous night and the last few days.

Gina broke the silence. "Are you okay?"

"Hell no, I'm not okay," I responded. "Are you?"

"Not even a little bit. I've been replaying that scene from last night in my mind over and over again, wondering if we could have done something different, or should have done something different."

"It's too late now to consider what we could have or should have done. It's over, and we can't change anything. I'm annoyed and angry as hell that Speirs made us watch him blow his head off. I doubt that's something I'll be forgetting anytime soon," I said.

"That bothers me too. Speirs could have 'offed' himself anytime, but it was as if he wanted us to be there, to witness that."

"You heard him, though. It was like he was two different people by the way he talked. His voice seemed to change too. It was like he was a spectator in his own body. It was almost like he was possessed."

"That's it!" Gina said, nearly lifting herself off of her chair.

"What, that he was possessed?"

"No, that he needed an audience. He needed us to witness his murder."

"Why? Gina, I'm not following you. No one murdered him. He killed himself. We were there, remember? No one forced him to wrap his lips around the barrel of that shotgun."

"I'm not so sure about that. I know Speirs did it in the physical sense, but was it really him? Think about what we've seen already. The cases of Multiple Personality Disorder caused by trauma and programming. Split personalities, including, not just what we've seen, but from the congressional testimony from the Church Committee back in the 1970s. Remember the words he used last night, 'Beta, Delta, and Omega?' They could have been 'trigger' words. And the way that his voice changed."

"Go on."

"Maybe he was programmed to do what he did not only because his job was done, but to send a message, a message to us." Gina stopped long enough for me to consider what she was saying.

"So, what's the message?"

"I'm not sure yet. Maybe to scare us off, to get us to back off, or something more. I need time to think about this and to look into some things. What are your plans for today, Marc?"

"Well, it's Sunday, and it's not like we're looking for things to do. I haven't thought about it yet, though. Why, what do you have in mind?"

"How do you feel about me spending the day here so the two of us can work together? We can finish reviewing all of the documents Jim got from the feds, look through the journal, and plan out our next moves."

"I'm game. But we need to change some things," I said.

Like what?

"I feel like we've been playing defense for the last week, and I'm getting more than a little irritated. It's time we change our strategy to an offensive one."

"I agree."

Gina stood up and poured the last bit of coffee into her cup. "I'll get dressed and be right out."

****

By 9:30 am., we had numerous stacks of papers strewn across the floor and on the tops of tables, including the copies of the FBI files Jim was able to acquire yesterday. A much smaller stack of papers sat on top of my desk that also required my attention. The stack contained the file notes for the insurance case we'd been working. Gina sat back on the leather sofa to survey the piles of sorted documents, glancing at the insurance case file. "We need to finish that report and get it to the client by tomorrow," she said.

"I can have it done in an hour or two at the most. I'll do it later tonight and drop the report off with the client tomorrow."

We spent the next few hours reading the FBI 302s, profiling notes, police and coroner reports, and taking notes of our own. We worked in relative silence, occasionally exchanging observations and thoughts about each of the recent and past events, trying to make sense of it all. By noon, we finished three pots of coffee and polished off a pack of cigarettes I opened early this morning. As usual, classical music from my radio provided calming, ambient noise.

As if matching our moods, the weather took a dark turn as storms moved in off the lake. The temperature dropped at least ten degrees in just a few minutes, as thick, low hanging clouds darkened the sky, and the north wind picked up considerably. I closed the windows and turned on a few lamps as the ambient light from the sun disappeared. Rain began coming down in large drops, quickly picking up in intensity and turning into a noisy downpour.

Just as Gina picked up Speirs' journal, a bright flash of lightning spread across the room like a strobe light, and a clap of thunder rattled the windows, causing her to jump backward with a shriek and drop the book on the floor.

"Wow, that couldn't have been planned any better," I said as I picked the book up from the floor and placed it on the table between us.

"Well, now I'm officially freaked out," Gina said as she rubbed her eyes. "I need to take a break."

"Me too. Are you hungry? Can I buy you lunch?"

"Sure, I could eat. Before we do, we probably should make a few calls, don't you think? I should check on my daughter, and you probably want to call Deana. We should see how Carr is doing, too, and check-in with the office."

"The office? It's Sunday."

"I mean, one of us should call Paul to tell him about what happened last night with Speirs. Oh, and when is the last time you talked to Deana?"

"I called her after our lunch date Friday and spoke to her again yesterday morning. She told me that she had a family gathering to attend today, so I asked her to give me a call when she got back tonight. Don't worry, I followed up with her after our lunch date."

"What do you mean you 'followed-up?'" Gina asked with a chuckle. "It's not like you closed a business deal."

"I guess that came out wrong. Anyway, everything is fine between us," I assured Gina.

"Maybe we should check on Martin and Mary, too, drop in unannounced. I want to talk with Mary alone, if possible. Something is bothering me about them, and I can't put my finger on it. I don't know what it is, but I've just got a bad feeling."

"Marvelous," I muttered. "One thing I've learned about you is that you've got some special kind of intuition, and it's usually right on the mark."

"Usually?"

"All right, always."

"Isn't that one of your 'rules,' to listen to that little voice in your head?"

"Ah yes, rule number one. Follow your gut instincts and don't ignore that nagging voice in your head that's trying to tell you something. It's usually right and can save your life."

****

Instead of calling Paul to let him know about last night's events, I decided to call Jim Carr to fill him in. He answered on the first ring and sounded busy.

"Jim, it's Marc. Got a few minutes to talk?"

"Not right now, but I will in a little while. My neighbor just stopped over. I think you know Tom Bauer. He helped me temporarily fix my window the night of the break-in. He's got out of town visitors and wanted to see if I had an extra bottle of single malt Scotch I wasn't using," he chuckled. "They're here on business, and single malt is their beverage of choice. We're having some iced tea Angie made for us while he's waiting for his friends to return. They're out running an errand."

"A business meeting on a Sunday? Must be pretty important."

"I didn't ask. Good neighbors don't pry into the business affairs of their neighbors. Can I call you back after he leaves?"

"Sure. Gina is here, and we've got a lot to tell you. But in the meantime, I think I'll take her out to lunch since we've been working all morning, so why don't you call me when you're free. If I don't answer, keep trying, and you'll get me eventually."

"Anything earthshaking, Marc?" Jim asked.

"Earthshaking? Yeah, I suppose you could call it that. Bone-chilling might be a more appropriate description."

Jim's tone notably changed. "Okay, I'll call you as soon as Tom leaves."

"Give us at least an hour."

"Will do." I could hear Tom's voice close by as Jim cradled the receiver, but I couldn't make out anything he said.

"Why didn't you tell him about last night?" Gina asked.

I stared at Gina after hanging up the phone. "That was odd," I said.

"What?"

"Jim. There was something odd about his behavior. He didn't want to talk while his neighbor Tom was there."

"Can you blame him?"

"No, but there's something else. Something's not right, Gina."

"Do you want to stop by to see if he's in trouble?"

I momentarily hesitated, considering Gina's idea. "No, let's wait until we hear from him. Maybe it's nothing."

Chapter 21

Gina and I decided to have lunch at the Towne Restaurant. Not only is the food good, but this would give us a chance to talk to Brenda, at Gina's insistence, about Lander's Friday visit. As Brenda is now the general manager of the restaurant, she works long hours and is there every day.

We opted to sit in the bar area near the window. When Brenda saw us sit down, she smiled and waved. After taking care of a customer at the bar, she walked over to us, exchanged pleasantries with Gina, and kissed me on the cheek.

"Marc told me about the two guys who stopped by to ask some questions," Gina said to Brenda as Gina shot me an irritated sideways glance.

"I was just about to ask you about that. Have you heard anything from them?" Brenda asked.

"Not yet, but I suspect we will. Have you seen our uninvited visitors around since Friday?" I queried.

"No, and I've given all of the wait staff and extra bartenders their description and asked them to keep their eyes open for them. I told them to contact me in the event they come in again," Brenda added.

"Thanks, hon," I said to Brenda and grabbed her hand that she left resting on my shoulder.

"Are you two eating?"

"Yes, and it's my treat," I said with a forced smile.

"I'll send someone over with menus. Just give me a minute." Brenda disappeared as she walked into the kitchen area behind the bar.

"Wow, Marc. You and Brenda seem to be very close these days. Have I missed something?" Gina prodded.

"Do you ever miss anything? She's become a very close friend."

Both of us were much quieter than usual while we ate, each of us thinking about the situation as it existed. As we finished our light lunch, Gina broke the silence.

"Marc, I think we need to confront Landers. We need to find out what he's doing here in Lakewood, how long he's actually been here, and if his presence is related to the murder of Jacob Tingsley."

"We need to find out where he's staying first," I said. "I'd much rather drop in on him and surprise him instead of him surprising us."

"Well, I think that ship has already sailed. It appears that we've got company," Gina said without looking up from the table. "Don't look now, but there's a Cadillac with the plate you identified parked across the lot. I can see two people sitting in the front, but it's hard to tell through the drizzle and window fog."

"Marvelous," I responded.

Landers parked his Cadillac in a corner space that faced the windows of the restaurant. Behind his car was a concrete municipal street pole that held an oblong streetlight. Landers and his 'cabana boy' assistant have a clear view of the restaurant and our position inside. Our car was parked on the other side and toward the rear of the restaurant, out of their immediate sight.

"Well, partner, how do you want to handle this?" I asked.

"I have an idea. Just wait here and pretend you don't know that they're outside watching us. I've got to go to the little girls' room," Gina said in a coy fashion to which I've become familiar when she's working a plan. Having worked with Gina and knowing her abilities, I didn't protest or even ask as she picked up her purse and walked toward the restrooms near the kitchen entrance.

Gina returned to the table a few minutes later with a sly grin. "I've got it handled," she told me.

"I gotta hear this," I said.

"Okay, here's the deal," she began. "I talked to Brenda and explained the situation. She's 'all in' and will help us leave without Landers on our tail. At least we'll have a head start," she added. "All you have to do is be ready to leave in a hurry when I say so. We're clear to leave the restaurant through the kitchen and out the back door. By the way, I already paid our bill and left our waiter a nice tip."

"How is that going to prevent those mopes from following us?" I asked.

"You'll see. Just follow my lead."

Just then, I spotted a young busboy pushing a large, commercial kitchen cart on wheels across the parking lot. The cart appeared to be loaded with a big bucket of fryer grease and other kitchen equipment. He was taking a somewhat circuitous route from the side door of the kitchen toward a fenced dumpster area at the rear side of the building. As he walked in front of Landers' car, the cart tipped and fell on its side, spilling the contents across the front of Landers' car and onto the pavement.

"Now! Let's go through the kitchen," Gina instructed. I could see Landers and his young friend getting out of their car, yelling and pouring their wrath on to the poor busboy. Fryer grease, an array of metal kitchen objects, and even some serving plates were strewn in front of the car, along with the metal cart now laying sideways under the front bumper.

"You idiot!" I heard landers yelling and instructing the young man to get out of his way. "I'm sorry, sir! I'm so sorry. I'll clean this up right away, sir," the busboy exclaimed. I could still hear Landers over Gina's stifled laughter as we exited the parking lot, driving in the opposite direction of my apartment. After fifteen minutes of taking numerous side roads to make sure we were not being followed, we arrived back at my place alone and without any problems. This time, I parked my vehicle behind my apartment in a makeshift parking space assuring it was not visible from the street. Both of us made it inside without being seen, even if there was surveillance on us.

Gina and I had just walked into the war room when the telephone rang. "It's probably Jim," I said to Gina, who was still grinning at the comedy skit she arranged at the restaurant. Gina slipped into the bathroom as I answered the phone. Whatever humor we derived from foiling Landers was tempered by Brenda's trembling voice.

"Marc, are you guys okay?"

"Yes, and I want to thank you and the busboy for having our backs. He deserves a raise for his performance," I said.

"That's why I'm calling. Robbie, the busboy, was just taken to the hospital by ambulance, Marc. He's unconscious and unresponsive like he's in a coma. They don't know what's wrong with him," Brenda said and began crying.

"What happened? Did Landers get physical with him? Hit him or run him over?"

"No, that's the strange thing," she said between sobs. "I watched the whole thing, and neither Landers nor his friend ever touched him."

"Then what happened to him?"

"The paramedics weren't sure, but they said his symptoms resemble a stroke."

"A stroke? How is that even possible? He can't be more than 18 or 19. Do you know if he has any medical problems?"

"He's 19, and no, he doesn't have any medical problems that I know of."

"Somebody must have seen something. Are you positive that Landers or his buddy never laid a hand on him?"

"Nope, Landers stopped yelling and was standing about 3 or 4 feet away from him. He pointed at him and said something. I couldn't tell and didn't hear what he said, but Landers looked angry and serious. Then Robbie just collapsed and fell on the ground like a rag doll."

"I spoke with Robbie's mom. His parents are on their way to the hospital. I'll know more after they check him out. His mother said she would call me as soon as she knows anything."

"Please call me as soon as you know something, Brenda."

"I will, and Marc, I've got to tell you that Landers is beyond angry. I've never seen anything like it, or him. While we were waiting for the ambulance, he walked over to me and said something I didn't understand. It almost sounded like some kind of curse. It was in a different language, Eastern European maybe, and his voice didn't sound 'normal.' I don't know what he said, but whatever it was sent a shiver through me as I've never experienced. That guy is pure evil."

"Were the police there?" I asked.

"Yes, but they left when they determined that it was just a medical call and not a fight or hit and run. The police didn't even take anyone's information. They weren't even interested in what Landers said to me. They just looked at me like I was a hysterical nutcase and just left."

"Yeah, that sounds about right."

"Marc, I'm terrified. I don't want to sound like I'm some sort of a fragile damsel in distress, but what I saw today..." her voice trailed off.

"Did Landers or his friend say anything else to you at all, or threaten you?"

"No, just whatever that curse or whatever it was, that's it."

"Do you want me to come back over?"

"No, I'm sure I'll be fine. Please, though, you guys be careful, okay?"

"We will."

"Promise me?"

"I promise. Remember, call me when you hear anything about Ronnie."

"I will."

Gina walked into the room as I was hanging up the phone. "Marc, what's wrong? You look like you've seen a ghost."

"That was Brenda who called. Robbie, the busboy who helped us out by distracting Landers, was taken to St. Elizabeth's Hospital. He collapsed at the scene and appeared to be in a coma. I'll know more when Brenda calls me with a report from the hospital."

"Could Landers have done anything to him when no one was looking?"

"I don't think so. Brenda said she watched the whole encounter. She said that Landers stopped yelling at him, suddenly became serious, pointed at him, and said something. She was sure that they were about 3-4 feet apart. After that, the boy just collapsed to the ground."

"Do you know what Landers said?"

"Brenda didn't hear what he said, and she swears that Landers never touched him."

"Did she say anything else?"

"Before he left, Landers walked over to Brenda and said something in a different language. Not only in a different language, but in a different voice and inflection. A deeper voice. She said it sounded like a curse."

"The change of voices and inflections. That sounds familiar."

Gina and I spent a few more hours working in the war room. We decided to wait to check on the Tingsleys, thinking that we would give them some additional time to themselves. Considering that we now have Landers on our tail, we did not want to lead him anywhere near Martin and Mary.

At 4:45, Brenda called. "Marc, I've got good news. I just spoke with

Robbie's mother, and it looks like he's going to be fine. They were wheeling him to X-Ray for a CT scan when he suddenly woke up. They still did a brain scan and found nothing wrong. The good news is that he didn't have a stroke or brain hemorrhage, but the bad news is that they don't know what happened to him. They're making him stay overnight for observation. Barring anything dramatic or unforeseen complications, he can go home in the morning and come back to work when he feels ready."

"That's great news. Did Robbie say what happened or what he remembers?"

"I asked his mother the same question, and that's the odd part. He told her that the last thing he remembered is that he was standing face to face with 'a monster.' That's precisely how he described it, and that's the word he used. He told her that Landers' eyes became entirely black and that he smelled like his high school chemistry lab. He said that it was the odor that made him pass out."

"His high school chemistry lab? What's that supposed to mean?"

"I wondered the same thing too and asked about it. The odor Robbie eventually described after he woke up was a rotten egg smell, or sulfur. He said that it was overwhelming. That was of some concern to the doctor, as often people who have strokes and recover will occasionally describe a peculiar odor, or experience sudden vision problems, you know, that precede the event."

"I understand. But his description of Landers and the odor, well, that's pretty freaky."

"I'll say. I can't tell you how happy I am that he's going to be okay."

"Me too," I said. "Brenda, how about you? Are you doing to be okay?"

"Honestly, Marc, I'm not sure. This guy Landers who's chasing after you truly is a monster. When he walked over to me and said something in a foreign language, he scared me. And the way he changed his voice was something I've never heard before. I can't believe you have to deal with these creeps. I don't know how you guys do it."

"Brenda, can you remember what he said to you well enough to try to write it out, even if it's just phonetically? If you had to guess the language, what language do you think it was? What did it sound like?"

"I'm not sure, but I could try. You already know that I took language studies in college. If I were forced to guess, I would say it was German or some other Eastern European dialect of that style. I'm somewhat familiar with German as I had to take it for two semesters, but none of the words I heard sounded familiar to me. You might think this is weird, but it almost sounded 'ancient.' I'll do what I can, though, if you think it's important."

"I appreciate it. Thank you, my dear."

IN THE DARK OF NIGHT

Chapter 22

The Journal

Gina spent the rest of the afternoon and evening perusing the book taken from Roland Speirs and what we ultimately dubbed 'The Speirs' Journal.' Parts of it read like the diary kept by Sirhan Sirhan, the man accused of fatally shooting presidential candidate Robert F. Kennedy in 1968. That first section contained nonsensical writings repeated words and phrases, and seemingly wild streams of consciousness. The second section contained words and phrases written in different languages, including Latin and German. A third section included rudimentary drawings and sketches of symbols, intersecting lines, and numbers that could be maps of some sort. In contrast, the latter part of the journal contained something that looked like a list, but it was written with a combination of characters that was useless to anyone who did not understand the code, if there indeed is a code.

The actual book appeared to be very old, judging by the binding and condition of the glue, paper, and the ornately embossed leather cover. The entries themselves seemed to be written by more than one person, based on different handwriting styles. The entries were also written in various mediums, from pencil to the blackest ink I've ever seen. A few pages contained words and symbols that appeared to be created by blood or a medium that mimicked the appearance of dried blood.

The Fidelity Mutual Case

Despite all of the activity relating to the unofficial case in which Gina and I were involved, we needed to finish the insurance case for Fidelity Mutual. The wrongful death investigation focused on the actions of a supervisor operating a piece of equipment at a local warehouse. The man was moving pallets of paper using a forklift when the weight of the payload shifted, overturning the forklift and crushing him under the unit. Lakewood paramedics transported the victim to a local hospital where he was dead on arrival due to traumatic crushing injuries to his head and torso. The employee's wife filed suit against the company, citing several issues involving the company's alleged shoddy operations and improper training. Although the incident happened two years prior, the pre-trial discovery is scheduled to begin on Tuesday. The exposure to the insurance company was at least five million dollars if they lost the case, and potentially more if a case of willful negligence could be made against the insured. We have to furnish our findings in the form of a written report no later than Tuesday morning. The person handling this claim on behalf of Fidelity Mutual is Angie Carr, Jim Carr's wife. If it is indeed a small world, Lakewood is a much smaller city than it appears to outsiders.

Although all of the evidence suggested that there was a limited recall of the forklift the employee used and maintenance that was not done by the Lakewood company, we found mitigating factors as a result of our investigation. A handwritten entry on the ambulance transport slip I received from Russ noted that the deceased worker had just started taking a new medication to treat his high blood pressure. Gina's follow-up investigation last week resulted in two significant findings that could mitigate the liability exposure to Fidelity Mutual. First, the deceased began taking the medication just three days before the accident. A known side effect of the medicine was lightheadedness and syncope, or episodes of passing out. Secondly, Gina secured a written statement from a co-worker who stated that the deceased complained of feeling lightheaded on the day of the accident but didn't report this to his supervisor.

It took us two hours to assemble the documentation we obtained since the case was assigned. I typed the report and two carbon copies on my Smith Corona typewriter under Gina's watchful eye. When we finished our report, we were sure that it would cast sufficient doubt on the deceased's physical ability to operate heavy machinery at the time of the accident, a fact that was barely a footnote in the hospital records. When we were sure that Fidelity Mutual would be pleased with the depth and scope detailed in the report of our investigation, we placed two copies of our report and attachments in a large manila envelope. We planned to deliver it tomorrow, along with our invoice for 38 hours of investigative time.

****

It was just after 7 pm. when the phone rang at my apartment. "Sorry, I didn't call you back sooner, but I got tied up again with my neighbor."

"What happened, did he need more Scotch?" I asked with a bit more attitude than required.

"No," Jim chuckled, "Tom's out-of-town company had car problems. A flat tire, I think. Tom wasn't sure when I asked him. He said that they were both agitated when they got back to his house two hours later than expected and didn't want to talk to him about it, so I guess he didn't press them. Then Peggy came over and complained to Angie, so let's just say my Sunday was not that peaceful. So what's going on with you and Gina? You said you had some important things to tell me."

As I was talking to Jim, Gina began motioning to me, then grabbed my arm. "Hold on a second, Jim," I said and turned my attention to Gina.

"Marc, I think this conversation would be better in person, don't you?" I nodded to Gina in agreement.

"I know it's Sunday evening, but a few things have happened over the last few days that you need to see and hear in person. You know it's important, or I wouldn't ask."

"How important?" Jim pressed.

"On a scale of one to ten, I'd say twelve."

"Hang on a minute," Jim said. I heard him put the receiver down on the corner and walk out of the room. He returned a minute later and picked up the handset.

"You know you're going to be paying our marriage counselor. Angie wanted to take Oscar for a walk now that the rain stopped, but I convinced her that this was more important."

"Trust me, I love Oscar too, but we need to meet. In addition to what we've got to tell you, we have something here that you need to see."

"All right, I'll be over in 15 minutes. Put the coffee on. On second thought, I'll stop and get my own." Jim hung up before I could say anything more.

****

By 8:30 p.m., we brought Jim up to speed about the events of the last few days. We explained what happened when we visited the late Roland Speirs and told him about everything that happened today. Jim just sat and listened, shaking his head in disbelief a few times and writing a few notes as Gina and I took turns narrating the harrowing events.

"You should have told me about this earlier."

"I did, remember? You were busy. And so were we." I responded.

"Yeah, I can see that. I also see that a lot of people you encounter end up in the hospital or dead."

"That's why we need to finalize our report and get it to the attorney general. We can always supplement our report as needed, but let's get all of this on their radar."

"I can call their office tomorrow and schedule a meeting with them toward the end of this week. I'll try to make it for this Friday. That gives us a few extra days to tie up loose ends and drop this bomb on their laps before the week is over," Jim said. "Right now, I have to go. I better break the news to her that I'll be taking a road trip later this week."

"In the meantime, Gina and I will work on the contents of the journal. If we get anything definitive from it, we'll add it to the report."

Jim wished us both good luck and left my apartment close to 11:00.

Sitting next to Gina on the sofa in the war room, I was spent from the events of the day.

"Marc, I'm exhausted and can barely keep my eyes open. If you don't mind, I think I'll go home and get some sleep. I can be in the office early."

"Why make the trip when you've got proper accommodations ready for you in the next room?"

"I don't want to put you out or worse, create any problems for you."

"I insist. There are extra blankets, clean sheets if you want them, and more towels in the closet. Help yourself to whatever you need. After all, what are partners for?"

"I'm too tired to say no, so I'll take you up on your offer." Gina bent over and tenderly kissed me on the cheek. "Good night, and thank you, Marc."

"Have a good night, Gina. Sleep well."

IN THE DARK OF NIGHT

Chapter 23

<u>Monday, September 14, 1987</u>

I was awake at 4:45 a.m., showered, dressed by 5:30 and back from getting a half-dozen muffins and other pastries from a neighborhood bakery for our breakfast before six. I quietly opened the door to my bedroom to check on Gina. I could just make out the outline of her body lying on my bed under the sheet and thin blanket, soundly sleeping away the stress of the last few days. I gently shut the door and went into the war room to get a head start on the day.

I started by reviewing the blood-spattered journal that once belonged to Roland Speirs. Between the front and back cover existed an unfamiliar world of indescribable darkness that seemed to border on insanity. Words written in black ink, others in an iron-hued maroon that resembled dried blood were spelled forward and backward and repeated without apparent reason. Partial sentences and phrases were written in cursive in English and other languages. Images that looked like ancient hieroglyphs and seemed to have been drawn with the precision of a draftsman appeared on other pages. I found about a dozen drawings that appeared to be partial rudimentary maps, each drawn in pencil with the graphite worn to such an extent that they were barely legible. Two seemed newer and were located near the rear of the book. I could only wonder what secrets this book contained and why it was so crucial to Roland Speirs.

It was 6:30 a.m. and not yet light outside. I was so immersed in Roland's journal that I did not hear Gina come into the room. She was wearing another one of my dress shirts and carried a cup of coffee in each hand, placing one of the cups on my desk in front of me. "Marc, I just want to thank you for letting me stay here again last night."

"What are partners for? I hope I didn't wake you when I checked on you."

"No, I didn't even hear you."

"Good, because I had flashbacks to Florida when you drew down on me with a shotgun!"

"That's right! I almost forgot about that," Gina said, stifling a laugh. "We could write a nonfiction book about some of the things we've been through, but I don't think anyone would believe it."

"I wouldn't, and I lived it."

"So, what do you think about the journal?"

"I think I need a translator," I answered. "I'm serious."

"So, let's get one. I know two professors at the university. One specializes in ancient languages."

"And the other?"

"Well, he is someone with a broad and exciting range of unique skill sets. Some people might call him 'eccentric.' He can help us with the symbols and even the satanic information written in the book. He would be good as the lead in this case, but a proper introduction should be made by the professor I know best."

"Would you mind calling your professor friend this morning to see if we can meet him as soon as possible?"

"Sure, no problem. We also have to drop off the report at Fidelity Mutual this morning. Is Angie Carr still the lead case agent on the file?" Gina asked.

"Yes, and Jim told me that she is meeting with supervisory claim managers who are coming up from Columbus tomorrow, so she'll have time to go through the report and ask us any questions she might have."

"I'm anxious about getting off to a running start today. Do you mind if I use your shower again? I promise I'll be quick."

"Take as much time as you need. I've been up for a while and already went out. In case you didn't see them, I brought some pastries and muffins from the bakery. They're on the counter by the coffee maker and were just baked this morning. Have some."

"You're spoiling me, Marc, but I need to watch my figure. I can feel my jeans getting a little too snug when I carry my .45 inside my waistband."

"That's why I carry mine in a shoulder holster," I said with a smile, and watched as she gracefully walked out of the office and into the hall toward the bathroom.

I spent the next half-hour trying to put together a coherent timeline of events from the independent cards pinned to the corkboard. For some inexplicable reason, I was having trouble visualizing the case map, so I decided to write out the timeline on notepaper. When I realized I could barely read my own handwriting, I opted to type the timeline with important names and other information. I used four sheets of paper and three sheets of carbon paper, typing carefully to avoid mistakes.

Rough Notes & Timeline
Date compiled: Monday, September 14, 1987

First Week of September: Anonymous Letter was written Sunday, September 6, 1987; 7 p.m.: Dead body found at the Bayfront identified as Jacob Tingsley, age 14. Mutilated and tortured. Killed elsewhere 1-2 days before being found. Body staged. Heart and left hand missing. The body was transported to and staged at this location.

Monday, September 7, 1987; Between 6:00–6:15 p.m.: Answering service received two phone calls from an unidentified woman who claimed it was a life-and-death matter, asked to speak to Marc or Angie.

-Dusk: Break-in at the residence of Jim and Angie Carr. Files and Baphomet pendant to be used as evidence were taken from the file-drawer safe.

Tuesday, September 8, 1987; Met with Lakewood PD Detective Jenkins - London, England murder of a woman, believed to be Sadie Cooper with Marc's and Gina's business cards found at the murder scene.

Wednesday, September 9, 1987; Second meeting with Jenkins - learned the identity of DB. FBI involvement in the investigation.

-Met with Martin and Mary Tingsley. Due to recent events and murder of Jacob, we suggested they stay in a safe house. They are staying at a cabin owned by Paul Kruger (Mary's uncle). Kruger owns a trucking/logistics company in Lakewood.

-An unidentified subject at Gina's house during the night. Possible surveillance/harassment - unknown if related.

Friday, September 10, 1987; Florida resident Porter Landers and associate, first known to be in Lakewood, contacted Brenda at the Towne Restaurant to get Marc's home address.

Saturday, September 12, 1987; Jim Carr surreptitiously obtains files from FBI agents and makes copies for our use.

- 11 p.m. - Roland Speirs commits suicide. We obtain his journal.

Sunday, September 13, 1987; Lunch at Towne Restaurant. Landers and his associate are conducting surveillance of Marc and Gina. Incident involving Ronnie, the busboy.

Undated/Misc: Possible missing infant from the Smith house - same location as missing Jacob Tingsley. Mother allegedly 15-year-old foster child, Maggie. The infant is determined to be 11 months. The Smith family denies.

Those were just the facts or the highlights: no added notes, only events. I left room for notes - my own and others. The telephone rang just as I pulled the sheets of paper from my Smith-Corona typewriter. I answered it on the first ring.

"Good morning Marc, it's Deana." A wave of nausea overcame me as she said the words in a way that suggested something was wrong.

"Good morning," I replied, "How are you?"

"I'm fine, but I've really been missing you. You never called me this weekend. I thought we were going to spend some time together."

"I know, and I'm sorry for not calling. It was a busy and rough weekend. Something happened Saturday night. I don't even want to tell you. I can't describe what."

Deana interrupted. "You don't have to describe anything, Marc. I don't need any explanations. Things always seem to be coming up between us. Things that are always keeping us apart."

"Deana, things are terrible right now. I wish I could tell you. About last weekend, do you forgive me?"

"Of course, I forgive you. I know how wrapped up you are in your work right now, which is why I'm calling. I decided to take a couple of weeks off work with the vacation time I've saved up and visit my sister in Wisconsin. It will give us some much-needed time."

"When?" I asked.

"Our flight, I'm taking my son, leaves this afternoon. I already cleared it through work."

"Can I see you before you leave?"

"I don't think there's enough time, and honestly, I think it would be best if we didn't."

"Deana, are you trying to tell me it's over between us?"

"No, Marc, I just need some time. I need time to think. Just know that I love you and will always love you. Look, I'll be back in a couple of weeks, and then maybe, maybe your schedule will give us more time together," her voice cracking.

"While you're gone, would you let me call you once in a while? Maybe you'd like to call me instead, but we should talk about things, about us. Please, at least allow me that much. I'll miss hearing your voice."

"Sure, we can keep in touch. After all, I'll be worried about you. You do know how much I care for you, I hope."

The conversation lagged as we both seemed to be out of words to say to each other. Deana gave me her sister's phone number and, at my insistence, her address. I wished her a safe trip and gently cradled the receiver. I sat in stunned silence, not knowing what the future held for us.

Showered and dressed, Gina walked into the office as I was gazing out the window, thinking about my conversation with Deana. "Marc, what's wrong?"

"Deana just called me. She just told me that she's taking a few weeks off of work and going to Wisconsin with her son to visit her sister. It was a spur of the moment decision. It had to be, or she would have told me before today. I think this is her way of saying goodbye to me, Gina, to get rid of me. I think it's over. It's my fault for not making time for her."

"You mean this wasn't planned? She never mentioned anything about taking a vacation before today?"

"No, and I'm sure she would have."

"Oh, Marc, I am so sorry. But look, it's only for a few weeks, and she'll be back. I'm a woman, and I know these things. If there were ever two people meant for each other, it's you two. I know that she is deeply in love with you.

Besides, maybe it's for the best, at least until we get through this case, or whatever this is. She and her son will be safe out of Lakewood."

"At least there's that, considering the way things have been going," I said in a moment of despair.

"Marc, look at me. You know that I know a thing or two about relationships. I know love when I see it, and I can recognize when love will last regardless of what is thrown at it. That's you two."

Gina was doing her best to make me feel better, but it wasn't working.

"What's this?" Gina asked as she picked up the typewritten timeline.

"Highlights from my case map, or a rough timeline. I'm having trouble with my card system, so I thought I'd try something different. Take a copy if you want."

Gina took a copy and placed it in her bag. I told her that no matter how many times we go over things, rehash events, and make notes it seems like we're not getting anywhere.

"The answers can only be found in the field, not behind a desk," I said.

"The field it is, then. Let's make a few calls first and head out."

****

Gina called the office and spoke with Annie and Paul. She brought Paul up to speed on the events of the last few days, making sure to let him know that we had completed the report for Fidelity Mutual and would be dropping it off along with the invoice later this morning. She also briefed him on the events surrounding our weekend experiences, to which he merely admonished us to be careful. Paul said that he would be traveling to the state capital to discuss a potentially large security contract with a state agency. He would be leaving shortly and would not be back until Wednesday at the earliest.

Gina then reminded Annie to keep an eye out for any sign of Landers, his Cadillac, or any indications of surveillance of the office. She assured us that she would, adding that she had not seen anything out of the ordinary since she arrived at the office just after 7:00 this morning. Annie then gave Gina the information for two additional assignments. One is a background investigation of a prospective employee for an executive-level position, and the other involved checking on the activities of a dock worker who reportedly sustained a soft tissue injury to his lower back. We were given ten business days to complete both cases.

Gina made a few more telephone calls, including one to her mother. She inquired about her daughter and asked if she could remain with her for a few more days. I could hear her mother's favorable reaction from where I sat, and Gina's response. "I'm glad she's been such a help to you, mom. Just make sure she does her schoolwork, and you two don't stay up too late watching old movies," she added.

When it was my turn to use the telephone, I called Brenda at the Towne Restaurant. Since she was promoted to manage the entire restaurant operation, Brenda arrives early every Monday to oversee inventory and handle other managerial duties, so I knew she would be at work. I wanted to check on her and Robbie regarding their experiences yesterday. It was at least six rings before she picked up.

"Brenda, it's Marc, do you have a minute to talk?"

"For you, I sure do!" She sounded much more chipper than I expected and a lot better than I felt.

"I just want to check on you and to see how Robbie is doing today."

"Robbie is just fine. I talked to his mother last night, and just a few minutes ago. He feels completely normal and wants to come back to work. His mom said that he could after he sees the doctor for a final check-up in a few days, so he'll only miss one day of work. The doctor still does not know what happened to him. All of his tests, including his blood tests, came back normal."

"That's great news," I said to Brenda.

"What's wrong?"

"Nothing, I'm fine."

"I can tell, and you're not fine. You know I'll keep bugging you until you tell me, so spit it out now."

"Deana called me this morning. She told me that she needs some time to think, so she's leaving to stay with her sister in Wisconsin for a few weeks. She just told me this morning, and she's leaving today."

"That's a bit sudden, isn't it?"

"Yeah, I thought so. I also thought things were fine with us, but I guess I was wrong about that too."

"Well, she's not breaking off the relationship, and it is only for two weeks," Brenda said.

"I know. I haven't been the best guy to be with lately, so I can't blame her. Maybe I'm just overreacting."

"I don't want to sound too forward, Marc, but we are friends. Is there anything I can do for you?"

"No, just please take care of yourself. Be careful. Watch your surroundings."

"It's you who needs to be careful. Have you seen your Florida visitors since yesterday?"

"No, and if I didn't thank you before, I want to thank you now for helping us out. Please make sure Robbie knows that I owe him one. I feel responsible for what happened to him."

"I'll be sure to tell him, but I hardly think what happened to him had anything to do with you or what he did yesterday."

"You're probably right. Anyway, I hope you know just how much I appreciate you."

"I do, Marc. Remember, I'm just a phone call away, and if you need me, I'll be there for you."

"Thanks, Brenda. I'm here for you too."

"There's one more thing, Marc. I tried to write out what Landers said to me, and I'm drawing a blank. I wish I could be more help."

"Don't worry about it, Brenda. Just take care of yourself."

I continued to hold the phone receiver in my hand long after she hung up, staring out the window in silence.

Gina interrupted my silent introspection. "C'mon Marc, we've got a lot to do today, and I need to use the phone again."

After getting the telephone number for the university from directory assistance, Gina dialed the number and was eventually connected to the office of Professor Eric Myers. He remembered her from classes there and an informal class reunion they both attended when she was still a cop. He received her unexpected phone call warmly. She explained most of the situation with the professor, who agreed to meet us today to look at the journal she told him about.

"He sounded genuinely intrigued," Gina said after hanging up the phone. We have an appointment with him today. His schedule is open, and he'll see us when we can get there. I told him we would try to be there at noon.

IN THE DARK OF NIGHT

Chapter 24

<u>Professor Eric Myers</u>

Gina and I walked into the atrium inside the front doors of the university. The campus security guard gave us instructions at the front desk to the classroom of Professor Myers. The guard picked up a clipboard and checked his class schedule. He doesn't have classes scheduled for this morning, but he's in the building. He's probably in his office.

"Thanks. I spoke to Professor Myers on the telephone, so he's expecting us," Gina said to the guard.

We walked down two hallways and through a gauntlet of students carrying textbooks and talking to each other. We located his office at the end of a long hall of classrooms. An engraved brass placard with his name was positioned just under a sizeable translucent window that comprised the top half of the large wooden door.

"Gina! It's great to see you again. How long has it been? Three or four years?"

"It's been at least that long, Professor Myers."

"Call me Eric. You look as beautiful as ever. I'm allowed to say that now that you're not a student anymore. And I assume this is your partner you told me about when you called?"

"Thank you for taking the time to see us, Professor. I'm Marc Stiles," I said, and held my hand out to shake his. He greeted my outreached hand with a solid, firm handshake that matched his rakish appearance. Appearing to be in his late fifties, he had a thick crop of black hair that was being gradually overtaken by silver, especially on the sides. He was wearing black-framed eyeglasses that nearly matched the color of his hair. He looked like a typical college professor in his grey herringbone sport coat with leather elbow pads, solid white shirt, and a thin tie. Professor Myers exuded a level of confidence that matched his knowledge of more languages than I even knew existed.

"As I mentioned on the phone, professor, we need your help with a rather unusual case we're working."

"I'll be happy to help in any way I can, especially for a former student."

"We'd like you to take a look at a book, well, a journal or a kind of diary that contains many handwritten entries that appear to contain words and phrases written in different languages. We can't tell what they are and thought you could properly direct us," Gina said as she reached into her bag and removed Speirs' journal. She held the book out to Myers, expecting him to take it from her. Immediately upon seeing it, he retracted his hand as if the sight of the book startled him. He instructed her to put it down on his desk.

"Where did you find that?"

"It belonged to a man who we recently met. Why?"

"I've seen it before. Well, not this book, but books with similar covers and markings, except for the bloodstains, of course," Professor Myers said as he carefully inspected the front cover. He sat down and opened the right drawer of his desk, removing a set of fabric gloves and a large magnifying glass. He gently glided the book to the center of his desk, pulled it toward him, and used the magnifying glass to inspect the front cover.

"Runes," the Professor said at a barely audible level.

"What are runes?" I asked.

"Not 'are' but 'is,' as in singular. Simply stated, it's an ancient alphabet, but it's much more than that. Much more indeed. The simplified explanation is that it's a type of symbolic alphabet that dates back to the early to the mid-first century. It even predates Latin and has its origins in the early Germanic languages, although there's some scholarly academic debate about that. It can be considered more of a set of symbols rather than a traditional alphabet, though."

"Sort of like the Chinese alphabet?" I asked.

"Not exactly, but I suppose you can dumb it down that way, no offense intended, of course."

"Of course, none taken," I said as I shot a look to Gina, who had a smirk on her face when our eyes met.

"The word runes itself means hidden or secret, suggesting that there is a hidden meaning within the runic inscriptions themselves. It was a type of language or communication that was used by an elite class starting around 100 or 150 AD, especially sorcerers. Some runes were used to create amulets or talisman objects, often carried or worn by practitioners of black magic, or magick with a "k" at the end of the word."

"Do you mean like pendants and things like that?" I asked.

"Yes, perhaps, among other things."

"Are you able to tell us the meaning of the symbols on the front of the book?"

"I'm sure that after some research, I'll be able to tell you a whole lot more. This is an extremely unusual book cover, specifically to have the symbols embossed into the leather. This looks like it could be one-of-a-kind, most likely handmade. If you don't mind me asking, where did you find it?"

"Professor, we don't mind that you are asking, but we need this to remain between us as it involves an active investigation. No one must know that we came to see you about this. No one can know that this book even exists. Can we count on your confidentiality?" Gina asked.

"Absolutely."

"Well, the owner of the book is deceased."

"I figured that might be the case, considering the apparent age of the book and the bloodstains on the cover."

"It belonged to a man identified as Roland Speirs. Have you ever heard of him?"

"No, I can't say that I have."

"As far as we know, the writings and drawings inside are all his, or at least the later entries. We think he kept it like a diary," Gina said.

"My dear, one does not keep a diary like this. No, it is something much more than that," he said, as he opened the book and briefly scanned the first few pages. "No, no, no, it is not a simple diary. I believe that this book is essential to somebody. I suspect that if the former owner is deceased, somebody is looking very hard for this book."

"What makes you say that?" I asked.

"Because of the information or the secrets it undoubtedly contains."

"Are you able to leave this book with me so I can study its contents?"

"Can you work from copies?" I asked.

"It would be better for me to study the original work."

"Can you make us a copy of the entire book, including the cover, with the equipment you have here at the university? We'll work from copies, but we must maintain a proper chain of custody."

"Yes, I can do that. It's going to take me about twenty minutes or so as I will have to use the new Kodak color imager in the lab. We've only had it for a few weeks. The college put it into service right before the start of the 1987 school year. You'll be amazed at the color reproductions it makes. I'll make three copies. If you're satisfied with the reproductions, I'll sign a receipt or whatever paperwork you need for chain-of-custody purposes."

"That sounds good to us."

"Great. Why don't you two wait in the faculty lounge while I take care of this? Come with me, and I'll let you in. If anyone asks, you're my guests. There are coffee and snacks in there. Help yourself, and I'll be back when I'm finished."

Professor Myers returned a half-hour later with four shirt-sized boxes, one containing the bound journal and the other three containing remarkable color reproductions of the book, including the front and back cover. The copies had the feel and appearance of professional photographs.

"I wonder what the administrator would say if he knew that I just used a twelve-thousand-dollar piece of equipment and about a hundred dollars of supplies for this," the Professor said with a wry smile.

"We won't tell if you don't," I said.

"Have you talked to or shown this to Professor Wolfram? For all of his eccentricities, the guy is a genius with this sort of thing. He has dual Masters in Classical Antiquities and Archeology. He has degrees in Egyptology and Artifact Studies. He spent several years in Germany and London, and five years on archeological digs in Egypt. That's just what I know about."

"Sounds like a fun guy," I said, a comment that earned me a light jab to my ribs by Gina's elbow.

"You really should get his take on this. He's also an expert on many of the Pagan religions and their ceremonies. I'd be happy to call him right now to set up a meeting if you'd like. I'm sure he'd be ecstatic to take a look at this. He hasn't been happy since he came here. His passion is working in the field."

"So why did he stop his fieldwork?" I asked.

"Oh, that's a story better left for him to tell. Would you like me to call him?"

"If you don't mind."

Professor Richard Wolfram

Fifteen minutes later and after an introductory telephone call from Myers, all three of us were in the home of Professor Richard Wolfram, located about a half-mile from the college campus. His house was one of the larger and older homes in Lakewood and reminded me more of a museum than a house. Professor Wolfram looked like a more senior and more rotund Indiana Jones and definitely fit the part. Even his home held my expectations, as I noticed an odor of pipe smoke and a noticeable layer of dust covering the many books and artifacts on display.

Skipping any extended pleasantries, he invited us into his study and asked to see the journal. Professor Myers opened the box and placed the journal on a large mahogany table situated below a bright fluorescent light.

"Oh my!" Wolfram loudly exclaimed as he gingerly opened the book and turned its pages. "This is absolutely amazing. I must know, to whom does this belong? And how did you come to obtain it?"

"It's ours, professor," Gina answered.

"Well, yes, of course, you have current possession of it, but from whom, I must ask, did you acquire this? Where? And how? I must know."

How the professor forcefully asked his questions alarmed me and startled Gina. His reaction to seeing the journal made us think that we were in possession of the equivalent of a long-sought missing Rembrandt painting.

"We can tell you that the previous owner is recently deceased," I said, "but right now, I'd prefer that his identity remain confidential as this is part of an active murder investigation."

Professor Wolfram looked up from the journal to me, then to Gina, as if he was sizing both of us up. His gaze remained on us for several seconds without anyone speaking. "Hmmph. All right."

"Professor Myers explained that he had made copies. However, I must insist that I am permitted to examine the original artifact. I trust that won't present a problem, will it?"

"Professor Myers, can you work from a reproduction?"

"Yes, although I might not need to insert myself into this investigation at all," Myers responded. "If it's okay with you, I'll keep one of the copies I made if any language-related questions arise, and defer the official research to Professor Wolfram. He's much better suited to handle this and should have the original. He should lead the research. Quite candidly, you don't need me. This is right up Dick's alley, and as I said, he's best suited to handle all aspects of the entire journal. To be clear, I'll act as back-up if needed."

Gina and I thanked Professor Myers for his assistance and turned to professor Wolfram, who was busily studying the inside pages of the journal. "How long do you estimate it will take you to give us a report on your findings, even if just a preliminary report?"

Without looking up, he said, "Two or three days for my initial analysis if I begin now, and as you can readily see, I already have. There is one thing you should know," Professor Wolfram said without looking up. "I guarantee you that somebody will be looking for this book, and they'll stop at nothing to get it back. Make no mistake about it. This journal is very important to someone. I don't think I need to say anything more."

Gina changed the name on the chain of custody receipt from Myers to Wolfram and provided all of our contact information. Gina and I left with the copies of the journal, leaving Professor Myers with Wolfram. As we exited the residence, I caught a glimpse of Myers motioning Gina to call him, who merely smiled and nodded in return.

"It looks like you've got a potential suitor," I said to Gina as we entered my car. I was referring to Eric Myers, who was more than a little obvious in his treatment of Gina.

"Oh, puleese."

"What do you think about what Wolfram said about someone looking for that book?" Gina asked.

"Unfortunately, I agree with him. The first question is, who wants it more, and why? The second is perhaps more important. What lengths will they go to get it?" Minutes passed in silence as we both contemplated our predicament.

"Let's go check on Martin and Mary," I suggested to Gina, before putting the car into drive. "Maybe we should show a copy of the journal to them. Perhaps something will look familiar to Martin or even Mary," I recommended to Gina, who was in complete agreement. "We gave them more than enough time."

IN THE DARK OF NIGHT

Chapter 25

<u>**Cabin Fever**</u>

It took 45 minutes in my car to get to the cabin where the Tingsleys have been staying since last week. As we approached the place on the long, winding, gravel and dirt road, everything looked normal and even serene.

"I could live out here. Oh yeah, I could live like this," Gina said as she took a deep breath, taking in the fresh pine scent from the surrounding trees. She carried a copy of the journal as we walked to the door together.

Mary met us at the door, showed us a forced smile and let us in. "I saw you coming from the road. You can see a lot from up here," Mary said as she let us inside. "I thought you two forgot about us," Martin said from his chair at the kitchen table. From there, the entire expanse of the front of the property was visible. "It's gorgeous here. For the last two nights, we've seen a family of five deer walking across the front of the cabin. One had a huge rack, and the other was a doe. Three smaller deer followed them. They're magnificent animals. I could get used to this," he said. Gina and I joined Martin and Mary at the kitchen table, which was made from solid oak.

According to Mary, their stay was uneventful so far. Their young children are faring equally well, enjoying being able to play outside as the warm weather persisted. A large, 36-inch television was hooked up to an enormous satellite dish outside that provided their inside entertainment. A well-stocked pantry and refrigerator have taken care of them so far, although Mary said that they need to go to the market to buy more perishables. "We were just about to make a run to the grocery store before you came," Mary said.

"Gina, why don't you take Mary to the store. I'll stay here with Martin." Hearing that a trip to the grocery store was being planned, the children ran to Mary, begging to go along. "Let's take them too," Gina said she smiled at Mary and the kids. "I'm content to stay right here," Martin admitted. I handed my car keys to Gina, and they were out the door within seconds, with the children leading the way. Now alone, Martin and I sat in silence and watched as the car traveled down the driveway, turning right toward town.

"Anything new on the case? Has anything important happened since we've been here? They don't deliver a paper here, and we don't get the local channels on the television, so I haven't seen the news. Has it been quiet?" Martin asked.

I saw no reason to provide details of the ugly events that took place over the last few days, so I was intentionally vague. I explained that we found a journal from a man who had some level of involvement with the people who trafficked in children.

"So how did you guys end up with it?"

"I guess you could say it was willed to us."

"So, the man who had it is dead?"

"Yes."

I explained to Martin that I wanted him to look through the copies made from the journal and gently warned him that it contained demonic-looking symbols, phrases, and other entries he might find unsettling. I told him that I thought it would be best to wait for Mary to return, but he insisted that he wanted to look at it with me, especially while the children were away. There was something in his voice that made me believe he did not want Mary around when he viewed the journal. Against my better judgment, I relented and opened the box containing the color copies of Speirs' book.

Martin looked at every page, some with more interest than others. He identified a few symbols that he had seen at the locations where he was abused. Martin also recognized some of the words and phrases that appeared in another language other than English, but otherwise didn't say much. I couldn't put my finger on it, but he seemed to have something on his mind but was hesitant to talk. He appeared and acted afraid, but I couldn't tell if it was from looking through the copy of the journal or from something else entirely. Something just seemed off.

As we finished with the last page, I spotted my car pulling onto the driveway headed toward the cabin. I gathered the copies and placed them back into the box. Martin exhibited a blank stare and sat motionless at the table, like a child who did something wrong while his parents were away.

"We're going to eat good tonight, I bought steaks for us," Mary said to Martin as she walked in the front door, carrying two brown paper grocery bags. "And the kids have their favorite cereal for the morning," Gina added with a smile. The women unpacked the bags and put the groceries away.

Gina and Mary returned to the table as the children ran outside to play. I told them that I showed Martin the copies we brought with us, although he provided little help. Upon hearing this, Mary became visibly upset at me for showing Martin the pages without her being present.

"You had no right to do that!" Mary yelled, standing up and pointing her finger at my chest. It seemed uncharacteristic of her to respond that way. "How could you? You could have triggered him!"

Gina tried to calm Mary as I explained that it was at Martin's insistence. Mary walked to her purse and removed a pill bottle, dispensing two capsules and placing them into Martin's hand and instructed him to take them right away.

"I don't need these, Mary. I'm fine."

"Take them anyway," she said with a disturbing forcefulness I hadn't heard from her before. She abruptly stood up, almost tipping the heavy, solid oak chair that matched the table, and walked to the sink where she filled a drinking glass halfway with water. Mary placed the glass in front of Martin and motioned instructions to him to take the medication. Without saying anything else, Martin complied. "Now I want you to go to the bedroom and lay down. You need your rest," Mary said in a way that sounded more like a maternal figure than a wife.

As soon as Martin left the room, Mary glared at me and demanded to see the copies made from Speirs' book.

Gina broke into the discussion, assuring Mary that she could see everything that I showed to Martin. She placed the pages in front of Mary, who began to look through each page rather quickly as if she was looking for something specific. Mary completed the task quickly and in total silence. When she reached the last page, she pushed the pile of papers back to Gina. "Make sure you take this with you when you leave," Mary said in a stern voice.

"Did you see anything familiar?" Gina asked.

"No, nothing," she said dismissively. "It's meaningless to me, but you shouldn't have taken that chance with Martin," she said, turning her head to me. Her anger was unsettling.

"Mary, I don't want to seem out of line here, but it seems that Martin is a lot stronger than you think." Before I could say anything more, Mary objected, saying that I don't know him or live with him, and I don't know what "they" go through. Before anyone could say anything else, Mary instructed us to leave so Martin could get his rest. She thanked Gina for taking her to the store but remained cold to me. I apologized and told Gina I would wait for her in the car. I placed the copies back in the box and quietly retreated to my vehicle. Gina joined me a few minutes later. Neither of us said anything until we were on the main road.

"What do you think that was all about?" I asked Gina. "Was I that much out of line for allowing Martin to look through the papers?"

"Not at all, Marc. Her reaction was pretty odd. I'd say that she was the one who was out of line."

Chapter 26

As soon as we got back to my apartment and the war room, I checked my answering machine for messages. One was from Annie, two were from Detective Jenkins, who said it was "imperative" that he speak with us right away, and one from Jim Carr, who also wants to talk "as soon as possible." Gina wrote the messages in her notebook while I listened. The final message came in about ten minutes before we arrived, and the voice on the tape immediately caught my undivided attention.

"Marc, it's Deana. I just wanted to let you know that we got to my sister's house without any trouble. I thought you might be worried, so I thought I should call. I'm sorry I left on such short notice." There was a period of extended silence. "I want you to know that I care very deeply for you, and I worry about you. I'll call you again soon, okay?" I detected a trembling in her voice before she gently hung up the receiver.

Gina looked at me and smiled. "See, I told you. Women know these things. She'll be back. She loves you too much to do anything else."

"Yeah, well, I think she could have handled it a little differently, don't you? She's got no idea the crap that's going on and how I try to protect her from it. Maybe it would be best if she just stays out there," I said, angrily tossing a folder across my desk. Without waiting for her to respond, I picked up the phone and called Jim Carr, deciding to call Jenkins last. I wasn't in the mood to deal with a pushy gold shield at the moment.

"Jim, what's going on?" I abruptly asked.

"Hello, Mr. Stiles." Jim sounded deliberately official. "I apologize, I'm unable to accommodate your request. Anyway, I'm in the middle of something important. If I have the time, I'll call you back."

"Sure," I said, deliberately keeping it short.

"Thanks." A click on the line quickly followed.

As I was explaining to Gina the oddity of the call, the office telephone rang. I picked it up on the first ring, and it was Jim.

"What was that all about?" I asked.

"I'll explain later. I'm calling from one of the payphones in the courthouse, near the front entrance. I need to give you and Gina an urgent heads up about a few things."

"Gina is here with me in the war room. Hang on, and I'll put you on speaker," I said and pushed the speaker button under the dial pad. "Okay, what's up?"

"The first thing you should know is that the feds are royally pissed off at the two of you for a couple of reasons. They mentioned that they might ask the county detectives to review and maybe even suspend your license to operate. They want a full investigation into how Marc got to a homicide scene before the police, and how both of you just happened to be with Roland Speirs when he blew his head off."

"Come on, Jim, you know how it all happened, and so do they. It's bull, it's nothing but a smokescreen, and you know it."

"I know that, so you don't have to kill the messenger. I'm just letting you know what's going on. They also think you tampered with a potential crime scene by taking something from Speirs' apartment after he killed himself and before the police got there."

"Now I find that rather interesting. What are they saying that we removed?"

"You know. They want the journal and are hell-bent on getting it, even if it means getting a search warrant for your office, and they will get one to recover that book. They're leaning hard on my boss, who is leaning even harder on the police chief. This means that you've become an annoyance to the district attorney and a rock in the shoe of the Lakewood Police Chief by inserting yourselves into active police investigations. You know what they say, it all rolls downhill."

"Active investigations my—"

"I know, I get it. The feds are also going to hold a press conference sometime this week to announce that the Tingsley boy was the victim of a multi-state serial killer and flat out deny the existence of any satanic rituals. As I said, they're taking it out on the district attorney and the police chief. They want you to stop, and they do not want any mention of anything remotely related to rituals or ritual killings."

"Marvelous."

"They are going to publicly deny much of the evidence to 'sanitize' the killing as much as possible. To keep the peace, and maybe their jobs, the DA and chief are going along with it."

"Wait a minute. Do you mean that they would rather publicly claim that there's a serial killer on the loose rather than admitting that there's a problem with ritualist sexual abuse? That doesn't even make sense and could unnecessarily panic a large part of the population in this area. Who are they protecting, Jim, and why?"

"Those are both good questions. I don't know, but whoever they are running interference for seems to have a lot of pull."

"Is there anyone who we haven't seemed to piss off?"

Jim chuckled at the question. "I can't think of anyone, but I'm still on your side if that means anything."

"Are you still clear to meet with the state Attorney General this week? Maybe that will take some of the heat off us." There was a long pause that left that statement hanging in the air. "Take me off speaker," Jim instructed.

I obligingly picked up the telephone handset, which clicked off the speaker and brought the phone to my ear. "Okay, you're off speaker. Now, what's this all about?"

"I'll explain when I see you two. We need to meet. I don't want to talk about anything over the phone. Don't mention any of our plans until we talk in person, and let's meet sooner rather than later as things are happening fast right now."

"Do you want to meet here?"

"No, at least not right now. Let me think a minute." There was some rustling on his end and a pause.

"Okay, let's meet in the parking lot of the Lakewood Landing Marina in thirty minutes. Pull into the lot and park on the west side, where people park their cars and trucks after they put their boats in the water. Stay in your car, and I'll come over to you. Got it?"

"Got it. Are you sure all this cloak-and-dagger stuff is necessary?"

"Positive. See you shortly."

Curious, Gina asked what is going on. I explained that we were to meet Jim at the Lakewood Marina in a half-hour, and he would explain when he saw us.

"I'm going to go freshen up before we leave," Gina said and walked to the bathroom. I transferred the page copies from the journal into an expandable pocket file and tossed it into my briefcase, along with other related notes and papers. I considered returning Detective Jenkins' call but decided against it until we met with Jim. My attitude was not the best, anyway.

Gina walked back into the war room a few minutes later, and in another fifteen minutes, we were parked at the marina. Jim pulled into the parking spot next to us and got into the back seat behind Gina. He spoke first.

"I'm sorry about wanting to meet like this, but I'm starting to get a little spooked by things that have been happening lately. I don't trust anybody, present company excluded, of course."

"Of course, but why not? What's going on?"

"I keep some 'red herring' files, or at least that's what I call them, at my office on people and events related to the broader aspects of this case. I keep them in a locked file drawer in a particular way. I do that for a few reasons, not the least of which is to screw with anyone who might find or otherwise see the files. They're also filled with papers with fictitious entries that would send anyone who finds them in all the wrong directions. No one else knows about them or has access to them, and I have the only key to the cabinet. My secretary doesn't even have one. This morning I could tell that someone had gone through those files, and who knows, maybe even copied them, and then put them back. They were noticeably out of order."

"Maybe you just forgot how you put them back the last time you had them out," I offered.

"No way. I put them back in the same manner as I always do. Somebody was in that cabinet," Jim stressed.

"Okay, but you said the files contained false information, so what's the problem?" I asked.

"If that was the only thing off, I wouldn't be so concerned. But I could tell that someone went through the files and papers I keep locked in my office at my house, containing the real information. Before you say anything, this was after the Labor Day burglary. It happened within the last few days."

"You're kidding. After the burglary? That raises a lot more questions. Is there anything else?"

"Yes, two more things. One, I think I'm being followed. Two, I think my office, my phones, and maybe even my house might be bugged."

"First, who do you think is following you?"

"I don't know. But I know surveillance when I see it."

"Do you think you were followed here?" I scanned the lot as Jim responded.

"No, I made it a point to make sure of it. Unless they're doing it electronically, I don't know how I could have missed it otherwise. When I called you back, I used the payphone downstairs. As you know, the second-floor phones by the DA's office are all monitored. I just didn't want to take any chances."

"Are you sure that you're not a little too paranoid, Jim?"

"I don't think so. You know we're talking about some of the most horrendous things going on here by some powerful and influential people, and I've worked cases against people who killed for a lot less. By the way, how is the kid from the restaurant doing? The last thing you told me was that he was fine. Is that still the case?"

"As far as we know," Gina responded. "Why do you think your phones are tapped?"

"I'm not sure if it's just my phones. It's hard to explain, but it seems that some people, especially the feds, are always one step ahead of me on everything. I overheard a conversation earlier today about our meetings at Marc's apartment. There's no way they could know that without me being followed or a tap on my telephone, or maybe both. I don't know, but until I find out, I'm not taking any chances."

"I agree. I don't think any of us should."

"Does Angie know about any of this?"

"You mean about possible telephone taps, bugs, and surveillance? Hell no, and I want to keep it that way. I don't want to upset her, and I can't afford alimony payments."

"Well, you're the boss, the one person able to get our documentation and evidence to the Attorney General to make a case against these madmen, so what do you want to do?"

"We've got to move now with the evidence we have before one of us, or all of us, turn up missing or dead. I think we need to gather everything we have, including Speirs' journal, put it together in a tight and coherent form, and get it to the AG as soon as possible. And I do mean soon, just like we planned."

Gina explained that we had just come from Professor Wolfram's home study and gave him the Speirs' journal to review for relevant clues about names and events here in Lakewood. He is working on it as we speak.

"Do you think there's any way that he can give us a preliminary report by tonight? I know that's pushing it, but we have to get all of this out of our hands. I'm willing to make one more stop at the war room this evening, meet the professor, get this all packaged up, and get it to the task force before anyone else gets hurt or worse. Your professor has to be there. Get everyone together, make sure we have everything laid out and updated, and let's get it to the AG by Friday."

"Okay," I said, "but if you're under surveillance, then it's likely that we are too. I know Porter Landers is trying to find us, and heaven knows who else. And now we have the feds to deal with," I said. "Do you think the war room is the best place?"

"What other options do we have?" Jim sighed. "I suppose we could rent a motel room somewhere, but that would mean that we'd have to transport a lot of paper and evidence with us. Our exposure might be greater on unfamiliar ground. I think the safest bet right now is your place. Just make sure there are no strange cars around, and make sure no one follows you when you leave here. I'll do the same."

"Okay, it sounds good as long as we can get everything we've got into the hands of the attorney general and let their task force do the heavy lifting."

"That's the idea. I'll be at the war room at eight o'clock tonight. I'll bring all of my files with me. I'll park in the back and knock on the back door," he said with marked determination.

"It's a date," Gina said in a subdued tone.

"Oh, there is one more thing I thought about, Marc. Do you still have that RF detector you used on that case for the paper company executive to sweep his office for bugs a few months ago?"

"Yep, I sure do."

"Use it at your place before we meet. Humor me, please."

Jim slipped out of the car and into his and was gone from the parking lot before either of us could get a word out.

Gina and I watched Jim walk to his car and leave the marina. An oppressive silence hung in the air as neither of us seemed to want to be the first person to speak.

"Do you think your place is a good idea?" Gina asked. "I've been thinking about the people we know or at least suspect are involved. How is it possible that no one has found out where you live? Think about it."

"Who said they haven't? Anyway, I think it's the best place that we have," I responded. "I've been thinking about it, and I think I have the answer. As a matter of normal operational security, I've maintained a few firewalls. My attorney's brother, who is also my friend, owns my apartment. All of the utilities are in his name too."

"Except the phone," Gina interrupted.

"No, even the phone is in his name, and the number is unlisted."

"Still, that would not prevent a reverse trace or even a check of the Cole Directory."

"Again, it's unlisted. I even checked a couple of weeks ago when I was at the library."

"That's good."

"On a more personal level, my father knows where I live, but he knows never to give my address or phone number out to anyone. Plus, he has never been here. The same goes for my ex-wife."

"Your dad has never been to your apartment?"

"You sound surprised."

"Well, it does seem kind of odd."

"Not really, considering our relationship, and I don't bring my kids here, either."

"That's… that's just sad, isn't it, when you think about it?" Gina's voice trailed off.

"I don't think about it."

After leaving the marina, I drove on several side streets and made a few U-turns on our way back to my apartment. The maneuvers convinced me no one was physically following us.

Once we got back to my apartment, Gina helped me perform a search for electronic listening devices. She is familiar with the devices from her stint in the major crimes' unit at the police department where she previously worked. Planting a device is not as easy as it appears on television unless a police agency does it under court order. Finding such a device would be a more daunting task. Locating a wired device is somewhat more straightforward, but the process is tedious and time-consuming.

I used the RF detector through the entire war room, paying specific attention to any potential power sources such as outlets, light fixtures, and lamps. The detector is about the size and shape of a walkie-talkie and has the capabilities to scan the most common "bugging" frequencies from 30 to 50 MHz and 88 through 108 MHz. It locates wireless bugs by emitting a high-pitched noise that increases in intensity as it gets closer to a transmitter. If the bug is hard-wired, however, only a physical search would find it.

Neither of us found anything, either wireless or hard-wired, anywhere in the war room.

Afterward, I returned the earlier call from Detective Jenkins. As the desk clerk was unable to locate him, he took my name and phone number, promising he would have him return my call. Less than five minutes later, my telephone rang, and an irascible Detective Jenkins greeted me on the other end of the line.

"It's about time you decided to return my call."

"I'm sorry, Ron, we've been swamped," I said as I placed the phone on speaker.

"You sure have been busy. You and Gina certainly have been stirring the pot quite a bit, according to my boss, the district attorney, and let's not forget the fine folks from the United States government. I've got more people crawling up my ass than I've ever had in my life, and they all want to shut you guys down or have you arrested and charged with obstruction of justice, among other things."

"Marvelous."

"Agents Ted Roberts and Marcy Liu want the journal that Speirs supposedly had with him when he met his demise, and they want us to bring you and Gina in for questioning about his death. They also want to know about your presence at the Bayfront murder scene."

I heard all of this from Jim at the marina, I thought to myself.

"And, as if that's not enough, the London police finally verified that the murder victim believed to be Sadie Cooper from Lakewood is definitely not her," he added.

"Who was it?

"A woman named Annie Chapman," Ron said.

"You're kidding, right?" Gina asked with a loud chuckle.

"No, I'm not. Why, is that so funny?"

"That was the name of one of the victims of Jack the Ripper," Gina replied.

"What? How would you even know that?" Ron pressed Gina. "Never mind, don't tell me, I don't want to know."

"What can I say? I've read a lot about the Whitechapel murders. What's the story behind the identification?"

"I told you before that the London police weren't satisfied about the identity of Cooper's body and the police there were keeping her on ice for the requisite time. When the news that a woman's body was found cycled through the newspapers and television over there, a woman who claimed to be the dead woman's sister identified the body as Annie Chapman. She claims that her sister had gone missing several days earlier and provided pretty compelling evidence that it's not the body of Ms. Cooper. The surviving sister came forward the day before her sister's body was to be unceremoniously buried."

"Annie Chapman's sister. She must be pretty old," Gina said. "It sounds like a sick joke."

"C'mon, Chapman, that name can't be that uncommon," Ron said.

"Agreed, but what are the odds? Who has the ability to get away with something like this? Just think about it," Gina added. "There's got to be a message in that for us. The Jack the Ripper case is still officially unsolved a century later. As I recall from our previous conversation, the alleged murderer's name is Andrew Forsythe, correct?"

"Correct."

"He definitely hung himself and is absolutely dead and buried, correct?"

"Yes, that's right."

"That's all very convenient, wouldn't you say? Now your department doesn't have to reopen an investigation into her accident in Lakewood or her husband's death. No more questions. Case still closed, nice and tidy, as everyone likes it."

"There's still an issue of Sadie Cooper's passport and your business cards."

"Well, I'm sure that will readily be explained, or perhaps left unaddressed now that the case is closed. As I said, nice and tidy."

"You know, there's a lot of screwy stuff going on, and your names come up almost every damn time."

"What do you want us to do, Ron?"

The conversation ended in a ball of frustration deeply felt by all three of us. I felt terrible that Ron Jenkins has been forced into the unenviable task of balancing his job and our long-standing friendship. Nonetheless, he knows what's at stake, and has done an excellent job running interference on our behalf as much as he could.

Before the conversation concluded, however, he suggested that we turn over Speirs' journal after we had the chance to elicit as much information as possible from the book. Again, he cautioned us to be careful as we seemed to be stepping on the toes of some pretty powerful people. He promised to keep us informed about any new developments and asked that we keep him in the loop as well, further promising to keep whatever information we provided to him in confidence. He was able to do so as he knew that we would never place him in a bad position within his department.

Before the hastily scheduled meeting, Gina said that she wasn't surprised that the feds were after the journal and was not too bothered about the threats to review and pull our license. "They're just using that as leverage."

"I'm confused about Sadie Cooper, though," Gina said. "That victim identification is pretty far out there. Could it be Sadie Cooper they found or is that sister identification of the body actually legit?"

"I've got a better question for you. Seriously, who remembers the names of victims from a hundred-year-old murder case, even if it is the high-profile Jack the Ripper case."

"I think you'd be surprised. Plus, I think that's a devious yet subtle message to anyone poking around. You know that Jack the Ripper not only murdered his victims, but tortured them? Removed their organs?"

"Sounds familiar. But a hundred years later, what does it matter?"

"Don't you think it could be a message? I'm not convinced it was Sadie Cooper. Maybe it was her sending the message?"

"Well, at this point, I wouldn't rule anything out. Sadie seems to have more lives than a cat," I replied. "Considering what we've experienced here, there are more than a few people who want to see Sadie dead. If she's on the side of good, maybe she's got a list of her own. Either way, I have an uneasy feeling that we're going to find out before this is all over."

IN THE DARK OF NIGHT

Chapter 27

Annie arrived first. She knocked at the back door and was let inside by Gina. Figuring we could use all the help we could get, Gina told me that she asked her to attend tonight. Before Jim arrived, Gina and I updated Annie on the events of the day.

"Unfortunately, we couldn't get Professor Wolfram here tonight. He said that he was making progress on the journal and didn't want to stop. He said that if we needed him, we should conference him in by telephone. We don't want to rush him, and he already knows how important and time-sensitive this project is to us. We'll see what Jim has to say when he gets here."

A few minutes before eight, Jim knocked at the back door. After making sure it was him, Gina let him inside. They both walked into the war room where I had all of the files ready for review. I already added a copy of Speirs' journal to the package intended for the attorney general.

Less than 30 minutes into what we hoped would be our final meeting of the Carr Club, Jim's pager went off. The alert was from his house. As soon as Jim looked at the message, he jumped up and lunged for my desk phone, quickly pressing the numbers to his home. The call was answered right away, and a look of horror replaced the need for any words to be spoken. "I'll be right there."

"Marc, call Lakewood Ambulance, tell them to get to my house right away. There's something wrong with my wife, she's having severe stomach pains and is on the verge of passing out. She sounds bad and needs to get to the hospital right away. I'm headed to my house now. I'll call you when I know what's going on," Jim barked as he grabbed his keys and ran out the back door.

I called the emergency number for the ambulance service, which I knew from my time working there. Russ was on duty and answered the call, took the address, and knowing him as I do, was handling the call it as if was a member of his own family.

Gina, Annie, and I attempted to finish what we initially set out to do in

Jim's absence. After a half-hour of working in virtual silence, we realized that we weren't going to get anything done. Annie offered to go to the hospital to keep Jim company, but we all decided against it until we had more information. It was just before nine when Annie left, leaving Gina alone with me in my apartment.

I turned to Gina, not knowing what to say. The intensity of the last several days suddenly came down upon her like a mental battering ram. She collapsed back on the leather sofa and began to sob. "Marc, what's happening to us? I've never felt so much evil and so afraid before in my life. I don't know if I can take it anymore." I walked over and put my arm around across her shoulders in a compassionate attempt to console her. She buried her face in my chest and continued to cry until she seemingly ran out of tears.

"Gina, please go into my bedroom, lay down and get some rest. I'll wake you as soon as I find anything out." She grabbed my arm, "Please don't leave me."

I considered going to St. Elizabeth Hospital to keep vigil with Jim but figured that he would still be in the exam room with his wife and that I would not be permitted to be with him.

"Please, don't leave me, Marc," Gina again pleaded as I walked her into my room. Her eyes were red and glassy, amplified by the dark circles under them. I assured her that I wasn't going anywhere and would be in my office until I heard something.

"No, please stay with me. Right here with me," she begged. I gently helped her into the bed and walked around to the other side and laid next to her. We were both mentally and physically drained. She held onto my arm and drifted off into much-needed sleep, beating me by only a minute or two at most.

Chapter 28

Tuesday, September 15, 1987

I was jarred awake by the phone ringing on my nightstand. I looked at the digital clock next to it, and although my eyes were still not adjusted to the darkness, the red digits brightly displayed 4:19 a.m. "This is Marc," I answered, trying to sound as alert as possible.

"It's Jim. They put Angie through a bunch of tests, and although it's inconclusive, they think that she was poisoned."

"Poisoned? How? With what?"

"They don't know exactly how or even what, at least not with any degree of certainty. The doctors did a battery of tests and a toxicology screen, but everything came back clean. We're still waiting on the results of some additional blood work to come back, but the admitting physician believes that some kind of toxic substance was introduced orally, through something she either ate or drank."

"What symptoms did she have besides stomach pain? What's her condition now?"

"When I got home, I found her curled up on the kitchen floor, barely conscious. The ambulance arrived seconds later. She was able to tell me that she began to feel nauseous, which was followed by increasingly severe abdominal cramps. Then she had what appeared to be a seizure in the ambulance on the way to the hospital. Her heart rhythm was out of sync when they connected her to a monitor. They started an IV and gave her a bunch of medicine. I don't know what all they gave her, but they got her heart rhythm back to normal and seemed to stabilize her. Now they're just waiting on the lab results."

"Do you want me to come down?" I asked.

"No, visitors are restricted to immediate family only, and only for short intervals. My daughter Daria and her husband are with me now. My other two children will be here soon."

"Is there anything I can do?"

"No, but thanks. Once things settle down a bit, I'll go back home to change clothes and make sure Oscar is okay. I'll have plenty of help from my kids too."

I was trying desperately to make sense of what I was hearing. "Jim, could it be food poisoning? I mean, what else could it be? You don't think that she was deliberately poisoned, do you?"

"The doctor has all but ruled out traditional food poisoning, or what we would normally consider food poisoning if that makes sense."

"I guess it does, but poisoning by other means, that seems rather unusual, don't you think?"

"I don't know what to think. I really won't know until the doctors can identify what we're dealing with here."

"Please do me a favor, Jim. As soon as you know anything, please let me know. Gina and I are at your service. We'll do anything for you and Angie."

"You can do something for us right now. Pray. Please pray as you've never prayed before. I'll call you later." Jim's voice was shaky as he conveyed his request and hung up without saying anything more.

Gina was awakened by the phone and heard most of my part of the conversation and some of his. She sat up on her elbows and listened as I explained what I understood the situation to be. When I was finished, Gina silently pulled me over to her side, causing both of us to slide off of the bed in a single motion. I suddenly found myself on my knees next to Gina with our elbows resting on the bed, and we began praying for Angie's recovery, strength for Jim, and God's guidance for the two of us.

****

It was four hours later when Jim called from the hospital with an update about Angie. I was sleeping in my office chair where I moved earlier, and Gina was still asleep in my bed. Angie's condition was improving, and Jim sounded much better and more relieved compared to our last conversation. He explained that tests taken by the admitting physician found that Angie ingested a significant but non-lethal dose of Lycorine, a substance that comes from the Narcissus plant.

"The narcissist plant?" I asked.

"No," Jim replied with a slight chuckle. "The Narcissus plant, it's a certain type of daffodil. The toxicity is mainly found in the bulbs. The weird thing is that shortly after I called you, another doctor was just getting ready to leave the hospital after handling a new admission. He was looking at Angie's records and lab results at the request of the admitting doctor and offhandedly said that it reminded him of how sick his dog became this past spring when he got into a flower patch. His puppy dug into a patch of daffodils and chewed on the bulbs. He took his dog to the vet, and from all of the information provided, it was evident that the pup got sick from ingesting parts of the bulbs. From there, Angie's doctor ran additional tests and identified the properties of Lycorine. It's not effective as a poison to humans, but it will make you pretty sick, and depending on the dose, it could cause liver problems."

"That's pretty bizarre and hard to believe. How did this happen? I'm no gardener, but I do know that it's not spring, and daffodils are not in bloom. Secondly, I can't imagine Angie digging around in the garden chewing on daffodil bulbs like the doc's puppy," I said in an attempt to sound a bit more light-hearted and hopeful.

"The doctor talked to Angie. She told him that last evening, Peggy brought over some snack food, a 'care basket' of sorts, because, you know, I've been working late and stuff. She brought a bottle of wine, some homemade bagel chips, and an onion dip. Peggy is quite the little homemaker and cook. She's also an avid gardener and raises a variety of plants and flowers. I know how crazy this sounds, but it's possible that what Peggy thought were onions were these toxic bulbs, especially if she stored them near each other. She could have used them by mistake as they look very similar. Peggy left, and Angie started to feel sick rather quickly, and you know the rest."

"Oh, come on, that just sounds—I don't know how that sounds. Ridiculous comes to mind. Are the doctor's sure? I'm having a hard time wrapping my head around this whole thing, Jim."

"Yeah, well, you're not alone. The doctor said that he's never seen a case like this. He even called Poison Control for additional information. About 15 minutes ago, he called the police and asked them to meet Daria at the house, hoping to find any leftover food and wine for additional testing, just to be sure. They are also checking on Peggy to see whether she is suffering from any similar problems. I haven't heard anything yet, but I'll let you know when I do. I think it's fairly good news."

"Why did they call the police?" I asked.

"I asked the same thing. The doctor said it's primarily a hospital liability issue, and police are also tasked to perform wellness checks in cases like these. It's the hospital's way to cover their backside sort of thing, I suppose."

I wrote down what I could on a legal pad during our conversation and looked down at the paper. Food from Peggy. Lycorine. Narcissus plant. Daffodils. Onion dip. Avid gardener. Wine. Bulbs may be confused with onions. It didn't help because I was having a difficult time understanding how anything like this could happen.

The phone call from Jim awakened Gina, who was now sitting in the chair across from my desk. We were both wearing the same clothes from yesterday, and both of us were still hazy from the little sleep we got. I explained what I knew from Jim, and Gina was equally puzzled.

"I'll make us some coffee, maybe that will help," she said.

"Yeah, maybe."

Gina reappeared in the war room, carrying two mugs of coffee. "I feel like I'm a character in the plot of an Agatha Christie novel," Gina said, "although the various poisons she uses are much more lethal in her books. At least she uses some of the more traditional poisons too."

"That's what makes this bizarre. If this was an attempt to poison Angie, it certainly wasn't a very good one. Maybe it was an accident or a mix-up," I said. "I suppose it could happen. I'm not exactly sure how, but I suppose it can't be ruled out. What purpose would this otherwise serve? All that was accomplished, aside from making Angie sick, was that it caused all of us a bit of a scare and a delay."

"If you don't mind, I'm going to shower and try to clear my head. I've got one more change of clothes from my bag, Gina said, then I'm either going to have to go back home, or you'll have to take me clothes shopping."

"Go ahead and jump in the shower. I'll be right behind you." As soon as I said that, Gina shot me a sideways glance.

"I guess that came out wrong. You know what I mean. I'll shower after you're done." For the first time in a while, we both smiled at the same time.

After both of us were once again presentable, Gina and I decided to finish what we barely started last night before Jim had to leave and we sent Annie home. Taking our usual places, Gina sat on the leather sofa and I sat on my office chair.

"Marc, I just want you to know how much I appreciate all you've done for me. You've made sure I've felt at home and have taken great care of me. I don't know how I'll ever be able to repay you," Gina said.

"None is necessary. It's what friends and partners do."

Gina spotted Jim's pile of papers on the floor next to the chair where he sat the previous evening. "This incident with Angie isn't sitting well with me. What you said about creating a scare and causing a delay is making me think."

"Nothing that happened over the last ten days is sitting well with me either," I said as I walked into the kitchen for more coffee. Just then, the telephone rang. Gina sprang up and answered it. When I returned to the war room, she was sitting at my desk, cradling the handset between her shoulder and ear and writing notes on the legal pad I had left. I could tell from her side of the conversation that she was speaking with Professor Wolfram.

"Okay, professor, thank you. We'll leave right now." Gina picked up the pad, pen, and her purse and told me to drive. "Wolfram's got a lot to tell us, and he sounded as freaked out as someone like him could be."

"Marvelous," I uttered.

IN THE DARK OF NIGHT

Chapter 29

The professor opened the door for us before we even had the chance to knock or ring the bell. "Come this way," he motioned. I noticed that the professor was dressed in the same clothes he had on when we first met him yesterday. We followed him into his study where he had the journal positioned in the center of the large mahogany table, along with several other and much larger reference type books opened around it. A table-top style lighted magnifying glass, thin fabric gloves, a note pad, and several pencils were also on top of the table.

"After you left yesterday, Professor Myers stayed and we collaborated for a few hours to review the book and its contents. He confirmed the translations of some of the more traditional and recent words and phrases written inside, specifically those written in Latin and Greek. Of special interest to me are the symbols, archaic phrases, and words written in this journal and how they appear to have specific and even dual meanings and purposes. I suspect what might be of special interest to you are the rudimentary maps and names this book contains. Professor Myers told me that this book is somehow related to a murder investigation you are conducting, is that correct?"

"Yes, but names and maps?" I looked at Gina, who told the professor that we did not see anything that resembled maps or any names.

"They're encoded in here, but you have to understand what you're looking at, and equally important, what you're looking for. I'll spare you much of the scholarly commentary on ancient historical writings, as I'm not sure you're that interested in the origins of Futhark, more commonly called the runic alphabet or its more mundane uses. Nonetheless, you do need to understand a bit about the symbols on runestones and talisman-type objects and the thaumaturgical, or supernatural formulas, they were said to possess."

My blank stare in response to what he just said was not lost on the professor. He smiled at me and offered to explain what he meant in plain language.

Professor Wolfram explained some of the history of this ancient language and began discussing the debate among historians about the time when runes first came into use and its relationship to Latin. I nudged him back into the present with my stare.

"For the sake of relevance, I suggest we skip ahead to this century. Specifically, I'm talking about the more modern uses of the runic alphabet, of which you're more likely familiar and contextually used in this journal. For example, take a look at this and tell me if you've seen this anywhere before." The professor pointed to an embossed portion of the leather cover and asked if we recognized the symbol. It was worn and weathered and flattened through age and use. Both Gina and I hesitated before we answered as if we were being quizzed for a class grade.

"Don't worry," Professor Wolfram said slyly, "the questions will only get harder as we continue."

"It looks like a thick bolt of lightning, but it's difficult to tell because of the condition of the cover," I finally said.

I was partially correct. The symbol embossed into the upper right portion of the cover contained two identical bolts of lightning, or what is known as the sig rune. The professor explained that symbol is the runic insignia of the Schutzstaffel, or the Nazi SS. "You've probably seen pictures of this symbol on certain Nazi helmets and uniforms, most likely in history books or movies," Professor Wolfram explained.

"Now, look at this and tell me what you see." The professor pointed to an entry in the journal the resembled a 1960s style peace sign. Both Gina and I replied similarly and in near unison to his question.

"It's known in rune as the Tod, which was a symbol used by the Nazi SS to represent death on documents or other objects. Twenty years ago in the 1960s, young people across campuses and just about everywhere carried it on signs as a peace symbol, clueless about its history. It's also identified as the 'Cross of Nero,' an upside-down or broken cross that signifies the defeat of Christianity among those who engage in the occult."

"So, are you saying that the man who owned this journal was a Nazi?" I asked.

"It's far from being that simple," Professor Wolfram replied. "How well do you two know your history? Are you familiar with the occult practices of the Nazis, or the various initiatives used by our government to bring Nazi scientists to the United States after World War II?"

"Do you mean 'Operation Paperclip?'" Gina asked.

"Ah, so you do know your history!"

"Not much more than that, which is the reason we're here," I added.

"This also goes far beyond 'Operation Paperclip,' which was the secret government initiative that brought over 1,500 Nazi scientists into the United States. There's a natural evolution of government programs that one can follow in this journal if one knows where to look. It contains an interesting application of other secret black projects of the government, including the MKUltra program of mind control."

"Mind control?" Gina and I looked at each other, sharing an absolute vindication that neither one of us was 'unhinged.' At that moment, we knew Professor Wolfram would be a tremendous asset to us as we unraveled some of the most shocking crimes that have taken place in Lakewood and elsewhere. We told him as much and explained our findings since we first opened a case file on the murder of my uncle last spring. Our narration provided not only clarification to his question about us investigating a murder, but even more context to the journal he inspected. We explained that our investigation, which began with the murder of my uncle five years ago, branched off into the areas that include satanic ritual abuse, or commonly referenced as SRA, human and child sex trafficking, and even rituals being conducted here in Lakewood.

The professor nodded his head and stated that he felt that might be the case. Furthermore, he noted that this journal seems to contain a historical record, even if only a partial description of such activities.

"Wait, do you mean that this journal contains records of human sacrifices, the dates, and names? Things like that?"

"Yes, and even more, which is the reason I'm positive that this journal is being sought."

Even with the professor's acceptance, I was more than a little hesitant to mention our discovery of photographs of men in robes seemingly engaged in human sacrifice and the accounts of sexual perversions that went along with them. As it happened, I didn't have to be hesitant as Gina brought up the subject directly with him, describing in gory detail the photographs and the accounts of torture and sacrifice.

"None of that surprises me at all," the professor responded. "I don't know how much you know about my work, but I conducted research in Egypt for about five years. There, I found a connection to the occult practices of the Nazis, which led me to Germany. I stood inside the castle of Wewelsburg where Heinrich Himmler, who was most dedicated to practicing the occult, dedicated the structure as the 'spiritual center' of the world. A lot of bad things happened there when Himmler used the castle as his headquarters and center of power for the Nazi SS. It was following my experiences there that I returned to the United States. I'm in the process of writing a book on this very subject."

"Professor, you mentioned mind control. It seems like a big leap from the Nazi practices you described. How does that apply here?" Gina asked.

The professor explained that peripheral overlapping philosophies are driving an occult agenda. He talked about the philosophy of Friedrich Nietzsche of Übermensch, something called *Thus Spoke Zarathustra*, the Nazi version of Übermensch and the occult desire of men to become gods. He explained that to create a superior, god-like race, many people had to be exterminated. Others had to be in control, while others still had to be controlled. To achieve world domination by a satanic power, various programs and rituals were introduced and practiced by people who, for example, worshipped Satan as their god. This involved satanic ceremonies and even human sacrifice, where the practitioners obtained power from the act of the sacrifice as well as consuming the blood and internal organs of their victims.

"That's hard to believe that would exist today," I said.

"It might be hard to believe, but if I'm correct, and I am, you've got documentation of these very practices within this journal," he replied. "That's why I wanted to meet you right away. This journal contains more than ancient symbols. It also contains the identities of individuals who either were or are involved in such practices, names of victims, and at least one location where such death rituals were held."

"Do you have the names?" Gina asked.

"It's not quite that easy, but I think I can identify them with more documentation and corroborative research. Look at this page. It's a list of names written in code based on the runic alphabet. There are 13 names on this page, one per line."

"Okay, I see it."

"Do you see the symbol next to each name?"

"Yes, the peace symbol. What did you call it, a Tod?"

"That's correct. That suggests each one of those people are dead."

"What about the ritual location? Is it just one location or more than one?"

"Just one as far as I can tell, at least right now, identified by the two drawings in the back of the journal. They are the most recent drawings. Finding the ritual location might be a bit easier than identifying the people," he replied, "and it's going to take a bit of puzzle-solving to pinpoint the precise spot. I've already identified it as being in this county and near the state line by using old maps copied from the courthouse and brought back to me by my intern."

"How much longer do you need, and what can we do to help?" I asked.

"When I left Germany, I promised myself that I would not get involved in this type of research again. After seeing this journal, I've decided to make an exception."

"May I inquire as to what changed your mind after seeing this book?" Gina delicately asked.

"There are references to the sacrificing of children. Young children. The blood of the innocent. I cannot and will not turn my back on that."

After a period of uncomfortable silence, Professor Wolfram explained that it would benefit him to see all of the research and field investigations we had done to add context to the more recent entries made by Roland Speirs. We explained to him the voluminous amount of documentation and asked if he would mind if he could visit us in the war room. We offered to pay a consultation fee if he requested it. He declined payment but accepted the offer to meet. "I'd feel insulted if you didn't ask."

Before we left, we recounted the circumstances surrounding the demise of Roland Speirs, and his description of other "soldiers" like him. We also told him that Speirs repeated "Beta, Delta, and Omega" before gruesomely taking his own life.

The professor opened the book to the last page and pointed to the Greek symbols represented by those words. "He was conveying to you that he concluded his mission," Wolfram said.

"I'd say that was a reference to him being a participant of the MKUltra program. As far as more "soldiers" walking around out there, or people like him, you can count on that. Without intense investigation and understanding what to look for, you might never know who they are until it's too late."

"I'm sure Jim will agree, and Marc concurs that we'll give you complete access to all of the documentation and evidence we've collected. How soon can you meet us at the war room, and how long do you think you would need?" Gina asked.

"How long, you ask?" The professor looked down at his table and thought for a moment. "That depends. As to how soon, well, considering what's at stake, what I've already seen, and the events you described, we better make it as soon as possible. I can clear my schedule and start right away, which I think would be most appropriate. I have a feeling that every day that goes by that this journal remains out of the hands of whoever is looking for it, the more dangerous things will become. As it stands right now, there is one hell of an intense storm brewing, and you guys are directly in its path."

"Marvelous," I said, recalling similar words spoken and thinking that we're already in a storm.

"Let's make our initial meeting later today if you are free, unless you think that's too ambitious," Gina said.

"Not at all. I'll be at your place at 7:00 p.m."

Chapter 30

We left the professor's residence and drove to Gina's so she could pack some more clothes, as we decided it would be best if she stayed with me for a few more days. Although she is fiercely independent and I prefer solitude, it just made sense with all of the hours we've been putting in to prepare the information for submission to the state Attorney General.

While I double-checked the exterior of her residence, Gina checked in with the office and also called her mother to check on her daughter. Everything appeared to be in order and untouched, inside and out. All was well with Gina's daughter, and it was quiet at the office. Gina brought Annie up to date about our meeting with Professor Wolfram and invited her to the impromptu meeting this evening.

Considering our schedule, Gina asked Annie to come after she closed the office and to stop at the diner on her way over for the three of us. When Annie asked Gina what we would like, Gina told her, "Surprise us. Anything quick will do."

As we drove back to my apartment, I made a slight detour and stopped at the spot at the Lakewood Marina where Deana and I had stopped several times before during her lunch breaks. I drove my car into the parking spot I previously staked out and used as it offered one of the best views of the bay and provided sufficient privacy for whatever one might intend. "Why are you stopping here?" Gina asked.

"I bring Deana here sometimes. Once in a while, I stop here by myself for the serenity. I thought that this would give us a few minutes to think without the mental clutter and to talk," I said. "It also has the bonus of allowing us to determine whether we're being followed."

"Are we being followed?"

"Not that I can see."

"Why not?" Gina asked. The way she asked the question was almost comical, but it is a legitimate question. "That's another thing that's been bothering me. What happened to our tails from Sunday? Where do you think

Porter Landers and his sidekick are, and what are they doing here in Lakewood?"

"I don't know, but we're going to find out. This time, I want it to be on our terms when we do," I said.

We talked for a half-hour about the case and our strategy going forward, yet again rehashing the events of the last nine days. It seemed like the compression of nine months of surreal events and raw emotions.

We're missing something, I thought. Everything we experienced had taken an emotional toll on both of us, and we were both struggling to stay grounded in facts and reality. It was a difficult task at best, especially when emotions run high and are charged by the hideous nature of crimes against children and the innocent. A stillness existed between us for an extended period.

"You miss her, don't you?" Gina asked, breaking the silence.

"What?"

"You're afraid that you're going to lose her, aren't you?"

"I don't want to think about that right now. I can't afford to think about that right now."

Gina placed her hand on my shoulder and said, "She'll be back."

"And if not?"

Gina didn't respond, at least not with words. She moved her hand to the back of my neck and drew my head close to hers, my face to hers, our lips first touching and then joining with an animalistic fury that was reciprocal, followed by a tender and compassionate embrace.

"I'm sorry, Marc," Gina whispered as she pulled back. Her eyes were quickly welling up with tears. "It's just that we've been through so much together. Who do we have to talk to, except to each other? Who do we have that could understand about any of this?" She asked as a single tear streamed down her cheek.

I gently wiped the tear away and placed my finger over her lips, conveying that I understood. "No apology necessary."

Yet another period of silence and stillness enveloped us. I placed my arm around Gina's shoulders, allowing her head to rest on my chest for as long as she needed. The beauty of the waterfront and the movement of wildlife in front of us was serene and mesmerizing. It served as a stark contrast to the ugliness of the blood, gore, and pure evil that seemed to encompass our lives.

IN THE DARK OF NIGHT

Chapter 31

The Meeting with the Professor

Annie left the office shortly after 5:00 p.m. and was at my apartment 45 minutes later, carrying a grease-stained bag of six chili dogs and three orders of fries. "The dinner of champions," Gina remarked as we dug into the food without regard to our intestinal well-being. We had just enough time to eat, clean up, and prepare for our meeting.

Annie talked to Jim at the hospital, who said that Angie was feeling much better and should be released tomorrow. Considering the news, Annie told Jim about the meeting tonight with the professor. "I want to be there," he replied.

Professor Wolfram arrived promptly at 7:00 p.m., followed by Jim Carr less than a minute later. Jim looked as exhausted as he felt.

"How's Angie?" Gina immediately asked Jim.

"Much better and believe it or not, her doctor said that he would probably release her tomorrow. She's understandably tired and wanted to sleep, so I said goodnight to her early and decided to come right over. I'm beat myself, so I won't be staying long. That was quite a scare."

"What about Peggy, your neighbor?"

"She's fine. She just drank a glass of wine but didn't eat, so she was spared from her own mistake."

Gina introduced Jim to the professor, who overheard the conversation about his wife. Inquiring further, Jim provided the professor with a general overview of the events of the previous evening.

"Please forgive me if I'm out of line for asking this, but did I hear you correctly when you said she was poisoned by the Narcissus plant?"

Jim explained the situation in more detail. "Why do you ask?"

Wolfram said that he had seen an incident involving the Narcissus plant while he was in North Africa.

"Although it is not a plant commonly used as a poison, it does have its place in the occult and specifically, in witchcraft. Persephone, the queen of the underworld according to Greek mythology, was distracted by the beauty of the plant, which enabled her ultimate abduction by Hades. It's pretty obscure and merely anecdotal, but I thought it was worth mentioning considering why I'm here," he said.

"You don't think Peggy would intentionally use it to poison my wife, do you?" Jim asked.

"Frankly, I've never seen or heard of the bulb from that plant used as an intentional toxin. Domestic animals that dig up a garden bed and consume enough of it, yes, it can be fatal, but rarely humans. However, I would suspect that it would be rather difficult to diagnose and cause someone a lot of pain and a good scare, just for that reason. I don't know or don't know enough yet. The entire incident does seem rather odd," the professor added.

"Odd doesn't even begin to describe it," Jim said.

"On another unpleasant note," Jim began and halted as he pulled an envelope from his jacket pocket. He removed a two-page report, stapled at the upper left corner, from the envelope. The FBI logo was visible on top of the front page, and what appeared to be a graph with numbers and percentages was visible through the back of the second page.

"I just received this from Ed Gajewski, my friend from Quantico. It contains a summary analysis of the composition of the medium used to write the letter sent to Marc."

"What letter?" Professor Wolfram asked.

I explained the circumstances surrounding the letter to Wolfram, adding that I didn't want to disrupt his analysis of the journal unnecessarily. I handed him a copy from my desk, which he read while Jim was about to reveal the findings from the FBI lab.

"I'm not going to read all of this to you. I'll just give you the sick and twisted bottom line. The ink is not ink at all, but a concoction of human and animal blood, breast milk, and seminal fluid. The blood gave the ink its rust-like color, which was slightly lightened by the inclusion of the other components."

The room went completely still as no one moved upon hearing Jim's words.

"Eww," Annie uttered with repulsion.

"That's perverse," Gina added.

"Perverse but not without precedent, isn't that correct, Mr. Carr?" Professor Wolfram asked while looking directly at him, already knowing the answer. "I'm sure this is not the first time the FBI has identified this type of emulsion or a very similar ratio of components."

"You're right, but how did you know? That's law enforcement sensitive information that's not disseminated outside of certain divisions within the bureau."

"Perhaps, but it's not new. It's been used in one form or another in occult ceremonies since the dawn of time. Your friend from the FBI probably told you their lab obtained and processed several such mixtures from at least a dozen or so crime scenes over the last few decades."

"That's right. It's usually found at murder scenes involving victim mutilation or where there's a sexual component in the murder."

"Especially piquerism," Wolfram stated with authority.

"Yes, according to the unofficial analysis of the bureau profilers."

"Piquerism?" I asked.

"Yes. It's a form of sadism or sadistic torture where the perpetrator derives sexual satisfaction by stabbing another person, often to death."

"Now, that's just marvelous."

"I should also tell you that the analyzed ink contained the concoction of bodily fluids and was used as the medium of choice for a few entries in the journal."

"Unreal," Gina uttered.

"Very real," the professor replied. "Are you starting to see a pattern here?"

"What's your initial assessment of the letter's message?" I asked.

Wolfram spent a few minutes reviewing the letter.

"For starters, do you see the part where it says 'dark to light?' That's a reference to a black light, and bodily fluids glow under a black light. Like the letter, certain entries in the journal were written using the same or similar kind of writing medium."

He then walked to my desk, where he picked up the journal.

"Do you see this star inside the circle drawn at the bottom of the letter?" He asked and pointed to the symbol. "It's an inverted pentagram that represents the Baphomet. It is also used as a symbol of authority by Satanists. You're dealing with some hardcore Satanists and not 'posers' or 'dabblers' by any means. This is authentic. Do you know who wrote this letter to you?"

"I was hoping you might shed some light on that, professor."

Without addressing my concern about who wrote the letter, he asked if I had a commercial calendar he could see.

I reached into a drawer of my desk and handed him my Daytimer datebook. He looked through the section that contained holidays and other significant dates.

"According to this letter, there will be at least three ritualistic killings done by this satanic group of killers before September 23rd, which is the Autumnal Equinox referenced in this letter."

"You were right, Annie," I said.

"This is one time I wish I wasn't," she replied.

"Do you think that the three ritualistic killings mentioned in the letter include Jacob Tingsley, the boy whose body was found over the Labor Day weekend?" Gina asked. "It was written before the murder," she added.

"It's possible, and I would say it's even probable," Wolfram stated. "Especially when one considers the manner that the boy's body was staged."

"Do you think the writer wants to be caught? I mean, why write a letter like this that tells us there will be three murders if there isn't even the slightest desire of being stopped?" Gina asked.

"It's a taunt. The writer wants you to know that there will be three ritual murders. They want you to believe that there's not a damn thing you can do about it," Wolfram said. "There's another part to that as well. They believe that if they tell you what they intend to do and do it, the murders are on you as they 'told' you, and by not stopping them, you gave them your tacit approval."

An uncomfortable silence hung in the air as everyone seemed to contemplate additional deaths.

"So, we've got about a week to save at least two lives," I said.

"Less than that, I'm afraid. There's the process of selection and abduction of the victims. That could whittle the time down by a few days. We don't have much time at all."

IN THE DARK OF NIGHT

Chapter 32

"What can you tell us about Speirs' journal?"

"The book was created or bound sometime around the turn of the century," he said as he paced around the room like he was giving a private lecture to his students. "The earliest writings also seem to match that period in terms of the style of language that was used. As I already said, one of the mediums used to make a few of the entries matches that of the letter. Other entries were written by pencil and normal ink."

"I've determined that at least three different people owned the book, perhaps passed down generationally. It contains three distinct types of coded writing, possibly from its three different authors or owners. I'm unsure whether the book was kept within a single family or bloodline if you will, or its recipients were chosen using some other criteria. Regardless, its theme is consistent throughout, which makes it an occult death book, or some might call it a book of the dead."

Professor Wolfram continued. "I say that some might call it the book of the dead as it contains a few seemingly obligatory passages from the *Necronomicon*, also known by that name. Have either of you heard of that work?"

"No," Gina and I replied in near unison. Jim also shook his head.

"As I said, the *Necronomicon* is also known as *The Book of the Dead*. It is purportedly a fictional book referenced by several authors of horror stories and grimoire tales, initially referenced by writer H.P. Lovecraft in the 1920s. The book has since taken on a life of its own, no pun intended, and has been the subject of much lore in the occult world."

"That aside, I suppose you've seen the contents of the book, including some of the drawings and symbols." Everyone nodded in unison. By this time, the professor was wearing his protective gloves and had his magnifying glass in hand.

He identified each of the several drawings, including a neatly drawn representation of the Baphomet, also known as the Goat of Mendes, which further represents the male, female, and animal in one. The Baphomet head also sketched separately in the front part of the journal on the opposite page of the full figure, is also considered the universal symbol of Satan.

"Professor, we've seen that symbol several times before in this case. That particular symbol was a pendant made from .999 gold and was given to us by Sadie Cooper. The SS marking you earlier described was etched on the back of the pendant. That was also a pendant worn by Porter Landers on a chain around his neck," I added.

"May I see the artifact that was given to you by Ms. Cooper?"

"Unfortunately, it was taken in a burglary as we prepared to provide our evidence to the task force newly formed by the Attorney General."

"When was this?"

"On Labor Day. We have color photographs if they will help."

"Sure, I'll look at the pictures, but I will tell you that it's significant that the pendant was stolen."

"How so?"

"The Baphomet pendant, depending upon its provenance, is said to amplify the 'powers' of the wearer. Again, I must remind you that it's not important whether you believe it, but what the occultist or Satanist believes."

I retrieved two color photographs of the pendant and placed them down in front of the professor. "Oh yes, yes indeed, this is an authentic rendition of Baphomet. It was made by Nazi occultists based on the inscription on the obverse. You're dealing with satanism, Satanists and the evilest of evils that are related to the Nazi occultists, Heinrich Himmler, and the ceremonies at the castle of Wewelsburg. It also connects some of the writings in the journal and is consistent with my assessment of that book. I must tell you that people don't know what really went on at Wewelsburg. I think I've seen every documentary and read every history book on the subject, but nothing comes close to what I learned while I was there."

Professor Wolfram also identified a hagal rune drawn in the journal. It appeared to be one of the earlier drawings made. The hagal rune appeared as an "X" with a straight horizontal line drawn through the center where the two lines of the "X" meet and drawn inside a hexagram. "The last time I saw that was at the castle in Germany," Wolfram said. He added that not too many people are familiar with that rune or that it was one of five runes on a unique SS ring. The sixth symbol, and the largest and considered the centerpiece of the ring, was that of a skull.

"During your investigation, did you see anyone wearing a silver ring with a skull as the centerpiece?"

"Not that I recall, and I think I'd remember that," I said with assurance. "Why?"

"Interestingly, those rings were personally issued by Heinrich Himmler to SS members. There were between 14,500 to 15,000 authentic rings crafted. When the recipient of one of the rings died, that SS member's ring was sent back to Wewelsburg Castle, where it was placed into a coffin-like chest with others. Himmler ordered the production of the rings stopped in late 1944. Those that were returned upon his instructions were sealed into an unmarked hillside near the castle. However, nearly 4,000 of the remaining authentic rings are still missing. Some historians believe they exist as talismans and are worn by Satanists."

"Wait a second!" Gina exclaimed as she walked quickly to a nearby file cabinet. After searching through folders, she pulled out one with the label "Cooper, Benjamin" on the tab. She rifled through the photographs taken at the scene by police forensic examiners and pulled one out of the deceased man seated at his desk, his head, and left arm lying on the desktop. "Professor, may I borrow your magnifying glass?"

Gina carefully examined the photograph, looking at Cooper's partially visible left hand. It was partly out of frame as the subject of the camera was intended to be the head wound. "Professor, please take a look at this. Look at his left ring finger and tell me if this could be the ring you're talking about." The professor took the magnifying glass and the photograph from Gina, studying it for several seconds. "It could be or could be a fancy wedding ring. I can't tell from this angle. Do you have any better close-ups?" Gina looked through the file but could not find any other photograph that would permit positive identification. She removed the coroner's report from the folder and looked at the items found on the body. Among the things listed included an inventory of each item of clothing, shoes, and a well-worn ornate silver band with various symbols. It was further described in the coroner's report as blood-encrusted and present on the ring finger of his left hand. Gina removed a second piece of paper from the folder.

"Now look at this. Here's the inventory of items from the funeral home where the Cooper's body was taken. No wedding ring or ring of any kind appears on the inventory sheet." Gina said. "How does that happen?"

"It was either removed at the scene or the funeral home or somewhere in between," I said. "We're going to have to take another look at this later. It could be something, or perhaps nothing at all. Based on the fact that it's missing, though, I think it is something."

The professor agreed, then referred back to the journal. He again noted that the journal contains a coded list that contains the names of individuals who are a group of satanic practitioners. However, the characters were written and coded in such a way that only the author could readily identify. "I'll try to decipher these, but it will take more time than I'm afraid we have."

"Well, enough is enough. I'm taking our investigative findings to the attorney general's task force this week. I'll personally deliver it on Friday. Would you have the time to write a general summary of the journal that I could send with it? I think your credentials would go a long way in terms of the credibility of this information," Jim said, breaking the silence.

"Already done," the professor said as he produced a two-page typed document. "I was made aware of the deadline by Gina and Marc, and figured you would be asking for something, so I took the liberty of having this typed up. It affirms the authenticity of the journal and the fact that you are dealing with satanic rituals, Satanists, and; of course, murder, based on the entries contained in the journal. I provided my credentials separately. This is yours to keep, and I made a half-dozen copies for everyone here and myself," he said as he gave the original to Jim.

"Thanks, professor. If you all don't mind, I'm going home to get some sleep. I don't think Angie would be too happy if I overslept and was late picking her up from the hospital tomorrow. Please keep me posted. Marc, I'll call you tomorrow afternoon," Jim said, although he did not attempt to stand up from his chair.

Gina asked if there was any way to identify the ritual locations.

The professor pointed to two different pages, separated by several other pages between them, both containing two drawings of straight and curved lines.

"Here, put these two images side-by-side, you have a very rudimentary, recently drawn map that points to a ritual location. If we can locate this spot, we might be able to find sufficient evidence that would warrant an anthropology team from the college to investigate. It might be inevitable as our anthropology department is usually contacted by the police to assist in digging up bodies that have been long buried but found due to unplanned circumstances such as new construction and the like."

"Why are the drawings on two different pages?" I asked.

"You wouldn't want things to be easy, would you? Let's say, for example, that you and Gina just came across this book by accident. You would find it interesting, perhaps, but not instructive. It's simply the author's way of just making it more difficult to the uninitiated to make sense out of what they're looking at," Wolfram explained.

The professor pointed out symbols for water, which appear to be a small pond, and an access road from a paved or typically traveled road. The drawing also indicates a barn or similar structure near the pond. Another line appears to be a boundary marker, perhaps a county or even a state line. "It's definitely out in the sticks," he said. "It's far enough out of the way that there could still be markers on trees indicative of ritual sites or black masses. It's also possible that the bodies of additional ritual victims might be buried there or close to that location."

"As in victims of human sacrifice?"

"Either animal or human, or both, as both have been used in rituals."

"Human sacrifice? I don't mean to sound rude, but you do know that this is 1987. I could understand if you were talking about rituals taking place in ancient history, but now? This seems to be a far cry from modern-day sexual predators or even serial killers. But you're telling us that satanic masses complete with human sacrifice are still taking place? In the United States?

Perhaps even Lakewood?"

"Sadly, yes."

"Again, professor, with all due respect, you're not in Egypt, Africa, or some undeveloped region on the planet where these things happened in the past. Look around. We live in a normal city in an industrialized country."

"With all due respect to you, and with everything that you've personally seen and experienced so far, why are you having so much trouble accepting the fact that animal and even human sacrifices are still taking place? You attend a church, don't you?" he asked but continued without waiting for my response. "You're a Christian and believe in the God of the Bible. And so do I. That is your religion, and it's mine as well. It's your belief system. Mine too. You must understand that not everyone has the same set of beliefs as we do. Like different faiths, this is their belief and their church. I'm not here to convince you. I'm here to help you. If you believe in good, it stands to reason that you believe in evil."

Professor Wolfram continued his schooling. "You mentioned serial killers. Did you know that there have been ritualistic and even demonic elements found in some of the most prolific cases involving serial killers? Consider this as a refinement to those elements. There's more organization to this."

Jim held up his hand to stop the professor as there was a natural pause in the air. "Okay, guys, it's for real this time. I'm wiped out and need to head home for some sleep. But before I go, I'd like to take this opportunity to officially welcome Professor Richard Wolfram as an official member of the Carr Club, assuming; of course, that he accepts."

"I do indeed. Now that you've officially invited me, I wish to say something that I've felt since we first met. I feel like this is something I was put here to do. If I may say so, my involvement with all of you was not by accident, but by divine providence." We all agreed.

"One last thing before I go, professor," Jim said, as he placed his briefcase on his lap and looked through it for a specific folder. When he couldn't find it, he looked at Professor Wolfram and asked whether he ever consulted with the FBI on the ritual aspect of serial killings.

"I was contacted by the FBI once about a year ago," the professor replied. "The inquiry was about the abduction and murder of two teenage girls. As they were kidnapped and transported across state lines, and the case appeared related to another active missing person case, the FBI was the lead investigating agency. They permitted me to look over their files. I told them that the evidence at the scene and where their bodies were found had all the indications that they were the murder victims of a satanic ritual. The FBI agent who initially contacted me thanked me for my assessment, and that was the last I heard from them. It was as if they did not want to consider the ritualistic aspect of their murders," the professor said.

"Do you recall the FBI agent's name?" Gina asked.

"Not offhand, but I do have it somewhere in my files. I remember that she is an FBI profiler. A petite young lady, and I remember that she appeared to be Asian and had a name to match."

"Could it have been Agent Marcy Liu, perhaps?"

"Yes, that's it. I'm certain. How did you know?"

"She's one of two agents in Lakewood right now looking at the homicide of Jacob Tingsley. They are here because of that incident," Jim chimed in.

"If I may ask without being out of line, do you know if they have a suspect?" asked the professor.

"They haven't said anything to the district attorney that I know of."

"And I suppose that you think that this journal is somehow related to that murder?"

"That would seem logical, wouldn't it? I don't think it's that big of an assumptive leap. We are trying to determine how all of these pieces fit together." I added.

"Based on my experience, I strongly suspect that the journal, the letter sent to Marc, and the homicide are all connected through a single group of satanic practitioners operating in the shadows in Lakewood. Of course, that's why I'm here, to decode and connect whatever dots we can to identify the members of this most perverse demonic club. At this point, I believe that it's possible to uncover evidence that could implicate more than one person, more than one homicide, and more than one type of crime. There may be implications of several individuals and at least twice as many crimes, from the present backward maybe a half-century or more."

Jim Carr removed a folder from his briefcase. He provided copies of investigative reports we had compiled on the Tingsley homicide, asking Wolfram to read the material to see if it has any bearing on the information contained in the journal. He also produced a list of five people suspected to be involved in activities that suggest the involvement of satanic rituals that have taken place in and around Lakewood. He then gave the professor a separate list of four additional names, including Porter Landers, of individuals likely involved in human trafficking from Florida. Neither list excluded the activities of the other. "Is there any way to determine whether the journal names those individuals?"

"This will help, but as I already said, I'll need more time. Remember, the names in the book appear to have been written in some sort of code that is unique to the person writing it. Of course, knowing the names of the suspects will be helpful. Also, you must remember this is not only a linguistic translation issue. It's also a decoding issue."

"Maybe it's just my exhaustion talking, professor," Jim said in a defeated-sounding tone. "But the reason I'm taking our findings to the AG is we don't trust local law enforcement and certainly don't trust the FBI. This report must serve as the predicate to open a state-level investigation that the local authorities apparently cannot do, and the federal agencies are unwilling to do."

Professor Wolfram said he would do his best to decode and compare the information and lists to the names in the journal as soon as possible.

"Good night, everyone," Jim said as he walked out the back door to his vehicle.

"Drive safe and get some sleep," Annie said as she got up from the leather chair that seemed to envelop her. She had been quiet throughout the entire meeting.

"Professor, may we see the map?"

Wolfram pulled two pages from the copies made by Professor Eric Myers from one set stored at the war room, carefully taping them together in a near-perfect overlap that produced an area map of a potential ritual site. Annie watched as he held the map at its two upper corners and looked at an empty area of one of the cork boards.

"Allow me," she said and pinned the map in a prominent position amid the array of index cards, pictures, and papers connected by colored yarn.

Gina stood a few feet in front of the map, her arms folded, cocking her head to one side and then the other. "I've seen this area before, but I can't put my finger on it. There's something not right about this map. It looks 'off,' but I'm not exactly sure how," she added. Annie agreed.

She then turned her head to look out of the office window, watching Jim's taillights move away from the apartment. Then, it was nothing but darkness outside. Suddenly, Gina refocused her eyes to the interior reflection and our movements inside the war room. She saw the reflection of the map from the pane of the window. She was standing at the perfect angle to see the drawing reflected in the window. The darkness outside and the light inside created a mirror-like reflection of the paper map hanging from the board.

"That's it!" Gina exclaimed. "Guys, that's it!"

"What's it?" Annie asked.

"Stand here and look at the window."

"What's wrong? Is someone outside?" I asked.

"Don't look out the window; look at the window—look at the image reflected by the window. Look at the reflection of the map in the window and tell me what you see."

I joined Annie as she moved to stand next to Gina. Professor Wolfram followed. We all studied the image in the window.

"It can't be." Annie was surprised.

"No freakin' way."

"It is."

"Damn! You're right," I said.

IN THE DARK OF NIGHT

Chapter 33

Professor Wolfram walked over and looked at the image Gina, Annie, and I stood looking at. "It's a reversal, or mirror image, of the hand-drawn map caused by the window reflection. I take it from your reaction that you're familiar with this location?"

"Familiar with it? We should be. We were there twice, including yesterday. It's the cabin where Martin and Mary Tingsley and their children are staying. They're using it as a safe house at our urging. We knew about the barn but not the pond. Until the image was reversed, it didn't seem to fit the general layout, especially the property boundary lines."

"We've got to get them out of there now," Gina said as she checked her weapon and rushed to gather her things.

"Wait!" Professor Wolfram held up his hands. "I know I'm the junior member here, but may I give you my input before you guys go off storming the cabin?"

"Why wait? They could be in danger, and we put them there," Gina said.

"Maybe," Wolfram said. "Then again, maybe not. By rushing in there, you might be creating a greater danger for them, or worse."

"What do you mean, worse? How?" I asked.

"You could be walking into a trap. Please indulge me," Wolfram said in a scholarly manner. "Tell me, how long have they been staying at the cabin?"

"A little over a week."

"And they were fine yesterday?"

"Yes, but Mary acted a little odd when we showed her the copies from Speirs' journal," Gina said.

"Odd? She was downright hostile," I insisted. "She was furious that I showed Martin the journal when Gina took Mary and the kids to the store. Upset that she wasn't there. She all but threw me out of the cabin after she sedated Martin and made him go to bed because I upset him by making him look at the pages of the journal. I wanted to see whether he recognized anything," I said.

"Did you?"

"Did I what?"

"Did you upset Martin by anything you showed him? Did he show any reaction at all?"

"No, none. I observed him, and although he recognized some of the symbols, he was far from being upset or triggered by anything he saw."

"Who owns the cabin where they're staying? Is the cabin part of the property that includes the barn and pond?"

"Mary's uncle, Paul Kruger, who also owns a large trucking company here in Lakewood," Gina responded. "Here is a copy of the tax map of the property I got from the courthouse after we expanded our background checks."

"I see," Wolfram casually said as he pulled his pipe from his vest pocket. "Do you have a background file on this Kruger fellow?"

"Professor, I know you want help, but aren't we just wasting time? We've been over this information countless times, and now we've finally got an actionable and quite important piece of the puzzle. Lives could be in jeopardy." Gina was tense and forceful in her delivery.

"Oh, my yes, lives are in jeopardy, but not the lives you think," he said, continuing his scholarly tone. "I think they're your lives." His words hung in the air like the thick smoke from his pipe.

His response gave me pause and caused Gina and Annie to pay close attention. "I've seen a similar situation when I was in Germany, and I ask that you hear me out before you do what you're planning."

Annie lifted the file on Paul Kruger from one of the piles of papers and folders on my desk and gave it to Wolfram, who moved behind my desk and sat in my chair. "You don't mind if I sit here, do you?"

"Be my guest," I said, having little choice since he was already seated.

Annie suddenly shifted from being a quiet observer to a forceful participant. "I really think we need to listen."

The professor put another match to his pipe, taking a long and deep drag. The aroma from the burning tobacco wafted through the room as he quietly inspected every page in the file.

He asked for the background files on Martin and Mary Tingsley, the homicide file on Jacob, and all of the copies of the investigative documents Jim Carr had secreted from the DA's office.

"And if it's not too much trouble, I'll take a cup of coffee if you have any left. Just cream."

After fifteen minutes and two cups of coffee, Wolfram finally looked up from the paperwork. "Gina, may I see the background file on Benjamin Cooper and this Porter Landers fellow you and Marc encountered in Florida?"

"Sure, but I still think we're wasting time we might not have." Gina pulled one folder from a stack on the floor, and the Landers report from a file cabinet and put them both on the desk. Tension filled the room.

"Thank you. Now, please, give me just a few more minutes."

"Professor Wolfram, may I ask what you're looking for?"

"I'll explain momentarily."

Another quarter-hour passed in near silence and growing uneasiness. For whatever reason, watching the professor work made it look like he was grading papers, adding to the tension. He finally broke his self-imposed silence.

"May I see the list of suspects compiled for Jim that you've reasonably identified as participants in the rituals in Lakewood?"

"Yes, but they are all just suspects. We don't have hard evidence tying them to any crimes."

"So, what makes you think of them as suspects?"

"There's a boat load of circumstantial evidence, including photographs given to us by Martin and Mary."

"Don't forget about the three pictures Roger Braun gave us before he died," Gina said.

"I saw them. They're right here on the desk." Wolfram picked them up and used a magnifying glass to look at them. "May I see the list?" Wolfram asked again from behind his magnifying glass.

Gina handed him a single sheet of paper with names typed in the form of a list. Some of the people listed were quite familiar and also quite dead, such as Benjamin Cooper, Roger Braun, and Roland Speirs. Others were unfamiliar names, but they were rich, powerful, or both. A judge, an attorney, and two area businessmen who Martin Tingsley tentatively identified during our initial interviews with him. Some matched the general appearance of those depicted in our collection of photographs.

The professor looked up as he tamped down and re-lit the tobacco in his pipe. "You have more than you know."

"Are you going to tell us, or do we have to guess?" The tone of my question was a bit much for both Gina and Annie considering the glances they both gave me. I immediately apologized, rephrasing the question with more tact and diplomacy. "I'm just very frustrated, professor."

"Don't worry about it, Marc. I've encountered far more intractable people in my work than you. And that was a fair question that I fully intend to answer. Permit me one more minute," he said as he stood up and walked to the cork boards and whiteboards hung around the war room.

He stopped at the letter I received that began mockingly, Tick Tock Mister Big Shot PI. He tapped the letter with the stem of his pipe. "This ties a lot of things together. This will be their undoing."

"The letter?" Gina asked.

"Yes, and the hubris that exists in the letter."

"How?"

"It provides a type of location that corresponds with the map in Speirs' journal. It also gives us a timeline the killers are using."

"Killers, as in more than one?"

"Yes. It also gives us the identity of their leader."

"Who, Moloch?"

"Their human leader is found in the passage about the super soldiers and the silver ring. Look for the person wearing either, or both the Baphomet pendant and an SS ring."

"Okay," Gina sounded unsure as she responded to this information. "In total, how many more targets or victims might there be? Don't forget, an infant might be missing from the home where Jacob Tingsley lived."

"That depends," the professor said as he looked up from the letter.

"On what?" I asked.

"It depends on whether they are including you and Gina in that number."

"Marvelous," I uttered.

IN THE DARK OF NIGHT

Chapter 34

As the evening turned into night, the Carr Club, without Jim Carr but with the added expertise of Professor Dick Wolfram, firmly reaffirmed our objectives. Annie wrote our admittedly ambitious goals on a clean whiteboard:

* Identify each member of the Lakewood based satanic cult responsible for numerous abductions and murders of children and adults;

* Deliver useable evidence to the task force formed under the state attorney sufficient to enable successful prosecutions;

* Interrupt operations and rescue anyone endangered by this group, including anyone being held against their will;

* Identify any connections between this and other similar groups, wherever they operate, nationally or internationally.

Next, we discussed how best to complete these objectives while posing minimal risk to ourselves and others. We considered asking Lakewood Police Detective Ron Jenkins to provide us with assistance but decided against it due to the potential for conflict of interest and the FBI's restrictive presence. We could not request the FBI agents for their help for reasons evident to everybody. Finally, we agreed to give Jim some time to rest and make sure his wife got home from the hospital without complication. As we need Jim to be our point man with the attorney general and the state task force, we also agreed it would be best to keep him out of the fieldwork.

But first, we had to be able to separate the good guys from the bad, at least with reasonable certainty.

"Professor," Gina began, "you've had a lot of experience dealing with these kinds of people. How did you identify the killers when you worked in the field?"

"If they are involved in a real satanic cult, then they're all killers in one way or another. Each person has a different task from the leader or handler who organizes the rituals to those who carry out their orders. Some are programmed multiples, or individuals with multiple personalities in one body. They have various tasks, as well. Doctors have described this as a multiple personality disorder, disregarding the cause and completely ignoring or downplaying the demonic aspect. These are individuals who've been subjected to extreme trauma, usually starting at a young age. The result is a fractured mind. They have split personalities. They become programmable. An excellent example of this behavior was shown in a movie that came out in the 1960s called *The Manchurian Candidate*. Have any of you seen it?"

"We all have," Gina said. "Sadie Cooper strongly recommended it when we last met."

"In many cases, Western Intelligence agencies have experience in this area. You already know about the MKUltra programs by the CIA."

"Yes, but it's still difficult to accept," I said.

"Art imitating life."

"I guess if you want to call it that."

"I have another movie recommendation for you that you might find even more objectionable. Have you watched *Rosemary's Baby*?"

Almost in unison and with an audible groan or two, we all replied that we had. It was the second movie Sadie Cooper recommended we watch before she disappeared. She told us it would provide us with a better understanding of who and what we are up against.

The *Manchurian Candidate* would give us insight into certain aspects of mind control. At the same time, *Rosemary's Baby* is a primer into what is going on in Lakewood and elsewhere regarding Satanic cults, according to Cooper.

"There you are. No pun intended, but are you starting to get the picture? The situation you encountered or uncovered is like this nightmare of a double feature."

"So, who do we trust?"

"If you want to stay alive, you trust no one except for the people in this room and Jim, of course."

"Considering what you've seen and analyzed, who is our primary suspect?"

My question was not answered but instead met with another question.

"Where's Porter Landers?"

Gina and I looked at each other, a bit dumbfounded as we both sought the answer. "We don't know. Would you consider him the leader?"

"He could be the leader, or at least one of them. You need to find Landers. From what I've read, he has you in his sights. Until you locate him and anyone supporting him in Lakewood, you're at a disadvantage. He's certainly dangerous."

"What about Martin and Mary? They could be in the belly of the beast and in danger, along with their children. Don't you think we need to get them out of there now?" I asked.

The professor pulled a long drag from his pipe as he considered my question, smoke swirling around him. An extended silence gripped the room.

"There's something wrong with that situation. It just doesn't fit into my experience with similar groups in Germany."

"What are you implying?" Gina pressed.

"Implying? I'm not implying anything. I'm just making an observation. Like in all cases of serial killings, if we use the serial killer model as an example before adding the satanic component, we must go back to the very beginning. Such as the first killing, which gives us important information. In this case, we should look at the circumstances behind your first meeting with them. From what I read in your notes, they were reluctant witnesses."

"Wouldn't you be? He was treated as a party toy and tortured. Even his scars have scars. His mother died in a freakish car accident as she was taking evidence to the authorities, and the evidence magically disappeared. Now, his younger brother was tortured in the same way and murdered. He was initially reluctant; now, I think he's just damn traumatized and scared." I summarized.

"I don't disagree with you, but don't you find it a bit interesting that out of all potential victims that it was his younger brother who was supposedly hidden away by his deceased mother, who turned up dead? Consider the victimology in this case."

"Wouldn't the victimology support his murder, or that they selected Jacob as the victim based on the victimology?"

"That's exactly what I'm saying. And who has been around Jacob in the past and present? Who knows about the familial relationship?"

"Other than Martin and Mary, the attorney and judge? No one else should know."

"That's my point. Marc, I noticed that you have a set of guidelines you use. Stiles' Rules as you've called them. I read them from a paper on the corkboard over there. Allow me to paraphrase: 'Be aware that you will be played, and if you think you are being played, you're probably right.'"

"You don't miss much, do you? That's my rule #12, and you have it correct," I said.

"Often, we get so close to a situation that our perception becomes skewed. We become hobbled. I call it 'paralysis by analysis.' Occasionally it takes an outsider, or fresh eyes, to point out possibilities we haven't considered."

"Do you think that Martin and Mary are playing us?" Gina asked.

There was another long pause. Wolfram took another long drag on his pipe. His answer came from behind a cloud of thick smoke, decisive in its delivery.

"Martin and Mary? No."

"Since you've done a great deal of fieldwork, would you like to accompany Gina and me to talk to them? You can make an assessment and perhaps see things we've missed as you have more experience in the realm of satanic activity. If you think that they are safe for the time being and an emergency extraction is not immediately necessary, we could drop in on them unannounced tomorrow morning."

"I'd like that very much. It's been some time since I've actively worked in the field, but I'm up for that. Eventually, I'd like to see the interaction between Martin and Mary. I would, however, really like to look at the surrounding area. How sure are you that this is the area depicted by the map in the journal?"

Gina and I both agreed that it seemed to fit.

"And to recap, Porter Landers and his compatriot are what you guys call 'in the wind' at the moment?"

"For the moment."

"As I already said, you need to find them as soon as possible. Once you do, keep them under surveillance."

"What's your best guess, why haven't they come after us yet?"

"I'm certain that they already have, just not directly. I suspect that at some point very soon, they will."

"Remember one thing. They don't like you meddling in their affairs. If they can't get you directly, they will go after someone close to you. They want to slow you down, distract you, and even scare you. The closer you get to exposing them, the more vicious they will become."

By 11:00 p.m., we had our primary and contingency plans formulated. As we ended our strategy session, Professor Wolfram quoted Robert Burns and said aloud what we were all thinking, "Even the best-laid plan s of mice and men go awry."

Once everyone was gone, Gina asked to use the shower. "You've got to stop asking and consider it yours."

"You know, Marc, I'm still a guest here."

Thinking about everything that happened over the last several days, I wasn't sure how I felt about her gentle reminder that she was merely a guest. Maybe she was becoming something more.

I sat at my desk, pondering our plans as the telephone rang. It was a quarter past eleven and late by most standards. My terse hello was tempered by Deana's voice, telling me that she could not stop thinking about me this evening. She asked if everything was alright, if I was alright, and said that she missed me.

"You're the one who left me."

"I didn't leave you, Marc."

"That's funny; I don't see you around anywhere."

"You know what I mean. Please, don't be mad at me."

After telling her I was not angry, just confused, disappointed, and lonely, she said that she was going to be cutting her visit short and coming back this Sunday. Although she enjoyed being with her sister, she told me that she missed me, and suggested that we could use her remaining time off work to spend some time together.

"I'll even bake you some cookies."

"Is that code for anything?" I asked, smiling to myself.

Deana chuckled. "You're bad. Maybe we could spend some time talking about the future. I love you; you know."

"I love you too. Let's talk before you board, and I can arrange to pick you up at the airport."

"That sounds good. Get some rest, Marc, and have a good night."

"Good night, my love."

I was still sitting at my desk five minutes after I hung up, thinking about everything the professor said and the plans we made. Rarely, if ever, do plans go the way they should, I thought.

Just then, Gina walked around the corner in an oversized white nightshirt she brought in her go-bag. Her hair flowed down in front of her shoulders, accenting the contours of her face. She walked behind me and stood looking down at the notes I wrote during the meeting.

For a few seconds, the world seemed to slow as I breathed in the unmistakably delicate scent of her freshness. My world seemed to spin, and my head began to hurt from my carnal desires that I fought with every fiber of my being. However momentarily, my mind wandered and was mired in my confusion. Gina quickly but unknowingly brought me back to earth with her dire prognostications of the events ahead.

"I have a feeling that things are going to get a little dicey," she said.

Without answering her, I opened the top drawer of my desk and took out a new Walther PPK with a silver finish and placed it on top of my desk. "I decided that it was time to retire my .38 and upgrade. If this model is good enough for the late Elvis Presley and James Bond, well, why not for me?"

"Wow, that a beauty! When did you get that?"

"I picked it up last week. I took it to the range the same day to check the sights. I'm proud to say that I can make a tight grouping into a target at regulation distance. I figured I couldn't let you do all the shooting if things go sideways."

"Let's hope they don't."

"I've got to get some sleep, Marc. I have a feeling the next few days are going to be busy."

"There's an extra blanket on the closet shelf you can use if you want it."

"Thanks," Gina said as she hesitated at the door. "I feel bad taking your bed and making you sleep on the couch. At the risk of sounding too forward, you can join me if you want. There's enough room, and I don't bite. I promise I'll be good."

"I'd bet my life on that," I said with a wry smile. I stood up from my desk and walked to Gina, stopping directly in front of her. I gently held her face in my hands and stared into her eyes. "You're one beautiful and strong woman, and you're my partner. I would do anything for you to keep you safe and make you happy. But I'm scared," I whispered close to her ear.

"What are you afraid of?"

"Us," I said as I kissed her on her forehead. I pulled her close and gave her a warm and lasting hug, feeling the supple curves of her body against mine. I felt the moisture of a single tear on my chest, unsure if it was mine or hers.

Chapter 35

The man with the soulless eyes emerged from the thick woods and walked to the barn. He followed the yellow brick road that existed only through his eyes. He approached the main dual doors and encountered the three heavy-duty padlocks aligned vertically at the center of the closing. He counted, "1-2-3" as he opened each lock with a key on a ring of several other keys.

Noise from the woods, from the croaking frogs to the various other nocturnal animals and insects, covered the sound made by his whispers. He hated their sounds. The barn doors creaked open, and the man entered. It was just as he left it days ago. The van was parked exactly where he left it. The low hum of the refrigeration unit and chest freezer on the other side of the van hurt his head, which he cradled with both hands. He stood just inside, holding his head and rocking back and forth in a physical misery he could not describe. Just as quickly as his pain started, it ended, and he could think again.

There would be no forgetting his instructions this time. The pain Luke inflicted while Landers watched and laughed was seared into this memory. Clean the van. Remove the bits and pieces of flesh and organ meat and blood from the corrugated metal floor. Feed the fish. Throw everything in the pond. Scrub it clean. The fish are hungry.

He took a bucket, a rag, a container of bleach and opened the side door of the van. The stench from the air inside the van struck him in the face like a dead fish. It was offensive yet familiar. He stared at the pieces of flesh and hair mixed with caked blood. There was more left than he thought.

He used his fingers to pick at a piece, removing it from the metal and held it to his nose. It was too sour and hard and not as he liked it. He dropped it in the bucket and repeated the process, counting the number of pieces as he did it. Thirteen. He stopped at thirteen and was satisfied with that number. The last piece of Jacob Tingsley was a small piece of bone about the size of the palm of his hand, perhaps slightly smaller. He wiped it with bleach and walked to the altar, where he placed it next to other similar pieces on a shelf behind the wooden structure.

Next, he took the bucket of purification and walked it to the pond and fed the fish. He watched as the moonlight shone across the water, and the ripples spread across the pond. Satisfied, he walked back to the barn, trying his best to stay on the yellow brick road. He counted his steps. Thirty-three, from the end of the yellow brick road.

He finished his job with the rag, bleach, and the bucket. He was sure Landers would be proud, and Luke would not hurt him again. He concluded by putting the bucket and the bleach next to the wall and placed the rag inside the bucket. He left the barn, closed the doors, and counted 1, 2, 3 as he locked each lock.

He walked back into the woods, whispering, "I'm following the yellow brick road," and disappeared into the night. He was bothered by the lights from the cabin and angered by the thought that others occupied his rightful place.

Chapter 36

<u>**Wednesday, September 16, 1987**</u>

I had become accustomed to employing stealth-like movements in my apartment in the pre-dawn hours since Gina began staying with me. This morning was no different.

By 5:00 a.m., I had shaved, showered, and changed into a clean suit; all accomplished without waking Gina. As I dressed, I noticed that I was running out of clean dress shirts and made a mental note to make a trip to the dry cleaners. After making coffee, I sat at my desk and loaded two extra magazines for my Walther, tucking them into the inside pockets of my suitcoat. I spent about an hour writing up a checklist of to-do items for today and updating the boards.

Gina joined me in the war room early at 6:15 a.m., already dressed and ready for the day. She walked over to me as I was standing in front of one of the whiteboards. She put her hands on my shoulders and gently turned me so I would be facing her and softly wrapped her arms around my neck.

"About last night, I just want to thank you for being such a stand-up guy and a good friend." Before I had a chance to respond, she walked to my desk and said, "Well, come on, we need to get started." I thought that I detected a tinge of regret in her voice.

Gina called Jim at 6:30 a.m. per his request the previous evening. He wanted to make sure he was up to go to the hospital to get his wife and needed to be brought up to speed on the plans we made in his absence.

We put him on speaker and started to tell him about what he missed last night. Jim interrupted us before we could even begin. "I need to tell you something—."

He explained that he had been up for an hour and just finished taking Oscar on his morning walk. What he said next sent a chill down our spines.

"Because of my schedule and what happened to Angie, I've haven't been taking Oscar on his walks. This morning he seemed a bit agitated, more than usual. I just thought he wanted me to take him out. I walked him before it was light this morning and saw the vehicle you said is owned by Porter Landers parked near the end of our cul-de-sac. I'm not entirely sure it was his because I couldn't make out the license plate. I was going to get closer, but Oscar wasn't having any of it. He was pulling hard in the other direction. I've never seen him act that way before. The hair on his back was standing straight up. It was weird. He wanted to go back home, so we did. Anyway, I couldn't get any closer because of Oscar, and the other car was parked close behind it. Still, I think it's Lander's car that's parked no more than four houses away from mine. I didn't see anyone in either vehicle."

"Is Lander's car still there?"

"I think so, unless it left within the last few minutes."

"What about the other car? Can you give us a description?"

"It's an older model, Honda, dark color, in-state plates. I managed to write the license plate down. It's Y92908L. I'm almost positive that's the vehicle that has been following me."

I repeated the license number as I wrote it down. "Gina and I will be right down to set up surveillance. Do what you normally do or whatever you had planned for this morning, and we'll watch the cars and residences. What time are you supposed to pick up Angie this morning?"

"I'm supposed to call or check-in with the hospital after seven. That's when the nurses change shifts, and the doctors are making their rounds. I didn't hear anything during the night, so I'm sure that she'll be released today. I'll head down there instead of calling."

"Okay, we'll talk with you either at the hospital or your house. Leave us a message if you decide to go to the office or anywhere else."

"Thanks, guys. We'll talk soon."

"Jim, if you happen to see us on surveillance, don't stop or acknowledge us."

"Of course not. Be safe."

The phone clicked off. "Even the best-laid plans," I mumbled. Gina and I gathered our gear for surveillance and were in my car within minutes. It took us less than 15 minutes to arrive in the vicinity of Jim's house. We did a drive-by and saw both vehicles parked as Jim described at the base of the cul-de-sac between two houses. Gina snapped several still photographs of the cars.

"I didn't see this coming, did you?" I asked Gina.

"Not at all."

I parked on an adjacent street that gave us an unobstructed view of Jim's house and the cars parked nearby. We spent 90 minutes and observed Jim leaving his home, presumably for the hospital to pick up Angie. Neither Lander's Cadillac nor the Honda moved, and we saw no activity at that location.

"I'd like to get the ownership record on the dark-colored Honda, but I need to get to a payphone," I said.

"I could use a restroom too," Gina said. "There's a phone and a bathroom at the Seven-Eleven about a half-mile from here. Do you think we should break surveillance and chance it? It's still reasonably early, but it's your call."

"All right, let's do it. We can make it back here in under ten minutes."

It took only eight minutes for me to call TC and request ownership information on the Honda. I told him I needed the info expedited, and he said that I could call him back in thirty minutes for the information. Gina had returned to my car before I had completed my call.

We hurried back to our surveillance position and found both cars gone from that location.

"Damn!" I yelled as I pounded my hands on the steering wheel. "Can you freakin' believe it?" The recollection of our Florida surveillance where a similar event occurred entered both of our minds. "It was a rookie mistake," I said.

Gina apologized for not having the plumbing to take care of business in the vehicle. I apologized for breaking surveillance to call TC.

"Your excuse was better than mine," Gina said.

We spent the next 30 minutes checking gas stations, restaurants, and other businesses situated on the main road closest to Carr's house but failed to locate either vehicle. Lacking success, we returned to the war room to regroup and call my contact for the vehicle ownership information.

"TC, what have you got for me?"

"I think you owe me a steak dinner for this one, TC replied. I had to jump through quite a few hoops to pin this one down. The car is a rental."

"Damn. That's just our luck," I said as I began to complain when he talked over me, telling me to calm down. "I told you that I jumped through hoops on this one."

TC told me that he tracked the vehicle to the Hertz rental car agency at the airport. He called the rental agency on my behalf and promised the young lady a night on the town if she would look through the rental records to identify the person who rented the vehicle.

"It's a 1987 dark blue Honda Accord. It was leased on Sunday, September 13, 1987, by Porter O. Landers."

"That doesn't make sense. Landers has his own vehicle. Why would he need to rent a car?"

"Maybe he had car problems, or perhaps it wasn't for him. He named an additional driver on the rental contract. The other driver identified by the paperwork is a guy named Paul Kruger."

"Kruger? He's local and owns a trucking company. Why would he need a rental?"

"Determining that is your job. Mine is just to get the information for you. Good luck!"

After I completed my call, Gina walked over to my desk and picked up the receiver. She dialed a number that was answered on the first ring and updated the professor about this morning's events. After she hung up the phone, she said that he was on his way down, sticking with the plans that we made last night. He would just arrive earlier.

I picked up the receiver again, this time calling Detective Ron Jenkins at the Lakewood Police Department. Although I was a bit vague with the details, I told Ron that Porter Landers might be preparing to do something of an illegal nature within his jurisdiction. Dissatisfied with my explanation, he asked me for specific details. I could give him none. I merely needed him to be prepared to assist should we need police intervention.

Out of an abundance of caution, I also called Brenda at the Towne Restaurant. I asked her to keep her eyes open for any sign of Porter Landers or the new dark blue Honda rental vehicle. I also called Annie at the office and informed her about the events that transpired this morning. I gave both Brenda and Annie the plate number of the Honda and told them to call Detective Jenkins if either of them had any contact with Landers. Perhaps detecting the urgency in my voice, they didn't ask any questions and hastily agreed.

Gina and I talked as we waited for professor Wolfram to arrive.

"What in the world would Porter Landers and Paul Kruger be doing near Jim Carr's house?" Gina asked.

"I don't know, but it's close to Tom and Peggy Bauer's house too. Maybe they know each other. If they do, it would surely cast a different perspective on Peggy's poisoning, wouldn't it?"

"Do you think Peggy Bauer intentionally poisoned Angie? If she did, why not just use a more traditional and effective poison? You know, Agatha Christie style?" Gina asked. "Not only that, what about the break-in at their house?"

"I don't know. About the method of poisoning, maybe Peggy thought it would give her a measure of plausible deniability," I said. "Or maybe her intent was not to kill her. Or, maybe she just sucks at poisoning people."

Gina sat in the chair behind my desk, and I began pacing back and forth in the war room, trying to process this new information while waiting for Wolfram to arrive.

Gina picked up the telephone receiver again and dialed the number for the hospital. After going through an arduous process with the hospital switchboard and two nursing stations, she finally reached Angie, who was mired in the bureaucratic process of being checked out. Gina exchanged pleasantries with Angie and then asked to speak to Jim. After a few minutes of audible rustling from the receiver being moved around from the bed to the nightstand, Gina heard Jim's footsteps approaching the telephone.

As soon as Jim picked up the phone, Gina put him on speaker and gave him a rapid-fire update of the plans we hatched after he left the war room the previous evening. She told Jim that we were going to pay a visit to Martin and Mary with the professor, who would take a look at the barn and surrounding property while we kept the Tingsley family occupied. She told him that the map in the journal appeared to identify that property but left out how we determined that probability. Wolfram would know what to look for.

Next, she told Jim that the Honda he saw at his cul-de-sac was leased to Porter Landers. She identified a secondary driver as Paul Kruger. She also left out the part about losing both vehicles but asked him a question that was met with several seconds of silence.

"Is it possible that your neighbors, Tom and Peggy Bauer, know Porter Landers or Paul Kruger?

"Jim sounded like he was cupping the speaker part of the handset with his hand and whispered his disbelief to Gina. "I just thought of this. Tom might know Kruger. I had no reason to tell you this before, but Tom Bauer moved from Columbus due to the expansion of his commercial transport business. Kruger is in the same business. When did you say Landers or Kruger rented the car?"

"I didn't. If it makes a difference, though, the rental contract was dated Sunday, September 13, 1987. Three days ago," I said.

"Marc, that was the day Tom had business associates visit him from out of town and stopped by to borrow a bottle of Scotch. Do you remember me telling you Tom mentioned that his guests were agitated because they had some kind of car problem?"

"Yes, and do you remember what happened at the Towne Restaurant? Maybe Landers ran over some restaurant equipment in the lot when Robbie helped us slow him down. Maybe he was the one with car trouble," I said.

"What in the hell is going on? Should I even take Angie back home?"

Gina and I looked at each other. Without a word exchanged between us, Gina suggested that Jim keep to his schedule of taking Angie home, but remain with her. "You still have your weapon, don't you?" Gina asked.

"I sure do, and you can bet I'll be carrying it."

"Make sure you do. Also, please do us a favor. Call Detective Jenkins and fill him in on everything we just told you. Marc already spoke to him, but he'll take it more seriously coming from an assistant DA," Gina said. And call Annie at the office should you see anything odd. I have my pager, and Marc and I will stay together."

"Will do." The line clicked off.

A few minutes later, Professor Wolfram knocked at the door. We let him inside and explained everything that happened this morning, including the presence of Lander's car and a rental car parked near Jim Carr's house. The additional driver on the rental contract is Paul Kruger, the owner of the cabin and surrounding property. A look of concern washed over his face.

"Where's Jim?" asked the professor.

"He's picking up Angie from the hospital."

"We suggested that he kept to his schedule, although he might stay home with Angie today," Gina explained.

"That might be a good idea. I think Jim needs to be very careful. I also think the Kruger property is where we need to be looking. We need to get to that property to check things out."

IN THE DARK OF NIGHT

Chapter 37

"Considering what you know now, what do you expect to find at the cabin?" Gina asked Wolfram pointedly.

"It's not the cabin that interests me. It's the barn, pond, and the area around it. I'm not sure. I can only rely on my experience with similar cases I've worked in Germany. From my experience, the property would be a perfect location for holding rituals and even disposing of bodies. It's been under the radar since Kruger built up the property, and it's in the middle of nowhere. We must determine if anyone is using the barn for any nefarious purposes, see if Kruger or Landers are there, and later, check on Martin and Mary and their children."

"How will you be able to tell if it's a ritual site? If murders were committed there?"

"The first sign would be markings on the surrounding trees, identifying the location as being used for black masses and even animal and perhaps human sacrifices. I'll check the trees around the barn, look inside the barn for artifacts, and take a look around the pond."

"Do you think Landers or Kruger might be there?"

"If that's their base of operation for rituals and murder, they might be trying to clean things up before we or the FBI get there."

"What about Martin and Mary? Wouldn't they be in the way and in danger?"

"Not necessarily. If they stay inside the cabin, there's a good chance that they'll be safe. It's Kruger's property, so they wouldn't question him working in the barn if he shows up. There could be trouble if they see or recognize Landers, though. I think Kruger would make sure he remained out of sight. If they're together, that is."

"Why would Kruger offer to put up Martin and his family if Kruger is deeply involved in the activities that injured Martin? Does that make sense to you?" I asked.

"What is a better way to keep track of them? However, I agree that it wouldn't make sense to a person of normal sensibilities. These are men of incredible hubris and believe they are shielded or protected by the most powerful entities of the underworld. In the real world, though, they have police officers, attorneys, and judges in compromising positions, which helps if they are discovered or caught."

"Marvelous. How do you want to do this?" I asked the professor. Instead of immediately answering me, he unrolled the county map across my desk that he brought with him, which was a copy his intern got from the courthouse at his request. It was already marked with his notes, lines, and arrows, depicting possible points of ingress and egress and names of the property owners. The property where the Tingsleys were staying was outlined with a yellow highlighter. A black "X" was placed over the cabin, a red "X" identified the location of the barn, and a blue "O" noted the area of the pond.

"There's only one road to get to the property from the front, and a long driveway that takes you to the cabin. The barn can be accessed from the cabin by a makeshift driveway that extends from the side of the cabin where the main driveway ends, although I'm not sure of its condition. Did either of you notice the driveway extension when you were there?"

"I wasn't paying attention," I responded.

"I noticed it, but at the time, I thought that it was for farm equipment, like tractors and such. My guess is that cars can use it without any problems, and probably have. It looked like it had been used throughout the summer and is well-traveled," Gina said. The barn is not visible from the cabin. It's behind a tree line and sits below the incline of the property, based strictly on my memory and this map.

"What's behind the Kruger property? How about on each side?" I asked.

"The land that butts up against the rear of that parcel is relatively wooded. Directly behind there, about 200 yards north, is a livestock farm of some type. It's located on State Line Road. The west side is all heavily wooded, and there is a large pasture to the east. If you look at this map, you'll see that the power company maintains an easement between the parcel where the cabin is located, running north connecting the cabin road to State Line Road. It's on the west side of the properties between both parallel roads. Lines from the poles provide power to the few properties in that area, including the cabin and possibly the barn." Wolfram explained.

"The easement doesn't provide us with much cover," Gina noted.

"How about covertly entering from the north along the tree line, or from the property that abuts Kruger's property from the rear. It's a livestock farm. We can check out the barn and pond area first to get an idea of what's there. Once we determine what's there, we can approach the cabin like we are paying them a regular visit," offered Gina.

"I think we should skip visiting the cabin this time and just focus on the pond and barn. Also, we should split up," Wolfram replied. "I'll go in from the rear first while you two set up surveillance from a nearby location on State Line Road, north of Kruger's property. Both of you wait for me, cover me and give me about an hour to get in, look around, and get out. I'll take photographs of what I find, if anything."

"It sounds like you've done this before."

"I have," Wolfram said as he removed his pipe from the breast pocket of his tan vest that made him look like Indiana Jones. His hands shook a little as he lit it.

"Are you sure you're okay to do this?" Gina asked.

"Yes. I was just thinking about my time in Germany."

"How did that go?" I asked. Wolfram didn't answer but stared blankly ahead and held that stare for several seconds. Instead, he said that we could reminisce later.

"We'll keep in touch with the two handheld radios we have here. They'll give you adequate range," I added. "But we should limit using them to prevent being heard."

"Agreed."

Gina loaded up my vehicle with surveillance equipment while I changed my clothes from a suit to cargo pants, tan boots, and a brown sweatshirt. Gina also made some wardrobe adjustments, after which we double-checked our weapons and made sure we both had extra magazines. It was 10:45 a.m. when the three of us left my apartment and entered my vehicle.

Chapter 38

From Stateline Road, we dropped the professor off about 100 yards east of the farm behind Kruger's property and watched as he entered the heavily wooded area, walking south. A neck strap held a camera, and the two-way radio was tucked inside of his vest, hidden from view. To a casual observer, he looked like he could be on a nature hike and posed no threat to anyone. Within minutes, he disappeared from our view. We moved our vehicle to an area by an oil storage tank on the power company's property.

On a reconnaissance mission like this, waiting was always tense and challenging. Gina broke the silence by asking me about my rule that addressed threats coming from unseen directions.

"Do you mean Stiles' Rule #18? The most serious threat to an operation is the one you never see coming?"

"Yeah, that's the one."

"Why?"

"I don't know. I just have a hinky feeling about this."

"Marvelous," I deadpanned.

"Do you remember the case we worked in Keene, New York last year? We were in the middle of nowhere, at the northern edge of the Adirondacks, watching that convicted child molester? He lived in a trailer on a dirt road that had only two other houses on it. We should've checked property ownership before we started our surveillance. We would've found out that his brother lived in one house and his parents in the other. I think that was the first time we were blindsided by an ornery old man brandishing a double-barrel shotgun who demanded to know what we were doing." Gina had a slight smile on her face as she spoke of that encounter.

"He thought we were making out," I chuckled.

"Having a shotgun pointed at my face through the car window, now that was a rush."

"He told us that he could shoot us both and feed us to the bears, and nobody would know. He was probably right," I said. "You don't think that could happen here, do you?"

"No."

"Why not?" I asked.

"There aren't any bears around here."

Just then, the radio came to life. "Hey guys, I'm past the pond, about thirty yards from the barn. There's a single door at the back of the barn, and it looks like I can get inside that way. I don't see anyone around."

"Be careful and keep us posted," Gina responded.

"Holy crap," the professor said almost immediately. "I see a symbol etched and painted on a large tree that identifies that the area is used for animal or human sacrifice. I haven't seen anything like this in years." The professor took two photographs of the tree and symbol. "I guess I'm in the right place." The symbol Wolfram saw appeared to be a crescent moon on the left with two intersecting arrows that form a narrow "X" on the right, according to his description.

Gina and I discussed whether Wolfram needed to go any further as he already had photographic evidence of ritual activity.

"What would that prove to the police? Would that be enough for a search warrant? They'll pass it off as graffiti made by kids," Gina said. Wolfram must have thought the same thing as he continued to move forward. He crossed the clearing from the tree line that protected him from sight to the rear of the barn, stopping briefly at the door. He radioed that he was at the door and was about to enter.

"Okay, be careful," Gina acknowledged.

The next forty minutes of radio silence seemed like an eternity. Neither of us said anything during that time. We kept watching the trees ahead of us for any sign of the professor.

"I'm clear of the barn and back into the woods," Wolfram's voice crackled over the radio. "I'm getting my ass back to you guys right now. Give me ten minutes. Watch for me. Pick me up as soon as you see me." The professor sounded breathless and nervous, almost excited.

It took him seven minutes, not ten, to reach the road from the woods. He exited the woods about twenty yards farther away from us than we anticipated and excitedly waved to us. I had barely slowed down when Wolfram opened the back door and climbed in the car. "Let's go, let's get the hell out of here," he commanded.

"Did you have any problems?" Gina asked.

"No, but I've seen all I need to see," he responded. "There's a whole lot of evil right there. I used all 24 pictures on the roll and could have taken another roll. You've got to see these."

"Tell us."

"I have no doubt in my mind that the barn is used for rituals. There's a long table, or a makeshift altar inside. There's a van parked near the front of the barn, inside, by a set of double doors. It smells of decomposition in there."

"Is that what I smell from your clothes?" asked Gina.

"No. I was heading back and strayed too far west. There's a pig farm adjacent to the rear of Kruger's property, and I slipped when I accidently got too close to one of the pens. How fast can you get the film developed?"

"There's a photo store where we take our film. They'll do it right away for us."

Professor Wolfram talked about everything he saw and documented around and inside the barn. He explained that he saw at least three satanic symbols, not including the first one he saw on the tree, all indicative of black masses and sacrifice. There was a long piece of decorated fabric and robes neatly folded by the table. He photographed those items. He saw a refrigeration unit and a chest freezer, both stained by a reddish-brown substance that appeared to be dried blood and took photos of each.

Speaking of the appliances, I said that the substance "could be rust."

"Sure, it could be, but it's not. That's not a slaughterhouse in there. At least not a normal one."

We had the photographs developed and were back in the war room by 1:30 p.m. The developer made three copies of each photo for us, as we requested, and we studied each of them carefully. The professor explained what each photograph showed, and the meaning of the symbols depicted. Each picture was clear and in focus, although a few were darker than usual due to the low lighting inside the barn.

A raised wooden table appeared in four pictures. Wolfram said that the table was at the far end of the barn, or closest to the rear door.

"Does this look familiar?"

"It does. It looks like the same set-up we saw in the Polaroids Roger Braun gave us," I said.

"Are those handles on the tabletop? What are they used for?"

"Those aren't handles. They're shackles," Wolfram replied. He deeply sighed as he finished his sentence, "Just like I saw in Germany. Now take a look at this," Wolfram added as he reached into his vest pocket and pulled out a small, curved, dull-white object about the size of a hollow baseball that retained some of its curvature. A partial etching appeared on the outside of the curved portion.

"I purposely saved this for last. Do you know what this is?" he asked.

"It looks like part of a bone," Gina said.

"That's my guess too. Now look at the next to last photograph," he instructed.

"It looks like a shelf that has several of these types of things on top of it."

"That's right. This was on the end, and within my reach, so I grabbed it," he said.

"You stole that from the inside barn?" I asked with a bit of alarm.

"Yes, and if this is what we think it is, it will prove what's been going on in there. I think this is part of a skull, and the markings are part of a larger etching of a satanic symbol," he said.

"Is it human?"

"Laboratory tests will determine that. Whether it's human or animal, this should be sufficient to prove your case."

"We've got to call Detective Jenkins," I said. I looked at the professor, who appeared tired and drained. What he saw inside the barn had an impact on him.

"Are you okay?" I asked.

"I'll be fine. I'm just getting old, I guess."

About thirty minutes passed since we got back to the war room. Considering the evidence we found, I made the call to Detective Jenkins. This time, I would hold nothing back. I would tell him about everything we saw and suspected. Gina and the professor agreed that it was the best course of action, especially since assistant DA Jim Carr should have spoken to Jenkins by now.

I put the call on speaker so Gina and the professor could listen and chime in whenever needed. I didn't hold back on anything and used our longstanding friendship as leverage to gain his assistance. His reaction was not what I expected, considering his recent conversation with Jim Carr, which he acknowledged.

"Do you know how crazy all of this sounds?" Jenkins asked.

"No crazier than finding the mutilated corpse of a young boy at the Bayfront."

"I'll have to involve the FBI agents on this."

"And then what?" I protested, "They'll take over the investigation, and it goes into a black hole somewhere. Nothing gets done, and the investigation goes nowhere."

"What do you want me to do?" Jenkins asked. He sounded frustrated and equally defeated.

"At least find Landers and his sidekick, along with Kruger, and bring them in for questioning. That will keep them out of our way while we continue our investigation."

Jenkins balked at the idea. "Bring them in for what? Maybe, just maybe, I could ask Kruger to come down to the station as a potential informant to the Tingsley homicide based on family ties, but that's reaching. I don't think I could convince the chief of detectives to sign off on that idea, and I'm sure Kruger's lawyers would have a field day with me for even asking."

"I had to ask, Ron." I knew it would be a long shot. "What about the photographs and the piece of bone?"

"Do you mean the pictures you guys took while trespassing and breaking and entering? And the piece of bone, or whatever it turns out to be that you guys stole from inside the barn?"

"Yes, I do mean those photographs, and yes, that bone."

"Those pictures could be easily explained away, making them meaningless and worthless. The bone can be easily explained, too, if it is even a bone."

"Consider the larger context of what we're dealing with here," I insisted.

"That might work with the attorney general's task force, but not here. The only shot we might have is for Jim Carr to push the district attorney to somehow act on whatever evidence you guys think you have, but I doubt any action will be coming from this department."

"Ron, do you believe us?" Gina asked into the speaker.

"I believe that you believe there's a satanic cult operating in Lakewood. For all I know, there is. But that's not the issue. The problem is that I need to convince my boss, the FBI agents, and the district attorney's office."

The professor stood up and spoke toward the speaker. His voice bellowed inside the office. "Detective Jenkins, I'm Professor Wolfram, and I've been working on this case with Marc and Gina. ADA Jim Carr knows my experience and has a copy of my credentials. I've seen a very similar, if not exact situation during my work abroad. Is there anything I can do to convince you that you've got a major crime scene within your jurisdiction? One that involves serial murders. Ritualistic murders. I'm convinced that you'll find the evidence you'll need in that barn and in that area. You will find one hell of a major crime scene, the likes of which Lakewood has never seen."

A period of silence followed Professor Wolfram's statements.

"I know about you, professor, and I respect your experience. I'm aware of your previous consultations with the FBI, and you have a great reputation."

"That doesn't matter to you?"

"I didn't say that. It's just that there's only so much I can do."

At this point, we all reached our limits of frustration. It was clear that Ron felt that a system of procedural red tape tied his hands, and we felt that we had enough to convince the police that unspeakable criminal acts were and are still are being conducted. We thought that we were offering enough evidence for them to open a criminal investigation or advance their homicide investigation of Jacob Tingsley. We believed that we had enough for Lakewood PD to at least get a search warrant.

"Here's what I'll do," Jenkins offered. "I'm going to be tied to my desk catching up on paperwork today. If you see anything suspicious going on at that barn or anywhere else, call dispatch and ask for me. I'll personally respond, and maybe we can use our observations as the basis for a warrant. That's the best that I can do. Will that work for you guys?"

"Do we have a choice?" I asked, and then clicked the button that ended the call.

IN THE DARK OF NIGHT

Chapter 39

The tension inside the war room was palpable. Wolfram spoke first.

"I see now that there's no difference between continents and police agencies. You can point them to something so obvious, and they refuse to accept it because it is too horrific to comprehend. They will bury the truth along with the dead. The evil ones remain free to kill again because of some inexplicable cognitive dissonance of those in charge."

"Please, professor, explain." I pressed.

"We don't have time for this right now, Marc."

"I think we do, or at least we need to make time. I think it's important to our case in Lakewood that we at least know what you experienced a few thousand miles away and a few years ago. Maybe it doesn't have to end the same, however it ended. Tell us. Maybe we can learn from it and do things differently." The room stayed silent.

"Please," I paused, then added, "take the time."

Professor Wolfram took a long drag on his lit pipe and considered my question. The red-hot glow of the tobacco embers appeared to match the growing red color of his face.

"Our team gave them everything. We played by the rules and worked an investigation for two years that involved the disappearance of over fifty children and an unknown number of indigents who were sacrificed in satanic rituals. The police did not want to believe it. They ignored the evidence. We showed them that the Satanists, the Nazi occultists, were active and responsible for the deaths of nearly a hundred people over two years. The torture, the killings as sacrifices were too horrific to be believed."

"What did they do with your evidence?"

"They buried it along with the remains of the dead. The guilty still walk free because the people in charge could not come to grips with the horrors in their midst. Just like here. No difference."

"If you don't mind me saying so, it seems that there is something much more personal going on. What aren't you telling us?"

My belief that Wolfram was holding something back proved correct. He continued his narration as he stared out the office window.

"My niece was my student and a member of my team. Her name was Michelle, and she was twenty-two years old at the time. Two days after we identified the cult and cult leaders, and three days before we were scheduled to leave Germany, the cult leader we identified ordered her kidnapping. They killed her in a ritual sacrifice to their god Moloch, and her body was left for me to find."

"What did the police do?"

"They blamed the murder on a man they said was a serial killer who they arrested the next day. They did not want to confront the evil of the satanic; instead, they charged a known serial killer for the crime. They never charged the real perpetrator. Does that sound familiar?"

"That's what is happening here," Gina said.

"I'll never forget him for what he did."

"Who is he?" I asked.

"A Nazi in his youth who later engaged in mind control experiments under the MKUltra programs. His name is Rudolph Fleischer."

Gina and I immediately looked at each other as the immediate recognition of the name sunk in. Gina looked at the professor accusingly, "You knew all along." She stood up and pointed her finger at the professor. "Benjamin Cooper is Rudolph Fleischer."

Her voice raised, "You freakin' knew since the very beginning, but you never said a word!"

"I had my suspicions but wasn't sure until I studied the journal you got from Roland Spiers and your investigative notes. Then, I knew."

"Why didn't you tell us?" I asked.

"Because I didn't think it would matter anymore. Rudolph Fleischer, or Benjamin Cooper as he was more commonly known throughout Lakewood, is dead, as is his widow. Even so, I didn't think you would let me assist you. I thought you might see it as a conflict of interest."

"A conflict of interest? All you had to do was tell us. We would have understood. Don't forget that we're working this case today because of the murder of my uncle, which anyone would consider the mother of all conflicts." I added.

"I didn't tell you why they selected her as their victim. In addition to the fact that she was my niece, she was married to a fellow graduate student and was five-and-a-half months pregnant with a baby boy. They sacrificed the baby while she was still alive. They drugged her with ketamine and made her watch as she laid in agony, dying an agonizing death. They did unspeakable things to my niece and her baby. They passed around a silver chalice of the baby's and his mother's blood, just like in the photographs Roger Braun left you."

"I'm so sorry," Gina said softly.

"Well, professor, it looks like we've got a lot of work ahead of us. We can't allow this to happen again, happen here. We're glad you're aboard."

IN THE DARK OF NIGHT

Chapter 40

It was just after 1:00 p.m. when Professor Wolfram placed the artifact he took from the barn in a plastic evidence bag that we supplied. The professor summoned a graduate student at the forensic anthropology laboratory at his college who is familiar with these matters to pick up the item and run the appropriate tests to determine if the object is indeed a part of a skull and whether it was animal or human. Nicknamed "Bones" and, more formally, "the Bone Detective" at the college, he is good at his job and has a positive history with the local and state police departments. A chain of custody form was started and maintained for the artifact in case it was needed later.

Before leaving, Wolfram asked him to take a closer look at the artifact, pointing out a barely visible line on the small piece. He spent a few minutes using a magnifying glass before placing the object back in the bag.

"Well?" Asked the professor.

"I'll take it for proper analysis, but I suspect that it's part of a human skull," declared Bones.

"How can you tell from such a small piece and just by looking at it," I asked as I walked closer to inspect it myself.

"Do you see this slightly indented line right here on the outside of the curvature?"

"Yeah."

"This looks like it could be the coronal suture, which is located at the top of a human skull and extends to both sides. Also, the bone density suggests it's human as well. I'll know more after I perform more tests."

"Thanks, I think," I responded.

"Bones pushed his glasses up and placed the object back into the bag. As he did, he made certain all of the evidence spaces were completed. He smiled at the professor, who thanked him for responding quickly. Looking at me, he asked, "Do you know what bone inside the human body is rarely broken?" After a few seconds of considering the question, I blurted out, "A bone in the neck."

"That's close, very close, but can you be more specific?"

When I didn't reply right away, he said, "It's the hyoid bone, which we don't see too often. It's generally broken due to manual strangulation and accounts for less than two one-hundredths of a percent of all breaks," Bones added. Before he could say anything more, Wolfram thanked him again and led him out the door.

"He's a young genius, and we're lucky to have him. He doesn't socialize much, which explains the exchange you just encountered."

"I thought it was interesting," I replied.

"When he looks at a bone fragment and says it's probably human, it most likely is," Wolfram added.

Gina picked up the telephone and called Jim Carr's residence. She listened to Angie's voice on their answering machine that prompted her to leave a message. Her brow furled as she tried again, getting the same result. "There's no answer at Jim's house," Gina said aloud.

"Try his office, maybe Angie is sleeping and he went to check on his cases," I responded. I didn't believe that scenario for a minute but tried to reassure myself that there is a logical explanation before thinking the worst. After a few minutes of dialing and talking to a few people at the DA's office, she hung up the receiver and said that the DA's receptionist said that he wasn't in and would not be in until tomorrow.

"I'll try the hospital, maybe they're still there," Gina said with growing concern.

Gina dialed the hospital and spoke to the admissions department, who said that Angie Carr was released earlier today. She contacted the nurses' station on the floor she spent the night and spoke to the head nurse who knew Gina from another case.

"Angie Carr? Let me see. Oh, yes, she was released at 10:45 this morning. Two plainclothes detectives picked her up to take her back home. She's in some sort of protective custody," the nurse stated.

"Was her husband with her when she left?" Gina asked with more than a hint of urgency.

"Yes, I recall that he was. He seemed very upset and concerned about all the fuss," the nurse added.

"Thanks," Gina said and quickly hung up. Professor Wolfram and I were now paying close attention to the unfolding events.

Gina called the police station and asked for Ron Jenkins, who answered immediately.

"Ron, this is Gina. Did you guys send out two plainclothes detectives to pick up Angie and Jim Carr from the hospital and place them in protective custody?"

The look on her face told us the answer. She explained the process she just went through to contact Jim and Angie, and the information the nurse gave her at the hospital. "I'll send a marked unit over to Jim's house now and let you know what they find," Jenkins said, hanging up immediately.

We decided not to wait. Jim's house is only a few minutes' drive from my apartment, and we arrived at the same time as the marked police car. Unsurprisingly, Jenkins got there a few seconds after us.

The uniformed officer checked the house and found all of the doors locked and windows closed. He knocked heavily several times on the doors as Jenkins looked through the first-floor windows. He saw and heard Oscar, but nothing else.

"Nothing looks disturbed. I don't think Jim or Angie came back after Jim left this morning." Jenkins asked the police dispatch to call Carr on his pager. After several minutes, he said that Jim did not respond to his pages.

I thought about the letter I received, and the phrase, "There will be no one to talk for thee." Considering that Jim was to represent us as the "point man," submitting our investigation to the state's attorney and their task force, he seemed like a logical target. I shared my concerns with Gina and Professor Wolfram, who both agreed this was possible. I reminded Jenkins of the letter, and he was now equally concerned.

"It's been over three hours now since Angie was released," Gina said to no one in particular.

Jenkins used the radio in his car to contact dispatch. He identified the car Jim is known to be driving and requested the dispatcher put out a BOLO alert for his vehicle, and also for Jim and Angie. He added that two unidentified males might be accompanying them. Jenkins temporarily stationed a patrol unit at Jim's residence and left to talk to Jim's boss, the district attorney. He instructed us to immediately inform him if we made contact with Jim or Angie. We assured him that we would and asked him if he would do the same for us.

"We can't just sit around and do nothing," I said to Gina and Wolfram. "We've got to find them."

Professor Wolfram, having an eidetic memory, recalled the exact phrasing of the letter.

"'There will be no one to talk for thee' seems now to be a direct threat against Jim," Wolfram said. "Jim knows the evidence compiled by the Carr Club inside and out and knows how to present it to the state attorney and the task force for maximum attention. Thinking back to the reason Angie was hospitalized, Wolfram said that it was an effective way to get at Jim or at least slow him down.

"Maybe the poisoning wasn't accidental, just ineffective. When it turned out not to be fatal, intercepting them at the hospital, when they are both exceptionally vulnerable, might have been their next best option."

The three of us stood on the sidewalk in front of Jim Carr's house, contemplating different scenarios. "The fact that Jim saw the car registered to Porter Landers parked near his house this morning couldn't have been a coincidence," I said.

"Don't forget the Honda leased to Landers and Kruger," Gina added.

"You know something? We're assuming that Landers' vehicle was parked there because of Jim. But you know who else lives in this cul-de-sac, don't you? Peggy and Tom Bauer," I mentioned.

"Let's take a walk over to the Bauer's house and have a look around. We'll knock first to see if anyone is home, although I doubt it as they would have been over here asking questions by now," I said. Leaving my car parked behind the marked cruiser, we walked to Tom and Peggy's house.

Gina knocked on the front door and rang the bell, but there was no one home. Wolfram and I walked around back. I looked into the garage through the man door on the side of the garage, spotting the dark Honda. "We can scratch the Honda from our BOLO list," I said to Wolfram, loud enough for Gina to hear. "It's in the garage."

By this time, both Wolfram and Gina were standing next to me. I turned the doorknob and found the door to be unlocked. I let myself in. Gina and the professor followed me inside.

"We don't have a warrant," Wolfram nervously said.

"That's okay, we don't need one. We're not cops," I replied levelly.

There was sufficient light from the open door and the windows in the garage door that we could see without any trouble. Everything looked normal, although the hood of the car was warm, indicated that someone drove it recently. Also, the car was exceptionally dusty, as if someone drove it on a dirt road. I pointed this out to Gina and Wolfram, who both mentioned that the streets near the cabin were dry and dirt covered.

"It could be just a coincidence," Gina said.

"Could be."

I looked at the trunk area and saw a lot of fingerprints in the dust and near the key slot. There was also a small but perceptible red smear that could be dried blood on the edge of the lock.

"Marvelous," I uttered as a chill went up my spine and disturbing thoughts went through my brain. "Gina, would you ask the uniformed officer to come back here?"

"Won't he be a bit curious why we're back here?"

"Probably." I spent a few seconds thinking about how to best protect Gina and Wolfram. "Professor, why don't you step out of the garage, and Gina, you were never inside. I stopped you at the door. I'll take the blame for this if it comes to that," I said. "Anyway, there's a BOLO out for this car, so he should be thanking us."

"Yeah, that'll happen," Gina replied as she summoned the officer.

I stood as still as possible at the back of the Honda. I leaned toward the trunk as close as I could without disturbing the prints on the car but didn't hear any sounds coming from inside.

Seconds later, Gina returned with the uniformed officer, having told him that we located one of the two vehicles being sought. Although the officer wasn't impressed with our tactics and said as much, he was concerned by what he saw. "I'll call it in. We'll get a warrant to check the inside of the car and the trunk," he said.

"That could take more time than we have, officer," I said as I pointed to the fingerprints around the trunk, and the red smear on the lock. "The driver's side window is down. I know this model has a trunk release on the bottom of the dash to the left of the steering column. Deana has the same model Honda," I added.

The officer stood near the trunk, straining to hear any noise coming from the trunk. It was quiet.

"I thought I heard something moving inside before you got here," I told the cop, who rolled his eyes as I offered this information. I could almost visualize the argument he was having with himself as he considered his options.

Without further hesitation, he said, "Okay, Marc, use your pen or something to press or pull the latch that opens the trunk, but be careful not to touch anything else." He stood behind the car and waited for the lid to pop open.

I heard the click of the latch and watched as the trunk opened about an inch. The police officer used his gloved finger to guide the trunk to its fully extended position. I heard Gina gasp and the professor's head drop to his chest. I watched as the officer bent into the trunk, removed the glove from his hand, and reached inside to touch the woman inside. He put two fingers on her neck to check for a carotid pulse and yelled, "She's alive. I'll call for an ambulance," he said as he hurried back to his cruiser to contact dispatch.

I walked around to the rear of the car and saw Angie lying on her right side, curled in a fetal position. Her hands, legs, and feet were clasped tightly together with black zip ties. A piece of silver duct tape was stretched across her mouth, which I carefully removed to help her breathe. I used a cloth to make sure I did not contaminate the tape, which I placed tacky side up on a bench inside the garage. Just as I finished doing that, the uniformed officer came back and pressed the button on the wall to open the large door of the garage. Two paramedics, neither whom I recognized, then appeared and began to tend to Angie. We gave them room and accompanied the officer out of their way to provide him with the information he needed for his report. The officer told us that Jenkins was on his way to the hospital to meet the paramedics at the ER and talk to Angie as soon as she regains consciousness.

The paramedics wheeled Angie on the gurney toward the ambulance after briefly assessing her condition. "She's unconscious, but her vitals are stable. There are no visible signs of trauma. We'll know more when we get her to the ER," one paramedic said as they loaded her into the back of the rig. I glanced up at the ambulance unit number, which was A-1. I wondered the odds.

After we provided all of the information asked by the uniformed officer, he told us that we were free to leave. I told him to notify Detective Jenkins that we were headed to Kruger's cabin and asked him to send back-up, even if it had to be the county sheriff. I said that's where we thought the kidnappers took Jim. The officer agreed to immediately do so.

IN THE DARK OF NIGHT

Chapter 41

"Why didn't they take both Angie and Jim instead of just Jim?" Gina wondered aloud.

"I guess two hostages would slow them down more than one. Also, Jim is the one with authority and knows the people involved in this case. He's the bigger of the two targets to them," I said. "She's a nuisance. He's a problem."

"I think you're right," Wolfram said. "They're also following the plan to the letter, no pun intended."

"Kidnapping an assistant district attorney takes some brass ones," I said.

"And torturing and killing a young boy doesn't?" Gina retorted.

"We don't have much time to find Jim. We need to come up with a plan now," I said as we were still feeling the shock from finding Angie and dealing with the confusion and complexity of our situation. "So, let me see if I have this straight," I began, rubbing my forehead as I drove. "Jim Carr, an assistant district attorney in Lakewood, and his wife Angie were intercepted and kidnapped this morning at the hospital by two men posing as plainclothes detectives. Jim is still missing, but we found his wife Angie, alive but unconscious in the trunk of a 1987 Honda leased to Porter Landers. Paul Kruger, the head of a large trucking company and owner of the property where Martin and Mary Tinsgley are using as a safe house, is an authorized driver of the rented Honda where Angie was tied up and gagged. The car was parked inside the closed garage at their neighbors Tom and Peggy Bauer's house. The hospital released Angie after being treated for being strangely poisoned by an unknown source. Her poisoning followed a visit by her friend and neighbor, Peggy Bauer."

"And here we are," Angie said.

"Jim intended to take the results of our investigation of occult murders to the state attorney and their task force in just a few days. Which brings us to Jacob Tingsley being tortured, murdered, and found over the Labor Day weekend," I paused.

"That also follows a letter addressed to Marc that taunts us, and Roland

Speirs painting his brains all over his room with his shotgun when we dropped by for a visit," Gina added.

"That led us to his journal, which is the reason we asked for the assistance of the good professor here. Let's not forget the other oddities too" I added. "There was the break-in at Jim's home office where the thief took only material related to our investigation. Followed by the strange calls presumably from Sadie Cooper from England and her alleged murder with our business cards found by her body. Also, Porter Landers showed up at the Towne Restaurant asking about us, then his encounter with the busboy that put the young man in the hospital overnight. Oh, and let's not forget what Jenkins told us about the possibility of an infant missing from the same address where Jacob Tingsley was last known to reside. And Gina, I wouldn't downplay the importance of the boot prints found outside of your window, or Jim's feeling that we were under physical and possible electronic surveillance, either. It appears that he was right, someone had Jim under surveillance, at least."

"I agree," Wolfram said.

"Finally, as Jim and Angie were being kidnapped as they left the hospital this morning, Professor Wolfram found ample evidence suggestive of ritual killings at the Kruger property. Specifically, the barn appears to be the epicenter of this activity."

"That's correct," the professor interjected. "If you want my opinion based on my experience, I think that's where we'll find Jim and whoever has him."

"I think you're right," I said as I continued driving toward the Kruger property.

"Well, Gina, do you have any ideas on how we should approach the property without getting Jim or us killed?" I could see Gina working out different scenarios in her head.

"What about you, professor?" I asked. "Maybe we should drop you off before we get there."

"I think I could be of assistance to you guys."

"In what way? You don't have a gun and could be a liability should things get ugly."

"I didn't have a gun in Germany, and I made it out. I know how to deal with these people on their level. Furthermore, I trust that you two will have my back if it comes down to that."

"Professor, there's one thing that I don't understand yet, and that is how Martin and Mary Tingsley fit into the current situation," I asked as we continued toward Kruger's property. "There's no doubt that Martin was victimized by the same people who now seem to be protecting him. I know what you said before about keeping them close, but it still doesn't make any sense to me," I said. "And what about Mary?"

"What about Mary?"

"Wouldn't she know things aren't right?"

"Who said that she doesn't. I think that has been an assumption on your part."

"Do you think that she's part of this group of Satanists? If so, why keep Martin around? Wouldn't he just be a liability to her?"

"Right now, I see him as her alibi," Wolfram said, flatly. "Also, as a practical matter, he's a source of income for her through his disability. The truth, however, is that we don't know."

We were about five minutes out from Kruger's property and closing quickly. "How do you want to do this?" I asked to no one in particular. "We need a plan, and we need it now."

Professor Wolfram immediately spoke up. "Based on what I saw today, I would expect that they have Jim in the barn. If they're still there, Martin and Mary will be in the cabin and might not even know what's happening."

"Do you think that's possible?" Gina asked. "How are we going to find out?"

"Let's go directly to the cabin. Take me to Martin and Mary and introduce me as a victim-witness advocate working on their behalf as relatives of Jacob. If they are truly unaware of what's happening, they should be open and cooperative. I'll tell them I need to speak to them in private, and I'll ask you two to wait outside, and that it's the protocol as you are not family," Wolfram said. "You guys can then make your way to the barn to find out what you can while I keep them occupied."

"What if they are part of this thing?" I asked.
"Then I guess we'll have to switch to plan B."
"What's plan B?" asked Gina.
"I have no idea."

Chapter 42

We pulled onto the driveway at the cabin, seeing nothing to suggest anything was going on inside. Professor Wolfram followed behind Gina and me as we walked to the door. As we walked onto the porch, we noticed that the door was open slightly, and one of the chairs knocked backward onto the kitchen floor.

I gently pushed the door open and called out for Martin and Mary. Hearing nothing, I entered the cabin first, followed by Gina and the professor. It was too quiet. It was also a different kind of quiet, the type that places all of one's senses on high alert.

With our guns drawn, Gina and I checked every room for Martin, Mary, and their children. The beds were made, and nothing else, except for the kitchen chair, was disturbed. They were not anywhere inside the cabin.

Our attention was immediately drawn back to the kitchen area, where the chair was knocked onto its back. Gina noticed Mary's purse next to the leg of the table. An open lipstick container was on the floor nearby. Gina used a tissue to pick up and inspect the tube of lipstick.

"Look at this," she said about the contents that stuck far above its cylindrical holder.

The professor and I looked at the condition of the waxy, reddish substance. It was heavily grooved as if someone used it on a cheese grater.

"Is that the only thing out of her purse?" I asked as I looked down at the floor.

"That's all that I can see," Gina said.

I placed the heavy chair back upright at its regular place at the table. I got on my knees and looked at the underside of the massive oak table. "Professor, come take a look at this," I instructed.

Gina and the professor both got on one knee and looked at the rough surface on the underside of the homemade table. Someone had written the words "HELP US" and "BARN" in red lipstick.

The professor studied the writing several seconds longer before rising back to a standing position.

"It's not what you think. It's a setup!"

"What do you mean?"

The professor hastily explained that we are supposed to believe that whoever wrote that on the bottom of the table, presumably Mary, did so while seated at the table. They were trying to send a message that they are in trouble.

"Yeah, so?" I said.

"You can either believe me or try it yourself now if you want to take the time. It's almost impossible for anyone in a seated position to write "HELP US" and "BARN" in standard block lettering without some of the letters appearing backward. It's not normal. It's a setup!"

Gina looked up from the table and said, "He's right, look." Within the few seconds of discussion, Gina quickly tried to duplicate the message, but couldn't. We glanced under the table at her attempt and noticed that among other things that the "E" and "P" were backward on the message Gina attempted to duplicate.

"Whoever did this wants us to believe they are in danger inside the barn," Wolfram said. "They're likely in the barn, but we cannot trust anyone at this point, not Martin, not Mary, not anyone, except for Jim."

"One more thing," said the professor. "They'll be expecting you, whoever 'they' are."

We exited the cabin through the front door and walked along the tree line, doing our best not to make any sound as we encountered sticks and heavy brush.

Between the ominous dark clouds, heavy with unfallen rain that pushed them lower and stretched them across the afternoon sky, and the sun dropping lower as the calendar progressed toward fall, it seemed much later than it was. In the far distance, lights flicked on with the encroaching darkness.

The wind seemed to pick up as we neared the back of the barn, causing some of the old boards to creak with each gust. The sounds added to the creepy feeling we already had.

The three of us made it to the back of the barn and gathered by the rear door. We heard voices coming from inside the structure but could not discern what they were saying. Gina and I had our weapons drawn, prepared for any threat we would encounter.

"Professor?" I asked.

"What is it?"

"Just in case things go bad, we don't need any of those special silver bullets for this, do we?" I whispered. My question was meant to cut the tension but failed miserably, judging by the looks I received in return.

Wolfram, who had been at the barn earlier, pushed the door inward about an inch and looked inside.

"I see Jim," he said with excitement. "It looks like he's alright, but they've got his hands tied to one of the shackles on the altar. There are two other guys with him, one on each side next to him. We're about thirty meters away from them."

"C'mon professor, give it to me in normal numbers," I said.

"About a hundred feet or so," he replied.

"Got it. Thanks."

"Anyone else with them?" Gina asked.

"Not that I can see. I'm going to slip inside. I'll cause some sort of distraction. You guys come in and free Jim."

"Or you can get yourself killed," I said. Before the last word left my mouth, Wolfram was inside the barn, leaving Gina and me alone outside.

"Marvelous," I uttered.

"Let's go in," Gina whispered. "I'll break right, you go left." Like Wolfram, she was inside before I had a chance to object.

I followed Gina through the door and immediately broke left. It was apparent that we were making plans as we went, a tactic I disliked.

I was inside for only a few seconds when I heard Porter Landers speaking to Jim Carr. What I heard caused me to have flashbacks to the time in Florida when Landers delivered his lecture to Gina and me. It was a frightening flashback that I loathed to relive. As he spoke, a clap of thunder shook the barn, making the scenario even more difficult to believe. I saw Luke holding a gun on Jim. He was standing just to the right of Landers, whose hands appeared empty. There was no sign of Martin or Mary inside of the barn. A van was parked just inside the front of the structure, just as Wolfram described earlier. I also observed the freezer and refrigerator unit on the far side of the barn from my position.

Just then, I heard Luke call out to the front of the barn. "Who are you?"

I looked and saw the professor alone in front of the large closed front doors, standing as still as a statue. Landers stopped talking, and Jim looked up. As Jim raised his head, Luke brought the butt of his gun down on Jim's skull. I could hear the thud from my position. Jim slumped down upon being struck but still appeared conscious.

"I'm your worst enemy," Professor Wolfram said, his voice echoing off the walls of the barn. "I'm here to stop you and your group of sociopaths and psychopaths from killing anyone else."

Great diversion, I thought.

"Do we know each other?" Landers bellowed to Wolfram, an evil smile appearing on his face.

"I know you, and that's all that matters. I know everything about you and your group of queers." The professor did not move as he spoke.

Landers turned to Luke. "Get him and bring him to me."

There was another clap of thunder, and the wind picked up, rattling the loose boards of the barn. Luke started toward the professor and was far enough away from Jim that he posed little threat to him.

"Stop right there and drop your gun or I'll blow your head off," Gina said to a surprised Luke, standing up from a crouched position almost directly across from me.

Landers reached into his coat and pulled out his gun, training it on Jim. "Do it, and your friend dies."

At that moment, I figured it was my turn. I stood up and pointed my weapon at Landers, ordering him to drop his gun or die where he stood. I felt like I was an actor in a bad cop drama, but was doing everything I could not to show just how scared I was.

Another thunderous clap. This time, it sounded quite different and much closer than the thunder outside. With my weapon still trained on Landers, I watched a dark circular spot begin to form and grow larger on his white shirt right over his heart.

Landers stood expressionless at first, and then he looked down at the area that had now grown to a large, dark red blotch. An expression of surprise appeared on his face. A second or two later, Landers simply fell where he stood, dead from a single shot to his heart. I looked at my gun, puzzled. I was confused as I didn't take the shot. I looked over at Gina, who still had her gun leveled on Luke. She didn't shoot either. The professor, unarmed, never moved from his position.

Luke jumped and moved left, breaking free from Gina's aim and began running to the rear door of the barn. He pulled the door open and disappeared into the growing darkness. Neither Gina nor I ran after him as we were both still stunned from the shot that seemed to come from nowhere.

IN THE DARK OF NIGHT

Chapter 43

"In the name of everything holy, isn't someone going to help me? Untie my hands and find my wife!"

"Professor! Help Jim. Gina, we need to find out who made that shot!" I yelled.

"Jim, was there anyone else here with you? My voice provided a bit of cover for Gina to begin cautiously canvassing the barn.

"No. I don't think so. Wait! I don't know!" Jim yelled back. "I only saw Landers and Luke from the time they took us from the hospital until now."

The professor hastily approached Jim and cut his hands free with a dagger that he found strategically placed near the altar.

"Where's Angie?" Jim yelled to us, almost unaware of the professor's presence. I listened as Wolfram calmed Jim with his words of reassurance.

As Wolfram was tending to Jim, I began to assist Gina in searching the barn. Just then, a woman in a red overcoat stepped out from behind the van. All I could make out was red lipstick to match her coat and her right hand's red fingernails wrapped around the butt of a semi-automatic pistol. I brought my weapon up to her chest from about twenty feet away, shouting at her not to move. Gina swung around and also leveled her gun at the woman. I saw the professor gently moving Jim down to the floor, away from any potentially errant projectiles.

"I said, drop it, do it now, damnit!" As soon as I finished my command, I immediately recognized the woman.

"Gina?" I yelled.

"Yeah?"

"Are you seeing what I'm seeing?"

Before Gina could answer, the woman spoke up. "Come now, is this any way to treat an old friend and ally?"

As the woman spoke, she returned her pistol to her coat pocket. Neither Gina nor I moved. We both kept our weapons trained on the woman.

"Put those away before somebody gets hurt," commanded the woman in red. "I shot Landers. Oh, and by the way, you're welcome," she added.

Gina and I lowered our weapons, staring at the woman and looking at each other in disbelief.

"You do remember me, don't you? It hasn't been that long."

"You look good for a twice-dead woman," I said.

"Gina, check on Jim and Wolfram, I'll handle her," I said. I saw Gina nod and run to Jim. I quickly walked toward the woman, holding my gun at the down but ready position.

I walked up to her and simply said, "Sadie Cooper."

"In the flesh," she replied with a slight smile.

"I've got a lot of questions for you, such as what you're doing here, but for now, why don't you let me reach into your coat pocket and take your gun. For now."

"You still don't trust me even though I could've shot all of you before you knew I was even here. I'll keep my gun. Really, I insist. Now let's go check on your friend."

I considered the circumstances for a few seconds. I looked into her eyes and told her to walk in front of me. I ordered her to keep her hands out of her pockets where I could see them. She complied, and we both quickly joined Gina, Jim, the professor, and a dead Porter Landers. Instinctively, Gina kicked Lander's gun away from his hand and checked him for a carotid pulse. Gina could not find one. Satisfied that Landers no longer posed a threat, Gina moved away from the body and we turned our attention to Jim.

While all of our attention was on Jim, Sadie Cooper stood over Landers' body, straddling him. She reached down and grabbed his head by his hair, lifting him to a semi-sitting position. She straddled his lifeless corpse and appeared to be going through his shirt and jacket pockets, although the position of her body over his blocked our view. After several seconds, she released her grip on his upper body, vaulting his torso into a free fall against the barn floor. His head struck with a dull, lifeless thud. Without saying a word, she moved away from the body.

Jim Carr was now standing upright with the professor's assistance, using his right hand to nurse the lump on the back of his head. "That rat bastard hit me," he said, referring to Luke. "Where is he? He's still got a gun."

"He ran out of the barn once Sadie Cooper shot Landers," Gina said.

"Sadie Cooper?" Jim said in a painful and confused state. "What in the hell?"

"He's gone. I heard him tear out of here in Lander's car," Sadie replied.

"I need to see Angie," Jim said.

"That's convenient because you need to get that lump on your head treated at the hospital. You can see Angie there," I said. "Gina, did you see a phone inside the cabin?"

"Mary told us that there's no phone here, but I did see a telephone line running from one of the utility poles."

"Let's all go in together to see if there's a working phone. We need to get Jim to the hospital."

"I need to check on Angie," Jim repeated with confused determination.

We all walked to the cabin as a group, leaving Lander's body where it fell. We walked into the warm structure and assisted Jim onto a chair while Gina took a quick look around the cabin, finding a telephone jack but no telephone. "I'll look in the bedroom," Gina said and disappeared down the short hallway.

IN THE DARK OF NIGHT

Chapter 44

The man with the soulless eyes was confused as he watched the events at the barn from the tree line that separated the Kruger property from the livestock farm. His job was to tend to the pigs, although Kruger or Landers or sometimes others hired him to do important things for them. He liked to drive the van the best. He liked everybody except Luke, who often hit him and hurt his bottom and sometimes made him bleed.

As the dark clouds whirled above his head, he heard the claps of thunder and wanted to seek shelter but could not turn his eyes away from the events at the barn. He watched Landers and Luke bring a man to the barn and waited for either man to call on him to feed the pigs. Feeding the pigs was always his job.

He was always told never to ask any questions. It only happened occasionally that a man of his size would be brought to the barn. Most were very young and small and easier to handle. This would be different, he thought. He would have to open all of the pens.

Instead of Landers telling him to take care of things, this time he acted without instruction. He had to. Feeding the pigs was always his job.

He counted the number of people who went in and the number that came out, just like he did every other time. After watching Luke run and everyone but Landers walk out of the barn, the man with the soulless eyes quietly went in to investigate. The pigs were hungry, he thought, and this was the order of things. It was the end of the yellow brick road, he recalled Porter Landers tell him once. The pigs were already five days without food and hungry. He did not know it would be Landers, though, and wondered if Landers himself knew.

It only took him seconds to look around and find him, whose chalky appearance and pallor was familiar. After seeing the blood and watching the body and failing to see his chest to rise and fall, he instinctively knew what to do. He did not like the noise they made otherwise when the pigs began to eat. He hated the combination of the noise from the pigs and the food. Sometimes he heard it at night. The noise from the wind through the trees helped cover the sounds this night.

He moved Landers onto a heavy-duty hand truck so he could move him by himself quickly and quietly. It wasn't his first time and he was quiet and adept at it. He just did not expect it to be him. It didn't matter, though, as he was to follow the yellow brick road to the end like he was told. It was all the same.

Once he got Landers' body near the pens, he spent a few minutes looking at him. He liked him and hated him at the same time. He wished it was Luke instead, because Luke was the one who was very mean to him. He looked around for Luke but didn't see him, except when he ran from the barn, by the pond, and into the woods toward Lakewood.

In the end, though, it would be no different than handling the others. Step one was putting all of the clothes in the burn barrel and step two was dragging the body through the slop into the center pen, where the hogs were fat but still hungry. It was feeding time and they were restless.

The man with the soulless eyes hit himself on his forehead with his open palm, angry that he did not count his steps, except to the pen from where he prepared the meal for the hogs. Thirteen steps. He was satisfied with that number but wasn't sure why. He thought Landers liked the number thirteen and would be pleased.

He counted the number of pigs. Seventeen. He dragged Landers to the middle pen and opened the surrounding pens to release the hogs so they could eat. They went to him fast. Then, he started to count the minutes. He got to seven minutes, then to seven minutes and thirteen seconds. The sounds of the pig's crunching bothered him, so he stopped counting. They were done anyway, now just sniffing and snorting. There was nothing left in the slop except for some hair. He fought to put the pigs back into their pens.

The man with the soulless eyes then disappeared back into his quarters, which was nothing more than a shed of tools and hay that he used as a mattress for sleeping.

He would continue to watch until he was needed again.

Chapter 45

As darkness was quickly enveloping the house and winds were again picking up, a siren sounded in the distance, getting closer with every wail. "Better late than never," I muttered.

Jim moaned as he laid his head down on his arms on the tabletop.

"They got the jump on me. They took my gun. Getting hit on the head is not like it looks in the movies. My head hurts like hell and I can barely think," Jim said.

The professor collected ice from the freezer and a towel from the counter, wrapped the ice with the towel, and placed it on Jim's head. I went to the cabin's front door to open it for the local police who were summoned by Jenkins.

"That phone might not be necessary after all," the professor yelled back to Gina, who then came around the corner and walked over to Jim. "I think the police are here."

A blur of activity occurred over the next few seconds as two Lakewood County Sheriff deputies entered the cabin. We didn't know either deputy. Both had their guns drawn, however, holstered them as soon as we identified ourselves and said that we asked Detective Ron Jenkins to send back up.

"Is everyone alright here? Sir, are you okay," one of the deputies asked Jim, recognizing him as the Lakewood assistant district attorney.

"Hell no, I'm not okay, my wife and I were kidnapped, and I was almost killed. My head hurts like hell," Jim said.

Just then, a third member of the Lakewood County Sherriff's Department walked through the door. He identified himself as the officer-in-charge. He immediately recognized Jim as the assistant district attorney and said that he had just been in contact with Detective Jenkins.

"Sir, your wife is at the hospital, and she's going to be alright. She's conscious, alert, and unharmed. She's more worried about you than anything else. You can ride to the hospital with me or go by ambulance, but I'll get you there faster," the beefy commander said.

"Let's go," Jim replied. Wolfram steadied Jim and walked him to the sheriff's car, helping him inside.

"You're going to have to catch us up on what's going on here," Deputy John Cater said to us as we watched the taillights and the flashing lightbar of the sheriff's car head down the driveway. "Detective Jenkins wasn't very specific when he made the call, except that there was a potential hostage situation and that you two here are the good guys," he said, pointing to Gina and me.

I spoke first. "It's a long story that begins with the body of that young boy found at the Bayfront during the Labor Day weekend and ends with Jim Carr and his wife being kidnapped at the hospital earlier today with Jim being brought here. My partner Gina Russell, Professor Dick Wolfram, and I found Jim inside the barn being held by Porter Landers and his younger sidekick Luke."

"How were you able to free Mr. Carr from his captors?" asked Cater.

"That's a bit more difficult to explain," Gina said. "But I think Sadie Cooper can fill you in on the details as she was here before us. She was the one who shot and killed Landers. Lander's sidekick Luke ran from the barn as he must have figured he was outnumbered and outgunned. We immediately came in here to call for, or in actuality, wait for help."

Cater looked around. Seeing no one else, he asked, "And where might I find this Ms. Cooper?"

"She's right—," I stopped midsentence. "She *was* right here. Gina, do you know where she went?"

Gina looked around in stunned silence. "She could be back in the barn," I offered.

"Where's the barn? Cater asked.

"It's about 50 yards behind us, obscured by a line of trees and down an incline. You'll see it once you get near the trees," I said. "You'll also find the body of Porter Landers inside."

Cater looked at his partner, Deputy Vinaman, according to his badge, and ordered him to wait at the table with us. "I'll check the barn. Keep your radio handy," Cater said as he exited the cabin and walked across the back field toward the structure.

"Sadie must have gone back to the barn, but why?" I asked Gina.

"I don't know. How about you, professor, any ideas?"

"I wouldn't think she'd have any business going back there. I think the better question is how did she get there in the first place? How did she know when to come when she did? How did she know about any of this? And the biggest question of all, isn't she supposed to be dead?"

"Yeah, those are some great questions," I replied. "She's the only one who can give us answers, and right now, I don't see her around."

Deputy Vinaman's radio crackled with the sound of Cater's voice. "Where did they say the shooting happened?"

"Inside the barn, on the far side of the table near the rear door. Lander's body should be on the barn floor near the edge of the table."

"Vinaman, please escort all three of them down to the barn, forthwith."

"Yes, sir."

As we were walked to the barn, I wondered how long we would be detained by the deputies as we would undoubtedly have to explain a shooting death, separately recount details, provide our statements, and turn over our guns for ballistic tests. It wouldn't be a quick ordeal. I quietly hoped Detective Jenkins would step up and assist us with the sheriff's department.

We entered the barn through the back door and walked to where Cater was standing. He looked puzzled and acted as such. "Now, where did you say this Landers fellow was shot?"

"Right there."

"Do you see him with us now?" Cater asked in a critically mocking tone.

Gina and Wolfram walked over to the area where Landers fell. There was no body, gun, blood, or sign of a shooting.

"That can't be. He took one shot to the heart! There was no doubt about it, he was dead, and I mean quite dead," Gina said.

"Wait right here with them, I'll take a look around the outside of the barn," Cater said to Vinaman. His weapon drawn, Cater removed a long Maglite from his holster and exited the barn.

He returned a few minutes later and said that there was no sign of a corpse anywhere. No blood trail, no body where he could have collapsed after being shot, nothing. No sign of the shooter, or a woman in red, either," Cater added.

"Lander's car," Gina said. "Lander's car must be parked outside somewhere."

"There's no other car outside except yours," Cater said.

"What about on the other side of the barn?" I asked.

"Nope."

"Could Luke have taken it, along with Landers' body?" asked the professor.

"He must have. He drove Landers around like a chauffeur," I said. "That's the only logical explanation."

"No!" Gina exclaimed, nearly shouting. "We would have seen or at least heard him."

"Sadie Cooper seemed to be searching Landers' body like she was looking for something," I said. "Maybe car keys, which might explain a few things."

"I guess that's possible," Gina said. "But if Luke was always the driver, why would Landers have the keys? I just don't know anymore," she added, defeat in her voice.

"Well, I can assure all of you that I'm not disappointed. It certainly makes my job a lot easier, not having to deal with the paperwork that goes with shootings and killings and all of that. Is it possible that you didn't see what you thought you saw?" Cater asked with a bit more empathy.

We all stood and looked at each other. "Ask Jim Carr, the assistant district attorney who is the reason we're all here. You saw him, didn't you?" I asked in an equally mocking tone.

"Yeah, I saw him, but didn't hear him say anything about someone getting shot. What I saw was a guy with a hell of a big lump on his head. I would think the only thing he saw was stars, if anything at all," Vinamin said. "But, I'll radio the chief to make sure he gets his statement. In the meantime, I want each of you to write your names and contact information on this pad. I'll need you to come to the department to give me your statements tomorrow or whenever the sheriff wants. Then, we'll determine how we'll proceed."

"Wait, deputy, look inside the freezer and refrigerator." I didn't expect

Landers to be in either appliance, but I wanted someone in law enforcement to open them. My curiosity was intense.

He eyed the padlocks on both appliances. "I can't. No probable cause, and I doubt I can get a warrant."

"Okay, then just look at them. Do you see blood?"

"This is a farm and by the looks of it, an occasional slaughterhouse. What would you expect?"

"I would expect you to do you're freakin' job!" I shouted. "Do you see any livestock on this farm? No, because there is no livestock. So, what's being slaughtered? Or who might be the better question."

"Now you listen here, young man," Vinamin said as he pointed his finger into my chest. "There's only one reason you're not in cuffs right now, and it's called professional courtesy to Lakewood PD and Detective Jenkins. For all we know, you set this whole thing up for some reason."

"Why would I do that?"

"I don't know, maybe because you're a PI trying to make a name for yourself."

"It's private detective," I responded angrily.

"I don't like PIs, Mr. bigshot PI."

I resisted every temptation to say something that would likely land me in handcuffs. Gina was squeezing my arm so tight it started to hurt as she knew I was about to land myself in the rear of the sheriff's car. I stayed silent and was the last to write my name and contact information on the deputy's notepad.

"Aren't you going to rope off the area as a crime scene?"

"Tell me what crime occurred here, other than you folks breaking and entering, perhaps. When we rolled up, Jim Carr was seated with all of you inside the cabin. The sheriff will take his statement at the hospital and work with Jenkins on that end of things. I'll contact the property owners when I return to the station and get a statement from them. In the meantime, I suggest we all leave now so I can sort this out with Jenkins. Let me know if any of you should decide to leave the area before I have a chance to wrap this up," Vinamin instructed. "Let's walk back up to the cabin for a moment."

We entered the cabin and walked to the table.

"Here, look under the table, deputy," Gina instructed. "Tell me what you see."

"I see some kids playing around, maybe. How many kids use their mother's lipstick like a crayon?"

"What about the purse here that belongs to Mary Tingsley?"

"Didn't you say that they are staying here?

"I did, but how many women do you know leave their purse behind when they leave?"

Deputy Vinamin looked inside the purse. "Well, there's no wallet or keys in here, so it could be an extra purse. Who knows?"

We were getting nowhere fast. His use of the phrase, "Mr. bigshot PI," bothered me too, as it appeared in the letter I received. I just wanted to get out of there as quickly as possible.

Gina, the professor, and me left the cabin as Deputy Vinamin made sure the door was locked behind us. We entered my car and I slowly drove down the driveway. We all looked around us as I drove, looking for something, looking for anything. We all had much to say, yet no one felt like talking.

"Where to?" I asked.

"How about going to the hospital to check on Jim and Angie and talk to Jenkins?" Wolfram responded.

"I don't think it would be proper decorum for all of us to show up at the hospital. Why don't we go back to the war room and call Jenkins?" Gina asked.

"That's a better idea. We need to regroup and figure some things out," I said as my adrenaline level was starting to drop back to normal.

Chapter 46

It was now fully dark outside, and a steady rain followed a heavy downpour just as we left the Kruger property. Low hanging clouds made for a thick fog that matched our moods. I felt defeated but was unsure why. Jim and Angie are safe, and we're not dead or in jail. Yet. As it is said, of course, the night is still young.

During the ride back, the conversation consisted of questions and confusion. Gina wondered aloud where Mary and Martin were. The professor questioned how a corpse could disappear, and I simply asked, "What in the hell is going on?" The only thing I assertively stated is that we didn't know much about what just happened, something about which we all agreed.

The three of us entered my apartment through the rear door. Gina and I had our weapons out in case we of any more surprises. Considering what happened to Jim, the disappearance of Luke, the unexpected resurrection of Sadie Cooper, and a presumably dead but missing Porter Landers, we were not taking any chances.

A thorough check of my apartment found nothing amiss. Gina made a pot of coffee while the professor and I lowered the blinds in the war room. The red light on my answering machine was blinking steadily. Once Gina brought coffee for each of us and we settled ourselves, I clicked the play button.

Of the six messages, five were from Detective Jenkins, and one was from Deana, who said that she would be coming back home this Sunday. Each one of the messages from Jenkins sounded a bit more urgent, and his voice more strained. The most recent message came in just ten minutes before we arrived at the war room. He left his pager number and instructions to call him at once. "I guess Gina had the right idea," the professor said.

Gina picked up the telephone and called Jenkins' pager, punching in the war room's telephone number as the call back telephone number. Within seconds, Ron called back. Gina pushed the speaker button and was about to say hello.

"I'm just leaving the hospital and want to talk to you guys right away. Are you still all together?"

"Yeah, we are. Right now, it's Gina, the professor, and me," I said. "All three of us were at the Kruger property and spoke with the deputies."

"No one leaves. I'll be right over."

"Are Jim and Angie going to be okay?"

"They're fine. I'll be there in fifteen minutes." The line abruptly clicked off.

"Gina, let's get Annie here too. She needs to be brought up to date," I instructed.

A half-hour later, everyone but Jim Carr was in the war room, now with the addition of Detective Ron Jenkins.

"Want some coffee?" I asked Ron.

"Sure, bring in the entire pot. I need it."

"I'll get it," Annie said and brought him a large mug of coffee. Ron was already seated behind my desk and appeared deeply disturbed. I wondered how I kept losing my rightful place in the office, but I didn't push it.

Ron took a cigarette from his pack, ripped off the filter, and lit it as he brought the coffee cup closer to him. He looked like he hadn't slept for a few days and appeared to have aged a few years since our last meeting at the truck stop.

"Tell us how Jim and Angie are doing," Gina softly asked. Her voice was tender and reflected genuine concern and the closeness we all developed during this intense investigation.

"They are now both at home and have around-the-clock protection by Lakewood's finest until we can determine what's going on. Jim has a concussion and will be okay after a few days of rest. Angie is fine; the lab results determined that she was drugged with Scopolamine. At the proper dose, it incapacitates a person and wipes out their memory at the same time. A person would have no memory of what happened."

"Ah, yes, it's also very appropriately known as Devil's Breath," said the professor.

"How much do you know about it?"

"It's odorless and tasteless and can be used in various forms, such as powder or liquid. It's got an interesting history. The OSS, the predecessor to the CIA, used it on people for various purposes. It also has a reputation in mythology and the occult, especially across northern Africa and Egypt."

"Interesting," Ron said, raising an eyebrow upon hearing this.

"The drug must be administered by someone with experience as it can be lethal in high doses. Spies and the intelligence community have used it as a type of 'truth serum' or to 'brainwash' people and even make them compliant to instructions. During the Church Committee hearings about ten years ago, the CIA was accused of testing and using the drug on people. The revelations were not well received, and the majority of people believed it was an unfounded conspiracy theory."

"Okay, okay, I get it," Ron said. "Conspiracy theories aside, it would explain why Angie has no memory of anything after being discharged from the hospital until she 'came to' back at the hospital," Ron said. "According to the preliminary hospital lab reports, it was also found in Jim, although only in trace amounts."

"So, Jim's memory is intact?"

"Pretty much. Jim told me that you guys have evidence to give to the state attorney's task force and said that he planned to see the attorney general Friday."

"That was the plan," I interjected.

"Speaking strictly off the record, I hope you continue with your plan," Ron said, "although Jim might not be physically able to do it himself." Ron snuffed out his cigarette and immediately lit another.

"Kidnapping an assistant district attorney takes a lot of balls and has gotten the attention of a lot of important people. I've got the DA himself, my boss, the department's chief, the FBI, and now the county sheriff all crawling up my backside for answers. It's getting a bit crowded and quite uncomfortable up there. It would help me to know what you have, and maybe I can unofficially assist you as well. It might even give me a little bit of leverage to use if I need it. A lot of stuff just doesn't make sense right now." Ron was exasperated. "Let's work together on this."

"If you're willing to compare notes." Ron agreed before I could finish.

It was just the break we needed. For the next ninety minutes, we shared every event of the day at least twice from our own perspectives, which matched up reasonably well with Jenkins's information. He had copious notes and offered information from his police reports and database reports he ran on various people, including Porter Landers.

Ron confirmed that Landers maintains a post office box under the business name of Oz Enterprises in Lakewood, which we learned when we ran the plate on his Cadillac. He also informed us that Luke's legal name is Lucius Kruger, a fact that eluded us until now. Like Landers, his legal residence is in Florida.

"Kruger? As in Paul Kruger of Kruger Logistics? Do we know if they're related?"

"I'll tell you in a minute." Ron telephoned his department and spoke to someone in the newly formed computer records division.

"I thought so but wanted to make sure. Lucius Kruger, aka 'Luke' is Paul Kruger's son." We were stunned.

"I didn't see that coming," I said. "All of this time I thought that he was just a bit player in all of this. A combination of muscle and window dressing for Landers."

"That tightens the circles a bit more," Angie said. "So, just to be absolutely clear, Luke is the son of Paul Kruger, who owns the property where Martin and Mary stayed, and the barn where Landers took Jim?"

"Yes."

"There's got to be a physical address associated with the post office box for Oz Enterprises. Do you have that information?" I asked Ron.

He looked through his notes. "Yeah, right here. It's the same physical address as Kruger's Logistics company."

"So, was Porter Landers associated with Paul Kruger through his son Luke?" I asked. "Or do we have it reversed?"

"I don't think we can be certain at this point."

"Landers' business, Oz Enterprises, shares the same physical address as Paul Kruger's transport company, though. That should explain a lot."

"Or raise more questions. What does that tell us about Martin and Mary? Or maybe just Mary, considering that Paul Kruger is her uncle and Luke would be her cousin?" Gina asked. "And why weren't they at the cabin when we got there? Where are they?"

"I don't know, but it's about time that I have a chat with them at the station."

"Good luck with that," I said. "Martin is a walking valium and Mary has turned into a complete bitch," I said to Ron.

"Tell me again what all these 'Wizard of Oz' references are supposed to mean?" Ron asked.

The professor began to explain the idea of the film and trauma-based mind control, but Ron held up his hand and said the question was rhetorical.

"Okay, considering this new information, what exactly do we know?" Gina asked in frustration.

The professor spoke up. "I remember telling you guys once before that you have more than you know. Now, I'll say that you know more than you think you know," Wolfram said as he took a long pull on his pipe, smoke wafting around his head.

"What does that mean?" Ron asked.

"I know how these people operate. Detective Jenkins, you're still thinking like you're dealing with the pattern of a serial killer, and in a sense, you are. But these people are different as many are involved in this cult of human and child sex trafficking, torture, and murder."

"Go on," Ron said.

"Several powerful people have a lot to lose if someone found their names in a journal, journal copies, photographs, tapes, video recordings, or whatever. They're in positions of influence, such as in politics, the legal and medical professions, and even in law enforcement. They've been operating in Lakewood for a long time. It's multi-generational. Think bigger. They need to make sure everything is destroyed, not just one copy of a single report."

"That's why they didn't just wait to grab Jim somewhere when he was on his way to see the state attorney. We thought that's when they would make their move as it would seem to be more efficient," Gina asserted. "Jim leaves and simply disappears before he delivers the report to the state attorney."

"Exactly. That could work, but the cult members wanted it all, including the original information and not just the final report," Wolfram said.

"They figured they could grab Jim and Angie when both were vulnerable, drug them, get the information and take them back home after they got everything, and neither of them would have any memory of what transpired. They might have done the same thing with Gina and Marc."

"What happened? Obviously, something went wrong with their plan," Annie chimed in with her question.

"That's the interesting part. Jim said that someone unexpected showed up."

"Sadie Cooper is what happened," I said aloud.

"You're mostly correct. She somehow showed up at the barn, but a lot had to happen before then," added the professor.

"What's the deal with Tom and Peggy Bauer? We found the Honda parked inside their garage, with Angie in the trunk," Gina noted.

"We already interviewed them both at the station. Tom Bauer admitted knowing Paul Kruger, his son Luke, and Landers through mutual business contacts but denied connecting them with Jim or his investigation. Angie said virtually the same thing. Their names were never brought up by Jim or during any conversation between the two couples. Jim confirmed Tom's statement. They both appeared genuinely horrified that Landers would use their garage for something like that."

"Do you believe them?" I asked.

"The FBI agents do. They believe the location chosen by Landers was just an opportunity and unplanned. It was simply by chance."

"I think Tom and Peggy Bauer played hosts to Porter Landers and Lucius Kruger on the Sunday when Jim mentioned he had visitors who later had car trouble. Tom went to Jim's to borrow a bottle of Scotch for his guests, who were Landers and Luke. I'll bet they were Tom Bauer's guests. It fits with the incident at the Towne Restaurant and Robbie."

"What about the reason that Angie was in the hospital in the first place? She was poisoned with some obscure plant bulb, compliments of Peggy

Bauer."

"According to the agents, that was an unfortunate coincidence."

"And the break-in at their house?"

"Not related."

"And you believe that?"

"What in the hell do you want me to say?" Ron said defensively. Tension in the room mounted.

"Gentlemen," the professor interjected. "I know everybody is on edge, but let's try to stay focused."

"Let's get back to Martin and Mary," Gina said. "Mary is the reason we discovered the cabin and then the barn in the first place. She asked her uncle if they could use it as a safe house."

"What better way than to hide in plain sight," Wolfram said. "And what better way to lure all of you, or all of us into a trap."

"The professor has a point," noted Ron. "As I said, kidnapping an assistant district attorney and his wife tends to ramp things up a few notches. The FBI is now deeply involved and calling the shots regarding the abduction. Based on Jim's statements as a victim and witness, the feds got a warrant and are putting a team together now to search Kruger's property. They intend to dredge the bottom of the pond and even drain the damn thing if necessary to find Landers' body. That is, of course, if a search of the woods doesn't turn up anything. They're going to begin at daybreak tomorrow."

As we all contemplated what they might find, Ron's pager went off. He looked at the number and used the phone on my desk to call the station. Annie refilled our coffee, and Gina excused herself and walked to the bathroom. It was just the professor and me in the room listening to Ron's side of the telephone conversation.

"Uh-huh. DOA? Really? When? Where? Do you have the driver's name? A local farm truck. That's what he said? Okay, get a formal statement from the driver and make sure all possible forensic evidence is protected at the scene and on the body. Have the sheriff's department make the notification, it's their jurisdiction. Make sure a post-mortem is scheduled and let me know the time because I want to attend. What's the second thing? Okay, thanks.

Can you spare some plainclothes to watch them? Great. I appreciate it. Gina and Annie walked into the room as Ron hung up the receiver. He pulled another cigarette out from his breast pocket, ripped off the filter and lit it before he told us the news.

"Lucius Kruger is dead. He was hit by a local farm truck about a mile from his father's property about an hour ago. It was dark and raining, and the driver said he saw Luke walking on the side of the road. According to the driver, Luke looked over his shoulder, seemed to make eye contact with him, and jumped in front of the truck. The driver said it was too late to stop or swerve. Sounds like a suicide."

"Well, that's another thing I didn't see coming," I said. "This is getting ridiculous. I'm almost afraid to ask, but I will anyway. What was the second thing I heard you ask about?"

"It was nothing major. I had a uniform patrol car do a welfare check on Martin, Mary, and their kids at their house in Lakewood. They told the officer that they left the cabin yesterday or the day before. They appear to be fine."

"Interesting timing," Gina said. "We asked them to let us know when they left the cabin, but they didn't bother. I'm not too sure what to make of that."

"At least we know where they are," Ron said. "I suppose you heard that I asked for them to be placed under surveillance until we get a better handle on things."

"Is that for their protection or ours?" I asked but didn't receive an answer.

Chapter 47

It was precisely 10:00 p.m. when I turned on the television to seek mindless entertainment and divert my attention, however briefly. I was greeted by the opening credits from the television series *The Equalizer*, thinking that we could use the skills and Rolodex of Robert McCall.

Detective Jenkins was the first to leave just before 9:00 p.m., followed by the professor and then Annie. Ron went to the station, the professor to his home, and Annie to her apartment. Before breaking up, we all agreed to a conference call at 8:00 a.m. tomorrow after Jenkins had the chance to conduct a preliminary investigation into Luke's death and receive updates from the FBI agents and the Lakewood County Sheriff's Department.

Gina was still my houseguest until we felt we had everything under control. It felt like we packed several days into one, and we were all wiped out. After everyone left, the pizza that Gina ordered remained in the box on the kitchen table, missing just four pieces. Neither of us felt like eating.

"Aren't you going to call Deana back?" Gina asked.

"In all of the activity, I had forgotten she called. I will now," I said.

My conversation with Deana was brief, as she was just putting her son to bed. I had forgotten about the one-hour time difference. She said that she missed me and wanted to know if I would be able to break free and pick her up at the airport Sunday evening. I assured her that I would and that I was looking forward to having everything wrapped up by then. She could sense that I was trying to be optimistic and could tell the events of the last few weeks were wearing on me.

"Are you really okay?" Deana asked, adding that she sensed a strain in my voice that she hadn't heard before. I tried to reassure her by telling her that I was just tired from a long day in the field, sparing her the confusing and horrendous details. I wrote her flight number, gate number, and arrival time in my datebook, and reassured her that we would spend a few uninterrupted days together when she got back.

"I love you," Deana whispered softly. "I'll take care of you when I get back."

It was at that moment that I knew I wanted her to be my wife. I wanted to spend the rest of my life with the most beautiful woman I had ever seen and known. "I love you too," I said. Deana hung up, and I sat contemplating spending the rest of my life with her.

"Hey Romeo, are you done with the phone?" Gina asked from the kitchen.

"Do you realize that you haven't called me 'Romeo' in a long time," I said. "Yeah, I'm done with the phone."

"I'm going to call my daughter, if that's okay."

"Certainly, I'll be in the shower."

Gina called her mother, got a report on her daughter, and then spoke with her daughter for nearly half an hour. They were both enjoying their time together, and their close relationship delighted Gina and lifted the burden from Gina being a single mother.

When I came back out to the war room in sweatpants and a pullover shirt, Gina was off the phone and watching the last few minutes of *The Equalizer*.

"The local news is coming on if you want to watch it." I groaned at Gina's reminder.

"I guess we better."

The top story was about the pope's final day in the U.S., followed by news that the Lakewood County Council had voted in favor of increasing county property taxes. The video then switched to an on-scene report of a truck-pedestrian fatality of an unidentified man on a rural county road. The Lakewood County Sheriff's Department was investigating, according to the reporter.

"I wonder who that could be?" I sarcastically asked Gina.

"Do you think they found his gun? I wonder whether he lost it as he was running."

"What makes you ask that?"

"Wouldn't it be easier and more efficient for Luke to use it on himself instead of taking a chance with a truck?" Gina asked.

I agreed that it was an excellent point. Why step in front of a truck and risk not being successful when he was carrying a more efficient way to end his life? I walked to my desk and scribbled a note about the method of suicide. I also made a note to check the inventory of Luke's personal effects.

"I think we should ask to attend the autopsy," Gina said.

"Really? Why?"

"I'm not sure why. Something in my gut is telling me to pay close attention to this one," she said.

I took this opportunity to tease Gina about wanting to spend more time with Pete, although I could tell by her lack of response that her concentration was elsewhere.

"I'm in favor of that if we can swing it. Let's ask Ron in the morning if he'll authorize us to attend. He'll have to be there anyway."

There was a long and protracted silence that hung in the room. Gina turned down the television volume like she wanted to talk. I sat at my desk, writing a few notes in the diary portion of my datebook. I could feel her eyes on me and wondered what was on her mind.

"Do you mind if I tell you something personal, Marc? Fair warning, though, it also involves a favor."

"Sure, what is it?"

"I'm terrified. I've never been this afraid before, even during my time on the force. Don't laugh at me, but I think we're fighting against the supernatural. We're not merely fighting evil, but supernatural evil. I looked in Landers' eyes before the bullet went into his chest. I know I was quite a distance from him, but I swear I saw them change color. Then when I saw him lying dead on the barn floor, and his eyes were partially open, it was as if they changed again, like a demon was leaving his body. I know how crazy that sounds, but I don't care. If you told me that he got up and walked away from the dead, I'd believe you. The fact that we don't know where he is frightens me too. I'm scared."

"Now, may I tell you something, Gina?"

"Of course."

"I'm scared too. That's why I'm glad Deana is away, and I haven't spoken to my kids. I went to a seminary for four years, but I never learned anything about any of this kind of stuff. It seems to me they should teach a class or two about the demonic realm, if you ask me. It's all too real, especially when you see it up close and personal."

"That's the reason I'm glad Professor Wolfram is part of our group. I think he understands it better than most. I knew he would."

"I'm glad you brought him in. Using your female intuition in addition to your detective skills, do you think Ron understands the extent of what he's dealing with?" I asked.

"I don't know. I have a feeling he will after everything is said and done, though," Gina mused. "Marc, do you think that it's possible that Landers might still be alive?"

"Not a chance. I watched him die. So, no, I don't think so."

"Then where is he? What happened to his body?"

"That's why the FBI is dredging the pond. Maybe Luke tossed him in while we were in the cabin."

"Maybe, but he'd have to weigh his body down too. I don't think he had enough time."

"There are a lot of trees and heavy brush out there too. We should know tomorrow."

"I suppose."

"So, Gina, what's the favor?"

"Would you mind if I stayed with you tonight?"

"I thought you already were."

"No, I mean, do you mind if I slept in your chair out here while you sleep on the couch? I just don't want to feel alone."

"I can't let you do that. You take the couch, and I'll grab a piece of the floor. It's better for my back, anyway," I lied. "Why don't we let Johnny Carson put us to sleep."

"Are you sure? I know I sound like a baby."

"To tell you the truth, I'd like the company myself."

Chapter 48

<u>Thursday, September 17, 1987</u>

I woke up to the sound of Gina talking with someone. It was 5:45 a.m., and my body ached from sleeping on the floor. I saw Gina sitting at my desk with the telephone receiver cradled on her shoulder. She was busily writing in her notebook. In a hushed tone, I asked her if everything was okay. Without looking up, she nodded and kept listening and writing. In our business, calls at that time of day were not too unusual.

I walked into the kitchen to brew a pot of coffee and noticed that Gina already made it. I poured a cup and slipped into the bathroom to shower, shave, and get dressed. I returned to the war room twenty minutes later. Gina just hung up the telephone and reclined back in my chair.

I sat in the chair across from her and was fixing my tie when she told me that Professor Wolfram called fifteen minutes before I woke up.

"You must've been tired. You didn't budge when the phone rang," she said.

"Sorry about that. What's so pressing that Wolfram felt he needed to call us so early? I asked.

"He couldn't sleep last night, so he did some investigating on his own. He found several recent references to someone identified as 'the wizard' in the journal. The wizard presides over black masses, orgies involving men, women, and children, and blood sacrifices on specific satanic dates. Animals and people. He verified that this all takes place at the barn on Kruger's property."

"Has he identified this wizard person by name?" I asked.

"He's still working on that. Wolfram noted that the wizard has a wife who is also involved, according to his findings from the journal. He also found a hierarchy of people who have been programmed through Monarch, an MKUltra program. It's all part of the military-intelligence-occult complex going back to Nazi Germany and Operation Paperclip in the United States."

"Did he identify anyone we know?"

"Paul Kruger is definitely one of the leaders, but Wolfram is certain that he's not the wizard. He was also able to identify Benjamin Cooper by his German name as one of the journal owners."

"What about Sadie?" I asked.

"He said he searched using the Runic alphabet, German, and Greek codes that he identified but found no reference to her."

Gina explained that Wolfram also identified a man named Tobias Wagner, a medical doctor currently active in Lakewood. He has his own practice and has hospital privileges, which would explain the access to certain drugs, knowledge of medical procedures, and even access to medical records. His name appears in code using the Runic alphabet. Neither of us heard of Dr. Wagner.

"That's great information, but it doesn't make me think we're getting any closer to finding out who tortured and killed Jacob Tingsley. Don't forget the letter I got and the promise of additional murders. Do we have any idea who wrote that letter? No, we don't," I said, answering my own question.

"Instead of narrowing the list of suspects involved in whatever sick and twisted 'club dead' that's operating in Lakewood with affiliates in Florida and perhaps elsewhere, it seems like the list keeps growing," I complained. "And the game clock continues to wind down toward the promise of additional murders by next week. Meanwhile, the police and the feds are looking at this all wrong." I heard myself talking, which sounded more like a whine than a statement.

"I think we're making progress. This is bigger than one person, despite what the cops understand or what the FBI wants people to believe. We're not investigating just one serial or spree killer, but a group of murderers. This isn't merely psychopathic behavior. It's ritualistic in addition to the criminal psychopathy behind it."

"Wow, Gina. That's a pretty intense analysis to lay on me before my second cup of coffee," I chided. "You're right, though. I guess it's easy to lose sight of the bigger picture when the bigger picture is so perverse."

"I think you can now understand how difficult it's been for Ron to get a handle on what's going on," Gina said. "Remember Jim's learning curve.

Heck, remember ours, and we witnessed and experienced it! Consider Ron's reaction and approach to this investigation and compare that to Professor Wolfram, who has extensive experience with this type of crime. It's like night and day. It's hard for anyone to comprehend crime driven by the perverse ideology of Satan worship," Gina said. "And I think it's just as hard, if not harder, to believe."

"It feels like we're living inside a Stephen King novel."

Our telephone conference began at exactly 8:00 a.m. as scheduled. Gina and I were joined by Annie in the war room, while the professor and Detective Jenkins were at their respective locations.

A team of FBI agents and divers from the sheriff's department are searching the Kruger property right now. Although they got a warrant, Paul Kruger consented to the search after being notified of his son Luke's death.

A Lakewood detective and an agent from the FBI conducted a field interview with Kruger, who denies knowing about anything in which Luke was involved. He claims that he and his son have been estranged for a long time, going back to when Luke moved to Florida and adopted an alternative sexual lifestyle. Luke's mother, Paul Kruger's wife, died about six years ago, which is near the time that Luke hooked up with Landers. Luke has no siblings we could find. Paul Kruger claims that he never met Porter Landers, but knows the name," Ron said.

"You know that's a lie," Gina said. "The post office records prove that much. I don't think he was estranged from Luke at all."

"I know he's lying, but I'm not sure about the extent of his lies. I'll find out, though."

"Speaking of Luke, or Lucius to be accurate, an autopsy is scheduled for noon today," Ron said.

"Any chance of Gina and I attending?"

"I can check and let you know, which is the best I can do. I don't control the attendance, the medical examiner does."

"Fair enough."

"You'll find this interesting too. The medical examiner already rushed a drug screen and got some of the results back. Luke's blood tested positive for substantial amounts of gamma-hydroxybutyric acid, scopolamine, and benzodiazepines."

"That's not surprising. They all can be described as predatory drugs, causing the user to be subservient and open to suggestions depending on how they are administered and used," the professor interjected. "Don't forget that Angie also tested positive for the presence of scopolamine."

Wolfram repeated to everyone what he told Gina in the earlier call that he identified a local doctor whose name appeared in code in the journal belonging to Roland Speirs, adding that the doctor might serve as the provider of the drugs.

"Do you have a name, professor?"

"As I mentioned before, Tobias Wagner, MD. His family appears to be from Austria, and he fits well into this cast of characters. I'm curious, did Paul Kruger say anything about Tom or Peggy Bauer?" Wolfram asked.

"He said they know each other, but that was it. He was visibly upset over Luke. I haven't asked him to come down to the station for a formal interview yet," Ron said.

"So, is Paul Kruger behind all of this?"

"I think it's a safe bet that he knows a lot more than he's sharing if we find what you described on his property. It's hard to imagine that all of this activity is going on under his nose without having some level of knowledge, if not involvement. Despite that, the 'official' focus is on Lucius Kruger and Porter Landers."

"If I may inquire, Detective Jenkins, what are your plans for today?" asked the professor.

"I intend to lead the search of Kruger's property and attend Luke's autopsy. The rest of my day will depend on what they find from the search. If I can, I want to interview Martin and Mary, preferably at the station. Why, what do you have in mind?"

"If it's possible, I'd like to accompany you to the barn. You'll recall that I took photographs of the interior before Jim was rescued from there and identified some artifacts that I think would be relevant to your case."

"You and your team from the college would likely be called anyway if any artifacts are found. Can you meet me at the station in 30 minutes and bring the photographs with you? I'm sure the FBI agents and the sheriff would like to take a look at them too."

"I'll be right over," the professor said.

"Gina and I will also stop at the property if you don't mind."

"Marc, it's a crime scene, not a tourist attraction," Ron said with frustration. "You guys can stop by, but you'll have to stay behind the tape. Don't forget, both of you were part of what happened, and we can't risk any possible cross-contamination of the scene."

I immediately objected but was cut off.

"How about just waiting nearby so you don't ruffle the feathers of the feds and the sheriff, and I'll come to you and give you a personal update of the findings. Anyway, the professor can act as your eyes and ears on the inside."

"That's kind of you, Ron, and we are very appreciative," Gina said, shooting me a glance that stopped me from voicing any additional objections I had.

"I'm curious, Ron, have you heard anything else about the possible missing infant from Pennsylvania?"

"Are you kidding me?" Ron responded. "I've got enough going on right now," he added. After an extended silence, he sighed audibly and said, "I'll check on the status if I get the chance."

"I know your hands are full, Ron. I was just thinking about the letter I received."

"I'm sorry, I didn't mean to sound like I didn't care. In my defense, Marc, a lot has changed over the last 36 hours that's causing me to rethink things. Just make sure you guys get your evidence to the state attorney general's task force as soon as you can. I think that would be more effective than anything happening here, especially if I understand everything correctly. By the way, I think I'm beginning to see the bigger picture," Ron said.

The professor's voice seemed to blow through the speaker as he said, "I can assure you that you are, Detective. I'll see you in a bit. I'm leaving now." The professor clicked off.

"We'll see you later, Ron. You can let us know about us attending the post-mortem when we see you at the property," Gina said as we ended the conference call.

Chapter 49

I drove my car up the driveway on Kruger's property, driving on the extended path and moving beyond the cabin. I stopped at a clearing about 20 yards from the tree line that obscured the barn. Gina and I parked next to Jenkins' unmarked car. The officers set up a staging area near the tree line that blocked the view of the barn, and we saw about a dozen law enforcement agents spread out across the rear part of the property that encompassed the pond and barn. Detective Jenkins saw us drive up and walked over to us. Professor Wolfram walked behind him.

"The sheriff's department has a three-man diving team in the pond right now. Agents Roberts and Liu called in two other agents from the Columbus field office. They're checking the barn now. The rest of the officers are checking the woods," Jenkins said.

"Have they found anything yet?"

As soon as I asked that question, agent Roberts yelled to Jenkins, telling him and the professor to meet them in the barn.

"Stay behind the tape, and I'll let you know what's going on as soon as I find out myself," Jenkins said.

"I don't know about you, but I'm creeped out by seeing all of this again, even in the light," Gina said.

"Me too."

Gina and I carefully surveyed the area in daylight. Although there was reassurance in numbers and that those numbers consisted of a well-armed assembly of law enforcement officers, I nonetheless felt a sickening sensation deep inside my gut.

"We're really out in the sticks out here," I remarked to Gina. "Do you recall the property boundaries?"

"Yeah, I remember the lines from the county map. Kruger's property ends about 30 yards past the pond that way," Gina pointed due north, "and only about 20 yards past the tree line that way," she said as she motioned to the heavily wooded area east of us. "His property ends at the power company's easement to our west, and the road to our south. It's fairly straightforward."

We didn't have to wait much longer for Jenkins and Wolfram to give us an update. We saw them walking toward us about five minutes after they went into the barn. Their heads were down, and they didn't seem to be talking to each other. From my vantage point, both looked defeated.

"Well, you'll find it interesting that the barn is clean," Wolfram said.

"What do you mean, clean?" Gina asked.

"It's completely cleared out. It must have happened overnight. None of the artifacts in the pictures I took are inside the barn anymore. The van is gone too. Somebody cleaned that place out but good," Wolfram said.

"What about blood? Did you find any blood inside?"

"The forensic guys found bloodstain evidence in the area where the table was."

"Wait, what do you mean was?" I asked assertively.

"The table or the altar is gone too, Marc," the professor said.

"But you have the photographs."

"Yes, we have the photos," Jenkins said. "And the tests for the presence of blood are presumptively positive. The question is whether it's human, animal, or both. The techs will take the samples to the lab where they'll conduct precipitin tests and further analysis."

"What about the marking on the tree that the professor saw and photographed?"

"That's still there, as are a few other symbols and markings elsewhere."

"That should tell you something, and the photographs too."

"The FBI documented the symbols, and they have copies of the photographs that the professor took, as we do," Jenkins added. "A search of the woods to the property line found no sign of the body of Porter Landers, or any body, for that matter."

"What about the pond?"

Jenkins used his radio to ask for an update on the search of the pond.

"Nothing on the first pass," the voice on the radio crackled. "We're almost done with our second."

"Are they going to drain it?"

"What for?"

"Damnit! How in the hell could this have happened? We should have had surveillance on this place ourselves!" I felt angry, livid. It was another rookie mistake, I thought to myself.

"Ron, you've got to find out who cleaned this place up!" I heard myself nearly shouting at him.

"Marc, if Landers was supposedly shot, killed, and disposed of here, where's the disposal site? If he managed to get up and walk outside, where's the blood trail? You damn well know he'd leave one. If he took a shot to his heart like you said he did and walked into the woods like a wounded deer, we would've found his body. The deputies would have found him last night."

"I'm telling you that Sadie Cooper shot him dead."

"Yeah, about that," Ron dragged out the words a bit longer than necessary. "A 'dead woman' shoots a guy, and not only does his body disappear, but she does too, all before the deputies get here and check the barn and property? I put myself out on a limb, getting all of these guys out here today, and it's not going too well, as you can see."

"What about everything you said this morning?"

"That was before a platoon of officers and agents started asking me what they're doing out here. I put my butt on the line."

"It's not just Gina and me, or the professor and us, but Jim's statement, the word of an assistant district attorney. You've got to believe him, at least."

"Jim took quite a blow to his head. He could've been seeing monkeys flying around after that. It's not about belief, but evidence. You should know that."

"So, what are you saying, Ron?" Gina asked. "That we imagined everything?"

"No, look, it's not that I don't believe you. All I'm asking is that you consider it from my perspective. What do I tell the chief? How about the FBI? There's no doubt that two men kidnapped Jim and Angie. There's no doubt that Jim was brought here by two men. One is on a slab at the morgue and not talking. The other is gone, just gone. No body and no indication of a body. Or a shooting. I honestly don't know what happened last night, but shooters and bodies don't just vanish, especially already dead shooters and supposedly dead victims."

"I'm not entirely sure what happened last night, either, Ron," I said.

"The second pass of the pond is negative, sir," the radio crackled again.

"Okay, everyone, let's wrap it up," agent Ted Roberts instructed the others.

"Professor, I'll take you back to the station so you can pick up your car. I appreciate your help and the photographs," Jenkins said to Wolfram. "I'm sorry that there was nothing for you to do here."

"Me too," the oddly quiet professor responded.

"One last thing, Marc. I couldn't get authorization for you and Gina to attend the post-mortem. I'm not sure what you expected to learn that a report wouldn't tell you anyway. I'll let you know how things go."

"I'll see you two back at your place?" Wolfram asked as he pointed to Gina and me.

I nodded, and Gina replied, "Yes, please."

Ron turned and walked back to his vehicle with the professor in tow.

Chapter 50

The man with the soulless eyes hid carefully in the thick underbrush from the neighboring property north of Kruger's land. The sunlight hurt his eyes. It was different now, without Porter Landers and Luke.

He was glad the police weren't using dogs. He hated dogs because they would still show him affection regardless of what he would do to them.

As he watched the figures move about in the distance, he was sure that he didn't leave anything behind. He gathered everything exactly as she instructed him and placed everything in the large utility shed where the feed and tractor and tools were kept. He knew that she would order the two men to hurt him if he didn't do everything just right. He knew that she was just looking out for him. She was not like his mother, who told him he was different and wished that he was dead. He hated his mother, a despicable woman, and he was glad that she was killed, he thought. He hated all women, too, except her.

He kept watching as he was told. He thought of her and the wizard and the yellow brick road and each step on the yellow brick road. He counted the steps on the yellow brick road. Sometimes there were thirteen. Other times there were thirty-three. Thirteen to Dorothy's Paradise at the place where it was hot during the day in the summer and the trees were different. Where they made fun of him and hurt him and took pictures of him and burned him with the ends of their hot sticks, he remembered. Thirty-three here from the slop to his cot where they made him sleep. It was cold, noisy and it stunk.

He stayed in the brush until he was sure everyone left, like he was told. Until it was dark. Until no one was there.

He walked back to the utility shed where he put everything to make sure that no one found it and it was all still there. He was pleased with himself because he never veered from the yellow brick road.

She told him not to let anyone in this building, especially the short man with glasses she called Marc and the pretty girl with him she called Gina. She said that if the short man and pretty girl came around to the pond or the woods or the utility shed on the property north of the barn and pond, to sneak up behind them. He was told to hit them on their heads with the heavy shovel and tie them up and then to tell her. No one else but her. Delta. That was the word they shared. The word made him think funny, and he didn't know why.

She wanted to surprise them and see the looks in their eyes when they saw her. She promised him that he could take their faces and keep them with the others he collected. He wanted their faces, especially the girl's face. He collected them.

He walked back to the brush as he was told and waited and watched and waited some more. When it was almost dark, he looked at the pile of skulls, bones, and bone parts that he gathered from the barn and hidden away. He transferred them to a burlap sack that once held feed. The sack was full and bulky.

He carried the sack to edge of the pond and reached in and threw every piece from the sack into the middle of the pon d. Each piece one by one. Each tooth one by one. He watched the ripples of water gently caress the edge of the pond with every piece of the once living people he threw into the dark soup.

She said it was important for him to do things in exactly this order because they would never come back to look into the pond. Not again. Not ever again. He could still hear her laugh after she said it.

She wore the ruby slippers and had the power and knew what to do at all times. Maybe she would one day let him stay with her and touch her because he was so good at following her instructions. Delta.

He got rid of almost everything. He kept the gun that fell from Luke's grasp when he was running. She didn't know he found the gun. He felt funny not telling her, and it made his head hurt.

He knew that she would disapprove of him keeping the gun, still, he didn't tell her. He didn't tell anyone. He hid the gun in the utility shed where he was the only one who could find it. It would be his secret. Omega.

Chapter 51

Annie was already in the war room at 1:30 when Gina and I returned. She stopped at Art's Deli, where she picked up sandwiches and snacks on her way from the office. She made a pot of coffee and was in the process of updating our case boards when we came in.

"I heard it didn't go so well at the Kruger property," Annie said meekly.

"Who told you?"

"I just hung up with Pete from the medical examiner's office. He told me. Plus, they were just finishing up with the Kruger autopsy. Ron couldn't make it in time, so another Lakewood detective took his place. Pete was quite talkative today," she added.

"Tell us."

"As you can imagine, there were no surprises regarding his cause of death, which was massive blunt force trauma. You already know about the preliminary blood toxicology results. He had GHB, scopolamine, and benzodiazepines in his system. Because of Angie's test results, I asked Pete to go back and look at the test done on Roland Speirs. He also has the same drug cocktail in his system."

"That's interesting."

"It gets better. Jacob Tingsley had a similar drug combination, although his were in different concentrations. His GHB levels were higher, which law enforcement agencies and, in the worst-case scenarios, medical examiners across the United States are seeing in sexual assault victims."

"He told you that?"

"Yes, he's extremely intelligent and reads a lot of the documents sent to medical examiners and coroners in his spare time. There is a rise nationally in using these drugs, especially in certain combinations. They are calling GHB, in particular, a 'date-rape' drug. The use of scopolamine, though, is more unusual."

"My research confirmed that scopolamine has a rich history with the CIA, although its presence is not found a lot in post-mortem toxicology screens,"

Gina said. "I think we're onto something considering we're supposedly dealing with sexual perversion rituals."

"What were Kruger's personal effects when they brought him in?"

"A wallet with a Florida driver's license and his clothing. Before you ask, he didn't have a gun."

"Thanks, Annie, " Gina replied.

"You saw him with a gun, right Gina?" I asked.

"He most certainly had a handgun. I saw him carrying a semiautomatic, maybe a nine-millimeter or a forty-five. He could have lost it or ditched it somewhere between the barn and where he jumped in front of the truck. Or, the impact from the truck could have sent the gun flying. Both sides of that road are thick with brush."

"Did Pete say anything else?" Gina asked.

"Just one more thing. He asked me whether I thought you'd go out to dinner with him if he asked you," Annie said with a smile. "I told him that I was sure you'd love to."

Professor Wolfram walked into the war room after first knocking but not waiting for an answer. "You really should lock your apartment door," he said.

"We were expecting you."

"So, you spoke with Ron, how screwed are we?" I asked Wolfram.

"Ron and I had a good talk on the ride back to the station. He has a lot of respect for you guys, and Jim too. He understands what you're trying to do but thinks you might be trying too hard, which could be skewing your perception."

"You are now part of our team, and you were with us. Does Ron think the same about you, that your perception is skewed?" Gina asked.

"I asked him the same thing. He seemed to back down after that."

"What do we do now?"

"I asked Ron the same question. He knows all about the formation of the task force headed by the attorney general from his own department and through official channels. His knowledge doesn't only come from you guys. The chief is calling it the 'God squad,' perhaps not realizing or downplaying its significance, much like the feds. This is the first one of its kind ever to be created, so it will be mocked until it shows some level of success. Maybe you didn't know this, but Jim confided to Ron that he and the attorney general go way back to their college days. They roomed together for two semesters."

"Jim never said anything about that to us," Gina said.

"I think that's because Jim wants the evidence collected by the Carr Club to be viewed on its own merits. He doesn't want you to cut any corners, not that you would."

"What about the fact that they didn't find anything in the barn, the pond, or on the property? That's not going to look good for us and could call all of our findings into question. The attorney general and the task force investigators may not take our report seriously. Unless we somehow pull a rabbit out of our hat, it could irreparably damage our credibility and, ultimately, our effectiveness."

"Exactly," said the professor as he walked over to my desk and sat in the chair behind it. "And the bad guys didn't even have to fire a single shot," he said with extra emphasis as he lit his pipe.

Just then, the telephone rang. Gina answered, identifying the caller as Detective Jenkins. It was mostly a one-sided conversation as Gina just listened intently and wrote a few notes. The room was quiet as we attempted to interpret Gina's responses and body language during this unexpected call. A minute passed before Gina said anything. Then two minutes. When she finally was able to talk, she asked Jenkins whether he wanted to talk to me or be put on speaker to say anything to the group. Without handing me the telephone or placing it on speaker, Gina kept the receiver to her ear, listening for another few minutes. She hung up after uttering a half-hearted, "Thanks for the call."

Gina turned to us and gave us the news. "FBI agents Roberts and Liu, along with the Lakewood Police chief and the county sheriff, are closing the kidnapping and murder investigation of Jacob Tingsley. They are naming Lucius Kruger as the murderer," Gina said.

"They're putting together a press conference now that will be conducted in time for the six o'clock local news. Since Lucius Kruger is dead, there won't be an arrest and trial. Few people, if any, will ask any questions, and the matter will be closed, nice and tidy, just the way they wanted it from day one."

"What about Porter Landers?"

"They are going to announce that although they consider the case closed, he's still a 'person of interest' who might have information pertinent to the case and that they want him to come forward. That's it."

"To be fair, they're not entirely wrong," the professor said matter-of-factly.

"Landers is dead! Sadie Cooper shot him." As soon as I said that, I realized the depth of the proverbial rabbit hole in which we found ourselves.

"So that's it? Case closed?" I asked angrily.

"It is as far as the murder of Jacob Tingsley is concerned. The official story is that Lucius Kruger murdered the young boy and committed suicide rather than face arrest." Gina paused, looked at us, and then turned her gaze to the window.

"Nice and tidy," I repeated, dragging the words out in response. "I wonder if Lucius uttered the word 'omega' before he jumped in front of the truck? What else did Jenkins say?"

"Ron said that he spoke with Jim in person at his house and told him. Angie was there, so not much else was said, except that if word about the kidnapping incident got out, they would hang that on Luke as well," Gina said. "Ron said that Jim agreed with that course of action."

The professor lit his pipe again, this time causing a thick cloud of smoke from the fragrant tobacco to waft in front and above him.

"Again, and to be fair, they're not entirely wrong about that either," he said.

The professor observed my angry gaze. "I'm not saying that I agree with them, I'm just saying that Luke was involved in the boy's murder and kidnapping Jim and Angie."

"Why are they making this announcement now?" Annie asked.

"It's the best time to do it. The timing of the search played a part in the decision too. In the event any questions were asked, the search would be attributed to their investigation. As Lucius is dead, they don't have to say whether they found anything at the property," Gina said.

"That's convenient," Annie responded. "What about Paul Kruger? Won't he have a lot of questions for them?"

"Think about it. His son committed a brutal murder on his property and then killed himself. Do you think anyone is going to care about his questions?" Gina said. "Anyway, Ron said that Paul Kruger 'reluctantly accepted' the official account of the murder and his son's suicide." Gina looked at her notes. "Reluctantly accepted were his exact words, according to Ron."

"What about Martin and Mary?" I asked.

"A Lakewood detective and an agent from the FBI spoke with both of them at their house a short time ago. Ron said they were both very thankful that they could put the entire incident behind them and move on with their lives. Those were his words, quoting Mary. Those are the exact words she used."

"That was fast. Everyone sure is acting like they're quite content with the 'official story,'" I said. "There's something about Mary," I added.

"Mary doesn't want to talk to you anymore, Marc. According to her, it's to protect Martin. She doesn't want to talk to any of us. She wants to put it all behind them."

"But still," I began.

"You're still angry at her reaction to showing the journal to Martin, and the way she treated you."

Gina was correct, but is there something more, I thought. I paused before I spoke again. "I really don't care about how she treated me, but you're right about her reaction. That bothers me, and there's something we're missing here. How is it possible that she suggested the use of her uncle's cabin as a safe house, and it turns out that his son, her cousin, took part in the murder of Martin's brother? How is it possible for her not to have a suspicion about them? I'm telling you, there's something wrong with that picture."

"She wouldn't be the first client to lie to us," Gina said.

"Sure, they usually lie about little things, mostly inconsequential. Not about the murder of a family member, unless they have something to hide," I said.

"You can't tell me Martin isn't a victim of ritualistic abuse," Annie said.

"The photographs you took of Martin's injuries last May don't lie."

"Sure, Martin is a victim. But who are the perpetrators? I mean all of them. What about their associates and enablers? What about Mary?"

"Are you saying that Mary had something to do with Martin's abuse? Or Jacob's murder? I find that hard to believe. I was with you when they first came to see us," Gina interjected. "I saw the visceral reaction Mary had to Martin's tormentors. The hate she had for them. I don't think she can be that good of a liar to fake those emotions."

"Maybe that was the 'real' Mary," Annie jumped back into the conversation, her eyes growing wider. "The common theme I've seen among all of the victims is that their minds have been fractured, causing multiple personalities to be created and exist within one person."

"Great, now we've got freakin' suspects within suspects. In this case, we're not just dealing with Mary, but with whatever other identities exist within her mind," I said.

"Well, have we ever considered that Mary is a victim too?" Annie opined.

The professor cleared his throat after filling the area around him with his pipe smoke, getting our attention. "I know this can be, or I should say, is, difficult to understand and follow. I'm sure interviewing and even interrogating one suspect with one personality can be challenging, but when you are talking to one person with sub-personalities, it can be almost impossible unless you are able to identify who you're actually talking to. I sat in on an interview when a police captain in Germany interviewed a 'multiple,' or a man with multiple personalities."

"And?" I asked.

"I watched him change from a man talking normally to a man speaking in a woman's voice, which was one sub-personality. He exhibited at least two more sub-personalities during that same interview. When he first sat down to speak with the captain, he was very friendly. Within minutes, he was threatening to kill everyone in the room."

"That sounds like a scene from *The Exorcist*."

"That movie was tame compared to what I witnessed."

"Please, continue," Gina urged.

"The guards handcuffed him, put leg irons on him, and shacked him at the waist. They moved him to another holding cell, where there were a single metal table and chair, both bolted to the floor. It was a cell where the more dangerous inmates are interrogated or allowed to meet with their legal counsel. After he was secured in the room, and by secured, I mean chained to the desk and chair, the police permitted my associate to talk to him. My associate was experienced in dealing with cases of multiple personalities and demonic possession."

"So, what was he, a priest authorized to do exorcisms?" I asked. "As in the movie *The Exorcist*?"

"No, that's Hollywood. My associate studied the tactics used by intelligence agencies, including the CIA and its predecessor, the OSS, as referenced by congressional hearings on trauma-based mind control. He was skilled in the use of 'trigger' words and commands. He was also a minister who understood the connection between mind control and the demonic."

Gina prompted the professor to continue his account of the incident.

"This was about a decade ago, and the suspect was part of Himmler's inner circle. He was one of the original men from Wewelsburg Castle I told you about. I stood next to two guards and watched from behind the bars, which were also covered by a Plexiglas shield. My associate was able to determine the suspect's triggers and different personalities emerged. He was a programmed multiple. He was a business owner but was also a programmed assassin. He was programmed to murder."

"What did the suspect say? What happened?"

"He used some of the same words that were written in the letter to you, Marc. He said that there are 'super soldiers' who are walking and working among us, and they can't be stopped. He said they're everywhere, that they've infiltrated all parts of society, and they answer to a 'higher god' than ours."

"He could have called himself Hitler, so what?"

The professor shot me a look that made me feel like I was a student about to be sent to the office for my bad behavior. I apologized and asked him to continue.

"I was there, and until you see it, you might not believe it. In fact, you already have. Think about what you and Gina experienced in Florida with Porter Landers changing personalities, or have you forgotten already?"

"Not at all." My reply was meek.

"After extracting as much information from the suspect as he thought he could, my associate commanded the demons to depart from him 'in the name of Jesus.' The next thing I saw was a man who exhibited super-human strength. He ripped the table out of the cement floor. Imagine the strength that would take. At the same time, the plexiglass iced up from the inside as the actual temperature inside the cell dropped below freezing. Before the guards could see through the iced plexiglass and get inside, my associate was dead. The man snapped his neck like a twig, and the shackles were around his neck. The guards shot the suspect twelve times before he died."

"Do you think Mary might be a programmed multiple?" Annie asked Wolfram.

"I don't know, but I do have my suspicions. I'd like to talk with her, though."

"As I said before, there's something about Mary. But you can't talk to her if she doesn't want to talk."

"I'm sure there are ways," the professor said.

Chapter 52

Our conversation was interrupted by an unexpected and forceful knock at the front door.

"Are we expecting anyone?" Gina asked.

"I don't think so," I replied.

Annie peered out the front window. "How about a delivery? There's a Lakewood Expedited Delivery and Messenger Service van parked out front."

That company handles many of the deliveries made between law firms, banks, and other businesses in Lakewood, in addition to other personal deliveries to private residences. It is mostly used by professionals.

"I'll get it," I said as I walked to the front door.

"Are you Marc Stiles?" asked the young man dressed in a company uniform. He was holding a clipboard and an extra-large manila envelope. He didn't wait for me to answer.

"Sign here please," he instructed as he turned the clipboard in my direction, balancing it on top of the oversized envelope.

He handed me the package after I signed for the delivery. He was back in his van and driving away before I could ask him who ordered it to be delivered.

The envelope was well-padded, heavy and bulky, with a generic label affixed to the outside indicating that it originated from a local upscale hotel. There was no sender's name I could find on the outside of the envelope as I carried it to the war room and placed it on top of my desk. The professor got up from my chair and moved to a seat across from me. Eyeing the envelope, he asked me if I shouldn't check it a little closer before I opened it.

"Be my guest, professor, I'm starting to think you've got a better understanding of the state of things right now than I do. Just let us know if we should plug our ears or take cover when you open it."

The professor let out an uncharacteristically nervous chuckle as he carefully picked up the bulky envelope and studied it carefully. He reached into his pocket and brought out a folding knife, one like my grandfather might have carried, and carefully slid it under the top flap. After looking inside, he slowly slid the contents onto the top of my desk. Tissue paper hid and protected three items, each one several times larger than the other. Once Wolfram removed the items from the tissue paper, silence overtook the room.

Annie, Gina, Wolfram, and I were staring at the gold neck chain with the Baphomet symbol Landers was wearing and a silver Nazi SS ring we had previously discussed. Both items still had a few blood stains faintly visible around their edges.

"That's the chain Landers was wearing when Sadie Cooper shot him. That's his ring too. It's one of the missing rare rings worn by Himmler's SS men," I said, recalling our recent conversation about the ornate silver ring with a skull as its centerpiece.

"It could be the chain and pendant taken from Jim's house safe. It could be both, I suppose, if Landers was wearing the chain that was stolen," Gina said.

The largest of the three items was a gun. I recognized it as Jim's gun. I picked it up, dropped a fully loaded magazine from the butt of the gun and checked the chamber, which was empty. "I'm sure Jim will be glad to get this back."

"It didn't do him much good before," Angie said.

"Wait, there's a note," the professor said as he looked inside the envelope. According to this note, everything here was taken from Landers' body."

"What else does the note say?"

"Nothing, really. The note was short and to the point. 'These are from the body of Porter Landers. Don't lose them.' The note contains no name or signature," the professor responded. "But, I think I know who sent them."

"You're not going to tell me that—"

"Yes, I'm certain they're from Sadie Cooper. The not-so-late Sadie Cooper. It has to be her. If you recall, she was handling Landers' body like she was looking for something after he was shot. She lifted his head up, perhaps taking this chain, then appeared to be looking for his car keys. That's when she probably got his keys and I think she got this ring too."

"So that's how she got away?"

"Probably."

"I thought Luke drove all of the time. Why would Landers have the keys?"

"If you were Landers, would you trust Luke with the keys when he wasn't driving?"

"Good point. So, she's trying to help us?" I asked Wolfram.

"It seems that way. Otherwise, we'd all be dead, and she'd have no reason to shoot Landers."

The professor studied the ring using a magnifying glass.

"I haven't seen one of these in a long time. This is authentic and it's in good shape. These are the runes I was telling you about," he said, pointing out the ornate etchings on it.

"Well, if the AG needs hard evidence, it seems like he'll get it. The journal, the genuine SS ring, and the Baphomet talisman and chain are all original and authentic evidence of satanic worship in Lakewood. These items, combined with the photographs, witness statements and the expertise of you, Professor Wolfram, and the assistant district attorney should get the task force off to a running start." I said.

It was the first time I spoke with confidence, and everyone agreed that our case was much more solid with these items and the testimony of the assistant DA.

"I'll get hard copies of the toxicology reports from Pete to add to the report," Gina said. "I'm sure it will require another date with him, but it's worth it."

"Don't forget about the piece of human skull recovered from the barn," Wolfram added. "That will end up being equally important to their investigation. I'll have it brought to you right way with the analysis from the university's lab."

The professor said that he would be able to work from the high-quality images of the journal to complete his analysis, hopefully, identifying every name encoded in it. He would do the same with the letter as he already did an analysis of the medium used. We have reports on both that can be packaged for the attorney general, who would also have direct access of the original items.

"I didn't tell you that when I spoke to Ron, Jim told him that he wanted us to go in his place. The attorney general is expecting you and me tomorrow. He already notified the AG that we'll be taking his place," Gina said.

"That was fast. I guess having friends in high places cuts through the red tape," I said.

"Ready for another road trip, partner?" Gina asked, looking at me in anticipation.

"Let's do it."

By eight o'clock, Gina and I had collected every article of evidence we intended to turn over to the attorney general. It was now all in our possession, and all of our reports and the proper chain of custody forms were completed. Annie and the professor had left, and Jim remained at home recuperating.

"I've been thinking," I said to Gina. "I'm curious. Where did everything that was inside the barn go? If Landers' body wasn't in the pond and the police searched every square foot of Kruger's property, including the wooded areas, how did his body disappear so quickly and without a trace?" I wondered out loud. "There's got to be evidence that everyone's missed. Where's the best place to hide evidence sometimes?"

"In plain sight, I suppose," Gina replied. "Is that one of Stiles' Rules?"

"No, but maybe it should be. You know another great place to hide evidence?" I asked.

"No, where?"

"A location that's already been searched," I replied. "I'm also a bit curious about what Paul Kruger is doing right now."

"Maybe making burial arrangements for his son?" Gina answered.

"Not at this hour. It might be late, but it's still early, at least by our standards. Let's just take a ride by the cabin and barn to see if there's anything going on. The police are done and have released the scene. Just a quick look, I promise."

"Oh, Marc, are you sure that's such a good idea?" Gina asked.

"I'll even spring for a pizza and we'll pick it up while we're out. It won't take long."

"What about our evidence. I don't want to leave it after coming this far."

"I'll put it in the trunk. We'll keep it with us."

"I'm only going because I've learned to trust your hunches. You've got to listen to that little voice, you know," Gina said. "Plus, I'm hungry, so let's go so we can get back and eat."

IN THE DARK OF NIGHT

Chapter 53

It was now completely dark outside and there was no moon or other ambient light to guide us. As we approached the Kruger property, I put the car in neutral, turned off the headlights and engine, and coasted.

We had enough momentum to coast slowly in front of the property. At that exact moment, Gina and I observed a car parked next to the cabin. The interior light was on inside the car, clearly illuminating a driver and a passenger against the blackness. As I slowed nearly to a stop, we observed both individuals getting out of the car and walking to the cabin. Both were men based on their size and the mannerisms.

We watched the two men enter through the back door. Interior lights illuminated the back porch and the north-western side of the cabin through uncovered windows.

'How's that for luck," Gina said.

"It's called making our own luck."

I coasted a bit further and pulled off the road into a wooded area owned by Kruger's neighbor to the east.

"What are you doing?" Gina asked, sounding irritated.

"I'm curious, aren't you?"

"It's probably just Paul Kruger and a friend. It's his cabin and I'd want to check it out if I just had a multi-jurisdictional police search team on my property."

"Sure, but the police never entered the cabin," I stressed. "He knows that. He consented to the search and has a copy of the warrant. It was just for the barn, pond, and surrounding area."

"So?"

"So, what is he doing inside the cabin? And who's with him?"

"Alright," Gina sighed, "let's go check it out, but we can't be caught back here."

"I have no intention of getting caught."

I exited the driver's side door and approached the rear of the cabin heading north along the tree line. Gina followed closely behind and had her weapon out. I looked at her, looked at the cabin, and looked back at Gina as she held her gun at chest height, pointed toward the ground.

"Marvelous," I whispered and kept moving.

We crossed the clearing, moving west toward the cabin. Once there, we crouched under the back windows of the cabin and nearly crawled to the open back door. Gina remained close behind me. I lifted my head, looked through the window, and quickly ducked back below the sill. We were about ten feet away.

"Did you get an ID?" Gina whispered.

"Yeah, it's definitely Paul Kruger. But you'll never guess who's with him."

"Ah crap, another surprise."

"It's Tom Bauer, Jim's neighbor."

"You've got to be freakin' kidding me. Are you sure? I didn't think they were friends, just business acquaintances. What are they doing?" Gina asked in a hushed but strained voice.

"I don't know yet."

Lifting my head up again, I saw the backs of both men, facing away from the windows. I was able to watch a bit longer without being seen.

Wait," I said. "Kruger just took two packages of wrapped meat from the freezer and handed them to Bauer. Two vacuum sealed bags that looked like meat, anyway. He put them inside a plastic grocery bag. Whatever's going on, they seem to be having a good time. Both are smiling, almost laughing."

Gina lifted her head up to look for herself.

"What, you don't believe me?" I turned and asked.

"I had to see for myself."

As we crouched below the window closest to the back porch, my attention was drawn to a dull clanking sound coming from the porch area. The sound was like hollow sticks striking each other in the breeze. I looked in the direction of the sound and saw what seemed like discolored, brownish worn-out wind chimes.

"Gina, look at that chime and tell me I'm not seeing what I think I'm seeing," I said just above a whisper. "Are those what I think they are?"

"Please tell me they're not." Gina whispered back.

"Dear God, almighty. How did we miss that? Can we grab it without being seen? Before it disappears?"

Gina lifted her head and looked inside. "Not a chance. It looks like they're getting ready to leave. We have to get out of here now."

We moved quickly and quietly, making it back to the wooded area before they both stepped out of the back door of the cabin. They reentered Kruger's car and left the cabin, heading towards town. We decided not to tail them.

"Do you want to check the barn" Gina asked.

"Yeah, I do, but not tonight. I don't want to do anything that could jeopardize our meeting tomorrow. But I want to do one thing before we call it a night, though," I said.

"They were in Kruger's car, right?" I asked Gina.

"Yes, and Paul Kruger was definitely driving," Gina replied.

"Humor me then," I said, as I quickly drove to Kruger's street using an alternative route, blowing through stop lights and stop signs.

"What are you doing?" Gina asked.

"I want to beat Kruger to Bauer's residence."

"Why?" Gina asked as she was being bounced around in the passenger seat.

"I want to see if Bauer gets out of the car with the packages they took from the cabin."

I backed my car on the driveway of a house that is vacant and listed for sale, situated almost directly across from the Bauer residence. I turned it off and rolled my window down.

"I think I beat them back," I said to Gina who still had her arm wrapped around the center armrest and storage compartment after being jostled around by my erratic driving.

"Yeah, I'd bet on it," Gina said, weakly.

It took less than three minutes for my question to be answered. The headlights from Kruger's car illuminated the street ahead of us.

"Crouch down a bit," I instructed Gina.

Paul Kruger pulled his car onto Bauer's driveway, giving us a clear and unobstructed view of the activities taking place in front of us. We heard the two men talking and even laughing, although could not make out what they were saying. Thirty-seconds later, Bauer entered his residence, carrying the bag taken from the cabin. Kruger then drove off.

"You saw that, didn't you?" I asked Gina.

"Yeah, I saw it. I videotaped it too," Gina replied. I was so fixated on the events in front of me that I didn't notice Gina take the video camera from the center armrest and capture the incident on tape.

Chapter 54

The man with the soulless eyes watched the events at the cabin from his look-out spot hidden deep in the brush. His hiding spot was situated exactly on the property line that separated the pig farm from the Kruger property. He was alerted to activity at the cabin by Kruger's headlights that pierced the blackness of the night.

The man with the soulless eyes moved with almost superhuman speed through the woods to the position he used many times in the past without detection. He counted thirty-three steps three times to his position as he traveled the yellow brick road.

He hoped to see her, but instead saw Paul Kruger and Tom Bauer. He saw both men many times before with his handler, Porter Landers, who was now long digested. He felt lost without his "handler," a word with which he felt only a vague familiarity.

He watched Gina and Marc as they crept along the tree line, coming within fifty feet of him. He had plans if he saw them. He was holding a sharp, decorative dagger that he longed to use as he had done before. Gina's face was pretty, and after all, she promised it to him.

The man with the soulless eyes watched Kruger and Bauer take the meal Landers had promised him and was upset at them for stealing from him. He thought about taking it back as his hands tightened on the dagger, but his head hurt too much for that tonight. He knew there would be more soon. Fresh, not frozen, so it would be even better.

He remained still as he watched Gina and Marc leave, coming even closer to him than before. He was hungry and wanted to touch Gina's face and skin, but she didn't say that he could. Not this time. Not yet.

IN THE DARK OF NIGHT

Chapter 55

Thirty minutes later, Gina and I were picking up a large pizza with cheese and pepperoni and heading back to my apartment.

Gina carried the pizza inside while I removed the catalogue case from the trunk. Once inside, we walked into the war room and I turned on the television. An episode of the television series *Moonlighting* was quietly playing in the background.

Catching my eye, Gina playfully said "Hey, don't be thinking that you're Bruce Willis now."

"And you? Cybill Shepherd? I don't think so," I responded playfully.

Neither one of us said a word yet about what we just did or what we just saw. Instead, we pushed that memory from our minds, at least temporarily, so we could eat. Instinctively, we both knew what we saw and what that trip was all about, but neither of us wanted to confront the sick and perverse reality at this moment. Not now. We deserved a little bit of normalcy, even if it was just fleeting.

We finished most of the pizza and we each had a beer. We were both mentally and physically exhausted from the last several days and ready to get some sleep.

I walked to the kitchen and grabbed two more beers, handing Gina one and twisting off the cap on my bottle. I took a long pull on my beer and sat down at my desk, trying my hardest to maintain just a few more minutes away from the unthinkable. I was privately begging God for just a few more minutes. I found myself praying so hard that I said "please" out loud, with my hands wrapped together so tightly that my knuckles were white.

Gina saw me and walked over to me, gently putting her hand on my arm. I looked up at her. Tears had welled up in her eyes and began to drip down her cheeks.

"It's almost over," she said. "Tomorrow. Just one more day."

"That's the thing, Gina, it's not. It's only the start. You know it just like I do," I said, fighting off exhaustive tears of my own.

"But we won't be fighting this darkness alone."

"Are you sure about that?" I asked.

"Am I sure? No. But we have to have faith."

"Faith? In what, a task force? In an attorney general?"

"No," Gina said, now better composed. "Faith in God. Remember, the work is up to us. The results are up to God."

"You saw what I saw. You heard what I heard, that sickening noise made with each breeze. You know what that's made from, and you know what's going to happen to our "frozen" evidence. Is that really what God wants?"

"Of course not, Marc. But you said it best. We're not done yet."

A few minutes of silence hung in the air as we both considered tomorrow and the days ahead.

"Are you going to be okay?" Gina asked, breaking the silence.

"I will be now," I said, my strength renewed. "You take the bed tonight, I've got the couch," I instructed Gina.

"I'm sorry I've put you out so much, Marc, but thanks for being so kind to me. You're really a great guy."

"Just make sure you tell Deana that," I said as I watched Gina walked into my bedroom.

As soon as I heard the door to my bedroom close, I picked up the telephone and called Jim Carr. Our conversation lasted nearly an hour. It began with me recounting the events Gina and I had seen at Kruger's cabin and ended with Jim's assurances that he would meet with Detective Jenkins while we met with the attorney general. He and Jenkins would work out a plan to expose his neighbor and Paul Kruger. Before the conversation ended, Jim warned me of the potential consequences of me being wrong about Kruger and his neighbor.

"I'm not wrong, Jim," I assured him. "I just wish I was."

Chapter 56

Friday, September 18, 1987

It was 5:30 a.m. when Gina and I left my apartment and headed to meet with the attorney general. Jim assured us that the attorney general was expecting us in his place and would give us his full attention.

It felt like we were about to deliver a shipment of gold to Fort Knox, not in monetary value, but of importance. We've been working on this case nearly all year and were prepared to hand off our interim findings to a newly formed law enforcement agency with the necessary power to bring down the sickest and most heinous criminal groups Lakewood has ever seen.

The "windshield time," as I frequently call long trips, gave Gina and I an uninterrupted opportunity to discuss matters of importance.

"Thanks for last night, Gina," I said to her about fifteen minutes into our trip.

"Boy, if anyone else heard that they might think of something other than what you meant," she said with an infectious smile.

"You know what I mean. Sometimes I forget why we fight, why we do what we do. Sometimes the evil seems just so incomprehensible, it defies words."

"That's true, but we both know how it all ends. Never forget that."

The meeting lasted ninety minutes and included trading business cards and personal phone numbers with three task force members introduced to us by the attorney general. The hand-off of evidence and documents was successful.

The attorney general was impressed with the volume and quality of our evidence and assured us that the case would receive top priority with the task force. He personally looked at every piece of evidence and every report we brought with us. He carefully read the letter sent to me, checked the date on his calendar and called on his primary investigator to review that document, including the analysis of the medium used. It finally appeared things were about to get done.

We left the meeting with as much optimism as we've had since we started the investigation. We were energized. I called Jim after the meeting and told him how well things went. He was ecstatic. He told me that he had a long talk with Angie, and she promised to support him in our future endeavors.

After I gave him the pleasant news of our meeting, I brought up our conversation from the previous night. I asked Jim whether he spoke with Detective Jenkins about Tom Bauer's relationship with Paul Kruger, and by extension, Lucius Kruger. After a lengthy pause, Jim said, "Things have changed dramatically within the last few hours."

"Dramatically? In what way?" I asked.

"Let's leave that discussion for later, when we meet," Jim replied. "There are things you need to know."

"All I want to know is that you and Angie are okay."

"We're going to be just fine," he said.

"Then that's good enough for me right now."

Gina and I talked continuously during the drive back. We went over the many remaining questions we had and agreed to continue working on the case in tandem with the state task force.

Where is Sadie Cooper? We checked the hotel from where the package was supposedly sent, but they had no Sadie Cooper listed in their registry or anyone who matched her description staying in the hotel. They aren't supposed to give out that information, but a twenty-dollar bill convinced them otherwise.

What is Tom Bauer's role in this mess? What about his wife Peggy Bauer, who might have been responsible for the inept poisoning of Angie? And what's the real story with Martin and Mary? We realized that we had many more questions than answers.

The good news is that Porter Landers is dead. He won't be jamming his gun in my ribs like he did in Florida or delivering sermons to Gina and me anymore. We still don't know where his body is, but we're both sure he's dead. Lucius Kruger is dead too. What's left of him is on a slab at the county morgue.

We also picked up a new member of the Carr Club, Professor Richard Wolfram. He is well versed in all things MKUltra, Nazi occult, and Operation Paperclip related. He'll be quite an asset to us.

IN THE DARK OF NIGHT

Chapter 57

It was 4:20 p.m. when we got back to Lakewood. We decided to skip stopping at the office and go right to my apartment. From there, we could call Annie and let her know we were back. We would then call Jim Carr and inform him of how well the meeting went.

I unlocked the back door of my apartment and walked into the kitchen, followed by Gina. Neither one of us needed the bathroom as we stopped just outside of Lakewood to get gas and rid ourselves of the copious amounts of coffee we consumed during our trip. As Gina and I walked into the war room, I asked Gina to call Annie and we'd all speak to Jim.

We both came to a dead stop as we entered the war room. My high-backed leather chair was facing the wall away from us, and a thick puff of cigarette smoke billowed above the chair. In an instant, we both had our weapons drawn and trained on the chair, and both of us shouted commands to the invisible figure to turn around, very slowly and with both hands visible.

I quickly and silently moved sideways to the far right of the room while Gina held her position at the door. Another large plume of smoke rose from behind the chair as it began to slowly twist clockwise toward us. A familiar voice told us to relax, stay calm, and lower our weapons.

"Like I told you in that barn, I'm not your enemy. You should know that by now," Sadie Cooper said as she continued to turn my chair toward us. She had both of her elbows on the armrests, with a lit cigarette in one hand and a folder in the other.

I let out a flurry of expletives and lowered my weapon while Gina kept her gun on Sadie.

"C'mon Gina, we're on the same side, and as you can see, I'm harmless," Sadie said to Gina, who slowly lowered her gun and put it back into her holster under her shirt.

"You both look like you've seen a ghost," Sadie said, with a mischievous grin.

"How in the hell did you get in here?" I asked.

"You're kidding, right? I'm still alive because I've managed to fool Scotland Yard, Interpol, the FBI, and police departments on two continents. Do you really think a locked door would keep me from getting inside?"

"The polite thing would have been to call us, don't you think?" Gina said.

"I don't trust the phones."

"I don't trust you." Gina replied.

"So, what are you doing here?" I asked.

"I wanted to tell you that you made quite a positive impression at your meeting today. I wanted to personally thank all of you for everything you've gone through to make that happen. I guess you'll have to pass my message along to Jim, Annie, and the professor."

"You could have just sent a thank-you card." I said with obvious irritation in my voice.

"That wouldn't have had quite the same effect, now would it?"

"How would you know what kind of impression we made? We just got back."

"I have friends in high places."

"Apparently, not high enough. Innocent people are still dying."

"Hey, I'm not superwoman. The fight against evil won't be won overnight."

"You still didn't answer me. What are you doing here?"

"I'm here to help you connect some of the dots you seem to be having trouble with, and to provide you with some other important information. I cannot answer all of your questions because I don't have the answers either. I'll do the best I can, then, I'll leave you to your business."

Gina and I relaxed a bit and sat on the chairs opposite my desk. "We're listening," I said.

"Did you know that Jim's neighbors, Tom and Peggy Bauer, were active in feeding the homeless at one of the largest shelters in Lakewood?" Sadie asked. "They donate food. Meals."

"So what? What does that have to do with—Oh hell no," I said as I felt my stomach turning.

"I think I'm going to be sick," Gina said as she slowly stood up and turned toward the bathroom. She stopped herself, sweat forming across her forehead.

"Take it easy. They won't be feeding anyone anymore, except in a federal prison. They were quietly arrested and moved by U.S. Marshalls to a prison out of state."

"Do Jim and Angie know?"

"Yes, I personally made certain of it. I have a good friend in the FBI psychological unit who visited with them today. They don't know all of the details, of course, and I hope you can understand why. I trust you will be equally discreet."

"How did they take it?"

"Like you would expect. They were surprised, but as I said, they were not told everything. They've been through a lot. You'll be glad to know that Jim's still on board and Angie is behind him."

"Did Peggy poison Angie on purpose?"

"Yes, but not to kill her. To slow you guys down and distract you."

"What did you do with Landers' body?" I asked.

"Me? Nothing. He is dead, though. Quite dead, and his body will never be found."

"Where is it?"

"Let's take things one step at a time." I'll make sure you have the answers you are seeking in due time. I'll have more documents for you that will help you. You must understand that some things are just more difficult to, um, digest in one sitting than others, no pun intended." Sadie's pun went over our heads.

"What about Paul Kruger? Martin and Mary Tingsley?" Gina prodded.

"Like Landers, Paul and his son have been on a federal watch list for some time. Martin and Mary are an enigma. There are some things that even the feds don't know. That's why they've let you continue your investigation. You're doing well, sometimes better than they can do."

"So, you're a fed?"

"No, not exactly."

"Then what exactly are you?"

"Like I told you before. I'm someone who cares, just like both of you. We're fighting the same enemies, battling some of the same red tape, although some of us have an advantage."

"You haven't answered my question."

"That's the best you're going to get, at least for now. I do want to tell you something you might not know, something you need to know, especially as you begin to doubt yourselves, as you wonder if you're making a difference," Sadie said with much compassion. "I want you to know that you are making a difference and have already saved an innocent life."

"How's that?" I asked.

"Your involvement stopped a ritual murder of an infant. The heat that you two, along with Annie, Jim, and the professor, brought to this group of abusers and killers saved the life of the infant in that Pennsylvania group home."

"So, there was a missing infant after all?" Gina asked.

"Maggie was what is known as a breeder. Infants are bred for that specific purpose in groups like that. The baby was rescued and Maggie is now in protective custody. We rescued the infant first, then a team extracted Maggie from the home. It could not have been done without the heat you brought upon the operation here in Lakewood."

"Thank God," Gina exhaled.

"I'm sure you know about the anonymous letter I received that promised at least three ritual killings," I said flatly, looking at Sadie. "Who wrote that letter?"

"You had that letter analyzed with the Bureau who deemed it authentic."

"I know. Who wrote it?"

"I don't know. That's an honest answer. The profile suggests that it was written by a woman. We've ruled out Peggy Bauer, but no one else. That's something you'll have to continue to investigate."

"That's not very helpful," Gina said.

"Right now, that's the best that I can do. But you must know that your investigation stopped, or at least delayed, the ritualistic killings that were planned and referenced by that letter. That should make you feel good on some level."

"Not really, because we know that there are more of these sick bastards out there. More killers equal more victims," I said.

"That's why you can't quit," Sadie responded.

"What's in the folder?" I asked.

"Just some photographs and reports I'll leave with you. There's a picture of the bags of meat taken from Bauer today, marked as evidence. It's sometimes referred to as long pork. I'm sure you know what that is. Go through them at your leisure," Sadie said as she laid the folder on my desk. "Just to be clear, none of this will ever see the light of day on the news."

"Why the cover up?" Gina asked.

"It wouldn't fit in people's idea of a Norman Rockwell's world."

"I can't argue with you about that."

"Now if I might trouble you and if you promise not to shoot me, I've been sitting in that chair waiting for you two for a few hours. Would it be too much trouble if I used your bathroom?"

"Go ahead," I said as Gina and I looked at each other, then at the folder on the desk. "I assume you know where it is."

"By the way, I really like Professor Wolfram. I'm glad he's part of your team," Sadie said as she rounded the corner from the war room. "He's a solid addition," she said as her voice got farther away.

Gina picked up the folder and saw several photographs of what appeared to be rituals being conducted in Kruger's barn. We passed them between us, mesmerized by the evil they illustrated.

A report on FBI letterhead detailed characteristics of an individual known as "the wizard," but no names were associated with the profile. We thumbed through the rest of the documents but found no "smoking guns" that identify additional suspects in Lakewood. A handwritten entry indicated that the process was still ongoing. Several other pages consisted of information about MKUltra programs marked "CLASSIFIED" in bold, red letters that raised the little hairs on the backs of our necks.

The last page contained only one handwritten sentence. "I'll have more for you later. S."

Just then, the thought struck both of us at the same time. Gina and I simultaneously jumped out of our chairs and sprinted toward the bathroom. The door was open, and the room was empty. The kitchen was also empty, and the interior door was open.

We scanned the area around my apartment for several minutes, finding no trace of Ms. Cooper.

Sadie Cooper, along with the answers to additional questions that remained, was again "in the wind."

Chapter 58

<u>Sunday, September 20, 1987</u>

I arrived at the airport about a half-hour before Deana's flight was scheduled to arrive, which was listed as an on-time arrival for 5:50 p.m. I sat down in the arrival area, watching people carrying their luggage and returning home after their far-away visits. They were greeted by their loved ones with hugs and sometimes kisses, all seemingly glad to be reunited with those left behind.

I watched Deana as she walked down the ramp, juggling her young son on her hip. As soon as she saw me, she quickened her pace and we met in the middle of the arrival section and embraced each other. "It's so good to see you again," she said.

"The way you left, I wasn't sure that I would see you again," I replied. Before I could say anything else, she gave me a long and passionate kiss, and placed her finger over my lips. "That's in the past. We have our whole lives ahead of us, if that's okay with you," she said.

"It will be my pleasure," I said as we walked over to get her luggage from the turnstile. We picked up three bags. "All here," she said.

I carried her bags outside to the passenger pick-up area and told her to wait while I brought the car around. It took me about three minutes to get my car and drive to where she was standing. I loaded her luggage into my trunk as she buckled her son into the back seat. We both got back into my car at the same time. We embraced again, and she gently kissed me on my forehead.

"That was nice," I said.

"Oh, I need to give you this," Deana said as she removed a thick manila envelope from her purse. My name was written in cursive across the front of the envelope.

"What's this?" I asked.

"I don't know," Deana said. "While we were waiting for you to bring the car around, a woman came up to me and asked me if I was Deana Griffiths. When I said yes, she asked me to give you this envelope."

"You didn't know her?"

"I never saw her before in my life. I thought that maybe she was a client you arranged to meet here when you agreed to pick me up."

"What was she wearing? What did she look like?"

"She was older, in her 50s I'd say, wearing a long red coat. She had blond hair and was pulling a carry-on bag on wheels. She handed me that and walked toward the departure area."

"Wait here." I bolted from my car and ran back into the airport, sprinting toward the departure gates. It was a sea of people, each line moving quickly to their respective planes. I looked at the scheduled departures and saw planes leaving for numerous domestic and international locations.

I saw her in line for Zurich at the same time she saw me. She crossed the threshold onto the ramp that led to the plane, where she stopped briefly, looked at me, smiled and waved. It was unmistakably Sadie Cooper. A sea of people prevented me from reaching her, and in the blink of an eye, she was gone before I could get close.

I walked back to my car and got back inside, where Deana expressed both concern and confusion.

"Marc, you look like you just saw a ghost," Deana said, holding my hand tightly.

"Not quite, but I'm sure it's the closest I'll ever get," I said as I tucked the envelope above the visor in my car.

"Aren't you going to open the envelope?"

"I think I'll wait. Just don't let me forget."

VISIT
WWW.DOUGLASJHAGMANN.COM

PLEASE TURN THIS PAGE FOR A PREVIEW OF

DOUGLAS J. HAGMANN
THE DEVIL WITHIN
A MIND OF A KILLER
A MURDER INVESTIGATION BASED ON A TRUE STORY

BOOK 3

Chapter 1

<u>Monday, October 26, 1987</u>

It was just after 7 a.m. Monday and I had just gotten to my office. The telephone rang, jarring me from my thoughts about my weekend with Deana. The ringing actually made me jump and strike the phone with my left hand, knocking the receiver from its cradle and onto the floor. Startled and irritated, I leaned over, picked up the handset and responded with a terse greeting.

"Geez Marc, what'd I do, wake you up? Are you sleeping at your office now?" The male voice on the other end was Ron Jenkins, a good-humored but hardened veteran detective with the Lakewood Police Department. I could hear the wind and voices in the background as he struggled to talk to me over the noise.

"Sorry about that, Ron. What's up?" I asked as I untangled the cord from the receiver.

"Looks like we've got another one for you." I could hear him pause as he took a drink, most likely hours-old coffee he bought from an open gas station while on his way to the homicide scene. "A body was found a little bit ago in the old National Forge building. It's pretty bad and fits the profile of the previous ritual killings you've investigated. The attorney general's task force wants you to consult on this one, to be their eyes and ears, which is why I'm calling."

"They're not sending anyone?" I asked, referring to the state attorney's task force that was created especially for ritual related crimes.

"I spoke to their liaison before I called you. In fact, I got her out of bed. She said that they can't get agents here until late this afternoon, at the earliest. They want you to handle it until they can get an agent here. That's why I'm calling you."

"Marvelous," I uttered. "Coffee over a corpse with Ron Jenkins. Sounds like a great way to spend a Monday morning."

"Actually, it sounds like a morning public access program over a local cable channel. It's got sort of a ring to it, don't you think?" Ron replied. I could sense a slight smile in his voice.

"You're in luck. Gina just walked in the office for our Monday morning meeting. We'll meet you down there in fifteen minutes." I said, motioning to Gina that we had to leave.

"Come around to the rear of the main building. I'll escort both of you past the tape." The phone clicked off.

Gina Russell is an attractive, thirty-something, unmarried private detective who was a former police officer until budget cuts wiped out the department where she was employed. We've been working closely together on SRA crimes, an acronym for Satanic Ritual Abuse, that has garnered much national attention over the last few years. The task force started by the attorney general is the first and only such dedicated task force in the nation, specializing in satanic abuse, ritualistic crimes, and related murders. Gina and I met with the attorney general and three of the task force leaders in September about another case in Lakewood.

"Was that Detective Jenkins?" Gina asked, as she walked into the office with Annie, our young and intelligent office secretary right behind her.

"Yeah, he's got a fresh one down at the old National Forge Building. We'll be the 'stand-ins' for the task force until they can get someone down there later this afternoon."

Gina grabbed our evidence kit, still camera and four rolls of film. "The forensic kit is in the trunk of my car, along with my blood spatter equipment," I told Gina. "We've got extra evidence bags from the task force in there too," I added.

"Do you want me to let Jim know?" Annie asked as Gina and I were preparing to leave. Jim Carr is an assistant district attorney in Lakewood and the namesake of "The Carr Club," a small group of investigators who established a murder club to investigate occult crimes in Lakewood. Annie is a member, along with Gina, Jim, Professor Dick Wolfram (our newest addition), and me. The professor is sort of an "Indiana Jones" character, but extremely knowledgeable in ancient satanic writings and rituals. Our home base is a spacious office in my apartment we refer to as the "war room."

"Let's wait until we see what we've got," Gina instructed. "We'll let you know."

"Be careful," Annie replied as we walked out the door.

We arrived at the crime scene and spotted Jenkins holding a cup of coffee while talking to a patrol officer. He motioned us over. Another patrol officer saw us approaching and lifted the crime scene tape for us.

"Come in and take a look," Jenkins instructed us. "But I've got to warn you, it's bad."

"When is it ever good," I said.

"Okay wise-ass, but don't say I didn't warn you," Ron said in response.

Chapter 2

"Are you guys about done? Jenkins yelled to the forensic team processing the body and the scene. The coroner was also present and waiting for the body to be turned over to him.

"You can have the scene, we're through," the lead forensic technician yelled over the noise of a moving train near the building.

"Okay, let these two have it for a minute," Jenkins said, pointing to Gina and me.

"Who in the hell are those two mopes?" The voice came from an ornery, older police lieutenant. Jenkins introduced us as representing the state task force on occult crimes, but the lieutenant was not impressed. "What a load of crap," he said as he shook his head and walked away. "A couple of 'wanna-be' cops."

"Making friends wherever you go, I see," Jenkins said. "I'll walk you through what we've found so far." Jenkins removed a notepad from the breast pocket of his sport coat as we approached the body. The body was carefully covered by a white sheet after forensics finished, only to be disturbed by us again. Before the body is released to the coroner, it's our turn.

"What we have here is thirty-three-year-old Christine Osterman, a resident of Lakewood based on the ID we found in her purse, which is right over there," Jenkins pointed over his shoulder to an evidence marker. Her throat was slashed, and she was brutally raped and violated, both before death and post-mortem. She's got a rap sheet and was arrested this summer on prostitution charges."

"Sounds fairly routine. So, what do you need us for?" I asked as Gina and I gently lifted the sheet up and away from her body.

My question was answered before we had the sheet completely removed from her body. The victim was nude, although she was laying on her clothes that were cut from her front with either a serrated knife or scissors. A wooden cross was placed upside down near her left thigh, which was the instrument used to violate her. Human bite marks were clearly visible on both of her breasts and thighs, with sufficient skin and tissue missing to suggest cannibalism.

"We'll know if the bite marks were done before she died or perimortem, but there's enough blood flow to indicate that she was still alive. As you can see, there are defensive wounds from a knife on her arms and hands."

"Geez, this poor woman," Gina said.

"There's also a deep incision across her lower abdomen. We'll know more about that once the medical examiner takes a look," Jenkins added. "One more thing. Remember that letter that was mailed to you? You know, the Tick-Toc letter?"

"Yeah, I do."

"Looks like you got another one, only this time it was hand-delivered to you with the body." Jenkins motioned to a forensic technician who appeared to be holding a paper in a zip lock bag. The technician handed the letter to Jenkins, who showed it Gina and me.

The printing and prose appeared almost identical to the letter mailed to me, but the words were different. The letter was signed in the same fashion and included a hand-drawn inverted pentagram inside a circle. Gina snapped a couple of photographs of the letter and began taking pictures of the body.

"Marvelous," I said in response. "Do you have a time of death?" I asked.

"The best we can tell right now? It looks like she's been dead for about four hours, give or take, which would make her time of death sometime around three a.m."

ABOUT THE AUTHOR

Douglas J. Hagmann has been a licensed investigator in the private sector for the last 30 years. As a private detective, Hagmann has worked well over 6,000 cases and is recognized as a surveillance specialist and blood spatter analyst. He has also served as an informational and operational asset for various federal and state law enforcement agencies.

Doug Hagmann is a contributing writer for *Wisconsin Christian News, Canada Free Press*, and other publications. He also hosts a popular radio and video talk show each weeknight from 7:00-9:00 p.m. ET on the *Global Star Radio Network* that is heard in over 90 countries.

He is the author of *Stained By Blood, A Murder Investigation;* which is based on the true story of his investigation into the murder of his uncle. For more information, please visit his website at:

www.DouglasJHagmann.com